WAIT FOR THE TIGERS

Robert Chase

WAIT FOR
THE TIGERS

HEINEMANN : LONDON

William Heinemann Ltd
Michelin House, 81 Fulham Road, London SW3 6RB
LONDON   MELBOURNE   AUCKLAND

First published 1991
Copyright © Robert Chase 1991

A CIP catalogue record for this book
is held by the British Library
ISBN 0 434 65554 6

Phototypeset by Input Typesetting Ltd, London
Printed in England
by Clays Ltd, St Ives plc

Why, this is hell, nor am I out of it

Marlowe
Doctor Faustus

One

The English visitors called it the happy valley, because for most of their time there they were drunk, but for older Spaniards like Don Federico it remained, from days when the Rio Azaroso formed the front line of the civil war, the valley of the guns. When the rains came the valley shook to the rages of the swollen river, but on this day Roderick and Jessica Wardour looked down on the wide plain, in which the Azaroso ran, rapid and musical, through a tenth of its grey stony bed.

The Wardours were very much a couple. Sometimes they were even taken for brother and sister because of a shared tallness and a sort of predatory leanness both of physique and personality. Away from the formal clothes, the make-up and hair-spray of London, they were still well-groomed, handsome people. Their dark hair was well cut and youthful. Jessica had a candid blue-eyed gaze that would fix anyone approaching her from a distance and not deviate for one second until they met. Even in casual clothes her lips were neatly edged in pale pink gloss, her fingernails matching. Her face carried the slight anxiety of someone whose life has one overriding goal.

Roderick, in contrast, wore his talents and ambition lightly. His sense of his own destiny expressed itself in charm, in the smile which frequently followed what he said in such a way as to put his listener instantly at ease. His fine chin and almost feminine lips softened the steely authority that lurked behind the ingratiating facade. Extremely photogenic, Wardour kept his vanity well hidden, realising that it was a weakness which others could exploit. His grey eyes, alternately kind and forbidding, looked out on a world which was imperfect but which, through a mixture of action and imagination, he could make his own.

The Wardours paused at a cleft in the steeply climbing path

through whose tawny rocks they could look across to the white clusters of Robleda, and on from there to villages sprinkled like icing sugar on the foothills, and finally to the still white caps of the Sierra Nevada.

'From here,' Roderick Wardour said, 'the republicans shelled Robleda. The smallholders across the river were Francoists, whether they liked it or not.' But Jessica Wardour spoke Spanish, and while Roderick had been, as usual, devouring the political background, she had questioned Don Federico, the lizard-eyed old land-worker who tended the properties which the Conefort family had bought up in the valley.

She put aside the water flask and said: 'This path is the old track up to the lead mine. Don Federico worked there for thirty years. The men from the village were captive labour, it took them three hours up this hill to the mine, a twelve-hour shift, then three hours back again. The village women used to watch the miners' lamps coming back late at night, like glow-worms.'

'Trust you to get the good stories,' Wardour laughed.

Jessica said: 'Not only that. Don Federico offered to show me the gorge where they threw the Robleda villagers who refused to fight for Franco. I thanked him for the honour and said I'd ask you.'

'My God, Jessie,' Wardour said, full of admiration. 'If I ever become Prime Minister people had better watch out for you.'

Jessica gripped Wardour's arm and said, 'Listen.'

From above came the sound of goat bells. The Wardours climbed higher up the miners' track, through gorges whose ridges always opened up further horizons of ochre rocks beyond. On near-vertical paths a herd of goats browsed through the bluish light of distant crags, the varied clangour of their bells echoing softly down through the pure silence.

When the Wardours turned away, to look over monstrous outcrops which a hundred paces before had towered above them, their breath was stilled by the view they had finally achieved; the far-off Nevada whose white-horned crest now floated in some ethereal middle space, undreamt of by the inhabitants of the plain.

2

Roderick Wardour inhaled the thinning air and felt a great contentment. Everything was far off and yet simple – Robleda, London, the House of Commons, Belfast. Here his thoughts revolved around the lead mine, the gorge of corpses, the valley of the guns. Yet he smiled inwardly and tasted this moment of peace as if assured that the rest of his life would continue the same.

Then he noticed Jessica, fierce, proud, ambitious, watching as if she had caught him out in a moment of weakness. 'Just don't forget that Chinese proverb,' she said.

'Which?' Wardour asked.

'On each hill there is only one tiger.'

The Café Nemesis stood on the sloping main street of Robleda, between the Mirador bar and a seedy discotheque. The two Englishmen who sat drinking at an aluminium table on the pavement outside were fellow-parliamentarians of Wardour's and they had all come to Spain for the same reason, the wedding party of Archie Conefort's grand-daughter. The festivities were over now. The young couple had porsched away into the distance, and the small political clique that hung around Archie – recently ennobled and now Lord Conefort – had drifted down to the less touristy hill-town of Robleda, unmentioned in the Michelin guide, for a few days' tranquillity among the secreted *bodegas* and the orange groves of the Azaroso valley.

Over the years the Coneforts had brought up several *cortijos*, the timeless peasant smallholdings in the valley, merging and improving where necessary, and had found in Don Federico a useful steward. Barricaded by sierras, the region remained unfrequented. An Ulster protestant of the old school, who now found both England and Ireland bad for his blood pressure, Archie Conefort came here for the sun, the sherry-like local wine and the vines trailing overhead on his patio.

Today Archie had drunk too much, and the various wives and children, gripped by solicitude and fear, were back at the *cortijo*, hovering around him. The two men outside the Café Nemesis were Tony Gwyer, MP, and Herbert Conefort, son of

Archie, who everybody said had only entered politics to win his father's respect and had been publicly slighted by him ever since. They were keeping clear of Archie's unpredictable temper, enjoying the feeling of truancy and of the street which, although midnight approached, was still busy with crowds of shouting Robledans. At another snap of the fingers the sullen waiter brought two more beers and *tapas*, the greasy salty snack provided to stimulate thirst.

'Octopus again,' Herbert exclaimed. 'I hate bloody octopus.'

'Life's little surprises,' Gwyer said. 'You never know what your next *tapas* will bring. That's the name of the game.'

The two men were bored, their limited conversation exhausted. In a place like this the trouble was that you could end up trapped forever. Robleda was full of old characters shuffling through the same round of bars and alleys they had traversed for fifty years, sitting every day in the same corner of the square, their wrinkled faces immobile as the church clock's tuneless boom marked off the quarter-hours. Herbert was a bore like that, Gwyer thought, whereas he had clawed his way up and wanted to leave his mark. Towns like this sapped your strength. Give him the thrust of urban development any day.

Herbert knocked over a chair as he got up to seek the toilet. From the other side of the plastic strip which filled the doorway came the noise of Spanish TV and radio simultaneously, and the loud bleeps and gurgles of an arcade game. Gwyer lit a cigarette as the church clock once again clanged harshly above the shouted conversations from the pavement café.

Herbert had reappeared suddenly. He looked ill. 'You'd better come inside.'

'Why?'

But Herbert had not waited for an answer. With an intolerant snort Gwyer followed him into the dark garbage-strewn interior. They didn't need Spanish to understand the news item. On a big TV screen up near the ceiling they watched film of people smashing holes in the Berlin Wall.

From the centre of Archie Conefort's living room, crowded with

4

people watching the same news from Berlin, Roderick Wardour nodded to the two men who had hurried back through the Robleda lanes from the Nemesis. Wardour had the keen look and dilated eyes of a man whose hour was about to dawn. Archie Conefort was sprawled on a couch, a big dour man with a flushed face and dark jowls. He looked displeased at what was happening, and his displeasure had communicated itself. Lucy Conefort, Herbert's wife and Jessica's sister, was sitting where she did not have to see Jessica's face, with its triumphal certainty that she had married the winner.

'A celebration or a wake?' Gwyer asked.

Archie glowered and everybody else looked nervous. Only Wardour spoke. 'A dream come true.'

Jonah Sweetman, an old-style Tory in a wig and gaudy beach shirt, asked the gathering: 'But who's the enemy now?'

'If you keep to your principles,' Archie growled, 'your enemy is always the same.'

Roderick Wardour maintained the discreet silence of a guest. But his face revealed the calculations going on in his mind. Wardour was the politician as media star, and Jessica had the hunger of ambition. Together they were regarded as unstoppable. Six months earlier Wardour, a junior minister at the Foreign Office, had visited Berlin and given a much-reported impromptu TV interview in front of the Wall, in which he had hailed the tearing down of the Wall, then still a fantasy, and the emergence of a reunited Germany as the new progressive force in Europe. Wardour had the charismatic politician's knack of turning minor occasions into major events. At the time a lot of people, some of them in this room, had called Wardour *flash*, a sound-bite junkie who would do anything for a headline. But Wardour knew that back home the party old guard would be rerunning that clip now and playing a different tune.

'What do you think, Roddy?' Gwyer asked. Apart from being politicians in the same party, the two men could not have been more different. From their accents to their clothes and the cut of their politics, everything declared two incompatible human types.

5

Wardour turned his head to Gwyer with a statesmanlike calm which caused glances to be exchanged, an exchange to which only the Wardours were oblivious. 'Today Berlin, tomorrow – who knows?' he answered. Into which they all read, *Belfast*.

After a long silence Archie Conefort grunted that it was getting cold in the house now, and waited for one of the women to load wood into the stove.

Roderick Wardour would never have been at Robleda at all had he not been related to the Coneforts through marriage. As a rising politician he had been glad of a political family behind him, but as things went his way Wardour had become aloof – 'too clever by half' and 'young man in a hurry' were the sort of comments he provoked. He was known as an idealist, but those close to him made sure never to turn their backs.

After the Wardours had left Robleda, Roderick, more even than events in Berlin, became the focus of conversation. Archie said, 'That young man needs his wings clipping.' Later on Gwyer, Herbert Conefort and Jonah Sweetman gravitated once more to the pavement bar of the Nemesis. Over beers and the inevitable *tapas* Roderick Wardour and his works seemed to be on the minds of all three men.

Shortly before they had left Britain, a national opinion poll on the subject of who should be the next Conservative leader had given Wardour a twenty-five point lead over his nearest rival. This only confirmed a trend in the polls which had been gathering steam for two years. It reflected a popularity in the country which was not shared by many of the parliamentary party. To them Wardour – handsome, of impeccable background, intelligent, gifted with words, and well versed in politics into the bargain – had all the makings of a demagogue, a glamorous rogue male who could appeal over the heads of the party machine to a broad base of support in both electorate and media. Wardour was a politician whose hour was about to strike, a moment which too many people seemed to be awaiting too eagerly.

6

Herbert Conefort said: 'What we need is to catch Roddy in bed with someone. Gay, preferably.'

Gwyer shook his head. Having privately desired Jessica for some years, he knew that if anybody could have detected a crack in the Wardour marriage, it was him. 'Roddy's not a slap-and-tickle man. And they're not short of money. How do you screw a man who's incorruptible?'

'I take it,' Sweetman said, 'that we all agree that Roddy's next step will be to Cabinet level, and from that springboard he'll almost certainly be the next leader?'

'The bookmakers are already giving odds on him,' Gwyer agreed.

'Which for some of us means the rest of our days in the wilderness.'

'The British Gorbachev. A new start for Britain. Troops out of Ireland, God knows what else.'

'And Jessica queening it all over London.'

'He needs his wings clipping,' Herbert interjected.

Gwyer and Sweetman let their gazes meet for a moment. Whatever Archie thought a good idea one day, Herbert would come up with the next.

'Because,' Sweetman said, 'if we're serious about this, I met the most interesting man.'

The man Sweetman had met was Swiss, and although he had willingly given a phone number at which he could be contacted, he had insisted that his name remain undisclosed. Fortyish, slim, businesslike in a courteous way that made the withholding of his name seem acceptable, the Swiss had seemed to know things about Jonah Sweetman, although their encounter in a Marbella casino could not have been other than accidental.

The Swiss had appeared interested in and knowledgeable about politics. He and Sweetman had discussed at length the recent case of an American presidential hopeful whose career had been destroyed by a frolic with two young women on board a boat. 'In Russia or Germany,' the Swiss said, 'that would pass – bad luck to get caught, but reassuring to know that your leader is a normal man. In France it would be a career plus –

7

the man who doesn't have affairs is suspect. In Britain the wife would stand by her husband, who would promise never to be a bad boy again. But some basic innocence in the American psyche ordains that a man cannot be politically pure if he is sexually corrupt. And unless you have the clout of the Kennedys, you can't keep a lid on these things.'

Fascinated, Sweetman asked, 'And how do you see the British arena?'

The Swiss clearly knew his subject. 'In the United Kingdom it helps to keep your dirty linen private, but the crunch is *treason*. I use that word in its widest sense, the public school ethic of not letting the side down. You can be as incompetent and crooked as you like, but when the moment comes you must close ranks. The worst thing that ever happened to Britain was winning the battle of Waterloo.'

Huffily, Sweetman cleared his throat at this. But the Swiss was one of those urbane people it is impossible to protest against. And he plied Sweetman with questions that flattered as they probed, all the time showing that he was intrigued and honoured to have made the MP's acquaintance.

Recalling this episode, Sweetman repeated to Gwyer and Conefort one remark by the Swiss that had never left his mind. 'You may be familiar with the concept in American law of entrapment. Whenever a politician's career ends in scandal, I would guarantee you that in nine cases out of ten, this is not bad luck. Somebody has organised the event. Politicians are the tragic heroes of democracy. Once they topple, no fall is too far for them, no depths too deep. Believe me, I know this.' Somewhat the worse for drink and roulette, Sweetman had chuckled cynically. But no more.

'Sounds like a rum sort of character,' Herbert Conefort said, trying for the phrase that he thought his father would use.

But Tony Gwyer fixed Sweetman's eye and said, 'Follow it up.'

The only distinguishing feature on first acquaintance was that with his lightweight suit the Swiss wore matching grey gloves.

8

The three MPs met him in a Malaga bar run principally for German tourists, the cleanliness and order reflected in the prices. The Swiss felt that one of the three was serious and had eyes on him that were already scrutinising and making calculations. After a round of drinks and some banter in which the Swiss was careful not to appear either to know anything about the British politicians or to be offering any particular service, Gwyer said, 'Can we go somewhere less crowded?'

The place was almost empty. But the Swiss said, 'The evening light from the cliffs is beautiful. If you follow my car.'

When they arrived, looking down over the coastal lights and the pearly Mediterranean, the Swiss insisted that they check him for concealed recording devices. Conefort and Sweetman regarded this as ungentlemanly, but Gwyer accepted the opportunity, impressed by the cold way in which the Swiss took care of business. Nodding approval, Gwyer stepped back.

'You see,' the Swiss said, 'I wish you to be able to speak freely.'

'We intend to,' Gwyer said. 'Let's get to the point. If we gave you a commission – ' the Swiss nodded, signifying that he was in the market for just such a thing, 'your conditions would be – ?'

'First I must know the identity, in order to prepare the correct sort of operation. And then we will never mention him again.'

After a chill silence, Tony Gwyer muttered the name of Roderick Wardour.

Acting deaf, the Swiss murmured, 'Just so.' Then he continued, 'In return for an operation that could never be traced back, I require fifty thousand upfront, pounds sterling, and the same sum on completion. The money should be lodged in a variety of Swiss accounts in such a way as to draw no attention, and then I will instruct you when to transfer to an account held by me.' Nothing could be simpler. The Swiss looked from man to man. The Conefort son was the weakest. The Swiss observed how the others had welded him into the deal.

Herbert Conefort asked, 'What exactly do you *do?*'

The Swiss was almost bland. 'Believe me, my dear sir, the

9

scandal that works is the one where the victim's own point of weakness drives him headlong into the action which must destroy him. I apologise for sounding like a brochure, but it is a fact of life. In reality we do very little. Remember, it is not the rope that kills you, but the weight of your own body. All we have to do is fix the noose and release the trapdoor.'

Sweetman asked, 'Can we discuss this and come back to you?'

'Certainly. There is one more thing which you will need to consider. I will need a source close to the subject of the operation to keep me informed of his movements. This would only involve calling a foreign number and leaving messages on an answering machine. I assume you can manage this if you wish to go ahead.'

Noncommittally the men shook hands and split up, the two cars heading off in different directions. Sensing that total agreement might be lacking, the three MPs deferred discussion until the next day. Gwyer had the will, Sweetman the cunning, Conefort the money. The problem was Herbert Conefort himself. His success as a constituency politician was founded on his willingness to say what people wanted to hear, but in the wider sea of Westminster he was an uneasy figure who sought certainties that were rarely to be found. A similar lack of assurance blighted his personal life.

He had already prepared a story to account for his absence that evening, but Lucy Conefort did not even ask. Half undressed, his wife slowly removed her face, indifferent to Conefort removing his clothes behind her. The bedrooms they shared had become wider, colder spaces with the passing years. Herbert felt that Lucy despised him just as his father despised him, for not being somebody else – a Roderick Wardour, for instance. Like anyone with this classic dilemma, Herbert Conefort would gladly have changed, but had no idea how. Love affairs would have been an answer, to copy Tony Gwyer and take what he could get, sexually, wherever he could get it. But Herbert was too timid, and too straight for the Madame Whiplashes of Westminster patronised by ageing rakes like Jonah Sweetman. There was no way out, except to depend on Lucy's increasingly contemptuous favours.

Dabbing at her cheeks, she seemed more fractious than usual. Nervously Herbert asked, 'Is something the matter?'

To her own savage mask in the mirror Lucy said, 'That bloody woman.'

Herbert asked, 'Who?'

'Jessica, for God's sake.'

'Why? What's she done?'

Lucy spun round, years of frustrated competition with her sister surfacing in wretched fury. 'If Roddy becomes prime minister, *you* are resigning from politics and *we* are leaving the country. I refuse to live in England once Jessica gets Number Ten.'

'Oh,' Herbert said, 'old Jessie's not that bad – ' He stepped forward.

'Don't come near me,' Lucy said shrilly. 'All those years of humiliation – you just don't see it, do you? Let's face it, Herbert, I married the loser. And she's never let me forget it.'

Slowly, unthreading his tie from his collar, Herbert said: 'There's still time for something to go wrong. For both of them.'

Lucy was visibly interested. 'What do you mean?'

'Just something I heard.'

'Tell me more.'

'I can't,' Herbert said. But immediately he felt this secrecy conferring power on him.

Lucy disregarded her toilette and stood up. 'Anything that brings Jessica down is sweet music to me.'

'That's all I want for you,' Herbert said.

'I could make you tell me,' Lucy said. 'Or have a damn good time trying.'

In Herbert bashfulness fought with daring. The effect below his waist was beginning to show. A strange fierce glow rippled through Lucy's body as she stripped off her remaining clothes.

'My lips are sealed,' Herbert said.

'Are they?' Lucy answered. 'Well, mine aren't.'

The road hairpinned round the mountain-sides, climbing all the time, edging steeply along the rims of gorges, then looping back on itself before another stretch of zig-zagging gradient. Peaks sank behind as whole rocky landscapes disappeared into the mist of sheer valleys. Lucian Weidinger drove the narrow vertiginous roads with all the aplomb of his alpine background. On a good day they said you could see Africa from up here, but Weidinger had never been here on a good day, apparently.

There was an Irishman lived on this mountain, who had made it in fast food franchising in the Republic, and retired out here to bask in his fortune. His real business, Weidinger knew, was to serve as a link in one of those loose chains that channelled dope from the Middle East into northern Europe. Weidinger had phoned ahead to ask if another Irishman was still in touch, and had got a positive answer. There were vast spaces out here, but among certain strands of the expatriate community there prevailed a village-like awareness of each other's movements. Equally it was assumed that one man's business would always be of mutual interest to another, and ears were always ready to listen.

The mountain village was white-washed and picturesque. Weidinger walked patiently through a crowd of shrieking teenage girls on a school trip, and found Sean McDade nursing a drink in a shady bar on the main square. They shook hands and dispensed with preliminaries. In McDade's company Weidinger did not wear gloves, revealing the fact that on the third finger of his left hand there was no nail. The result of a boyhood accident, the blank finger-tip carried the scars of reconstructive surgery. Although sensitive about it with strangers, Weidinger had long ago concluded that to wear gloves all the time would make him more noticed than the occasional observant person spotting this feature. Ninety-nine per cent of humanity, Weidinger had concluded, possessed no powers of observation whatsoever.

He declined a drink, and within minutes his Alfa Romeo had taken him and McDade even higher, into a terrain of scrub oak and dwarf pine. Here, at a spot the tourist parties never reached, Weidinger pulled off the road in a shower of grit. The two men leaned on the car to talk.

'Are you still interested in a job, Sean?'

McDade, a small dark man who looked undernourished and was always between beards, hand-rolled a cigarette and said, 'Sure.'

'How is your personnel recruitment?'

'It's OK.'

'Capable men?'

'Guys in trouble with nowhere to go. If it's a job, they'll need a bit of upfront to convince them.'

'That's no problem. Get five together plus yourself.'

McDade spat and asked, 'What job then?'

As if to him it was an everyday sort of contract, Weidinger answered: 'A smear on a British MP.'

'What kind of smear?'

Weidinger shrugged off a direct reply. 'How active are your contacts in Spain?' He was referring to expatriate members of the IRA. Neither man needed to speak of the organisation by name.

McDade looked a little furtive, but answered, 'Fine, why?'

'That's the smear. These politicians are travelling all the time. There are two ways we could do it. One, we set a trap – our man walks in voluntarily. Or, we give him no option, we hit him over the head – figure of speech. Either way, he is photographed and taped, apparently doing business with an illegal organisation not unknown to the British government. All we need is the right calibre of Irishman, enough for a crucifixion. Can you raise a couple of names?'

McDade grinned, 'Sure, crucifixion's our business.'

The men parted soon after.

McDade had been uneasy at Weidinger's question for reasons other than what the Swiss thought. The IRA were strong in Spain now. Apart from Gibraltar's permanent attraction as a British target, they had climbed into bed with ETA, the Basque separatists, who only that week had blown up a prominent Spanish businessman using Irish explosive and advice. But the last thing McDade wanted to do was let expatriate IRA men know who or where he was.

13

When he had first fallen into Weidinger's orbit, McDade had boasted that he was on the run from the British. The fact that it was the IRA he was hiding from, was something he preferred Weidinger not to know. The Swiss had a way of holding aces for the right moment, then slapping them down, and while McDade needed the kind of work and money Weidinger offered, he had no illusions about his humanity. If Weidinger learnt that he could sell McDade back to certain people in Belfast, their business partnership would soon be on a meathook.

But perhaps the strangest force binding them was the knowledge that the men who cooperate most profitably are those who observe reticence in what they know of each other. McDade habitually gave the thinnest of clues about himself, Weidinger none, but they had collaborated in the chains that operated below the surface of a so-called law-abiding Europe – drugs, weapons, people who were disappearing by choice or otherwise. They knew each other's mettle.

The offspring of a rich Swiss family, Lucian Weidinger was cosmopolitan, rootless, a man contemptuous of order, bored by many academic years spent studying power. Attracted by the real thing, Weidinger had the personal wealth, the social ease and range of contacts, to act as go-between for men of power who required and appreciated discretion. Morality, Weidinger believed, was a device through which those without power rationalised their helplessness. He sought the environment of those who lived without mortality. And in the darker depths of Weidinger's soul lurked one other compulsion – he knew he could not be psychologically whole until he had killed another man. The one thing that magnetised him to McDade was the certainty – although this had never been explicitly declared between them – that McDade had killed. Through the clockwork of Weidinger's rationality ran a streak of hero-worship that bordered on infatuation.

Edmund Hendry was a former professional soldier, an enlisted paratrooper who had made lieutenant by the time he left the service. A tough, wiry man with thinning hair and a blond moustache, Hendry had always believed what they had told him, that with a good service record he would find the doors of the civilian world opening respectfully for him. A man who could hack it would always find his niche, they had said. But maybe the glint in his eyes was too hard, or potential employers feared that his drive and performance would make them look bad. All Hendry got were rejections. The ability to hack it seemed the one thing nobody in contemporary Britain wanted.

Robin Knight was the other ex-serviceman on McDade's team, although all personal details including surnames were rigorously excluded when McDade assembled his five men together. Knight was a naval man who had failed at the last ditch to qualify as a submarine commander. In accordance with regulations he was removed from the test submarine and heli-coptered immediately back to Faslane. The options did not need underlining. Aspiring commanders who failed were bad for morale, and Knight knew the rules. He would never go to sea in a submarine again. Rather than keep up appearances with an admin job in the surface navy, he had cashed in his time and bought a hardware store in a small town where he could conceal his life's humiliation. Widowed young and out of touch with life outside the navy, Knight had found the dusty shelves and slow-moving stock not enough to live for. A punctilious man, he hired someone to mind the shop during his absence. But the object of his trip to Spain had been to kill himself.

Dickie Loman felt that he had already committed suicide. His false step had been to expose a complex and clever fiscal evasion in the financial services giant in which he occupied an executive position. The fraud was costing government several million pounds annually. But in the process of exposing it, Loman soon discovered that the issue was sensitive. In other words, it involved respected and newsworthy names. After a few quiet resignations, nothing more happened. Except to Dickie Loman. First Loman's job functions were cut off. Then his title was removed, and with it his secretary, desk and carpet. Finally he was refused entry to the company building. Defied to sue for unfair dismissal, Loman wasted thousands of pounds and a year of his life on a case that won him scant compensation and no return of his job. Other applications went unanswered. However much he lowered his standards, told himself and his bewildered family that he was facing up to reality, Loman was forced to realise that his future in the City, in any city, had become non-existent. By now a paunchy, hollow-eyed wreck with a valium addiction and a bad case of paranoia, Loman wanted to get even.

So much for what McDade, although he had no liking for the type, thought of as the officer class. The 'men' consisted of two – Griffin and Nevis. Griffin was a crop-headed muscular young man who in McDade's estimation would do anything for money, and was in no position to ask much. Nevis was an amoral south Londoner with the build of a granite mountain. He allowed people to call him Ben, but his small thick-lipped mouth and permanent scowl defied anybody to make it a joke.

These were the men McDade had gathered. Apart from acquaintance with the Irishman, they all possessed one other common factor – exile, and a sense of being rejected by their country for doing precisely what it had demanded of them. The Costa del Sol was awash with men whose grievances against life, realistic or otherwise, focused on society's refusal to acknowledge their talents. They were out here because the sun made failure softer, on open-ended vacations, drifting or working casually, seeking any reason for not going back. Without being criminals they were all, in their way, desperate men.

Having got to know them individually over a period of time, McDade now called them in. They were the kind of team McDade had assessed he would need. Loman had the polish, Knight the dignity, Hendry the discipline, Nevis the touch of villain with a heart of gold, and Griffin the blank-eyed psycho look that might be necessary at some point. A team for all contingencies, although where McDade came from men like these would not rate highly. They were all English – Brits to McDade, although he kept the word to himself. So in the end he felt nothing for them except perhaps a lazy contempt, which he hid beneath flattery and enthusiasm and the hard cash payment of £1000 to each.

'On account, boys. Take it, and you've signed on. A wee float to say we're in business. No limit to what's to come. How about it?'

The large Nevis, mean stupid eyes twinkling, said, 'What's to stop us just taking the money and disappearing?'

'Because, my friend,' McDade replied, 'if you take the money and then don't deliver, disappear is exactly what you will do.' The answer seemed to draw satisfaction from the others. The one man people like these never wanted to work for was a weakling.

'Just asking,' Nevis said.

'Sure,' said McDade, 'no offence. Any more questions at this stage?'

Each man was then required to give McDade a slip of paper with their name and a contact telephone number; for future payments, further employment if suitable. While the men watched, McDade placed the slips in an envelope unread, sealed the envelope, and dropped it into a mailbox. Thus their anonymity vis-a-vis each other was preserved. After that the only complication was that Hendry and Knight had to return to England. They could be back within the week. McDade declared the timing fine. There would be a gap before he needed their services. All they had to do for now was wait.

The Wardours had driven away from Robleda leaving their hosts with the belief that they still planned to drive back across Spain to the port of Santander. But a few kilometres into the mountains Wardour pulled the Jaguar into one of the rare stopping places. What ensued was a staple of the Wardours' twenty-year relationship, a kind of wrestling match in which both partners forced each other to win.

'The nearest airport is Malaga, and that's where you're going,' Jessica said.

Wardour answered: 'All my life I've wanted to see the Alhambra, and you're asking me to give that up for a quick dash back to London.'

'With this Berlin business you should be there.'

'The Berlin wall will collapse without me.'

'The media must be dying for you,' Jessica said. 'You can't be on holiday at a time like this.'

'And you, what will you do?'

'I'll drive and see you back in London. And when I get there, make sure you've created a stir.'

Wardour asked, 'How if I said that the pleasure of driving back through Spain with you outweighs the next stage – the next ten stages – in my career?'

'Then I'd know you really were mad,' Jessica said. 'Now let's get you to Malaga, and on the way you can talk me through your thoughts on Berlin.'

Two days after Roderick Wardour flew out of Malaga, Ed Hendry pulled up in front of the airport terminal, over which the sun was just melting an early haze. Along the cab ranks the palm leaves were making a tinny rustle. The car-hire rep was late, so Hendry went to find a baggage trolley. Then he recognised the other man. Awkward, Hendry thought, although situations like this never taxed him. But the Irishman had told them not to pal up, even when they were finally called to the job. Until then, they didn't even know each other. It was unlikely that at this time of day, and off-season, there would be more than one London flight, so the Irishman's order was about to be put to a classic test.

The man Hendry saw – travelling even lighter than he did himself, and that was some achievement – was the one in the group he had felt least easy about. They were all recognisable types, and no doubt that was one reason they had been selected. The one Hendry was watching now had *officer* written all over him, and although Hendry himself had made it to the rank of lieutenant, one of the reasons he had left the army was that he had never fitted into the officers' mess, had never been able to match the public school slang and invitations for weekend shoots of his newly acquired colleagues. This had left Hendry with a certain resentment, but also the ability to spot an officer at a hundred paces. Life had taught him to avoid getting personal, but Hendry disliked this higher caste on sight.

Taking instructions from an Irishman (Hendry knew from the accent McDade was a Catholic) was also something which several tours of duty in Ulster had programmed him to find objectionable. But he looked forward to the test of self-control involved in refusing to acknowledge his fellow-Englishman now. The tougher the better. Hendry had just bet himself that chance would have them in adjacent seats on the plane.

Then everything changed. As the officer-type passed through the automatic doors, someone tried the collision trick – a momentary bump as the glass doors slid apart, a fleeting apology, a face lost in the spaces of the airport. Only the English apologise for being robbed, Hendry thought. He had seen the wallet vanish into the thief's pocket.

Hendry had a second in which to act, or not. *Not* meant he could maintain his distance. But everything else in Hendry drove him to action. Above all, from twenty years of barrack rooms where every item of personal property was invaluable, Hendry hated thieves. He also hated smart-arses, and the jovial-looking Spaniard, bald, moustached and avuncular, was clearly a smart-arse from way back. He couldn't wait to explore his trophy. Hendry ran diagonally through the cars.

'Hey, Paco! *Momento!*'

The Spaniard looked round. He was near his car, keys already in his hand. He made as if Hendry was addressing somebody else, although no other person was nearby.

Hendry communicated through a mixture of English, sign language, and physical threat. The Spaniard, outraged, protested, so Hendry did what all along he had known he would have to do. Also assuming that the thief might pull a knife, Hendry made it plain immediately that he was not just a member of the public. The channelled violence of the paratrooper was never far below the surface. Hendry shook the Spaniard about by his clothes, slapped his face a few times, beat him against the car, all the time indicating that in the thief's pocket was something he wanted. Anticipating what was about to hit him, the Spaniard opened his hands in surrender and handed the wallet back. He watched mournfully as Hendry examined the contents. There was no apology, because from the Spaniard's point of view it was just one thief robbing another. At least the Spaniard had done it with skill. When Hendry pushed him away the Spaniard threw back a volley of gestures and curses.

Hendry returned to the airport entrance. His car-hire contact had turned up, one of a little rank of such men waiting by the arrivals exit. They had watched the whole thing, and as Hendry approached they all stood erect and applauded. Embarrassed, Hendry explained to the car-hire man that he would be back in a minute, and went inside.

The man Hendry wanted was called Robin Knight. Rather than chase around, Hendry went to an information desk, told them he had found the wallet, and asked them to call Knight over the P.A. system. Hendry saw this as a way of preserving non-contact with Knight. Unfortunately Knight himself had been to this desk only a minute before, and the uniformed girl noticed him in the distance. Thinking she was doing both men a favour, she caught his eye and waved to him. So they were forced to meet.

Accepting fate, over a drink on the cafeteria balcony the two men waited for the flight and exchanged token information about themselves. They kept off the subject of their return to Spain. At Heathrow they met up briefly again, and it emerged that Knight had no car. A simple, practical man with not much to do, and those mostly things he would prefer to avoid, Hendry offered to take Knight back to the country town where he lived.

Here Hendry saw the hardware shop into which Knight had sunk his navy pay-off. Knight himself admitted it was humdrum, but after all those years in submarines the place gave him the quiet and space he required. He didn't sound convincing. Hendry felt relaxed by Knight – a real officer and gentleman, but a man in a predicament, somehow. Undemanding, though, which was what Hendry needed. It didn't take a business genius

20

to see that the shop was a dead end. The shelves had a stagnant look, the smell of merchandise that had collected too much dust, the sort of place that reps dreaded or avoided visiting. Knight had come here to hide, and as he made tea in the flat above the shop, there was an atmosphere of time hanging heavy, of life going nowhere. Yet this man had once, not so long ago, been a senior officer on board submarines, had come within a whisker of piloting enough warheads to destroy mankind around the oceans of the world. It all went to show, Hendry reflected, what could happen once you let things slide.

As Hendry was leaving, Knight said, 'I suppose we'd better keep this secret.' Hendry agreed. Knight asked, 'What do you think it's all about?'

'I never do that,' Hendry said. 'I never think what it's all about. I just get on and do it.'

As the taxi rolled down Whitehall towards the House of Commons, Roderick Wardour looked, as he always looked when he passed this spot, at the bus stop opposite the Horse Guards. The sight always gave him an inescapable inward shudder.

The best part of two decades ago, as a postgraduate student, Wardour had caught his usual bus from that stop. As it had pulled away into the jostling traffic of a late winter afternoon, the crowd had shuffled forward. One minute later, jammed at Parliament Square, he had heard the noise as the bomb went off. Only two people had died. The outdoor placing of the bomb (they had packed it into a civil service briefcase) and the angle of the doorway in which it had been left, had mitigated the effects of the blast. But in addition to the two killed, some thirty had been injured, losing limbs or eyes, or minds.

Later that evening, with the bombing all over the TV screens, Wardour had visited his girlfriend of that time, an Irish medical student called Bridie. It had been a tormented relationship at best, but that evening they had plumbed new depths of guilt and doom. Nowadays, whenever Wardour confronted the Irish problem, he always thought of Bridie weeping in front of the

TV set, and of the bomb that had so nearly shattered his own life.

Wardour had been a junior minister at the Northern Ireland office when his supreme moment came, during the Gorbachevs' official visit. Raisa Gorbachev's tour of London's historic spots had been placed in the hands of the Education Secretary, a polished but two-dimensional man to whom Wardour, whose short-service commission in the Guards gave him the right presence for an equerry, was assigned as aide for the day. But the Education Secretary had gone down with a virus and had to be replaced at the last moment by an even lower minister who had had to be briefed in the taxi and had looked sick and unhappy by the time he shook the hand of the Russian First Lady. The day had threatened to fall somewhere between a bore and a disaster when Wardour, too careful to speak to Mrs Gorbachev directly, had got into conversation with the interpreter, a dour man who preferred the heavy coin of summit meetings to chit-chat about tourist sights. Missing nothing, Raisa Gorbachev had turned to Wardour exclaiming at the fact that he spoke fluent Russian. Always underplaying his hand, Wardour had answered, 'A little.' A brief exchange had ascertained how little, after which Mrs Gorbachev had given the interpreter the day off and requested Wardour to be her guide. After politely shadowing them for an hour, the British team had withdrawn and left Wardour and Mrs Gorbachev attended only by the security men.

While reading for his Cambridge economics degree, Wardour had studied Russian in his spare time, ploughing through books, listening to dialogue records, even hiring a conversation coach. He had visited the Soviet Union three times and was able to talk with Mrs Gorbachev about places they both knew. He was also well informed on some of London's more out-of-the-way history, and presented a *glasnost*-flavoured view of the British past which was not quite the diplomatic stodge Mrs Gorbachev had been expecting.

On that one day Wardour had made one very powerful friend, a meteoric reputation, and a lot of enemies. Just the idea of a

British politician, let alone a Conservative, speaking Russian, was outlandish enough. But Wardour had made a point of not peaking too soon. There was nothing worse than making cabinet minister before you were forty. At present he was a contented parliamentary undersecretary of state at the Foreign Office, a department which had became devalued by the little-England-ism of the Thatcher years. But Wardour had proceeded to make his own mark there. When the Russians left Afghanistan, Wardour said to the House, 'A great nation is one which can bring its troops home from an unjust and unwinnable war.' RAISA'S POODLE, the hostile section of the Press said. But an increasing number of other people were saying that Wardour would lead the country into the third millennium.

The televising of Parliament meant that a natural orator like Wardour no longer had to be bound by the few dozen bored faces scattered about the emerald leather in front of him. Now, every time he rose to his feet, he was at least potentially address-ing the nation. Always a diligent attender, Wardour now haun-ted the Chamber compulsively, losing no chance to speak, embracing the privilege which television conferred on the man of destiny.

The House was preoccupied with the breaching of the Berlin wall. Master of the short speech which left at least one phrase ringing in his audience's ears, Wardour cut through all the waffle about triumph of democracy, death of socialism, fear of renewed menace from a strong Germany, with a few unscripted sentences. 'Perhaps, Mr Speaker, the age of Europe's night-mares is finally over. The people streaming through the Berlin wall send us one very clear message, which is that governments erect these monstrous barriers, but only the will of the people can pull them down. When we stop applauding the courage of the real actors in this drama, we should ask ourselves what we have contributed to the destruction of this wall, and how we propose to live in a Europe which is no longer governed by the dead hand of outmoded prejudice.'

Everyone knew what he was talking about. Wardour was too shrewd to mention Ireland by name, but the coding of his speeches rarely left anyone in doubt. The TV cameras tracked along the government front bench to the frozen face of the Prime Minister. The rest of the House, instead of responding with its usual monkey-house noises of agreement or dissent, let Wardour speak and sit down in respectful silence. In the press gallery the journalists scribbled gleefully.

It all seemed a long way from the Café Nemesis and the hills of the Alpujarras. The three MPs who remained there, seeing out their mid-session break to the end, Berlin crisis or not, had turned the square of Robleda into an extension of those cosy Westminster bars where gossip was the main business of the day. As the waiter padded round with long glass tubes of beer and plates of *tapas*, the three men waited for the Swiss to arrive. It was the middle of the afternoon; the children had returned to school, the adults to work, but the atmosphere of perpetual lunchtime which was the charm of those places, still lingered.

Weidinger's Alfa Romeo pulled up. He was prompt, and no respecter of *dolce far niente*. Soon they were speeding along the foothills of the Nevada, Weidinger at the wheel. 'Well, gentlemen, we have a deal, yes or no? Subject to my proposal, of course?'

His languor always hinting at something more vicious, Tony Gwyer said, 'It looks as if we do.'

'The money is OK?'

Gwyer and Sweetman looked at Herbert Conefort, whose enthusiasm to do Wardour harm had been transformed over-night. 'As soon as we get back to London,' he confirmed.

Weidinger kept his eyes fixed on the serpentine road. A former lecturer specialising in international terrorism, he still kept his file on European politics in good shape. 'Very well, gentlemen. Mr Wardour's weak point is a certain – let's say, sentimentality on the Irish question. He sees himself leading a national change of mood. Let's see how he likes it when he wakes up in bed with his terrorist friends.'

The three MPs exchanged looks and sounds of approval.

Weidinger continued, 'I will give you a foreign number to

ring. An answering service, that's all. Messages to be left anonymously. But I will need constant updates on Mr Wardour's activities. Travel arrangements in particular.'

Then Weidinger stopped for them all to shake hands and regain their breath above a spectacular Spanish landscape. In their faces he saw the fear and elation of men who have steeled each other to momentous action. The English were always cleverer than they appeared, and Weidinger assumed that these were here as agents for a stronger faction within their party. A man who had grown terminally bored with security, Weidinger enjoyed the whiff of danger their commission brought with it. And if they were buying him today, he would sell them tomorrow. 'Well,' he said, 'as always it's a wonderful day for doing business.'

Two

For Jonah Sweetman's sixtieth birthday party, Archie Conefort
lent him Shearwater, the family house on the river in Berkshire.
With lanterns strung through the trees and a band playing
traditional jazz somewhere in the grounds, the place buzzed to
hundreds of voices and the constant movement of guests through
a still warm evening. The political and social mix around Sweetman was always interesting: television people and the press,
who revered Sweetman as one of the last real characters in the
House; property men and occupants of the fast lane of the
financial world; women of various social and sexual descriptions
wearing the most expensive dresses they could afford, enormous
hats and flashing eyes.

Except Jessica. She had come in a simple dress of pale grey
with no ornament. Hatless, her make-up perfect, she carried
herself with regal simplicity. Roderick Wardour wore an open-
necked shirt and cravat with his old Guards blazer, an image
calculated to offset Jessica's austere beauty. A Ph.D. thesis
could have been written about the language of clothes at such
a gathering, and its salient point would have been the arrival of
the Wardours.

'The shy one at the orgy!' Jonah Sweetman exclaimed.
Instantly excited by this blatant bid to upstage the finery of
every other woman there, Sweetman – a raddled, rotund man
whose wig was already cheerfully awry – headed straight across
the lawn to bow over Jessica's hand and clasp himself to the
chaste ampleness of her bosom.

The Wardours' marriage was rock-solid, which was another
affront to the many quietly and not so quietly desperate,
unstable relationships on show tonight. A bachelor himself,
Sweetman had a taste for decomposing marriages, since none of
them was his own, but seemed to feel that the Wardours' evident

affection for him was a kind of priestly absolution for the darker side of his life. Meanwhile, the Wardours' marriage was one of the most highly profiled in Britain, glamorised and analysed in the colour glossies at all levels of the market. A relationship of twenty years, that had produced two children and the usual run of devoted supporters and family pets, beautiful houses in town and country, an efficient political partnership, and no scandal, had been hyped into something approaching a modern wonder of the world. The Wardours had charisma, so what was dull in other people, in them acquired an ineffable sparkle.

For Roderick Wardour Jessica's appeal was something he basked in, the complete antithesis of the jealous husband. But they held hands, sometimes even kissed, in public, especially when cameras were around. It was a marriage made for public consumption with the same aura of non-stick classiness that had characterised Roderick's political progress. Everybody who met the Wardours came away feeling good, blessed even. Charm, as those who lack it soon learn, is the politician's deadliest weapon.

So Sweetman's birthday celebration, although enjoying its riotous corners, became increasingly a lordly parade for the Wardours. Too many people wanted Rod as a future friend for it to be otherwise, and the only sure way to Rod was through, as 'in' people advertised themselves by calling her, Jessie. Even those in competition might one day need to join the bandwagon, and on this evening they kept their less charitable feelings to themselves.

At a point in the proceedings when the jazz still played but the air was cool and cars had begun to rev up and wind their way back through the Shearwater park, the three men who had sat together at the Café Nemesis met up again. The Wardours had just left and, as if this gave a signal for the party to fall flat and the postmortems to begin, Tony Gwyer drew Sweetman and Herbert Conefort to one side. As the host, Conefort put discretion above his saying-goodbye duties and took the other men to an undisturbed den in Shearwater's east wing, where they could nurse their brandies and talk in peace.

A thin man with a disarming toothy smile which gave him

the look of a vulnerability he was not burdened with, Gwyer was the politician as anti-politician. He detested the theatricals of the Chamber, the old boy atmosphere which said that party differences were less important than belonging to the best club in London. For Gwyer differences were everything, not only between parties, but within parties themselves. An outsider candidate, he had fought a by-election in a safe Labour seat which happened to include an army camp. During the campaign they bombed the camp, and Gwyer was elected on an hysterical anti-terrorist platform. It was the kind of simple, single issue this self-made millionaire handled well. Having raised his horizon, he now saw his destiny in the Conservative party as an extension of his asset-stripping expertise acquired in the business world. His weakness in ideology became his greatest strength. No tolerator of complex argument, Gwyer had long ago learnt that life went more effectively without it. His approach was clear: cut out all the mush and slush and those who made their careers peddling the same. What Margaret Thatcher had started, strong men were needed to continue.

'So,' he asked, 'how did we like the king and queen?'

'Problem is, old son,' Sweetman said, 'everybody wants to screw Jessie. The women would like to do it with a pineapple.'

Gwyer looked at Conefort in mock disapproval. 'I myself, I must confess,' Sweetman added, 'find the presence of her body an enchantment. And we all know about you, Tony.'

'Absolutely not,' Gwyer lied. 'Not my type, Jessica. Much too clever.' His sarcasm concealed years of longing for Jessica Wardour, kept in order by fear of rejection by her.

'Don't look at me,' Conefort said. 'I'm a happily married man. I'm getting everything I can handle.'

Gwyer and Sweetman guffawed. 'Handle!' Sweetman repeated, slapping the table. Herbert Conefort touched his face nervously, unsure of the hazard lines when men were discussing women.

As the amusement died away, Gwyer said, 'I heard from our Swiss associate. He wants me to confirm that we still wish to buy in his service.'

Jonah Sweetman's blotched, drink-reddened face looked apprehensive. The set of his wig was a millimetre out, and its fresh strawlike weave made the rest of him look much older than sixty, mocking his body like astroturf in the garden of a derelict house. 'Roddy's very strong. I don't fancy him as an enemy. Although I admit that any escapade that scuppered him and left mud sticking to the terrorist bogtrotters would be good for the country.'

'Herbert?' Gwyer turned to Conefort.

'I'm for it,' Conefort said, with surprising decision. 'Providing our names are kept out of it.'

'Nothing easier,' Gwyer said. 'The IRA will come to Roddy, and being the crypto-paddy which we all know him to be, he'll fall for it. Evidence will be collected and undisclosed sources will make sure that the press pick it up at the right time. What we want is a story that can never be disproved, which Roddy will spend the rest of his life struggling to get from under.'

'The classic smear of the innocent,' Sweetman said.

Gwyer smiled, no respecter of resounding phrases. 'But he's not innocent, is he? On the other hand, if the steak's a little *tartare* for you – '

Sweetman shook his head impatiently. 'My dear boy, politics is the butcher's yard. Nothing you can tell me about that. No, what I fear about Roddy is his energy. Too many people are getting caught up in it. We have to burst the Wardour snowball before it rolls any further.'

'This Swiss chap,' Conefort said. 'Do we have any references on him?'

'I'll vouch for him,' Gwyer said. 'When someone's my kind of person, that's all the references I need.'

In bed that same night Jessica said: 'Guess what I found. You remember the envelope?'

Wardour grunted, sleepy. 'Mm-hm.'

'I came across it today. I'd kept it so safe I'd forgotten where it was. Your forecasts all came amazingly true.'

At the last May Ball of their Cambridge days, the twenty-one-year-old Wardour had written on the back of an envelope a timetable for his future which had ended with 'Downing Street – 2000'.

'Past tense?' Wardour asked.

'I found you terribly impressive that night, the way you just wrote it down, had it all worked out.'

More awake now, Wardour said, 'Politics is a sort of zen; if you get it right in your mind, reality falls in step.'

'The envelope was for me, wasn't it?'

'How, for you?'

'The way you handed it to me. It was a proposal, a challenge, a way of saying this was Roderick Wardour, if I wanted him.'

'I seem to recall it as a public advertisement,' Wardour said.

'You mean I was the only customer?'

'The shrewdest. Or the most desperate.'

'Or the one who really believed in you.'

'I've always been grateful, Jess.'

'We've done well together.'

Wardour kissed Jessica's cheek, but the kiss had the formality which typified all their closest encounters. Their sex life had become a repertoire of amiable gestures. 'We haven't even started yet,' Wardour said.

Jessica fondled the muscle of his chest and shoulders, as she would have touched and admired a thoroughbred racehorse. 'Can I say one thing?'

'Of course.'

'Leave Ireland alone.'

'It's already alone.'

'Don't risk your career for it. It's not worth it. And there's no answer to that problem, you know it. Mm?'

Wardour smiled. 'How do you see my epitaph: *A great man, he took a penny off income tax*? Believe me, no prime minister who fails the Irish challenge is worth a damn. "History is a nightmare from which I am trying to awake".'

'Who said that?'

'An Irishman.'

For the moment Jessica let the matter drop. In twenty years

30

she had never failed to persuade Rod of her point of view eventually. She would plug away at it again, until she won.

They lay still, not avoiding touch, but not touching. The few minutes between waking and oblivion when a sleepy, routine kind of sex might happen, once again passed unclaimed. For both the Wardours sex had yielded its passion and credibility to the wider horizons of power of which they dreamed daily.

Several days later Wardour was driving back from his Surrey constituency. As a junior minister he rated a government car and driver, but according to opinion polls the public found it sexy that a man in his position drove himself, especially when, as in Wardour's case, the cars in question were always Jaguars. During Wardour's political career three newspaper articles had been written referring to his car habits: Wardour knew good image-accessorising when he saw it. The darling of the forecourts, one article had called him, referring to the fact that when Wardour drove into a petrol station the arrival of this tall, physically appealing man in his sleek automobile stopped everything. Everyone looked, some people spoke or requested autographs. His appearance made their day, and Wardour, a man possessed of both humour and humility, knew how to bask in the experience without overdoing it.

On this particular day Wardour was pulling out onto a main road when another car shot by. Only after following for some miles did Wardour register that it was a black, medium-range VW, driven by a woman who was alone, because every time he attempted to overtake, the narrowness of the road, or oncoming traffic, prevented him. At a roundabout the road widened into two lanes for a brief stretch of dual carriageway, and Wardour was finally able to pull up parallel to the black car. He met the eye of the woman driver for a moment before shooting forward. The Volkswagen took the roundabout at the same time, and when he next checked his rear-view mirror, Wardour saw that she was now following him. For a time they both held sixty, as traffic ahead inhibited Wardour from letting the Jaguar take off. Then she was in the inside lane again, seizing a gap which was opening up. As she drew level with Wardour, the woman glanced sideways. The look was neither curious nor triumphal. Wardour was used to being stared at in public, but this was different, a look which seemed to declare that the cars had taken over, were following each other for pleasure.

The road became single carriageway again. When a moment came, Wardour eased forward and overtook and then slowed again. In his mirror the road unwound to reveal the black car still in his wake. For some reason this made Wardour glad. When the following car accelerated, flashing to overtake, instead of speeding himself or blocking the way round, he let the VW go. From the corner of his eye he saw the woman pointedly not looking at him, no doubt watching him in the same covert way. Once ahead, she slowed again. If ever two cars paraded for each other's arousal, this was it.

Then she was gone. In the traffic build-up Wardour's view of her was momentarily lost. He was gripped by an unreasoning sort of possessiveness: the cars had become each other's playthings, no longer free to vanish as easily as they had appeared. Wardour began to drive badly as he searched for a further sight of the black car, but there were other black cars and cars of every colour obstructing his view as he hunted the VW at speed. Irritation set in. For just a moment something had flashed across the window of Wardour's life and before he could decide whether or not to seize it, it had swept away again. For a man with a hundred things ahead of him that day, Roderick Wardour felt strangely desolate.

Needing a fast drive, Wardour decided on a fast burst on the M25, the motorway ring round London, but after a few minutes at a hundred mph, Wardour saw the ominous signs in the distance – traffic slowing, brake-lights winking, cars bunching as a lane somewhere closed down in a forest of orange-and-white cones. The next exit was miles ahead. He might get there at a crawl and sneak into London via the airport. But fifty yards and ten minutes later Wardour abandoned further fantasies of speed. He took off his jacket and loosened his tie, selected a new cassette, phoned ahead to his next appointment and warned that he would either be late or would phone again in half an hour to cancel. These M25 jams were always packed tight with stressed young men in shirt sleeves and powerful cars, barking into cell-phones. One of the icons of contemporary man, Wardour thought. Perhaps it was a good idea for a politician to share it.

The cars were boxed for miles. All engines were off, and in either direction the motorway was solid metal. Fortunately the day was overcast, warm but not hot enough to make people rage. In the opposite three lanes there was some traffic movement, but it was sporadic, as if a mile or so away, surface works and contraflow had combined to jam a thousand cars a minute into an almighty bottleneck. Or even a pile-up. But so far there were no flashing lights or screaming sirens.

Wardour reached for his attaché case and portable recorder. Might as well dictate replies to constituents' letters. Minutes later, stuck in the middle of a reply on the subject of street litter – how to evade committing himself to anything while making the recipient feel flattered to get a letter from Roderick Wardour MP – he realised, somewhere in the blankness of his mind, that he was staring at the car in the next lane.

Wardour's heart kicked. It was the black Volkswagen. Trapped by the jam, both drivers now had all the time they could wish for to study each other. Unable to accelerate away, they enacted this in a manner that was simultaneously intimate and coy. Their brief car chase had stripped away most of the normal formalities. The woman in the car had the same bored look, the enforced passivity, of everyone in the traffic jam. But something fleeting in her eyes, for a reason he would never understand, struck Wardour as powerfully familiar. It was not a face from his past, but that was how it felt. An uncanny recognition flooded his veins.

Momentarily Wardour's conscience took over. He was in the habit of looking at other women, of course. But only in the way that most men look at other women. Otherwise his marriage to Jessica was in better shape than most approaching their twentieth anniversary. Even if they had nothing left to discover, there

33

was still the occasional excitement, usually after weeks apart. And Wardour had never been unfaithful, a fact which obscurely embarrassed him. There had been the odd *almost* flirtatious exchanges of charm during conferences and trips abroad. But for one kind of woman Wardour was too straight, for another too dangerous, and if infidelity meant being body to body with someone else, alone in a room where they could explore total nakedness, he had spent twenty years in absolute fidelity to Jessica.

So what now, and why? This was not the normal routine of checking out an attractive female body, covertly admiring breasts or watching thighs as legs were crossed. Wardour sat trapped in his Jaguar awaiting the moment when all the traffic would start to move again. A terrible fear had descended on him, the dread that he would spend the rest of his life recalling that woman's face, wondering who she was, regretting the new world of possibility that had flickered by but eluded him. She would anguish his dreams forever.

Unable to see her number plate, Wardour solved his immediate panic by deciding that, as soon as the cars moved, he would quote her registration into his microtape. He would then, somehow, trace the number, and then – he could go no further now, but he knew that he could not let the traffic flow carry them apart with no chance of ever meeting again.

Perhaps he was staring too obviously. The woman looked over at him. She gave a wry smile, shrugged, then looked away again. Wardour's heart misted over: he forgot who he was, forgot the Foreign Office, the parliamentary career, he was no longer a future Prime Minister or Raisa Gorbachev's favourite western politician; he had become a vessel for forces stronger than himself, the victim of one of those glamorous moments which turn the rest of one's life to ashes.

He noticed a cell-phone in the woman's car. It gave him an idea. On a sheet of paper he wrote his own code, and the next time the woman looked his way she saw Wardour displaying the number and pointing to his phone. They could have wound down the windows and talked across the one-metre gap, but phone to phone from the privacy of their cars tendered a different kind of intimacy. The woman looked uncertain, then responded.

His muscles tingling, Wardour could tell from her face that she was not just going to enquire politely what he wanted. She liked the idea. The phone bleeped. Wardour's heart pounded as he took the call.

'This is crazy,' she said, in an American accent.

'Yes,' Wardour said, 'I know.' That was what Holly Odell liked about the English, the way they *knew* something but pushed blithely on regardless. The snarl-up had lasted an hour, by the end of which they had become incapable of letting each other go. After the first available exit from the M25 they took narrow roads through well-tended villages into wooded countryside. Neither of them had any clear idea where they were going. Yet they would know when they arrived.

They had introduced themselves as Rod and Holly. No surnames, no litter of detail to puncture this supernatural togetherness. Wardour even struggled, as he drove, to remove his wedding ring and with that one faithless gesture he realised that things were happening beyond his conscious control. The ring bit into his knuckle, but the desperate act of trying to remove it told him everything, both what he wanted to know, and what he did not.

They parked in a clearing at the end of a track, and walked through woods of brown and green bracken.

'Are you always this crazy?' Holly asked.

'Never,' Wardour said. Did she know who he was? Nothing gave it away.

Wardour took her hand. Holly wore no wedding ring. It didn't necessarily mean . . . but Wardour had stopped caring. All that preoccupied him now was, how did he kiss a woman who was not his wife? Not kiss the way he did hundreds of women socially, but kiss with surprisingly intense desire?

Holly's face was not a girl's any more. It had thinned, acquired a few lines, a pretty and tough face, not over-feminine. Her deep grey-green eyes stripped Wardour's soul. Joined in a

35

congruence like the perfection of an art form, their lips drew the rest of their bodies together in a welling of hungry fire.

'Do you feel it as well,' Wardour asked, 'that we've always – ?'

'Known each other.'

'Yes.'

'Yes.'

It was tempting to detach themselves, joke about it. But the woods wrapped them in a solemn stillness. As they made their way through the soft undergrowth, words would have been an intrusion. Even Wardour's reflex about his schedule disappeared – he had phoned to cancel that appointment, the M25 had its uses. The rest of the day was open. Jessica was out of town, nobody was expecting him. He could be where he liked, with whom he liked, doing what he liked.

On dry leaves and crushed bracken, indifferent to their clothing, they sank into a world of wide-eyed daring and timeless pleasure. The only words they spoke, murmurs of lust and endearment, sprang from a lifetime's fantasy carried on a wave of total and unbelievable release. Even the earthbound mechanics of cleaning up and rearranging clothes rested within their romantic aura. Only as they walked back to the cars did their hands become uncertain of each other's touch, and their voices take on the more distant timbre of separate worlds.

Wardour's defiant panache had deserted him. He was now in a mortal terror that some woodland stroller would recognise him – might even take his car number, Holly's number. But at the same time he felt neither regret nor guilt. He had found the partner who had haunted his dreams, the partner that Jessica had somehow never been. But how did he say goodbye to someone he had always known, and hence would always know? As if she sensed his hesitation, Holly took over superbly. As they shifted from foot to foot and toyed with car keys, she admitted to knowing who he was. Wardour was relieved, but looked sorry. For that hour he had wanted to be nobody, nothing more than the man who was lying on a forest floor with a woman who needed no name other than Holly.

'It's all right,' she said. 'I'm not impressed. Much.'

Dry-mouthed, Wardour asked: 'What are we going to do?'
'Live off a wonderful memory.'
'And?'
Holly raised her eyebrows. Wistful, gorgeously ironic.
Wardour said, 'You can always reach me at the House – '
'Yes, well, my name's Odell. I'm in the phone book.'
They both imperceptibly checked the clearing to make sure
there were no witnesses. Then, one more time, they embraced.
Their eyes said, don't let's speak any more. The road went left
and right. With a wave they drove separate ways.

Holly Odell was a thin, tallish woman who had all but stopped
using mirrors, except for functional purposes. In two years she
had found no satisfaction, much less pleasure, in looking at or
cultivating the image of herself which she found there. Now she
was unsure if she had fallen in love, but she felt the next
strongest thing, that someone had fallen in love with her. And
it was easier to be swept along by this feeling than by the more
fragile tremor of her own emotions.

In her early thirties, years of premature widowhood had
brought out a natural gauntness in Holly's well-proportioned
face. Assessing herself now, for the first time these two years,
she decided that she looked as good now as she ever had. She
had large, deep-set eyes, a wide mouth with thin, chiselled
lips which as soon as they parted revealed large teeth and an
impression of smiling as she spoke. But her mouth had a down-
ward cut, and experience had underscored this gravity with lines
that gave her beauty in repose an ascetic quality. With her short
fair hair and self-contained, independent manner, Holly had
always been taken for a lesbian by a certain section of the men
she met, an interpretation she had accepted readily for the
freedom it gave her.

Why now, and why Roderick Wardour, Holly would never
know. But she had served her time in the desert, and some
phenomenon of the same kind must have happened for him.
Maybe it was seducing each other verbally, from within the
modern world's supreme ego-box of separate cars, that had done

it – whatever, it had been the great emotional flood of her life, the end of winter.

Even if they never met again, this would always remain true.

Holly watched Wardour on TV, addressing a half-full House of Commons. Seeing him in that setting, she couldn't believe what had happened between them. Recalling it, and she recalled it all the time, she had difficulty believing it was her, either. Two years without a man, and of all the ways for it to happen! By definition it was unrepeatable, so even if it had made it possible for her to sleep with men again, no other man or occasion could ever measure up to that sexual torrent.

On returning to her flat, Holly had looked through all the pictures of David, the husband whose presence still haunted the place, and wept. But now she felt that once again she could weep tears that were warm. She wondered how Wardour had dealt with it. Had he returned to his wife, his political career, blanking it out, the way you had to be able to blank things out as a politician?

Holly was glad she hadn't replaced her video after the last burglary. If she had one now, she would have jabbed it on and captured these images of – God, was that his name? – the Honourable Roderick Wardour. Then she would have played them over, freeze-framing in a lonely late-night search for the vanished lover who had plucked her from a motorway jam, from the drifting sands of her life.

Or had she plucked him? Better not to debate it. Certainly better not to have pictures of him to torture herself with. Let the past go. Yet here she was, lapping up the parliamentary broadcast and feeling elated when she caught Wardour making a speech.

The phone rang, Holly deadened the TV volume and upset a stack of mail, readers' letters vibrant with pain and aching for advice. Today Holly was working from home. The letters were work: once, she had been a serious journalist, with all that that implied; the commitment to truth, facts are sacred, news, news, news. Then David had been killed, and his death was news too, and Holly had not been able to take it. So for two years she

38

had sunk, making out as best she could. A hard-working independent woman could always get a living.

The phone call was her father, speaking from Boston. 'Dad?'

Holly never called him Pop or Daddy or anything but that straight businesslike address.

Barron Odell called his daughter Hol. For a long time she had hated it but now, as they respectively faced old and middle age, Holly was getting to almost like it again. These monosyllables now sipped a tenderness from time.

'What do you mean, Ireland?'

'This is it, Hol. I'm coming over. It's time to go back.'

Back? He had never been there before. And for what, Holly wondered, the 150th anniversary of the potato famine? The next thing coming was, 'We can meet up.'

Wardour was on his feet again, gesturing silently on the TV screen. Holly cursed and wished she had replaced the stolen video, 'Great, Dad.'

The camera panned across other MPs' faces, laughing in dumb show, then back to Wardour, who had drawn his blood and now sat down again, smiling and finally showing the face that Holly recognised.

'I knew you'd like the idea, Hol.'

'When?'

'Maybe a month from now.'

Tell him business, Holly thought, claim to be checking your diary and invent an unbreakable work engagement. Across her silence Barron Odell was saying, 'I knew you'd like it.'

'And you'll come to London?'

'No, no, the way I figured it – ' He had no way of knowing why she didn't want to go to Ireland, even to the South. 'We could find our roots together, Hol – '

He's terminally ill, Holly thought. Or feeling old, which, for once, she herself was not. But his enthusiasm made her grimace. Who could she ever tell the truth to now, she who earned her living answering letters from newspaper readers whose lives had gone wrong? Even her father had only been told that David had died in an accident at a railway station. Embarrassed at never having met Holly's husband, Barron Odell had refrained from asking for further details. Exactly what Holly, unable to admit both the horror and triviality of such a death, had counted on. Railway station was right, accident too, in its way. But the bomb had been no accident. Planted at that quiet station whose main clientele were soldiers from a nearby army camp, it had killed two corporals on return from leave, injured several other people, and annihilated the man Holly loved and still, more than two years later, expected to walk in the door on which his coat still hung.

The IRA had claimed credit for the bomb. Nothing her father said or did would get her to Ireland. But for the moment it was easier to say yes.

Unaware of this conflict in his daughter, Barron Odell relinquished the phone agreeably. She had accepted, that was all he wanted for now.

But a few seconds' thought decided Holly. Even to humour his atavistic fantasy, she would never meet him in Ireland. Apart from her own bad associations, there were too many gaps in her relationship with her father – the divorce when she was a child, the later discovery of her father as an overpowering unhappy but emotionally extravagant man who needed his daughter to take away guilts she could not even understand. No, she would see him in London, on her own turf. The saddest index of their relationship was that even before he left the States, Holly was plotting how efficiently and painlessly she could get him on the plane back.

The doorbell rang. As soon as Holly opened the door wide enough Pumpkin, the tabby cat, gave her familiar squeak and walked in, erect tail pointing at a messenger who proffered a bunch of neatly tailored roses. Among the roses a card, unsigned, said that the sender would be in the same place at eight o'clock that coming Sunday morning.

At the same moment Holly had been watching Wardour speak in the House of Commons, he had been thinking of her, even as he was on his feet and rolling out the supremely articulate, unscripted sentences for which he was noted. If he was even better than usual, the image of Holly – Holly in the traffic jam, Holly in the Surrey coppice, Holly somewhere now – gave him an exhilaration and clarity of mind that did not go unnoticed.

Wardour himself had no doubts. A keen observer of himself as well as others, he had remarked two exceptional symptoms. Normally he did not look directly into the eyes of others, but followed the movement of their lips as they spoke. But with Holly he had looked nowhere but into her eyes, for as long as it was possible, and he had found there a relaxation, the promise of an endless, welcoming truth that communicated even above what their words or limbs were saying. Also Wardour had a facility for calling to mind the faces of people he knew, even those only met briefly years ago, as accurately as if they had materialised in front of him. But the struggle to conjure up Holly's face kept him awake at night and still defeated him. For Wardour, being in love could have no deeper definition.

The roses were a conventional gesture, but Holly would be there, Wardour was sure. Although he knew nothing about her private life, this certainty possessed him. She would be there because she had the choice of meeting him or not, and if she let the moment go, he would never get in touch again, and she would torment herself for ever about how it would have been a second time. He knew this was how she would work. For the same reason Wardour had swept aside the doubts, the risks, the shadows of guilt that played around the edge of his own mind. He wanted her again, and he would damn well do it.

Everything was well fixed for that Sunday: Jessica was at the country place with Josh and Tamsin home from school, and Wardour was to join them at lunchtime after a morning's work in town. The Sunday roads were quiet, only the odd newspaper-buyer or dog-walker on the suburban streets as he drove out into Surrey.

One complication arose on the way. As Wardour pulled into a petrol station to tank up the Jaguar for the journey out to Buckinghamshire later, another car stopped on the forecourt. Its window buzzed down. 'Hullo, Roddy!'

Wardour's hand went slack on the pump trigger. In a dead voice he said, 'Jonah.' He knew he looked troubled, and a trace of irritation showed.

'Early morning spin?'

'Sort of.'

'Jessica in the Ladies?'

'I'm alone.'

'I see,' Jonah Sweetman gave a knowing look.

'And you?' Wardour asked.

'Golf, old boy.'

'Perfect alibi, eh?'

'Too old to need alibis,' Sweetman said.

They laughed and went their separate ways. The encounter and the trite but pointed dialogue disturbed Wardour, and started him thinking.

By the time he reached the wood, it was raining. Holly was already there. Wardour pulled up alongside and they leaned out and kissed, awkwardly, through open windows. The rain was coming down harder all the time.

'Damn it,' Wardour said. 'Bloody annoying.'

Holly said, 'It wouldn't be the same in mud.'

'If you want to know,' Wardour said, 'I've never made love in a car.'

'Is that a suggestion?'

'Not really. I imagined a perfect replay of what happened before. A car wouldn't quite live up to that.'

Holly seemed pensive, then said, 'Look, follow me.'

Half an hour later she was letting him in from a quiet early-Sunday-morning street in west London. Rain washed red brick and raised a warm smell from the dusty tarmac.

In the doorway Holly turned to Wardour and kissed him. The kiss both expressed and overcame apprehension. Wardour, too, had been getting nervous as well as excited as he followed Holly's car and realised where they were going. Although he was already telling himself that he would have to be careful not to be spotted when he left, the freedom of Holly's flat aroused a terrible lust in him. He felt like a teenage boy, suddenly aware that his first seduction was about to take place.

Holly led him in. Almost the first thing Wardour's observant eye noticed was a man's coat, several in fact, on the hall rack. He played with the cat in an attempt to brush aside his unease. Holly had not actually said that she lived alone. Elsewhere there were photographs of a man, both alone and with Holly, which clearly answered the question in Wardour's mind. He tried not to stare.

Noticing his glances Holly said, 'I'd better explain.'

Afraid that what he would hear might spoil what remained of the romantic occasion, Wardour insisted not. But moving about the flat, looking at or touching the things which she knew disturbed Wardour, Holly told him about David. 'I didn't put anything away, because there was no reason. I'm not upset by them any more. In fact, as the pain has worn off, they've become rather friendly things. I'm sorry, this is rather an abrupt way to get to know someone. Not everyone has their lives on display like this.'

Wardour was shaking his head, burdened by the belief that his own feelings should now be completely set aside.

'Don't,' Holly said, knowing what he was thinking. She touched him randomly, her hand lingering. 'You haven't stumbled in on anything. It was me that brought you here, remember.'

Wardour hugged her. He was not used to women whose emotions were open yet strong at the same time. Slowly the consciousness of why they had come here overtook them. Before Wardour went into the bedroom, Holly put away all the reminders of David. It was not the coy or guilty act she had always feared it would be, but an embrace of the person she had become during her long empty night.

And suddenly everything was possible, feeling Wardour's nervous hands slowly strip her, unclothing him to revel in his long naked body, wanting and discovering things buried a lifetime ago. The rain beat down outside. Through the window all they

43

could see was a sky whose breaking cloud symbolised an infinity of spirit.

Their luck with each other, too, that special luck of two bodies that through a benign accident of nature fitted from the first moment, physically, rhythmically, anticipated and affirmed feelings unasked. That good fortune now demanded exploration, somewhere to grow, but Wardour was too recognisable to risk a return to Holly's flat. It would have to be something else.

Wardour had to go. First he had to clean himself up for a family lunch in Buckinghamshire. Before making a furtive, hasty goodbye at the door of Holly's flat, Wardour said, 'You know, what we need is to disappear.'

Three

Since the Channel Tunnel had got off the drawing board, Jonah Sweetman had assiduously bought reasonably priced properties in the Calais hinterland, whose resale ought to see him through a comfortable old age. Together on the terrace of the House, Wardour casually asked Sweetman if he still had his own place in France.

'Don't talk to me about France, Roddy. Must own half of it by now. Looking for a *pied à terre?*'

'I need somewhere for a very sensitive meeting. Out of the UK.' Wardour's candid manner and general gravitas forestalled any nudging or winking, any stray thoughts of improper conduct. 'You used to have a place in Normandy.'

'Dear old St Benoit, yes.'

'Even Security aren't going to know about this. And that includes Jessie.'

Sweetman chuckled, one man of the world to another, and said, 'Well, my little hidey hole has total seclusion. A crone from the village goes in once a week and does it over. But if I ring and announce guests, she just sticks a load of Perrier in the fridge and keeps out of the way. When do you want the keys?'

'It depends on my contact. I can't give much notice.'

'Only too glad to help,' Sweetman said. 'You name it.'

The quality which had both made Jonah Sweetman a formidable politician and, early on, limited the path his parliamentary career would take, was his capacity for intrigue. A man who would have been happier in the eighteenth century's corrupt world of big well-rounded personalities, he loved secrets, gossip, the machinations of the backstairs. Any misgivings Sweetman had entertained about the scheme to bring Roderick Wardour down, evaporated the moment Wardour involved him in this private drama he was playing on his own account. Sweetman had no doubt that Wardour was using him in a way he could not yet divine. But that only made the idea of a counter-play all the more piquant.

Sweetman sought out Gwyer. 'Tony, my dear boy, we have him.' Sweetman explained everything. Gwyer looked quietly triumphant.

'But what's he up to?'

'It could be something legit,' Sweetman said. 'But it's underhand, and when he came to me he knew he'd got the right man.'

'Let's take it as a challenge,' Gwyer said. 'You remember what our Swiss friend said? It's your weight that hangs you. I think Roddy just put his head in the noose.'

It was Gwyer's bloodthirsty arousal that set off the first tremors of doubt in Sweetman's mind. Perhaps things were falling into place a little too neatly. 'What do you think will happen? What if these people turn out to be a bunch of – ' Sweetman cast around for the correct word ' – psychos?'

Gwyer's response to introspection was always the same; stamp on it. He laughed. 'Some of our finest public servants are psychos, Jonah. Look, you just do your part. You've got the phone number, pass on relevant information about Roddy's movements. You're not breaking any law. Look at it this way – we suspected Wardour of devious actions, we set up a check on him, and lo and behold, what does he do but start acting deviously. QED.'

'But are you sure these people will get the result we want?'

'I talked some more to our Swiss friend,' Gwyer said, patiently impatient at Sweetman's wavering. 'His job is to produce evidence that Wardour is dealing privately with the IRA. Roddy has this obsession with Ireland, OK, let him pay for it. They guarantee he won't be hurt, physically, but you know how it goes, Jonah. Once the mud sticks, Roddy will spend the rest of his life trying to scrape it off. And nobody will want to know. The smear stays for ever. That's the beauty of smears. To be a

46

successful politician these days, you have to be smear-proof. If you like, we're just putting Roddy to the test.'

Once the scheme took hold of him Wardour let it run, enjoying it more as it gathered speed. He had no intention of spending a weekend with Holly at Sweetman's French retreat. While Wardour was laying the smokescreen, Holly was making the arrangements they would actually follow. A place in France, certainly, but booked under other names through an agency. Wardour was not fool enough to weekend with a woman in a place where a fellow-MP had eyes and ears. His plan was to drive over to Sweetman's place and leave some small evidence of having been there so the alibi would stand up should it ever be checked. It was essential, for instance, to rumple the bedclothes. But not the sort of rumple which lovers would make. Wardour derived great satisfaction from such fine detail.

Then, as the date approached, he instructed his secretary to make a reservation at the Belfast Europa under an alias. He said he would take care of the flight and security aspects himself, but asked his secretary to phone him at home to confirm the booking. If he happened to be out it was all right to leave the confirmation with his wife. Wardour then made sure he was out, and Jessica duly took the call.

Jessica said, when he returned, 'You're not going over there again?'

'It's only for a night. Two, if things go well. It could be a breakthrough. There are men over there who still trust me more than the people they currently have to deal with. I'm sorry it's come up so bloody suddenly.' Wardour kissed her, gave her body the light cosy fondle of many years' familiarity. Jessica took little persuading, she approved without question anything that might aid his political advancement.

'Don't get hurt, will you?'

'I'm flavour of the month, Jess. The first person to ask me the time will be mown down by Sergeant Rottweiler of the Special Branch.'

Jessica gave a tight, prim smile. Not a subject for joking, an

47

inane remark, but if he'd made it to Holly she'd have laughed aloud. Wardour couldn't help making the fatal distinction. But Jessica's desire to be Mrs Prime Minister remained both Wardour's strength and her own weakness. She wouldn't ask why he was going, and she knew better than to trespass on the classified areas of his political life. Whatever won and maintained power was right, she would look no further.

If Jessica ever found out that he had not gone to Belfast, he would say that Belfast had been a blind all along, and the meeting had taken place across the Channel. Jessica had only the vaguest idea of who or what the IRA were, but she knew that dealings with them required all kinds of underhand practice. Wardour would claim St Benoit as the true location, and if Jessica ever requested verification of the story, Sweetman would have to confirm Wardour's account that he had indeed been there. And Jessica was sufficiently hungry for power to value, if she ever discovered, the fact that her husband had been lying about Belfast. She had sometimes openly wondered if he was sufficiently cunning and ruthless to survive in the political jungle. Perhaps, Wardour felt, she was waiting for him to prove something after all.

With Jonah Sweetman, Wardour candidly paraded a sort of honesty. When Sweetman handed over the keys and asked when Wardour planned to arrive, Wardour safely told the truth. Sweetman also asked casually which crossing Wardour planned to take. Feeling good at being able to respond confidently without any subterfuge, Wardour answered, 'Dieppe.'

Fine and slender as a web of platinum wire, the plan was put together. From the time which Wardour had given as his expected arrival in St Benoit, Sweetman calculated in reverse to the ferry on which he would be likely to cross from Newhaven, and from there to the probable time of leaving London. Sweetman reasoned further that if Wardour wanted secrecy he would hardly be taking his Jaguar. Sweetman put the theory to the test at a chance meeting in the House.

'Regrettable spate of car break-ins in these remote villages – foreign vehicles the main target. Better watch out for your Jag.'

To which Wardour readily replied that he would be hiring a car for the trip. The essence of subterfuge was to be straightforward in all particulars except the crucial – bury the lie in a shroud of honesty. Having listened with apparent indifference, Sweetman now went away and transmitted all his information to a recording machine on the overseas number which Weidinger had given them. Although he suspected an African country, Sweetman refused to check the international code. Being clever was fun, but being too clever could be dangerous.

The recording machine was in fact in Algiers, where Weidinger paid an expatriate contact for the use of the service, which included playing all taped calls back to a second machine at Weidinger's base in Switzerland. The Algerian number was an office premises that could be decommissioned at extremely short notice. In case of anyone ever coming on their trail, Weidinger felt safer behind this break in the communication chain.

Wardour could hardly have been more cooperative if he had been playing along deliberately. He had made it clear to Sweetman that his trip abroad would be alone. Destination and timing were no secret. Weidinger could not believe his luck. He had the men, and the victim was about to deliver himself. All Weidinger needed was premises, and a way of bringing about the means of Wardour's destruction. The question of location was easily solved. Sous-bois was a country house, not a chateau of the tourist brochure kind but a solid, rambling haut-bourgeois mansion which originated in the Napoleonic era. More important, it was empty, hidden within a several-thousand-hectare estate, and its ultimate owner, untraceable behind a labyrinth of holding companies, was a drug-dealing cartel which owed Lucian Weidinger a favour.

Then, after the quick shot of sedative with which Weidinger had supplied McDade, to ensure that Wardour's transit through the French countryside was trouble-free and left to memories, Weidinger had orchestrated what would happen to Wardour on arrival. Certain amiable Irishmen would attend Wardour as he recovered. If he showed signs of regaining consciousness too soon and becoming difficult, there was always the option of further dosage. If, on the other hand, he felt relieved to be safe and in friendly company, and gave a positive response to their questions, the operation could run very smoothly. Whichever way, everything would be taped and photographed. The Irishmen's faces were already on the British anti-terrorist files, and Wardour's complex position on Irish matters would create an instant atmosphere of distrust. Then the compromising material would be made available to interested parties. Wardour would be accused of secretly attending a top-level meeting with representatives of the IRA. The senior echelons of the IRA themselves would never deny this, once they saw the confusion it would cause at Westminster. In spite of propaganda to the contrary, progressive MPs like Wardour were in the long term the IRA's worst enemy. And then, besides, denials such as those Weidinger anticipated from Wardour himself would only serve to confirm the accusations. In the age of the lie, the only safe man was the one who could prove the truth. On that basis, Roderick Wardour was doomed. He had been doomed from the moment he came into Lucian Weidinger's sights. Or so Weidinger complimented himself.

Once McDade had the details, he assembled his team. Following the times Sweetman had given, the six men were put in place. From first light the Wardour house in Regent's Park was watched by Griffin and Knight, and the driver of the cab which cruised up when Wardour appeared on the street had been well paid to make sure that another car, occupied by Griffin and Knight, tailed them to their destination. The destination was an Avis rental south of the river, and as Wardour headed out of London a call to a prearranged public call-box on the south coast alerted the two men there as to his leaving time and the make and registration of his car. On the approach road to the ferry terminal a high-powered Nissan picked up Wardour's Peugeot and stayed with it all the way onto the boat.

Two men waited either side of the water. At the British end Dickie Loman drove, with Ed Hendry. Loman had no idea who the Peugeot's driver was, or why they were about to snatch him, but something about the driver's personal style, his relaxed movements, the way he drove with his left arm draped across the empty passenger seat as if fondling an absent lover, soon told Loman that they were not in for a car race here.

Having made their call, Knight and Griffin screamed down the Brighton road, returned their car in Newhaven, and met up with Loman and Hendry on the boat. The four men in the Nissan followed Wardour into Dieppe and almost immediately, before any choice of route presented itself, slowed down to let McDade's BMW into the crawling line of traffic. The number of Wardour's car had been phoned through to the Dieppe team, and the pursuit began.

None of them knew the identity of the occupant of the Peugeot. It was just, as McDade said, a nice soft pluck. The two teams were excessive to requirements, assuming that one man could hardly give so much trouble. But all six were aware that among other things this was a blooding operation in which judgments of each operative's abilities would be made, and from which other assignments could follow. Tidy as a lace hanky, McDade said, as he slid the BMW between Wardour and his unsuspected tail.

But seconds later the Peugeot's brake-lights flashed and a woman stepped forward off the Dieppe street corner. The driver leaned over, opened the door, and she quickly got in. The car pulled away with hardly time for a gear change, although the couple inside had managed one rapid, hungry kiss.

To the five men under his command McDade never expressed irritation or anger except by lowering his voice. 'Did you see that now?' he muttered. His voice had become very quiet. He got on the car phone to the Nissan. 'Target picked up a woman. Plan goes ahead.'

The job of Nevis, riding with McDade, was to wrench the car door open, or if it was locked, terrify the driver into opening it. Failing all else, he had to smash his way in. Then to restrain the target for a few seconds, long enough for McDade to stick a hypodermic into Wardour's thigh. McDade thought fast and

51

answered the fears before Nevis could voice them. 'Ben, you get the girl out the car and into here. Then proceed as normal.' By radio to the Nissan he ordered, 'Dickie and Griffin, you take over my car and drive on up the road, after the pluck, understand? Griff, hold the girl down while I put her to sleep. We don't want screams, and we don't want either of them to see what happens, OK? Black hoods on and everything smooth as a baby's bottom please, boys.'

Wardour's reasoning had been that in a more out-of-the-way place he would attract less, or possibly no, notice. Where people didn't expect to see the famous they were less likely to recognise them. He passed most of the long journey on deck, softening his profile with a cap and a scarf inside an upturned collar. The journey was made less tedious by the fact that Holly Odell was on the same ferry. Killing time around the boat, they exchanged nothing more than silent glances and the occasional flex of expression that no third party could ever have intercepted. By the time the ferry berthed their minds were in a ferment, their bodies humming for contact.

Once Wardour cleared passport control in the hired Peugeot, he stopped for Holly, who was already waiting ahead, to get in. They trailed slowly through the industrial approaches to the port, railyards and grimy gull-shrieking streets.

Navigating, Holly said: 'We don't have to keep to the motorway.'

'No more delays,' Wardour said.

'Suddenly we've got all the time we want.'

'You're right,' Wardour said, easing his foot on the pedal, 'this is stupid.' In fact from the moment he landed in France every nerve in his body had been unwinding. Getting out of England had been a superb idea. Here there were no trip-wires. 'We'll take the next exit,' he said.

The French countryside was sinking into a mild dusk. They didn't need to wait for their rented bedroom, they could just lose themselves on a quiet road that led them nowhere except to each other.

A car overtook the Peugeot and disappeared round a bend ahead. A half-kilometre more and the same car came into view again. There was a car behind, too. Some quiet road, Wardour thought. Still, the next deserted lane, off we go. But the front car seemed to be coming back towards them. And the following car was gaining. Then full-beam lights came on. Wardour's eyes recoiled from the sudden glare in his mirror.

'My God,' Holly cried, 'what's wrong? What is it? My God, what is it?' She screamed as the cars closed in.

As soon as they had screeched to a standstill, bumpers inches apart, Nevis was out of the BMW and heaving the door of Wardour's car open. He thrust his hooded face close to Holly's and said, 'Stay pretty, lady. Not a sound, right.' His fist clenched her upper arm.

Holly turned to Wardour, but he was already shouting at other faces in the nearside window.

'What the bloody hell – ?'

Nevis dragged Holly from the car. On the other side Hendry and Griffin were ripping Wardour's seat belt off, and hauling him out. Holly resisted, kicked and turned her head and yelled, 'Rod, for Christ sake help – ' But that was all. Nevis slammed a meaty hand over her jaw and wrestled her along to the front car.

None of the hooded men spoke. Unlike Holly, Wardour was controlled, apparently more passive. Apart from having seen enough violence in his life to know not to resist, his mind had made a rapid calculation. This was no mistake. They wanted him, not Holly, they couldn't have known about her. Bewilderment at why they should want him and who they were kept fear of what they would do to her at bay. For the moment, he reasoned, he was of value to them. A sense of his own dignity also preserved him – a minister of the crown didn't submit to manhandling by greasy thugs. Once out of the car, Wardour tried to brush them aside. 'Leave the girl alone, she's no use to you,' he said, imperiously. But they ignored his words, showed no interest in his physical cooperation. Strong forearms pinioned him against the car, Wardour felt something against his right thigh. Any reaction he might make had been anticipated and as he suddenly panicked and tried to struggle, he felt several powerful bodies enforcing his immobility. There was no pain, only stillness, the waves of panic receding, as they held him there. At exactly the moment when Wardour's mind cried out, *they're killing me*, his nerves and muscles relaxed into a tranquillity that made the hooded men's grip feel like an embrace, like nothing more than a strange cuddle, as he sank against the car, his chin sliding down the curved steel of the roof. It was the cosiest bed he had ever known. Wardour felt he would collapse all the way to the ground, but the strong bodies behind relieved him of gravity, and eased him into a dark grateful sea of sleep.

Holly struggled to look round for Wardour, but all she was aware of in the gathering darkness was silence – no crying out in pain, no violence, no shots or sounds of beating. This puzzled her more than anything, and it flashed through her mind that Wardour might somehow be involved in all this. A few hours of stolen ecstasy didn't count as *knowing* somebody. What was he part of? Or had she blundered into something worse? The car's engine started, they were going to drive her away from here, she hoped, dump her by a roadside as if she didn't exist. They had no use for her. Holly begged gods she had never believed in that these people would have no use for her. But in the back of the car other hands kept her still as they drove a short distance and tightened their grip as something pierced her leg. For a minute nothing happened, they weren't going to hurt her, and then everything was a sweet velvety blackness.

McDade tapped Loman's shoulder, signalling to pull the car over. Separating the man and woman had been a precaution, in case one witnessed what was happening to the other. As the woman grew limp beside him McDade cursed the problem and wondered how he hadn't foreseen it. Did he use initiative now, or go to Weidinger for instructions? They would have to keep the girl. But what happened when the IRA boys turned up? This was an uneasy thought in several ways. With no idea of what their assignment would be, McDade's men had welded together into a group, and apart from a few superficial personality abrasions, no weak link had been exposed. But five fit and physically hard men, hyped up by the job, were going to be a problem now, locked up with a woman who, according to the plan, didn't even exist.

A tricky one for McDade too. If the little Irishman's tastes had to be given a label, he was a sadist. If he liked female bodies, it was to see how far they could be pushed. That had been part of the trouble in Belfast. As he slid the needle into the girl's leg, McDade had felt the stirrings of his old temptation. He had made a good job of it, he thought, efficient, but in fact the girl was too terrified to feel normal pain, and once the syringe was out and she slumped against him, McDade wanted to use it on her some more, in ways that had nothing to do with medicine. But maybe later. For now they returned to the other groups, and packed away the needle and the sedative. With hoods removed, and Dickie Loman at the wheel of Wardour's Peugeot, they drove their cargo of two heavily sedated bodies into the night.

Four

The three cars drove the 150 kilometres to Sous-bois by carefully chosen separate routes. Speed was essential, and while a trio of fast cars crashing through sleepy towns in cavalcade might arouse attention, individually they would be ignored. Every stage had been rehearsed, and within twenty minutes all three cars had pulled up in front of the house. Only McDade had entered the place before. He opened up, switching on no more lights than were necessary for the other men, moving with silent efficiency, to carry the limp unconscious bodies of Roderick Wardour and Holly Odell into the musty-smelling interior.

The woman had not figured in the plan and every step of the way McDade kept rubbing up against this fact; the allocation of beds and mattresses ran to seven, not eight. McDade quickly ordered things to be rearranged so that the victims were isolated in rooms at opposite ends of the house. A couple of the boys would have to split a bed and mattress somewhere else. It was only for two nights. The guard routine also had to be modified. Instead of two men with Wardour, one in the room and the other outside, McDade detailed Hendry to go in with the girl and Nevis to watch Wardour. After an hour the team would change. The object was to detect signs of recovery from the drug. Even split between the two captives, the lorazepam compound ought to keep them under for some hours. McDade had further dosage, enough to keep Wardour out for two days if necessary, but divided in half that time now had to come down to a maximum of twenty-four hours.

In a small study in a corner of the ground floor, McDade sat in a threadbare tapestry chair whose back was dark with ancient hair-cream, and took the call he had arranged to come through at this time. Only the message was unexpected.

Another Irish voice, scratchy over the long distance, said, 'The party's off.'

McDade said, 'What?'

'We picked up heat.'

'Heat? What fucking heat?'

'We reckon the Brits are onto us. Somebody's waiting for us to move. So we're breaking up the cell. Sorry and all that.' With no time for further explanation, the line went dead. McDade gripped the receiver as if strangling a serpent, then jabbed it down. Sonofabitch! Various obscenities formed on his lips, but his mind had already raced ahead of them. He sat back for a moment.

McDade had felt confident about his role in the Wardour smear. The prospect of working with some boys from the movement, always glad of a few grand, had drawn great energy from him. And activities deep in mainland Europe were remote enough for certain people in Ulster not to get wind that Sean McDade had raised his head. But the woman – he had been unable to work out any way of fitting the woman into the plan. She was the one thing they had not counted on, an independent corroborator of Wardour's story. Dumping her and keeping Wardour would be messy. Although maintaining a front for the benefit of his men, McDade had been getting sick with unease over the woman.

But this sudden failure of his contacts to materialise gave McDade a chance of the one bottom-line escape – they would simply take Wardour and his girlfriend to some deserted spot and leave them to come round in their car. If they ever reported what they thought had happened, who would believe them? McDade breathed more easily with this way out in mind. But first he had an arranged call of his own to make, to a hotel some kilometres out of Zurich. When it answered McDade stuck grudgingly to the agreed code.

'Herr Mauer?'

'This is Herr Mauer.'

Once he had confirmed that it was Weidinger's voice, McDade switched into normal language. Bugger what it did to Weiding-

57

er's code, he wanted some help out of this mess. Into a silent receiver McDade gave the curtest of summaries. Then Weidinger's cold, clear voice sounded. 'Don't panic. Sit on everything. Keep your men calm. Tell them everything is on target. I'll be with you soon after daylight.'

Weidinger hung up.

After he sent the boys downstairs for the meeting which he could not put off much longer, Sean McDade took a brief moment to look at the two sedated bodies he was suddenly trapped with. The stress of getting the precise timing of the kidnap right had eclipsed from McDade's mind the idea of these victims as anything other than a cargo for which he was the middleman. Now he had to ask who they were, and why somebody wanted them.

Although the windows were shuttered, lights were kept to a minimum, in case some poacher or trespasser on the estate had his curiosity aroused. McDade swung a torchbeam across Wardour's face, smoking thoughtfully as he gazed at the unconscious MP.

McDade had never bothered much with British politicians. In Ulster they tended to come and go, bright boys on the way up or premature wrecks on the way down. Either way, Ulster was just a dirty pond they had to wade through to get somewhere else they would rather be. Wardour was somehow different. During his brief shining passage through Northern Ireland, he had created the impression that at last someone had the intelligence, the energy, the right manner with all the different groups involved, the connections and the will, to unfreeze the deadlock. He had also shown a grasp of the fact, not widely acknowledged among politicians, that times change, and this year's unthinkable can become next year's inevitable, given the political courage. The joke had it that this was why they had shifted Wardour to another department, but such a man had value on all sorts of markets. Coming from nothing with nothing, McDade knew he could find an angle through all this. The problem was those boys downstairs. Running through various ideas, McDade went to take a look at the woman. She lay outside the bedclothes, not an inspiring sight. McDade stared at her with the detachment of a man whose feelings about women had always been confused, who was only happy with women when they were at his mercy. A dribble of saliva ran from her mouth, and her breath came uneasily. She wore a light dress, rucked up over bare legs. A gentleman among them had removed her shoes, revealing neatly painted toenails. Just as McDade feared she might vomit, the woman turned on her side and began to sleep more comfortably; the sedation was wearing off. But as his eyes coldly noted these incidentals, McDade's mind was unrolling the years – fifteen, twenty – to the time when he had known this woman before.

This had to be salvation. McDade moved to the side of the bed, to see the woman's face more clearly. He knew her, God-damnit! A mystical quiver in his blood declared the fact. A quick look in her bag told him the rest. Name of Odell! Barron Odell's daughter. McDade's stunned recognition permutated the sweetness of this coincidence. Until now McDade had not wanted to know who his captives were. Now he had no choice. Somebody somewhere had to be waiting for these people. McDade gave himself two hours. By then the rest of the world would be starting to catch up.

The kidnappers met in the kitchen, which was still in appearance a dark, echoing domain of hacking, grilling and roasting, where only servants had actually eaten, although dust now coated the scarred grease-darkened surfaces. Awaiting McDade the men shuffled on the flagstones.

Nevis, the corpulent Londoner with a mane of greasy hair and small, fleshy, ignorant mouth, shut the door. He spoke quietly, but a note of defiance conveyed that he didn't care if McDade heard anyway. 'I don't know about you boys, but I don't like it.'

Loman stepped in, 'We have to keep calm.'

Griffin said, 'There's something wrong. I can smell something wrong.'

Nevis looked across and nodded as if this one endorsement had made his own view supreme. 'This Irish git don't tell us enough. If he goes down the fucking toilet, I don't want to go with him. You know who that was we just carried in here?' None of the kidnappers had wanted to say it, but they had all recognised Roderick Wardour.

'Plus,' Griffin said, 'there's some skirt we never bargained for. I mean, who's she? And when do we get out of this place?' Unsure what to say next, he turned to Hendry. 'You're a bit silent, mate.'

Hendry was by nature and training taciturn. He also disliked mutiny, not from any respect for authority, but because mutinous men so rarely measured up to their words. 'I think you've signed on,' he said. 'I think you're in it up to your necks whether you like it or not. I think you should keep your mouth shut.'

The hostile silence was broken by Robin Knight's attempt at diplomacy. 'We have to stay together, for our own collective security.'

Dickie Loman added, 'We can't expect money for nothing.'

To the contempt that remained on Nevis's face Hendry added, 'If this gets tough, I better be able to rely on you the way you can rely on me. If there's a weak link, I say let's take it out now. Then let's give the Irishman a chance.'

The ensuing absence of words decided it for the moment, if not the long term. Nevis stabbed at an ancient chopping-board with a broken-bladed kitchen knife. As if on cue, McDade entered, showing no sign of having heard anything that had passed between the five men.

'OK boys, let's get it on.' McDade was a deliberate hybrid of the casual and the imperative. 'Straight to the point, our sleeping beauties upstairs. First, there are twice as many as we catered for. Next, it looks like we may be stuck with them.' In the muted light the five men listening formed a statuesque tableau. Much of their efficiency as a team, and their individual salvation, depended on nobody giving away reactions. Now, beneath the forced impassivity, each man's mind raced through the implications of what McDade had said. As they waited, the Irishman lit an untipped French cigarette and smoked pensively

60

for a moment, then continued as if everything was so plain it hardly needed saying. 'What we got to decide, in just a wee bit of a hurry, is what we do with the merchandise. Now we're all good democrats here, isn't that right, so we all have to go along with whatever happens. Or get out now.'

In the silence the only movement was somebody shifting weight to the other foot. Robin Knight asked, 'What do you suggest?'

'I don't suggest anything. I'm telling you what I'm going to do. If you don't like it, you're on your way.'

Griffin, a man who looked none too bright, but did a daily work-out designed to keep his muscles impressively firm said, 'What do we get if we quit now?'

'You see,' McDade said, with a faint smile which they were learning to fear, 'the guys that employed us have handed things over.' McDade always maintained the impression that behind the six of them stood some shadowy but powerful organisation. These men were all frustrated authoritarians, happier if they felt part of a machine. He continued, 'We're our own bosses now. If you want to jack it in, pay back your advance and get the fuck out. No risk, no reward.'

Dickie Loman's prim over-educated voice said, 'You are not clear.'

'Here's how it is,' McDade said. 'We could drop the merchandise at the side of a road. They won't remember a thing. Maybe they'll think they had the fuck to end all fucks, and go home smashed but happy. That way we get nothing. Except maybe caught. Or, we say we have a few days' march on the people out there. These are two beautiful people. Somebody's going to pay to get them back in one piece. All we ask is payment for the job of returning them.'

'What if they don't pay?' Nevis said.

'My huge friend,' McDade answered, 'I don't know about you, but in that event I personally go back to zero. I've done all this for nothing. You may have a wonderful life waiting for you, but I'm looking for a way to improve mine. If there's a chance it'll pay, I'll make it pay. If all I got to sell is those bodies upstairs, I'll sell the bastards. So how about you?'

Nevis glowered in the shadows, but acquiesced. He hated two things, small people and his social superiors. This encompassed ninety per cent of everyone he met. His eyes moved malevolently to the left as Robin Knight spoke, with the clarity of a service briefing. 'We all know too much. Anybody who leaves now is a threat. If one man walks out of here, the other five would be insane to let him go more than a hundred yards.' A long pause allowed Knight's argument to sink in. During the resulting grunts of agreement, some less enthusiastic than others, occurred one of the fleeting moments when Knight and Hendry permitted their eyes to meet, carefully expressionless but checking that they didn't yet have any reason to avoid each other.

'OK, sweethearts,' McDade said, 'that's good. Now try this idea for size.'

Five

When Roderick Wardour woke it was dark and he realised that he had been tied. Not tied to the bed, he was able to roll about too easily for that, but his arms and legs were bound, so his elbows dug into his belly, and level with his crotch his wrists, separately roped, already ached from the constriction. He felt as if he had been physically worked over. Fear numbed any panic he felt. He soon dismissed the thought that this might be a terrible mistake, and clung to a more hopeful equation – if he was important enough for someone to do this, they would look after him.

Time did not exist, and the darkness robbed him of space. Wardour sensed a sparsely furnished room, in which he had been left alone. Every time he thought about Holly a mixture of guilt and angry revulsion swept over him. He had been so stupid! He had an impulse to shout her name so she would know he was there, alive, thinking of her. But already, in spite of his gummy mouth and the puzzlement clouding his brain, Wardour was weighing consequences. Shouting Holly's name would look like an act of rebellion to be punished, would seem the admission of a weak point they could exploit. Wardour rested silent.

His arrival in France was already no more than a vague memory. That this place was still France he had no doubt. Generations of garlic-infused cuisine and Gauloise tobacco had imbued the walls with an unmistakable odour. As light began to penetrate the shutters, Wardour tried to reduce his tension with deep breathing. But the tight nylon rope refused to yield. Whatever else had been blanked from his mind, he remembered Holly, their last minutes in the car, and their reasons for coming to France. His imagination suddenly ran wild and pictured where they should be now, what they should be doing, as if his present bondage was some esoteric sexual spell from which Holly was about to come and release him. The dream died in ashes, laced with fear of the unknown and a painful flash of embarrassment at what this would probably do to his career.

Wardour's need for a toilet was desperate, but pride and perhaps caution – as if he was safest while they thought him unconscious – stopped him calling out. In the end a sense of his own dignity refused to let him soil himself. He was about to snap when quiet footsteps paralysed the cry on his lips.

The short man who came in was wearing a black hood. Somewhere, beyond Wardour's vanished recall of the previous night, lurked figures in black hoods. Eyeholes and a crudely cut shape for the mouth gave the hood the face of a childlike monster. Silently the figure untied all the ropes except those on the wrists, and beckoned Wardour off the bed with what the MP now saw was an automatic pistol. 'Don't make a sound, OK?'

The Irish accent provoked a tremor in Wardour's gut at the reminder that the IRA were everywhere in Europe – the Gibraltar bomb plot, attacks on servicemen in West Germany. As the fear mounted, Wardour told himself that if they wanted to kill him, they would have done it by now. But Holly? She was no part of anybody's scheme, she had no value to them. For a moment Wardour thought he was going to lurch forward and vomit in front of the gunman. As the nausea passed he took one private, redeeming oath – he would only give them information in return for guarantees of Holly's safety. It was the least he could do.

The gun prodded him into a room, a toilet cubicle with ancient but once-opulent fittings, stained hardwood seat and carved handles at the end of a tarnished brass chain. Wardour was left alone for a minute. But the frosted window, narrow and mildew-blotched, offered neither escape nor view, and the doorbolt had been removed. It was impossible to get the bound hands round to one's rear, but for the moment Wardour could live without that. The warm voiding of his bladder made him feel briefly optimistic, but when he turned at a rap from the automatic, he caught sight of his face in a small mirror mounted on the door. Sometimes the body knew things before the mind. What Wardour saw was a haggard, unkempt nonentity. He stared at his image in appeal, but the lined, unshaven face offered no pity. The gun rapped again. Stiffly, the blood throbbing in his legs, Wardour obediently shuffled forward.

A similar arrangement was made for Holly in another part of the house, timed so that by then Wardour would be back in his room, tied up by Griffin while McDade held the automatic, and no chance sighting or sound between the victims would occur.

At the conclusion of the kitchen meeting, still only a few hours' sleep in the past, McDade had summarised, 'The woman has to be the weak spot. She's no idea why she's in all this. He was probably just giving her a lift somewhere. So, Robin, be nice and gentlemanly to her and get her to spill the lot, eh?'

During the group's consolidation period, Knight had become known as the one who was good with words – glib, and very slippery. This, and his social background, made him the outsider. But Knight was finding his feet. He was the only one who could handle the woman with the right manners and verbal approach. Moreover, Knight was openly pleased by McDade's recognition of this fact. The protection of a hood made it even easier, like watching somebody through a one-way mirror.

'What we would like you to do,' Knight said, and he could see she was surprised at the precise, civilised voice coming from inside the hood, 'is to write a letter to the person who would most want to get you out of here.'

Holly's voice was strained, and Knight was surprised to discover that she was American. 'What am I doing here?'

'Do you know the man you were with?' Knight's assessment was that she knew, but was going to shield Wardour's identity. He had recognised the MP himself, of course, but kept quiet about it.

'Do I have to be tied up like this?'

'What would you do if we let you loose?'

'How long am I being kept here?'

'It depends.'

'On what?'

'On you.'

Knight was gentle, insistent, but behind his control he had doubts. As a submariner he was used to fine calculations, and he had primed himself for no more than twenty-four hours as a kidnapper – after that, money in the bank and time to think again. But McDade's words had disturbed him. Being suddenly unable to see an end to this business troubled Knight's love of orderliness. He asked again if Holly knew who her companion was. This time he elaborated. 'You understand, *we* know who he is. Tell me about your connection with him.'

'I never met him before. He gave me a lift.'

'You don't even know his name?'

'No.'

'You arrive in France, and off the boat the first thing you do is start thumbing lifts?'

'Why not?'

'You don't look the type for a hitch-hiker.'

Suddenly Holly was angry at being forced to lie here, confined by ropes, while some smooth-mannered ghoul in a hood picked holes in her inconsistent story. 'Fuck off, then. If you're going to kill me, kill me. Just don't expect me to lie here and talk like a normal human being. You bastard.'

Knight waited out the rage. He was grateful for the hood. Extremes of female emotion had always embarrassed him. In Holly's face it soon gave way to inverted anger and depression.

'All we want is for you to write a letter.'

'Shove it.'

'I'll dictate,' Knight said, and he could have been talking to himself when he added, 'You don't have a choice.

Tied up again, Roderick Wardour tried to use the sharpest talent he had, the skill with which he had cut through the jungle of politics: that ability to locate the other man's ego at its softest, and persuade him that he, Wardour, was its champion.

'You know who I am,' Wardour said, 'or I wouldn't be here. Is that correct?'

'It's not for you to question me,' McDade said. He wore a

66

denture, the result of once losing some teeth to a paratrooper's rifle butt, and its lack of fit made his *s*'s whistle.

'I can't believe you're IRA,' Wardour said. 'I know too many of those people.'

'Is that right, now?'

Wardour tried for the soft spot. 'I'm more sympathetic to the Irish problem than you might think.'

'And your wife?'

'What are you getting at?'

McDade indicated Wardour's wedding ring, the ring he had been unable to prize off for his meetings with Holly. 'The lady you were with is not your wife. I've been through your baggage, so don't let's waste time on that. But you are going to write to your wife, and we are going to deliver that letter. This other young lady doesn't exist, OK? But my guess is, your wife doesn't know where you are. Would that be correct?'

'You cheap little shit,' Wardour said to McDade's hooded face. 'None of your bloody business.'

'I'm asking again,' McDade said, 'and this time you'll please answer. It's Saturday morning now. When does anybody expect you back?'

McDade had to wait nearly a minute for the reply, but in the end, having rapidly assessed the jeopardies of non-cooperation, Wardour admitted, 'Tomorrow evening.'

McDade took a walk in the garden. It was still visibly a *jardin anglais*, with symmetrical flower beds and concealed arbours, although everything was now well tangled with weeds and in need of attention by a professional gardener. The Irishman sensed eyes on him from the house. He felt like a great military leader, watched at a distance by apprehensive marshals unable to predict his next *coup de foudre*. Well, McDade was starting to feel brilliant. Let them watch and wonder.

From his pocket he took a letter, reread it and sealed the envelope. When Dickie Loman joined him, McDade gave him the letter and said, 'We have time on our side, thirty-six hours before anybody wants to know where these two people are. The guy is an MP – '

'Yes, yes,' Loman said, always over-brisk, brushing off suspected condescension.

McDade continued, 'Train to Paris, flight to London. Get to the wife. Show her the letter but don't let her keep it. Make your own set-up about communicating, but don't let her lay a trap for you. Where will you stay?'

Loman recalled the family home, the wife who no longer welcomed him. Home had become a less-than-genteel bedsitter in Wimbledon. 'Can you sub me for a hotel? Nothing fancy.'

'Sure. But only keep in touch on public phones. If you've got to stay an extra night, change hotels. We want to shift this guy fast, in one piece. Make sure the wife gets that, *in one piece*. The price is half a million in random numbered notes. Shit,' McDade laughed and slapped Loman's arm, 'you're the money man. I can leave that to you. But come back here to confirm details of the handover. If we don't hear from you within twenty-four hours, we quit this place, and we never heard of you.'

'Don't worry,' Loman said, prickled at the suggestion that he might be unreliable or, of all things, dishonest. 'I won't let you down.' Half an hour later, Nevis drove Loman to a stop on the Paris line thirty kilometres further on than the local station. McDade was now joined in the garden by Ed Hendry. His briefing was similar, except that Hendry was to fly to America with a letter addressed to Barron Odell. The trauma of the kidnap, and the dislocation of time, had driven from Holly's mind the fact that on Monday, two days from now, she was due to meet her father at London Heathrow after his trip to Ireland. Meanwhile Robin Knight phoned the transatlantic number which Holly had also provided. A secretary answered that Mr Odell was in a meeting and took the message that a Mr Edmunds would be contacting him within the next forty-eight hours on urgent personal business. Hendry's instructions were to go to Boston, make contact with Odell and give him directions for paying the half a million dollars and for collecting his daughter. When Knight had objected that her family might not have that

68

kind of money, McDade seemed untroubled and said, 'Let's try it. I get the feel this is not a poor man's kid.'

The trip was to be financed with Roderick Wardour's credit cards, a plastic Jacob's ladder of Diner's Club, American Express, Visa – Wardour had the lot, and his credit limit had to be gigantic. By the time the accounts came through, this business would be over. If Wardour was still in good enough health to pay them, he would consider the bills cheap at the price. Hendry soon mastered the style of the MP's signature.

Between Hendry, the officer who had come up from the ranks, and McDade, the urban terrorist, a peculiar, powerful bond had developed, although neither of them knew anything of the other's background. Hendry's problem with leader figures was overcome by McDade's striking mixture of fey gaelic detachment and ruthless task-dedication. The dictatorial geniality with which he issued orders had impressed the ex-paratrooper. At a deeper level, although it was an iron rule that none of the men knew about each other's pasts, Hendry and McDade seemed to recognise in each other an almost shared experience, as though at one point they had been on opposite sides of the same Belfast front-line street, scalded by the same terror and hate. They were the hard men who fought on for the sake of fighting, all other objectives forgotten, who came back relentlessly again and again, who could never be defeated, who would die in their enmity.

But in the end the occupying soldier and the urban guerrilla converged, more like each other than they could ever resemble the civvies, the public, the normal people in the supermarket queues. Nobody could understand them any longer except other people like themselves, veterans of a war that nobody could end. Below the level of everyday, the minds of Hendry and McDade had met and declared this truth.

They shook hands as they parted. For Hendry, who lacked McDade's occasional touches of lyricism, the moment was emotionally difficult. He had the urge to salute, repressed it, but felt frustrated at having done so. Then Nevis returned to drive Hendry to the station in Angers, from which the Paris train conveniently ran past Orly airport.

Lucian Weidinger made contact from a small town on the way to Sous-bois, and gave McDade a map reference at which to meet. As part of their preparation they had equipped themselves with identical maps. Some twenty miles from the chateau McDade explained the changes.

Weidinger's reaction was angry and scornful. 'I thought you IRA men were such good mechanics.'

'That's right,' McDade sneered back, his temper on a short fuse. 'That's why we didn't go ahead. If they were likely to bring heat, they did us a favour by not showing up. And I did my part exactly like I said.'

Weidinger cooled down. He had the minute-to-minute outlook of the truly amoral. Instead of wasting energy on what might have been, he preferred to seize advantage from the situation as it now stood. 'What do you suggest?' he asked McDade.

'Wardour was sneaking off with a woman when we bagged him. Now, I should guess he's loaded – '

'He is personally rich,' Weidinger confirmed. 'His wife's family too.'

'Worth a few, to hush everything up and get him back quietly?'

'No doubt. And the girl?'

'Daddy's a millionaire. She says.'

'And your team can handle it?'

'So far they've been perfect,' McDade said. 'The skills they got, I reckon deserve a better class of job.'

'And you?'

'Never sharper.'

'How long do you think you need the house?'

'Days. Could be a week.'

'All right,' said Weidinger, 'the house is OK. I want to stay out of this. We'll cut the money later. What are you asking?'

'Half a mill. Each.'

Weidinger could not have been more composed. He did not need to tell McDade to keep in touch. All he said was, 'Well, a serious price always commands respect.' He buzzed up the window of his car, and within seconds all that remained was petrol fumes in the air.

The captives were propped up to eat and drink. It was easier to feed them than keep going through the rope routine. Their two wallets combined had yielded enough French money to feed six people for at least a fortnight, so Griffin took the other car from town to town, paying cash for unobtrusive amounts of provisions that would get him out of places fast and make no impression on shopkeepers. For the moment the policy was to treat the captives with dignity, avoid involvement with them, turn down their requests – both Wardour and Holly were soon asking to see each other and demanding information – but keep them comfortable.

Hooded – they kept to the hoods like some monastic emblem – McDade carefully spooned yoghurt past Holly's lips. She had overcome resentment at this manner of feeding by arguing to herself that the road might be long and tough, and the more food she got inside her, the better she would weather it. McDade took trouble to get the rhythm right, not to smear the side of her mouth.

She wouldn't remember his voice, but after all this time McDade still feared that she would know his face. Her father, McDade flattered himself, would remember. Mary and Joseph! What a turn-up! The daughter of one of the IRA's most solid fund-raisers in the north-east, in the days when McDade, young and on his way up through the organisation, had been a bag-man between Belfast and Boston, flying in untraceable money for the big boys to make their weaponry deals. Odell was an ex-policeman who ran his own security firm – dignitary protection, they called it, bodyguards for show people or high-flying executives. That was then. Whatever Odell did now would hardly be peanuts. When McDade said a half million he wondered if he was keeping the price-tag low for old times' sake. But he was already germinating another idea, which was that if things fouled up here, he could always run with the girl, call it a rescue, and make a deal of his own. Thoughtfully McDade spooned out the last of the yoghurt. Fruits of the forest, it was called, whatever they were.

None of the team spoke French. Robin Knight had the *franglais* retained by any middle-class product of the British educational system, but not enough to follow TV. So the one set in the chateau remained switched off. Had they watched it they might have learnt of a twenty-four-hour strike by French air traffic controllers. They heard about it soon enough when Hendry phoned in. He proposed to check into a Paris hotel then get airbound as soon as possible the next day. There was nothing McDade could say except, fine.

Across the Channel the British weekend had struck. Dickie Loman found a hotel room off Bayswater, then rang the number which Wardour had written, with his address on the envelope. There was no answer, and Loman took to the London streets, trying the number from every call box he passed. Still a blank. Wardour had given another number, which Loman recognised as a Buckinghamshire code. Wanting to appear helpful, Wardour had said it might be a possibility, but Loman was reluctant to use the number. It didn't suit him for Mrs Wardour to be out of London. To take advantage of the anonymity of the city, he would have to insist that she came back to town, which meant inventing reasons. Then Mrs Wardour would have to make excuses, and people might be alerted. To Loman's cautious mind the number of things that could go wrong was monumental.

An hour later, his nerve crumbling, Loman tried the country place. The voice that answered sounded like the housekeeper, humble, standing at respectful attention by the antique table which she had just finished buffing. No, Mrs Wardour was not there this weekend. Who was calling? 'It's all right,' Loman said, and hung up.

Loman took a bus out to Regent's Park. He walked along the

72

street where the Wardours lived, a large white terrace set back from the road, opulent but not showy. The apex of the social heap, where people led civilised, irreproachable lives while all their dirty work was done by others. Although to pass along here was potentially risky, Loman felt that in seeing the Wardours' house he had taken a step nearer making contact with the MP's wife. Loman also knew exactly who Wardour was, and the depth of water he had got himself into. A punctilious man with a comb-over hair-style which ineffectually concealed a large bald area on top of his head, Loman knew he would not initially arouse suspicion. He persuaded himself that this quality was his greatest asset in the delicate work which lay perhaps only five minutes, perhaps many hours, away.

The Wardour house triggered off the right kind of signals in Loman's mind. It was in such a mansion, in Highgate, that the chairman of Loman's firm had lived, and at which the Lomans had sometimes been guests. Until Dickie Loman had done what any honest man would have done, and then found all those gleaming doors shut in his face. Life's formulas were simple, Loman thought. He had paid. The Wardours would pay.

At Sous-bois, McDade convened a further night-time meeting in the absence of Hendry and Loman, to update the other three on their reports, and assess progress so far. 'Tomorrow looks like a dead day. But till Monday nobody knows where these two should be. So cool, boys, eh? Time's still working for us.'

Griffin asked, 'What do we do about the guy? His talking drives me fucking crazy.'

'Talking about what?' McDade asked. But the Irishman knew the answer. While he still had the energy Wardour was trying to get under their skins – not to annoy, but to empathise with them. After all, they had a common objective, to bring this kidnap to a successful conclusion. With McDade himself Wardour tried to provoke a discussion of Ireland, a subject on which McDade had refused to be drawn.

'What we're going to tell Mister and Miss,' McDade said, and again the team members were visibly struck by the boldness of his thinking, 'is that if they give us a nice peaceful time till, let's say, midday tomorrow, we're going to let them be together. And I mean, *together*.'

But when Knight told Holly of this offer, she was silent and unhappy, with the remote look of someone whose dreams had re-enacted some childhood anguish and left her with nothing but bitter helplessness.

Wardour pounced more sharply on McDade's offer. 'For how long?' Instantly the MP realised that, just as they were brought together, they would be separated again. The stick-and-carrot approach was brutally clear.

McDade answered, 'Let's just say, a while.'

Until now Wardour had maintained the convincing facade of a man almost disdainfully on top of what was happening to him. Now a crack had appeared. 'Just let us be in the same room,' he asked, 'and I'll give you my total cooperation.'

Casually McDade replied, 'I thought you were doing that already. The thing is, do you want to see the girl or not?'

'Of course I bloody well do.'

'Right, then,' McDade said, 'we're in business.'

Six

Time, having lost all meaning, lay gathered like an incalculable mass of water behind a vast dam. For Wardour the dam suddenly burst when two hooded men entered his room, untied him, and led him away at gunpoint, with all the timed efficiency of executioners.

It was Sunday. The days still managed to retain names. Wardour thought with pain of how many times he had lived in advance the pleasures of this day. His legs carried him stiffly outside, initially towards a gleaming new car. For a moment this made Wardour think that perhaps someone had already paid the ransom money, and he was on his way to freedom. But they steered him away from the car. He was not going anywhere.

A movement elsewhere in the garden made Wardour realise that they were bringing Holly out. The first thing he felt was fear, and he realised that captivity had already drained him of warmer emotion. All he felt now was what a trapped animal would feel, bewilderment at the unknown, a vacancy which led to terror.

The hooded men withdrew to keep an armed vigil from the further corners of the garden. Close to Holly, Wardour felt paralysed by guilt. Like people contemplating each other from a wasting sickness, he and Holly kept their bodies clinically apart while accusation and despair flickered over their haggard faces. Then Wardour suddenly started to cry. For a minute tears shook his body. Holly looked on, in frozen disbelief that any of this was happening. She recognised the tears for what they were – the frustration of a man who was used to unquestioned power, and now found himself stripped of control. For herself, Holly felt washed out but calmer. Women didn't have so far to fall.

They walked. Walking was better than standing staring at each other. 'What now?' Holly asked.

'They've sent a ransom note.'

'Me too.'

'You?' Wardour was surprised. The gentleman in him refused to ask if Holly was worth a lot of money. But he had still failed to answer the question of what this kidnap was about.

'What's going to happen?' Holly asked. But already the passivity of capture made the question flat, almost bored.

Wardour put his hand on her shoulder, drew their heads together. The gesture held no intimacy. They were both aware of how little they knew each other. 'They're probably listening to everything,' he whispered. 'Don't give anything away.'

Holly looked scared. Was that why they had been allowed together? But what did she say now?

A distant buzz in the sky heralded the approach of a light aircraft. Moving in quickly, the hooded men directed the captives back to the house. At the prospect of renewed isolation Holly broke into a hysterical scream. 'No – no – no – nooo – ' The yell shot from her like vomit, an uncontrollable, physical force. A gun in the back, a soft Irish voice telling her, 'Quiet, lady, or you'll never be let out again,' brought her down. Sobbing morosely as they hustled her inside, Holly turned her head for one last look. But Wardour had gone, led in by another door. Holly felt the wing of madness brush her mind, at the thought of being tied up again in the solitude of that room.

But they were no fools, these people, because the Englishman with the smooth voice came back soon after they had bound her up and said in a menacingly persuasive voice, 'Try and stay calm, and let's hope this is over as soon as possible. If you get upset, we have plenty of tranquilliser and we'll be forced to inject you.'

Holly's compulsion to scream ebbed away. She shut her eyes. For ever, perhaps.

Jessica Wardour had always wanted her husband's career to go as far and as fast as possible. She believed in his energy and his vision. She was also enough of a psychologically healthy woman to enjoy living with a man who was fulfilling himself. The glow of his well-earned gratification lit them both. Jessica had her own ruthless ego too. Her philosophy was simple – you only had the one life, and not to realise its potential was the ultimate crime. But now this career wife's code became her greatest enemy. Sunday evening, when Rod had said he would be back, dragged on into night. He had not returned. The code started to fracture.

The phone rang. Sure it was him, Jessica quietly congratulated herself on how well she had stood the mystery of his absence. Then the crack in her world yawned once again as she heard the voice of a distant aunt, half senile, who rang once a month for the same family conversation, identical phrase for phrase, they had every time. Aware that the one time Rod might try to get through was when the line was engaged, Jessica got rid of the old lady as fast as she could, simply to return to her own growing despair.

Three more times, in spite of the first disappointment, hope flared when people phoned, but no Rod. One of them was Jonah Sweetman, asking for a word and enquiring when Rod would be back. Jessica had to admit she couldn't be sure. For Jessica to be uncertain of anything spoke a volume to people who knew her. She kept the TV on, barely audible in the background, taking comfort from the absence of disaster bulletins. But if Rod was not dead or injured somewhere, why didn't he phone? He was always punctilious, and Jessica had always joked about how easy she was to manipulate or deceive – all she required was a regular communiqué, a coherent-sounding account of what he was doing, and she would never question further. That was how the code worked.

She felt very lonely now, in the big, tasteful, and somehow never homely house. By one in the morning she was getting tired of repeating a few more minutes and he'll be here, of looking out into the street as if interested in the white facades opposite and the moon rising above the trees. Once she even took a few steps outside, pretending to be walking, trying not

77

to scrutinise the cars that cruised by. When a man leaned out and asked directions, Jessica claimed not to know the district. When she went back in, the house was even more tomblike than ever.

She had to decide now – bed, or what. Jessica was afraid of sitting up. Except for their career value she had never liked parties or the life of the small hours. Her set mode of life was to sleep well, be up early and at something, usually following a list of tasks she had written on the back of an envelope the night before. The last thing she wanted was for Rod to come in at three or four o'clock, whatever the reason, and find her sitting alone, drawn and hysterical, screaming at him in a mixture of relief and reproach. That wasn't the woman he had married, or the person Jessica had any intention of being.

And here the code functioned at its deadliest. Jessica knew that all the normal options for people in her situation were closed off to her. She could phone the police, the airline, she could get friends out of bed and pour out her anxiety, but such actions might compromise Rod. If somebody knew something, the information would reach her soon enough. She had to cling to that cold consolation. She took his silence as a clear instruction to keep quiet, stomach her fear, not stir anything up. Finally, taking a large glass of dry sherry with a single ice cube, and a book which she knew she would not read, Jessica went upstairs. She left a single downstairs light on for when he returned, the light of domestic strength that said everything was fine.

Jessica undressed hastily, almost with a kind of anger, then lay in a plain night-gown on top of the bed. She had already drunk half the sherry. Having to go downstairs for more would seem like weakness. But she knew she would go. The one possibility she did not dwell on, was another woman. It wasn't Rod's style, he wasn't casual enough. Besides, the irregular hours of politics gave him all the scope he needed for that. All she could remember, from when he left for that depressing behind-the-scenes work in Belfast, was that he seemed quietly elated, in a high-strung sort of way. Nothing she could put her

78

finger on, but definitely something. And Belfast had always been such a grim note in their lives. As she faded into a troubled sleep, Jessica wondered if in fact Rod had suspected that he might not be coming back.

At Heathrow airport, having flown in from Dublin, Barron Odell had waited three hours for his daughter, never moving more than a few yards from where she had said she would meet him. The wait had left him in such a temper that it was better, now, if she didn't show up.

Odell gave it one more chance – a look round the crowded concourse area, moving slowly so he could be spotted. But the truth also was that he moved slowly because in the one year since he and Holly last met, he had aged ten. There had been no major illness, and Odell was only sixty, but when at nights now he woke up to empty his weakening bladder, he lay staring at the darkness as if no doorway of light would ever open it again. He still carried himself well, people occasionally mentioned his appearance of fitness. A powerfully built, mildly paranoid man, Odell had the ready-for-trouble presence that nobody was ever going to confront on the street. Above his mottled sausage-skin complexion, the blue eyes had a malicious glitter and the rapid sardonic tone of his deep, nasal voice gave people an instant idea of a man who could be good fun or an awful lot of trouble. But Barron Odell had long since ceased to enjoy being who he was. Men he would once have despised or derided, he now observed with the same dour tolerance he tried to extend to himself – just guys with problems, thinking themselves lucky if they survived, demanding little else; the people who made the world's machinery run, just wanting no hassle, unable to absorb the punches any more.

What really distressed Odell about Holly's failure to meet him was his own helplessness. He had smoked his way through a couple of cigars, trying to make that a reason for being there. He had checked and rechecked the notice-board by the Terminal One information desk, reading other people's messages, from the cryptic to the tender, through all four of the alphabetically

79

divided quadrants. There was nothing for him. The airport heat brought out a deep, sullen ache in the veins of his calves. It was possible to sit down, but if he surrendered the seat for one moment it was grabbed by domineering, loud-mouthed children or Walkman-eared backpackers. Hassle, the human race was wallowing in a big pit of hassle and didn't know how to get out.

If she was there, Holly couldn't have failed to recognise him. Externally, Odell knew, he hadn't changed that much in a year. Nor would she make him wait deliberately. In earlier years, meeting through the gaps in the fence of divorce, they had found contact difficult. Only now, later in both their lives, had they started to discover each other. However, Odell's sentimentality towards his daughter was not fully reciprocated – Holly was a cool, hidden woman and he had never really understood her. In the end Odell got a taxi, although her phone hadn't been answering. He had to check his pocket-book to remind himself where she lived.

Secretary for Northern Ireland was one of the twenty-two Cabinet posts in the British government, but it was a hard-luck job usually meted out to senior politicians who had earned the leader's displeasure and a public downgrading. Word sometimes flitted around that the position was due to move up-market – all it needed was an occupant with the right vision and flair – and, of course, it would be a useful promotion with which to bury the ambitions of an uppity young Turk. Either way, the name most on show in these muttered conversations was that of Roderick Wardour.

The motorist who ran down and killed the current Minister of Northern Ireland in Marsham Street, Westminster, was neither a drunk driver nor an IRA hit-man. The Minister had suffered a mild stroke while running across the street to escape a shower, and slipped on the greasy road into the path of an oncoming car. This was the first most members of the public had heard of him.

The accident was all over Monday's breakfast-time TV, and in the Wardours' Regent's Park home the phone started ringing.

By then Jessica Wardour had already been called by a number of Rod's colleagues and journalists after a comment or a lead. After a night numb with dread – he had been killed, or he had left her – Jessica still hoped that each call was her husband, about to explain it all away. Instead she had to tread water, embarrassingly forced to admit that she had no idea where Rod was or when he would return. Whatever his excuse, she began to hate him for putting her in this position.

Finally it was the Prime Minister. 'Where can Roderick be traced?'

'I'm sorry, I don't know. He went off for a few days on his own.' Belfast had been a lie. Of all the people who rang, nobody, *nobody*, had referred to it.

'He left a number, surely?'

Jessica thought quickly. Instinct warned her not to expose anything. However it sounded, she would have to deny. 'I'm afraid not.'

The incredulity and irritation at the other end was palpable. 'Keep in touch, Jessica, please. It's very important we find him.'

Superstitious, Barron Odell had not kept the taxi waiting, but now found himself rapping the door of Holly's flat and getting no answer. Her failure to keep their appointment made him boil inside. Like many people with a self-control problem, Odell was rattled when the clockwork of the world around him went haywire. Somebody came up the communal staircase of the pleasantly faded Edwardian block, a pleasantly faded elderly man who might have been one of the original occupants.

'I believe the young lady's away,' he courteously informed Odell.

Odell said, 'She's my daughter. Do you know anything about her movements?'

'I heard her telling the milkman not to deliver till Monday. She always has just the one bottle of blue-top.'

'Today's Monday.'

'So it is. When you're my age it doesn't make much difference.'

The old boy offered to take a message, but Odell said no, fine, he would try again later.

He found a hotel within half a mile of Holly's place. After a wash, a rest and a meal, he began a series of phone calls that was to last all day. Holly never answered. Then he decided to call Boston. His secretary gave him a message to the effect that a Mr Edmunds needed to contact him. An English accent, the caller refusing to give reasons, but he wished to meet with Odell the next day. In Odell's line of business phone calls from strangers were how the work came his way. He told his secretary to keep Edmunds on ice. For the moment Holly's absence preoccupied him more.

Odell had wanted her to meet him in Ireland. The female line of his ancestry had passed down to him a deep visceral resentment of Irish history, stretching down like a bony claw from the famine, the evictions, the forced emigrations, the civil war. Odell had needed Holly to be there with him when he went to what he still called the Free State, in search of these spectres of his past. But Holly had not inherited the red hair and the anger, and at the last moment she had pleaded inability to get away from London.

Alone, Odell found the Irish Republic peopled with genial folk anxious to please the tourists, and on a brief trip to Belfast he saw urban rundown that reminded him depressingly of the South Bronx. But in Ulster he could blame the squalor and bitterness on the combat-clad soldier-boys, who prowled the streets with automatic rifles at the port, and stared at everything with those army-issue, endlessly restless, eyes. And here Odell learnt why his grandmother, herself the grandchild of Patrick Odell, who had been driven from County Clare by starvation while the landlords gorged and soldiers stove in the turf roofs of the cottages, and why his own mother had passed the hatred down the generations. It was because only by passing the hatred on could you make sense of it, survive it. And that was why, without Holly to share his obsession, take the torch of vengeance from his own hand, Odell found himself at the mercy of this rage of ghosts, endlessly demanding tribute.

82

Failing to find Holly in London was the ultimate frustration. But as the day went by, Odell began to worry. He called the police to run a check through their accident file. This turned up nothing, no Holly Odell killed, injured or otherwise known to the Metropolitan Police.

Odell gave up. He had business back home. And then there was this Mr Edmunds. Odell revised his flight booking. If nothing else happened, he would return to Boston the next morning.

Jonah Sweetman had been a political and social uncle-figure to the Wardours for many years. He amused Jessica, and his company was a relaxing contrast to the ambitious fellow-climbers with whom Roderick was obliged to play social and psychological games.

The dark side of Sweetman's attachment was that he found Wardour's style of flexible conservatism repugnant. To Sweetman, Wardour was a pinko, a shade increasingly blending with the equally suspect colour of green. In Sweetman's world the only approved colours were red, white and blue, clipped together in a tidy rectangle. These preferences were complicated by Sweetman's attraction to Jessica, a woman out of time, a throwback to the sterling womanly qualities of his youth, what in his day they had called a *gel*; the sort of girl nobody could find fault with. In addition, Jessica had wonderfully shaped athletic legs and large breasts which pushed tightly against her clothes and which Sweetman could not help eyeing so avidly that after his visits the Wardours always had a laugh about it.

A generation ago the cause of gossip himself, Sweetman was now its receptacle. Nothing passed him by for long. After a sympathetic call to establish that Jessica was staying by the phone, Sweetman drove over.

'My dear Jessie – ' Sweetman accompanied his usual kiss of greeting with a long hug that enabled him to press that powerful, gorgeous bosom against his own sunken chest. Jessica seemed grateful at his offer to make coffee, and told him of Rod's story about Belfast. It was the first time she had told anybody. To her surprise Sweetman confirmed the story.

'His secretary booked the tickets.'

'Why did nobody tell me?' Jessica asked.

'I'm sure they're just tying up details.' But Sweetman had already heard word that Wardour's seat on the plane had been empty. People were talking. And anyway, a junior minister going into bandit country without Security being alerted? Everybody knew it was a ruse, probably just designed for Jessica's benefit. Poor girl, Sweetman gloated.

He had known more than this all along. But that morning he realised he knew less than he thought. At the first news of Wardour's absence, Sweetman phoned his housekeeper in St Benoit and asked if his guest's weekend at the cottage had gone well. The sharp-voiced old Frenchwoman informed him that nobody had turned up, no Englishman, *personne*. Almost hourly she had checked, nobody. All that food she had got in, going to waste. So either Sweetman had been fooled too, or something had happened to Roderick Wardour. And now, as he patted Jessica's arm and caressed her breasts with his eyes, Sweetman's own nerves began to jangle. Things were happening.

'I'll stay in touch, my dear,' he reassured Jessica. 'And let me know everything that happens. Everything.'

Jonah Sweetman had just left and Jessica was alone again when the phone rang. A voice, sedate, responsible, a voice you would leave money with, said, 'Mrs Wardour, inside your front gate there is a letter. I want you to read it and come back to the phone. Don't speak to anybody. If you have company in the house, don't tell them about this. In two minutes I'll call again. You'll find the letter between the hedge and the wall.' The line clicked.

Like a sleepwalker she went outside. A fine rain wetted the street and the letter, carefully placed so no one would discover it accidentally, was damp. Jessica took it inside and had barely read it, hands shaking, when the phone rang again.

'Are you alone, Mrs Wardour?'

'Yes.' Jessica cleared her throat. 'Yes.'

'Are you satisfied the letter's genuine?'

'Yes.'

'Do you accept the terms?'

'Where is my husband?'

'Mrs Wardour, at exactly nine-thirty I want you to call this number. You'll simply say yes or no. If the answer's yes, we'll make further contact later. Meanwhile, don't bring in anybody else. It may be difficult, but don't speak to anybody about this. We both have the same objective, to get your husband back safely.'

'And if I say no?'

'It will be the last message you send your husband.'

Dickie Loman, working on his own initiative now, was learning that for all the honesty that had sunk his own career, the world of so-called ethical finance had schooled him well for intrigue. His next stroke he found particularly pleasing.

London was full of *people* these days, not the normal population of decent workers and solid career men such as he had once been, but people on the street. They gave the city a bad and menacing atmosphere – dossers, squatters, scroungers, Loman didn't know or care what they were called. He had passed their growing numbers with a steely face on his daily walk across London Bridge. A man who would die, or perhaps even kill, rather than beg, Loman felt only contempt for people who had allowed themselves to sink so far. But everybody had their place in the scheme of things, and Loman now approached a youth he had observed for several minutes, hanging about a doorway waiting for trade of some kind. The boy had a blond quiff above a sweet mid-adolescent face, but his eyes were hollow and his skin had the pallor of over-use. Loman approached and offered a cigarette, to replace the one whose stub the boy had just flicked into the gutter.

'Looking for business?' he asked Loman.

'In a manner of speaking,' Loman replied.

The boy showed no expression. Posh businessmen were his most common clients. 'Anything you like.'

A different note entered Loman's voice. 'Not quite what you

think. I want you to answer a phone for me.' The boy looked suspicious. 'One minute's work, ten quid,' Loman coaxed.

The boy shrugged and Loman led him to a public call box off Shaftesbury Avenue. He had chosen this box, and given Jessica Wardour its number, for reasons of visibility. He had also allowed enough time for the police to be contacted, to trace the number and be waiting for him. He gave the boy five pounds on account and, as nine-thirty approached, directed him to stand in the box, take the message without saying anything, and report it back. If the police closed in, Loman would disappear into the Piccadilly crowds. The boy's doped-up brain would provide them with nothing of value. Then Mrs Wardour would have to be taught that she had not acted in her husband's best interests.

But it went fine. The boy took the call, came up the street and unquestioningly told Loman, 'Some woman. She just said yes.' Loman handed over the other five pounds and walked away.

He called the chateau to notify McDade that Jessica Wardour was cooperating. They fixed a plan for Loman to meet Griffin, who would be coming over to London to assist in the mechanics of the ransom. But now another facet of the situation was opening up, unknown to those so far concerned in it.

Sparked off by the TV item – casual at first but gaining momentum with regular repeats throughout the day – someone called a national newspaper and claimed to have a story on the missing MP. After agreeing a price, the paper put together a story it could run. They let some hours pass in verifying details, and waited until the London papers were being put to bed before the editor conveyed to a good friend at Scotland Yard that evidence had come their way which might help the police in their enquiries.

The informant had been a fellow-passenger on the ferry by which Wardour had crossed to France. He had once met Wardour at a public function, and had no doubt of the MP's identity, in spite of the cap and scarf Wardour had been wearing. Although he had made no personal approach, the informant had observed Wardour a number of times on the boat, apparently

86

alone. But later making his way on foot through Dieppe, he had noticed the MP stop and let a woman into his car. Although he had no interest in cars, and had not noticed the make or registration, something about this incident had stuck in the informant's mind. Both journalists and police tested him further on this. The way the car stopped, the way the woman got in, had a slick, premeditated look. There had been no dialogue between Wardour and the woman. One minute she was on the pavement, the next in the car. Urged to recall more, the informant was fairly certain that she had been looking out for a particular car, as if the pick-up was prearranged. Delving deeper, he was almost positive he had seen the woman on the ferry, but remained unshakeable on the point that at every sighting on the boat the MP had been alone. Oh yes, and when the woman got into Wardour's car, the informant was very clear on this point, the first thing she had done was lean over and kiss him.

As darkness fell over London, Jessica Wardour received another call from Loman. She had spent the day in frozen silence, fending off enquiries that ranged from the consolatory to the prying. But still something in her heart and breeding told her that her refusal to cry for help was the best way of pulling Rod through all this.

The voice said, 'You've done well, Mrs Wardour. We've let your husband know that you're being sensible. At the end of your street there's a post-box. Taped inside the slot you'll find a sheet of paper. Go there now, on foot, and follow the instructions.'

The line buzzed. Loman was assuming that by now the Wardour phones could have a trace on them. He had phased this move so that anybody tapping the call would have too little time to get to the message before Jessica Wardour. The only snag might be surveillance on the house, but if the woman did as Loman said, he would soon expose that too.

Jessica put on a coat and went out into the dark. When she untaped the note from the post-box it almost slipped from her hand and dropped into the box. For one sickening instant she realised that getting Rod out of this mess was going to depend on her not faltering at any stage. She stiffened and took the folded paper to a patch of lamplight.

After walking twice round the Regent's Park bandstand, Jessica stopped in front of the entrance. She waited a minute – *don't turn round*, the note ordered – and then became aware of someone at her back. 'Mrs Wardour, hand the note behind you.'

Jessica complied. Loman took the paper, to shred down a drain later. He spoke to the back of Jessica's head.

'If you involve the police, you'll discover things that will wreck your husband's career.' Loman was saying this for effect. Lying low, he had missed the media flurry about Wardour's disappearance. 'We know what you're worth, you can raise the money, so keep it between your family and your bankers. In two days' time we'll contact you again to tell you where and how the exchange is to be made. We'll expect you to confirm that the money's available. Your husband's being well looked after. If all goes well, you could have him back by the end of the week.' As if talking to a child on a day out, Loman added, 'You've been very good so far. Don't spoil it.' Then he was gone, into the nearest shrubbery, where he stayed to see if the woman had brought any action with her. But it was all clear, as Loman, in his executive's mind, had known it would be.

On her return home tense and uncertain of the rightness of her actions, Jessica noticed a car in the street not far from the driveway of her own house. Two men in white raincoats got out. They clearly knew her. They wasted no time on ceremonies as they identified themselves as Scotland Yard and insisted on coming in. Her face must have declared something, because they also insisted on knowing where she had just been.

'A walk in the park,' she half-lied.

'Are you sure that's all?'

It had occurred to Jessica that they might have intercepted the phone calls, but she said, 'Of course.'

'We have something to tell you.'

Everybody sat uneasily on the edge of their chairs.

'Then tell me.'

One of the detectives took out a copy of a newspaper. The

headline and ensuing columns held back nothing on the 'mystery woman' angle. The detectives waited for the shock to take effect. 'We assume you already had some idea of this.'

They were lying. They knew that the paper had decided not to give Jessica Wardour advance right of reply to the story, in case she neutralised it with a totally innocent explanation for Wardour's reported conduct. Although she had denied all knowledge of his whereabouts before the woman on the ferry might be his secretary, a friend, a sister. Mrs Wardour might know all about it. The informant might have exaggerated some of the details. The paper had acted to protect the sensationalism of the story. But as the detectives observed, none of the suppositions materialised. Jessica Wardour was stunned.

'I don't believe it.'

'Do you have any other explanation for your husband's disappearance?'

Jessica lowered her eyes to the front page again, chilled inside at the thought of Rod with some other woman. She felt the bitterness of having been cheated. All those years of being a good politician's wife and suddenly a public fool.

'We also have reason to suspect that your husband has been kidnapped. Has anyone approached you?' In fact this was speculation, no more than a ploy. Jessica sat up straight and stared at the detectives, unmoved, unspeaking. They tried again. 'We suspect the woman may have been a decoy. A bait.'

The problem with kidnaps was that the families were always ordered to keep silent. The detectives had spotted a way of unlocking any such injunction. Jessica's face revealed that they had touched the right nerve. If the woman was part of the kidnap team, Wardour was exonerated, and the threat to her marriage removed.

Jessica began, 'My husband and I have been happy together for twenty years. If he was having an affair I'd have known. The woman *must* have been a decoy.' The detectives nodded and kept blank faces. The trick had worked. Something was coming. She continued decisively, 'I think you're going to need your notebooks.'

Seven

On the flight to Boston, Ed Hendry slept, except when the stewardess woke him to wish him a happy trip and to ask if he wanted anything. The stony look in Hendry's eyes silently answered her question. Hendry switched straight back into unconsciousness again.

Then, as he blinked awake near the end of the flight, Hendry became aware of eyes on him, large eyes in a large face that was ironic, chiselled, fleshy. A worn, friendly face, with curly black hair greying round the ears.

'That was some sleep.' An American. In West Germany, Hendry's wife had left him for an American army engineer. They had brought his daughter to live in New England, which gave this ransom-raising trip an extra edge. It also meant that Hendry was not too well disposed towards Americans. He nodded, silent.

'Quite a talent, to bomb out like that.'

Hendry wriggled stiffness out of his neck. 'Army habit.'

'You know,' the American said, 'I thought you were military. I'm ex-army myself, but I never mastered tricks like that.'

Hendry's small clear eyes probed. 'Vietnam?'

'Yeah.' Silence. The American said, 'So?'

'Nothing.'

Something in Hendry's face made the American insist, 'No, what's it to you?'

'A hell of a war,' Hendry said.

'You were there?'

'The world's biggest war machine, chased out by a bunch of gooks. If I'd been there I wouldn't admit it.'

The American's face rumpled in a smile, but it was a mean smile. 'Let me guess. You were in the Falklands, right?'

'Correct.'

'You British got lucky down there.'

'Care to be specific?'

'The Argentinos, conscript boys who heard a shell burst and threw their rifles down.'

'You should have been there, pal.'

'Come on, I saw the pictures. Fields full of helmets. Weapons abandoned all over the place. The VC never did that.' Hendry was starting to boil, but the American was enjoying the flow of thought. 'See, to attack an entrenched enemy you need superiority of three to one. The Argentinos outnumbered *you* three to one. I make that a probability of nine to one against you winning.'

Hendry said sharply, 'So how come we won?'

The American beamed condescendingly. 'Because those were terrified guys who didn't want to be soldiers in the first place. But you gave them a new motivation – restore wounded pride. They'll be back, pal, and next time you'll get a bloody nose and run home to momma.'

Hendry checked his watch. They were half an hour out of Boston. 'You want to make something of it?' he said.

'Whatever. Soon as we're off the plane?'

'Don't take your eyes off me.'

'You got it.' The American beamed again.

Hendry glared ahead as his muscles soaked up adrenalin with the concentrated violence of the paratrooper. All the bitterness of the projected scene with his wife focused now on hammering an apology from this grinning American, who thumbed his magazine as if they had never so much as spoken.

Once off the plane the two men self-consciously kept together, neither wishing to appear to be backing off. Waiting for the baggage, they finally squared up to each other. The American said, 'You want to fight Bunker Hill again?' They got as far as fists in the air, then the American's face creased. Ignoring the stares of other travellers he laughed, his big uneven teeth defying Hendry's knuckles, his laughter melting the Englishman's anger. Hendry maintained a fighting stance long enough to satisfy his own pride, then relaxed and smiled at the thought of what they would have done to each other if blows had been exchanged.

The American stretched out a hand. 'Bobby Stanger.'

'Edmund Hendry, Ed.'

'It's my town. Can I buy you a drink?'

Over bourbon and soda in one of the airport bars, Hendry explained the purpose of his visit to New England; the failed marriage, the American army engineer who had stolen his wife, the daughter he was going to fight for. Hendry was a buttoned-up man who could only reveal himself haltingly, and always felt weakened by it afterwards. Stanger was relaxed and open but gave away nothing, a fact which Hendry's self-absorption for the moment kept him from noticing. But they had learnt enough about each other to fix up a further meeting.

Stanger offered a view of the city from the Air Traffic Control Tower, but Hendry was anxious to check into his hotel and make telephone contact with his wife. So, from the Share-A-Cab stand they took a taxi through the harbour tunnel. Stanger declined payment when Hendry got out at the over-expensive Back Bay hotel into which an English travel agent had booked him. Hendry took a scrap of paper with Stanger's number and the address of a place to meet before he left Boston.

In his room, Hendry phoned his wife. In his straightforward way he imagined they would be standing there waiting for him, as nervous and adversarial as he was, but Eileen Hendry sounded more at ease than he had ever known her, and said they had an engagement for that evening. She invited Hendry for the next day. Disgruntled, he had to accept her terms.

He killed time in the city, trying to ignore all the signs that directed him to the Freedom Trail. To a man whose honourable discharge from the army was recent, and still left a huge gap in his life, Freedom Trail had all the wrong sound.

The next day, picking up some special Boston candy for his daughter, Hendry took a train out to Burlington. Eileen had asked him to phone from the station and they would collect him. Hendry waited in the forecourt, trying to take an interest in the different styling of cars this side of the Atlantic. A Buick station wagon pulled in, a comfortable not too new vehicle. The driver got out and came straight over to Hendry, who showed no recognition. Although the Hendry marriage had fallen apart in Germany, where they were both stationed, the two men had never met before.

Jim Kunzel was an engineer who had returned to civilian life, but unlike Hendry to a successful career. He introduced himself, but tactfully offered no handshake. 'I came on my own so there wouldn't be too much pressure at the house. If you want to punch me out you can do it here.'

Hendry could not accept the ironic olive branch. 'I want Lisa back.'

Kunzel was a plump thirtyish man in a big woollen cardigan. He said, 'Look, I feel awful about this. Whatever happens, if it falls my way, I want to do everything I can to keep you and Lisa together. She's a terrific kid, I don't plan to replace her father.'

'What do you mean, whatever happens?'

'Eileen still has to decide what to do.'

Hendry had come here for a fight. Now the target kept moving, threatened to disappear. But at least Kunzel had defused the situation. At the house it was difficult, but everybody had got together to make it work. Hendry's innate self-discipline helped him fit into the emotional orchestration being woven around him. When Eileen kissed him on both cheeks, he realised that she was no longer just *his wife*. Lisa, twelve years old with long dark hair, took Hendry to a paddock and showed him her pony.

'What's his name?' he asked.

'Soldier. Do you want to stroke him?'

Hendry patted the docile pony's head while Lisa mounted. She trotted round a few times to demonstrate her skill. Hendry saw a new woman emerging, still his daughter, but happier than his daughter had ever been. As they shared the Marblehead mints Lisa said, 'If we stay here, will you come and visit?'

'If I'm invited,' Hendry said.

'Soldier and I are inviting you.'

93

'Only if you come and see me,' Hendry bargained.

'Are you still in the Army?'

'No, I finished with all that.'

'Where are you going to live?' Lisa asked. She had only ever known her father as a soldier.

'I don't know,' Hendry answered, trying not to think of the empty maisonette he had bought for them in London.

'There's a house for sale along the street.'

Hendry kept a rigid face to suppress great emotion. Why were the kids always so mature, the adults so fragile? 'America's not ready for me.'

Back in the house a meal was prepared. Jim Kunzel had done much of it himself. Hendry noted the contrast between them. The occasion was running on smooth rails now, but behind it all Hendry sensed that Eileen's view of him had not changed. Why should it? For years she had complained that he was withdrawn and aggressive, of his mania for self-organisation, all the qualities that had made Hendry a success as a professional soldier. But he sensed a new element in her reaction to him, something he could never bear to live with – pity.

Whatever his other business, Hendry had intended to come all the way to the States for Lisa's sake. This fact allowed him to tell himself that he had not sat back and let his daughter be taken from him. He had come in a temper to fight, to storm and destroy and win, or at least not to lose. He went away thinking that the best he could do for Lisa now was leave her to grow up happy. This entailed his own graceful acceptance of defeat, a thing he had no stomach for. The soldier in him took surrender badly, but for the first time in his life Hendry knew he would have to embrace it.

Back in Boston, Hendry looked again at the paper which Stanger had given him. It quoted a time to meet at the Blue Diner, near South Station, corner of Kneeland. Stanger had enthused about the food and classic rock music on real juke-boxes. He claimed that for people like him and Hendry it was a restful place.

By the time Hendry arrived, Stanger was there, wearing an

94

olive corduroy suit with a black shirt. He had not shaved that day. He looked more than ever like a college professor with a sex or drink problem.

They drank, and talked warily. Hendry confirmed that he had visited his wife and daughter. 'Tough, I hate family cases. When you come down to it, every goddamn case is a family case,' Stanger commented.

'What do you do exactly?' Hendry asked.

'Dirty business.'

'Investigate people?'

Stanger shrugged a disclaimer. 'I sell information. First I get it, then I sell it.'

Insecure about what he would say or do when faced with the kidnapped woman's father, Hendry was about to ask if Stanger had any knowledge of Barron Odell. Then he bit his lip. He would do his usual thing, say too much then regret it.

Stanger asked, 'Your wife's new man, you want him watching?'

'No, too late for that.'

Stanger attempted to probe further, but there was definitely something Hendry did not want to discuss about his business in America. He was a bad liar. Stanger had a way with bad liars. He just smiled and let them get on with it. In increasing silence both men stared at the street scene rippling by. They fixed up no further meeting, but exchanged numbers and agreed to get in touch. Hendry reckoned to be in Boston a couple of days.

Dressed in suit and tie, Hendry could have been any executive going anywhere. He blamed much of his vulnerability when he visited Lisa on the casual clothes he had worn at the time. To meet Barron Odell, whoever Barron Odell turned out to be, Hendry needed to look and feel very businesslike. Using the Mr Edmunds identity, Hendry rang the number they had used in France when Robin Knight had talked to Odell's secretary. Hendry learnt that Odell was in town and prepared to see him, although the address the woman gave differed from that on

Holly's letter. From its location, Hendry inferred that this was Odell's workplace, although he still had no idea what the man did.

When he saw the glossy stylishness of the premises, Hendry began to feel that they had got things right. Class and money, and above all discretion, breathed out of this building on the edge of the Theatre District, with fashion-wear and jewellers on the street and a canopied entry with commissionaire. Cautiously, Hendry read the company plates by the door, but found no reference to Odell. His executive-style appearance kept the commissionaire happy, but a firmly cocked eyebrow suggested that he needed assistance.

'I'm looking for a Mr Barron Odell.'

'StormWind, third floor. Have a nice day,' the commissionaire said.

On the third floor a long carpeted corridor led to an imposing glass-and-chrome foyer. The door stuck as Hendry tried to go in. A computerised voice ordered, 'Please state your business. Thank you.' Hendry cleared his throat and spoke into the receiver. He almost fumbled the name, but got out Edmunds just in time. Somewhere a secretary was hearing without looking at him. Then she buzzed the door open.

Whatever StormWind was, it made money. Odell's walnut-inlaid office had a view of Boston Common in one direction, the Hancock Tower in another. Barron Odell was a brick-faced man with sandy hair. The check pattern of his suit and that of his tie did not match. He motioned Hendry to a chair.

Hendry passed Odell Holly's letter. Using an antique silver knife, Odell sliced it open. With the ominous silence of a big man, he read it twice. 'One question, Mr Edmunds. Why me?'

Hendry was taking a chance, but clearly Odell was not poor. He remembered McDade's confidence about the ransom. 'We understand you can raise the money.'

'Half a million dollars.' Odell sounded contemplative, but not angry as Hendry himself would have been. Maybe to him the sum was trivial. Hendry did not comment. 'You have my daughter in France.'

Hendry was startled and felt his ears throb. How did Odell know that? Hendry felt the American's eyes boring into him. He rubbed his face uneasily. 'It doesn't matter where she is.'

Odell went for another point. 'I could take you as a counter-hostage.'

'That would get you nowhere.'

Odell glowered and said, 'Maybe not, but it would sure as hell do you no good, Mr Edmunds.'

'I can wait for your answer,' Hendry said stiffly, 'but not long.'

'At least two days,' Odell demanded.

'And at the end of two days what do I take back with me?'

Odell dropped his stance of intimidation. The hour of revenge would come later. Reasonably, he answered, 'By then I hope we have a deal.'

'That's fine,' Hendry said.

'Then I won't waste any more of your time, Mr Edmunds. Thank you for calling. Goodbye.' Odell saw Hendry all the way to the office's outer doors. With an instruction to phone again, Hendry did not stop till the street swirled around him, its noise echoing his own amazement and relief.

From the corner of the opposite block, concealed by four lanes of traffic, Bobby Stanger had watched Hendry enter Odell's building. Having seen Hendry speak to the commission-aire, Stanger went straight across and made it worth ten dollars to tell him which business destination the Englishman was seeking. Stanger had tailed Hendry there because of a hunch that his purpose in visiting Boston was not simply the family matter he claimed. Nor was it straight business. When a simple man avoided simple answers it meant something was worth hiding. Stanger made his living from picking up such clues.

After speaking to the commissionaire, Stanger returned on foot to his apartment, which doubled as office for the unlikely consumers of his services who might want to consult with him there. At the end of a street of Chinese eating places, he went up to the first floor of a crumbling brownstone, where he shaved and changed into his one bureaucratic suit and a striped tie.

Stanger remained in the state of excitement that the location of Hendry's appointment had created. Although he had never actually pinpointed its headquarters, Stanger knew of Storm-Wind. The organisation, founded and headed by Barron Odell, himself a legend of sorts, had one objective only – the freeing of hostages and kidnap victims, at whatever cost, in whatever country. Mostly it remained private work, although rumours said that at times governments were involved. But Odell, the former Boston policeman, was able to call on a unique range of qualified personnel – retired or freelance police, military, intelligence, political – none of them, and this was the beauty of it, on the StormWind payroll. They did the job and disappeared until the next call. Stanger was impressed that Hendry was going there. His view of the Englishman had clearly been an underestimate.

To allow enough time for Hendry's interview to expire, Stanger ambled through the Combat Zone, the downtown club area where the city offered erotica, from nude dancers and peep-shows downwards, everything 'For Adults Only'. On which subject, Stanger wondered if Hendry knew what kind of organisation he had come to Boston to deal with.

On Stanger's return to the StormWind building, the commissionaire confirmed that Hendry had left some time ago. For credibility, Stanger mentioned Barron Odell's name and went up. It was worth a try.

Odell was still staring at the envelope in which Holly's letter had arrived. Its style proclaimed *dictation*. In his guess that Holly was being held in France, Odell had responded purely to one word in the envelope's address. Holly had given the name of the New Hampshire farm where Odell spent time away from his work in Boston. She had also given her father's office phone number, but, making it read as if it was the name of the farm, she had written the word *Reunion*. Even without an accent on the *e*, Odell understood the concealed message. For some years before his marriage broke up, he and his wife and the young Holly rented a house in France for the summer vacation. In this period Odell had left the police and set up a bodyguard agency for the rich and important, and the house in France represented a raise in status, a more expansive lifestyle. The name of that house was *Réunion*.

Although his background was street cop rather than detective, Odell had good antennae for clues. He also felt strangely flattered: there were many areas where he and Holly somehow never overlapped, but in coding the address like that she had shown that once a cop's daughter, always a cop's daughter. This tapped a vein of sentiment deep within Odell's overbearing and somewhat harsh exterior. He was turning his mind to the practicalities of the case when his secretary came through on the intercom.

'A Mr Stanger?'

'Don't know him.'

'Mr Robert Stanger.' Random callers at StormWind were very rare, and usually trouble.

'Some mistake?'

'He has your name and says he can be of use.'

'Have the guard check him over,' Odell ordered.

The secretary called an office further along the floor, and seconds later a uniformed security man approached Stanger. 'OK, friend, just routine.'

Stanger knew the ropes and cooperated. Odell kept a .45 magnum in his desk and normally scorned having the paunchy ex-cop on the landing vet his callers. Only with those not expected did he use this service. On a pocket radio the guard informed the StormWind suite that Stanger was clean.

As soon as he reached Odell's office, Stanger presented his card. Odell scanned it disdainfully. Whatever these people called themselves with their spruced-up adman verbiage they were all the same, private dicks, more often than not con-men.

'In what way can you be of use to me?' Odell asked.

'I can check out a man called Hendry for you.'

'I don't know anybody called Hendry.'

'The Englishman who was here an hour ago.'

Odell's eyes contracted slightly inside their pink, gingerlashed lids. 'OK, so you know his name. What else do you know?'

'What are you interested to find out?'

'Mr . . .' Odell glanced at the card again, 'Stanger, you work here in Boston, in the business. So you know who I am.'

'You're a man with a reputation,' Stanger said.

'That I am. I also run my own show. Can you tell me why Mr Hendry was here?'

'No, sir, I can't. But I suspect it's no good.'

'Well, let me tell you something. He's an investment broker who stopped by to update me on my European portfolio. I have no idea why he should be an object of such fascination to you.'

Stanger knew this was simply an invitation to walk. But he nodded sagely, as if a genuine mistake had been made. The reserves of menace corked up in Odell's large, hypertense frame bothered Stanger. 'And so,' Odell went on, 'if there's nothing else, we don't appear to have any business in common.'

'Well, you've got my card,' said Stanger.

Odell did not deign to comment. Feeling more cowed than he had in years, Stanger left the StormWind offices with a meekness that bordered on the obsequious. Barron Odell slid shut the drawer in which he kept the magnum. Then he lit a cigar. So, the Englishman who posed as Edmunds was also named Hendry. And this downtown hustler had brought him the information for free. Odell allowed himself a brief chuckle at such a windfall.

Barron Odell was a big man who moved slowly but thought at great speed. In early life he had suffered some inner block to his powers of self-expression, caused largely by the fact that his violent physical temper always reacted before the rest of his personality could catch up. Only when he learnt to control violence did the bleak but shrewd realism of his mind identify outlets for its abilities, which the morally ambivalent and often frustrating world of police work could never satisfy. Odell had no objection to crime. Crime would always happen. But he wished to inhabit a world where the criminal, however long it took, got what was coming to him, got it so decisively that it slammed him in the face and left him in no doubt that justice had finally caught up. So Barron Odell did his bit towards creating such a world. His targets were identifiable, their misde-meanours clear and the remedies capable of realisation. The abduction of minors, whether for ransom or to serve the ven-geance of those worsted in divorce cases, the taking of hostages or sequestering of victims for reasons political, sexual or psy-chotic, all reduced to the same simple formula. The kidnap victim deserved liberty, and the kidnapper deserved everything he got. For the right deal, Barron Odell undertook to organise both. Although the philosophy of StormWind was to achieve rescue by cunning and force, it was often necessary to play along with ransom demands as a foot-in-the-door tactic. To this end, the use of forged money was a strategic requirement, and Odell had contacts who could replicate any major currency within forty-eight hours. The US dollar, unchanged in design since 1929, lacking either a watermark or a metallic strip, was particu-larly easy.

Odell began making calls. Within hours of Hendry's visit both the ransom money and a rescue team were being assembled. All along, Odell was wondering what lay behind Holly's kidnap. For many years he had raised money, sometimes more than money, for the republican cause in Ireland. He suspected that this connection would eventually explain Holly's disappearance. But for now, speculation had to give way to the grit of detail. Whoever his daughter's kidnappers were, they had offended not only his status as father, but also his professional competence. It even occurred to Odell that the whole thing might be a scam by some business competitor, testing out whether StormWind could still cut it. These days the world was that crazy. Well, Odell thought, whoever you are, we're cutting it already.

Eight

The first editions of the next morning's national papers arrived as usual at the House of Commons in the late evening. The Wardour exclusive generated instant excitement, and every MP still present for the late night sitting was soon either hunting down a copy of the paper, or reading it, or seeking out someone who had read it.

Tony Gwyer, an MP whose career had been founded on the twists and turns of public opinion, made a point of scanning the first editions. A man who turned pale when excited, he felt the blood drain from his face at what he read on this occasion. He immediately wheeled away from the buzz of MPs who might notice his reaction to the Wardour reports. On his way back to the Chamber, agitation and a kind of glee contending in his mind, he met Jonah Sweetman. Gwyer took Sweetman's arm.

'I heard – ' Sweetman began.

Gwyer muttered, 'Come on.'

Sweetman, hurrying on short legs, followed the younger man out through the Members' Entrance into New Palace Yard. Ignoring the policeman's salute, they crossed through the late night traffic and exchanged no more words until, as it were, out of earshot of the House.

'A woman,' Gwyer said. 'Well, well.'

'You don't think our friends – ?'

'I don't think anything,' Gwyer said. 'I just know when I got lucky.'

Contriving, as they walked along the lamplit street, to get closer and speak even more quietly, Sweetman said, 'You know it was my place in France he – '

Gwyer looked sharply sideways. 'Yes. What about it?'

'He never arrived there.'

'So he went somewhere else. With a bit of nooky. That's what'll hang him.'

'But you don't think I should tell – '

The sudden acceleration of events was evidently rattling Sweetman. He needed stiffening. Gwyer said, 'You haven't done anything wrong, Jonah. Why start confessing?'

'Yes, I know you're right, but – '

'Jonah,' Gwyer said firmly, 'Roddy just self-destructed. There's nothing we can do but watch. Sit back and enjoy it.'

Gwyer took Sweetman to his flat near Victoria. There, fortified with a gin and tonic, Sweetman admitted, 'I was afraid we'd gone in over our heads. Did you never have any misgivings?'

'No,' Gwyer said, then conceded, 'maybe one. We might have provoked even more support for Roddy than he had before. But now he's been caught with his pants down, the public will do to him what it does to all fallen heroes. And when Roddy goes down, a whole bunch of hangers-on will go down with him. That has to be money well spent, Jonah my boy.'

By Tuesday, the day before Dickie Loman was to make contact again, the London police computer had received two missing person reports – one from the magazine on which Holly worked, and one from a friend who had seen her car standing unused in the same Kensington side-street for several days. They collated this information with Barron Odell's inquiry about possible police knowledge of his daughter's whereabouts. The magazine had a file copy of Holly's identity-badge photo, of the type carried by all staff as an anti-terrorist precaution. The informant who had spotted Wardour on the cross-channel ferry was called in again, and told the police that, while he couldn't be sure, it was more than possible that the face in the photo could have been the MP's companion.

The police now broke into Holly's flat, a three-room conversion partitioned out of the second floor of a once-magnificent Edwardian building. The place yielded nothing to link her with Roderick Wardour. In a waste basket they found a crumpled note-sheet with the words *Daddy – Ireland – NO*, the last word heavily encircled. The page was bordered with doodles, suggesting that it had been produced during a phone call.

The same two detectives again visited Jessica Wardour. When they tried to phone ahead, the line was continually engaged. On arrival at the house they found the MP's wife radically changed from the brisk and polished woman who had put them through their paces the night before. She looked, strangely, younger, not in years but in image. Without make-up, her hair unsprayed, the control around eyes and mouth slipping, Jessica was showing all the strain of her marriage being rubbished on the front page of a cheap daily, and of having to answer phone calls from all the well-wishers who had 'had no idea' but were dying to find out more.

Jessica let the detectives in reluctantly. She wore a Dior jogging suit, but everything about her was pale and washed-out. Absent-mindedly she made them coffee, but took none herself. She had been drinking the stuff till the smell of it made her nauseous.

'We have to ask you to keep the phone on,' the senior detective said.

'I can't take any more,' Jessica told him.

'We're monitoring all calls. We need to get these people on tape,' the detective said anxiously.

'I told you, they're coming back to me tomorrow.'

Patiently he explained, 'From now on they won't do anything you expect. Whatever they tell you, it's ninety-nine per cent certain they'll do something different.'

'What are you doing to free my husband?' Jessica demanded.

'We're working on leads. Do you know this woman?' They handed over the photograph. Jessica shook her head and returned it as if soiled by its touch. 'Does the name Holly Odell mean anything to you?'

'No.'

'Can you recall anything in your husband's recent conduct, perhaps something you overlooked at the time, that might indicate . . . a relationship?' The detective anticipated the reply that politicians are not nine to five people, and in any case she was not her husband's probation officer. But the answer was instant and uncompromising.

'No.' Why were they pushing this line again, except to rattle her? Jessica flushed with resentment.

'It might be a good idea if you went through your husband's private papers.'

'What happened to the decoy idea?' Jessica snapped.

'It's one possibility of many.'

Jessica was learning a hard lesson: that to solve their case, these public servants would put her through anything. She was raw meat for them, just as the kidnappers were. They would get Rod back in the end, but dead or destroyed, they didn't care. And beneath their show of forbearance, they didn't care about her either.

The door bell rang and Jessica opened the door to find a thick-set man in a rumpled suit, a man with the receding curly hair and pop-eyes of a mad teddy-bear. He apologised and asked if he could speak to the two men who were inside. Jessica heard the word 'Commander', and then the door shut. Whatever business they had was transacted on the street. When Jessica realised they were not going to return, she ran out to demand what they were keeping from her, but the cars were already speeding away. Jessica repressed the urge to scream, and barely made it back to the house before she collapsed weeping.

Jessica waited on alone in the Regent's Park house. She spoke to her children, both away at school, by phone. Josh, a boy of sixteen and Tamsin, a girl three years younger, both had the self-control and poise that their father's life of public service had instilled. They declared that they would prefer to stick it out at school, which saved Jessica the need to say that the house might not be a safe place for them any more. The local police were keeping an eye on their schools. Jessica politely refused the offers of friends, to come and stay or have her stay with them. If anything happened, she had to be in the obvious place, whatever it cost her.

The detectives knew Commander Mike Wiley from the top floor

of the Scotland Yard building, and they knew that he was connected with F5, the Intelligence section that dealt with Irish terrorism. The Commander had driven out here to avoid phone lines, and also because he wanted to see the detectives' faces as he relieved them of this prestige case. He didn't explain why they were being relieved. They would soon work that out for themselves.

An American connection having been established, and the identity of the girl's father being known, a routine enquiry was cabled to Langley, Virginia, to ascertain if anything was known about Barron Odell. Realising that by the time it hit top-level desks in London the information would be hot, the CIA insisted on full participation in the case from now on, and having gained it after an urgent meeting in Curzon Street, released their file on Odell, notably the fact that he was one of the best-known fund-raisers for the IRA on the eastern seaboard.

The equation clicked into place. Why Odell should have been in England, why calling the police about his daughter's disappearance, could be left for later. Once that threatening abbreviation had appeared on the wall, with its distant echo of *dies irae*, the explanation for Wardour's kidnap was irresistible. In government-watching circles Roderick Wardour was regarded as being soft on the IRA. Mixed with a determination not to let the terrorist bastards win this one, was a feeling in certain quarters that the MP had got his comeuppance.

Jonah Sweetman was there two or three times daily, 'just looking in' as he put it, exercising great tact in sidestepping the revelation that Wardour had been with another woman when he disappeared. Sweetman was solicitous, propping Jessica up with messages of support from the Westminster grapevine. Poor, innocent girl, Sweetman thought. Her innocence was her main source of appeal – not innocence about sex, but about people. Somehow it flattered Sweetman's own corrupt nature. He was not sure how far he wanted things to go; to have Jessica in bed? He couldn't quite confess that to himself. But his body had frequently declared what his mind would not yet admit.

Duty, and the police, insisted the phones be left on the hook. So Jessica took the calls, and all the calibre of being the wife of a senior politician showed through in the dignified restraint with which she answered. Jessica had refused secretarial help, refused to have anyone else taking calls aimed at her. It had become a test of herself, and Jessica was not a woman who let people down who believed in her.

While Jessica was entangled with a journalist who refused to get off the line, Jonah Sweetman went to the bathroom. On his way back along the first floor landing, he passed Roderick Wardour's study. The door remained symbolically open, and the cleaners had been told not to touch anything in there. As Sweetman went by, with an ironic glance at a room where so much fantasy of power had gestated, a phone rang – it rang from somewhere inside Wardour's study. Jessica was still talking downstairs. Sweetman paused. There must be a second line into the house, direct to Wardour's desk. Sweetman entered the room, intending to take the call. But before he could get there, the tone cut out, and an answer machine spun into action. The machine had been left on OPEN. First came Wardour's voice, cheerily regretting that he was out, then the beep. What ensued Sweetman could not believe, would never believe. Across a not very good line an English voice said, 'Roderick Wardour is being kept in a country house near – ' and there followed the name of a French town which Sweetman thought he recognised. Sweetman touched his wig, a reflex, nervous gesture: Jessica's conversation could not last much longer and Sweetman had no time to assess how much this message threatened him. Acting from instinct, he rewound the machine and put the tape on RECORD, blanking the message out.

Jessica was replacing the receiver as he went down. 'Did I hear the other phone ring?' she asked.

'A nuisance caller,' Sweetman said. 'I gave him a flea in his ear and got rid of him.'

'But it came through on Rod's private line.'

Thinking quickly Sweetman said, 'The number's no secret. I have it myself.'

'You do?'

'Of course. Rod gives the number out so people can phone day or night without disturbing you.'

But before he left Sweetman got Jessica to call her police contact number and check that they were tapping both lines into the house. They said they weren't. They hadn't noted the second line, and anyway the kidnappers always seemed to come through on the main house number. The police promised to look into it. 'The police know best,' Sweetman said, relieved, and took an unusually rapid leave of Jessica. Even the farewell hug and the furtive pleasure of her breasts against him were temporarily forgotten. The call Sweetman had intercepted was like an object of corrosive power that he had to pass on, physically get rid of, before it destroyed him. He rang Weidinger's answer machine in Algeria. A deep pang of self-preservation told him not to sit on this item of news. Without identifying himself, Sweetman described briefly what had happened, including the vital detail that he had neutralised the tape.

After he hung up, Sweetman felt suddenly cleansed. A creature of the jungle, he decided to lunch at his club, stroll around town a bit, avoid introspection.

At the chateau, Sean McDade, panic-stricken, was about to evacuate the captives. He had been in the empty, dust-caked library when he had heard the ping, signifying that the main phone was being used. Picking up the library extension, McDade had listened in on the betraying call. Then, immediately, he had ordered those remaining there to clear the chateau. The postmortem, the hour of reckoning, would have to wait until they had got away.

Releasing Wardour and Holly, restoring their circulation and commanding enough energy from them for this leap into the unknown, took longer than even McDade, the ultra-realist, expected. Two hours passed before they were outside. In this time further telephone connections were made. When Weidinger came on the phone, through his Swiss seriousness came what sounded like amusement, which actually signified near-hysteria. 'You'll never believe this. The recorded message was picked up by one of our people and eliminated before anyone else could get to it. The police weren't tapping the line, so you're clear. But you got a problem you better take care of, huh?'

McDade collapsed into a worn antique chair and inhaled cigarette smoke so deeply he thought it would kill him, if he didn't feel almost dead already. He leaned from the window and called to Nevis and Knight, 'It's OK, put them back in their rooms.'

Nevis stared up, a sullen shifty face. 'What's up?'

'Just a trial run. Sort of fire drill.'

Things at the chateau reverted back to normal for a few hours. Normality was a torpid silence in which Knight, Nevis and McDade prowled the house, lethargic with the tedium of superintending their captives. Holly and Wardour, for all the regular feeding, were by now emaciated, withdrawn figures, with dead eyes and a will to live that barely flickered.

But Hendry's call from Boston declared safe touchdown and ready to go. The only good note in a bad day. McDade passed on Hendry's news to Nevis, smiled at him and said, 'It's going to work out, Benny. These are valuable people. Nobody wants to put their lives in the balance.' He slapped the big man's arm.

Nevis grunted 'Yeah' and gave a thick-lipped smile. But he seemed less formidably strong than he had up to now.

When Nevis was feeding Holly, McDade got Knight alone and said, 'Our politician friend has a wedding ring. Relieve him of it. Use butter, anything, but just get it off his finger.'

Obediently, Knight went to Wardour's room. The catatonic state of both the captives, brought on mostly by isolation, seeing no other human beings except their black-hooded captors, made it easy for someone like Knight not to feel sensitive on their account. People became like blocks of wood, tied up like parcels, boxlike. Because they didn't express suffering, it was easy to believe that they didn't suffer.

Where Holly maintained her identity by increasingly keeping her eyes shut and retreating to an inner world, Wardour stared fixedly at everything as if hunting for a reason. His wide eyes, in deepening sockets, were becoming more crazed by the day. Wardour looked on mutely as Knight, without explanation, worked to loosen the gold band. When Wardour himself had tried to remove it at his first meeting with Holly, the ring had stuck fast. Now stress and reduced circulation had wasted the finger. Knight was able to twist the ring free over the knuckle.

Knight himself was itching for action. During long weeks of physical inactivity on a submarine, one's mind had to be fully engaged at every second, for reasons of safety. Crew members rubbed elbows and had each other constantly under watch. But what was getting to Knight through the tedium at Sous-bois was dependence on the men out in the field, men whose actions he could not monitor. Everyone on the team had another man he trusted least, and for Knight it was Loman. Every time he thought about the glib ex-financier Knight saw something going wrong. But Loman seemed to have McDade's confidence, and increasingly Knight had no option but to go where the little Irishman directed.

Knight delivered the ring. 'Stay with them,' McDade indicated upstairs. 'You may hear a noise, ignore it.'

'Noise?' Knight asked.

'Ask Mr Wardour how come our friend Nevis made a call to London telling interested parties the location of this place. Ask where he got the number.'

The lines on Knight's face deepened. Now he knew why McDade had got them ready to move out. 'But how did you – ?'

McDade gave a summary of his lucky break with the extension. 'It's OK, the call went to the wrong person. Dead and buried. Danger over,' he reassured Knight.

'And Nevis?'

'You ever killed anyone?'

Knight felt sick. What Nevis had done was exactly what he had thought of doing himself. 'No.'

'Well I have. So leave Nevis to me.'

Knight told Nevis that McDade wanted to see him in the garden. From the house it seemed dark already, but once outside the two men made each other out clearly, as he stood smoking in the dusk.

'How did you like our practice evacuation?' McDade asked.

'Good idea,' Nevis said.

'You reckon?'

'You never know.'

'Sure don't. I just want to know why.'

'Why what?'

'Why you did it.'

To McDade's surprise Nevis didn't react. 'Did what?'

Thick cockney pig, McDade thought. But the moment he had overheard the call he had gone to look for both the other men: Knight had been giving Wardour something to eat, Nevis, on the other hand, was wandering about. It had been Nevis.

McDade pulled his automatic. But even before the black shape appeared, Nevis ran. One bullet into the dark mass of his back sent him crashing against overgrown trellises. Nevis was still on his feet, bellowing with pain, when McDade took a few cool steps forward and shot him again, this time through the greasy moonlit shine of his hair. Dragging foliage with him, Nevis crumpled to the ground. McDade held up Wardour's ring and peered through it, then began matching it to the fingers of Nevis's outstretched hand. With a bit of jamming he got it to fit. McDade now took out his favourite toy of a lifetime, an ivory-handled flick-knife with which he proceeded to saw below the ring on Nevis's finger.

McDade and Knight covered Nevis's body in a shallow grave. Then, still struggling to mask his distaste, Knight took the train that would get him to Orly in time for the last flight to London.

Nine

Dickie Loman took advantage of London's sprawling size to stay hidden and avoid any patterns of regular, traceable, behaviour. This included telephone contact with the Wardour household, for which he used call boxes in outlying suburbs. Griffin had arrived, and they had established a timetable of rendezvous. Otherwise, for personal reasons as much as anything, they stayed apart.

The crop-headed Griffin, muscular, taciturn, was the team member who most worried Loman. For the ex-City man anything involving money was sacrosanct, even on the wrong side of the law. Business was business, and in Griffin Loman saw a man without the necessary finesse to carry through a transaction smoothly.

Loman had to put aside his misgivings and make the next scheduled call to Jessica Wardour. 'Is the money ready?'

Jessica gave the answer the police had told her to give. 'My bank has the money.'

'Right,' Loman said, 'get it split in two halves – '

'Before I hand it over – ' Jessica interrupted. A condition. Loman's nerves were drum-tight. Her words irritated him.

'What?' he snapped.

'I must see my husband.'

'He'll be freed after we clear the money.'

'I must see him,' she insisted.

'Mrs Wardour, do you really think we're going to let you set up an ambush? We don't want your husband. We'll be only too happy to release him once – ' It was a trace, Loman suddenly realised. She was keeping him talking while they traced the number. 'Follow the deal, or you won't see your husband again,' he snapped.

Calmly, almost coldly, Jessica repeated, 'Unless I see that he's safe, no money will be handed over.'

In Loman's own mind there lurked a seed of mistrust of Sean McDade. Fatally, he had begun to relate to this dignified, self-controlled woman on the other end of the phone. 'I'll call again later,' he said, then got out of the phone box fast.

When Loman put through a call to the chateau McDade was not impressed. 'She's bluffing. Tell her no dice. If they want to up the stakes, we'll up the stakes. She'll see her old man sooner than she thinks.'

McDade sounded in no mood to argue. Loman submitted and suppressed his puzzlement at the last remark. Today television and the press carried no mention of the missing MP. Once the kidnap had been confirmed the police had imposed a media blackout, believing that any publicity must damage Wardour's chances of survival. They were willing to wait for what they were now certain would be a major coup against the IRA.

At the Wardour house the doorbell rang. On the deserted doorstep Jessica found a small plain package. The Special Branch observation van along the street put a tail on the boy who had delivered it. His story, too crude to be a lie, was that someone had approached him in the West End and paid him for this service, promising him more work if he made a good job of it.

Uneasy at the unstamped package, Jessica shook it. No sound. She went in and tore it open. At the sight of its contents, she dropped it. Box, bloodstained lint, and the raw stump of finger with the gold ring, which she instantly recognised, fell to the floor. Jessica clutched her face in a long silent scream, then ran to the bathroom and released her hysteria in a torrent of vomit.

When Loman phoned again, the finger still lay where Jessica had let it fall. In a reasonable voice Loman began to explain that no concessions were possible. But Jessica cut him short with a cry that sliced his eardrum. 'You murderers – you bloody murderers!'

A mixture of sobbing, hyperventilation and incoherent words

113

followed this outburst and made it difficult for Loman to say what he had prepared. This change in the cool, businesslike woman with whom it had been so easy to deal, shattered him. Crumbling inside, Loman started to bluster. 'Mrs Wardour, it's imperative that you pull yourself together so that we can finalise our arrangement. I give you my personal undertaking that no harm will come to your husband, providing – '

But the protracted, anguished accusation continued. 'Butchers – sadistic bastards – '

Sweating, grinding his teeth, Loman was about to interrupt again. But the line went dead. At least, for a moment that was what Loman thought had happened. Jessica Wardour's cries stopped and only a few faint random noises broke the silence. Dumb with astonishment, Loman was about to terminate the call when Jessica spoke again. This time her voice was that of the woman Loman felt he almost knew. Through heavy breaths she said, 'I'm sorry, can we continue?' But now Loman sensed, as if they were jammed in the phone box with him, the presence of other people, of grim tight-lipped men standing beside Jessica Wardour and urging her with sign language to stay calm, keep talking, keep this kidnapper on the phone.

Murderer, she had said. Why *murderer*? Loman's hands shook. What did she know that he didn't? A car pulled up beside the call box. The coincidence was enough to panic him. He slammed the receiver down. As he lurched from the box a woman with mauve-rinsed hair leaned out the car window to ask directions. Loman strode brusquely away.

The problem was the basic suspicion between Loman and Griffin. When Loman described everything that had happened, the sceptical mask of Griffin's face conveyed a dissatisfaction with the account, which left the financial expert rattled. But the days of holding out alone in London had eaten away at Loman's nerves. He felt angrily let down by everybody, including Griffin.

Keeping his voice low, although they were in the open space of a London park, he demanded, 'What did she mean, murderers?'

'No idea,' Griffin said.

Loman looked at him, a small-time swindler caught in the act. 'No idea? That's your only comment?'

Threateningly Griffin answered, 'What do you want me to say?'

Loman answered contemptuously, 'Well, my friend, you better come up with something, because my guess is the police are in on this, and where does that leave you and me?'

'She was winding you up,' Griffin said. 'Ever thought of that?'

'For what reason?'

'Because she guesses you scare easy.'

Loman exerted great will-power to keep his temper. Through compressed lips he repeated, 'Why did she use the word *murderers*? What did you animals do to Wardour?'

'Last time I saw him he was sleeping like a baby,' Griffin said.

'And you're happy with everything?'

'Sure.'

'Well I'm not.'

'So?'

'You think you've just come over here to pick up some money and go back to France on a first class ticket. And I'm telling you this woman is stringing us along. There's a trap being laid. Why did she use a word like *butchers*?'

'Just a woman shooting her mouth off. Take no notice.'

'There was somebody in the room with her, I know it.'

'When's the handover?'

'Tomorrow night.'

'Time to check her out, yeah?'

'They know my voice by now,' Loman said.

Griffin gave a confident leer. 'Yeah, well, they don't know nothing about me. Trouble with you, Dickie boy', Griffin patted Loman's cheek, 'you worry too much.'

From an electricity showroom Griffin picked up some giveaway promotional literature and a card on which people could request estimates for converting their homes to all-electric. From a hardware store he bought a tool bag and a set of coveralls. By the time he got to the Wardour house he had written on the card the address of an adjacent property. He also wore cheap sunglasses to make his face less recognisable to hidden cameras on the street, and only removed them when faced with Jessica Wardour herself.

'Electricity.'

'I beg your pardon.'

Griffin dug out the card and flashed it under Jessica's eyes. 'Fault reported next door. Just got to check a main cable. Take a couple of minutes.'

'I see. Well, I suppose so.'

'Quick look upstairs, OK?'

Without quite closing the front door Jessica said, 'Yes.'

Griffin's main objective was to sniff out the Wardour place for police or other hostile presences. Griffin had always found that if you were sincere enough, people let you in anywhere. Although toughly built, he had the knack of a self-effacing manner which people readily accepted. His plan was to claim to have spotted something which would require a return to the depot, then come back later, having established visual familiarity, and if the coast was clear, take Mrs Wardour on one side and straighten her out.

Returning downstairs, with the casual indifference of a cowboy odd-jobman, Griffin asked, 'Fuse box?'

'I don't know. Outside, I think.'

'That'll be the meter. Give it a look anyway.'

Griffin took the opportunity to view the rear of the house. The woman knew nothing about wiring, but might soon rumble that his business there had nothing to do with the electricity supply. Outside he poked around for the sake of appearances, carefully eyeing the corners of the garden and the exterior of the building. On the point of going back in, Griffin worked on what he was going to say to persuade Mrs Wardour that he needed to come back later.

Then he glimpsed somebody else inside, a man with curly hair and big staring eyes. But the angry teddy-bear face was

116

watching Griffin in a manner as unlike a cuddly toy as you could get.

Griffin did not even look round. Once they saw him seeking escape routes he was finished. He guessed they had the back entrance covered. He pretended he had noticed nothing and went back into the house. Mrs Wardour was nowhere to be seen. The teddy-bear-faced man confronted Griffin in the hall.

'Morning, guv,' said Griffin.

As Griffin brushed past, Mike Wiley's arm swung out, a stiff arresting barrier. 'What are you doing here?'

Griffin acted indignant. 'Hey, come on, mate, what's this? I got a job to do. What's your problem?'

'What job?'

Griffin gave him the wiring story.

'Identification?'

'Subcontract, guv. They just call us in, there's a job, get on and do it, claim later. Paperwork's in the van. You the man of the house?'

'No,' Mike Wiley said, 'but you're a bloody liar. Where's this van?'

'Couple of streets away. Straight up, I'll show you.'

Through a compact device in his chest pocket, Mike Wiley ordered back-up from the observation van. Griffin seized his moment, swiped Wiley's head with the tool bag, then kicked him in the groin. The Special Branch man had anticipated an attack, and managed to catch hold of Griffin's coveralls. Griffin ducked and swung sideways, delivering a savage head-butt to the Commander's face. Amid a shower of blood, outraged yells of pain, and footsteps running towards him, Griffin took off. He could probably outrun most policemen. Anyway, he had figured that if caught, he could always admit to being a conman, gaining entry by deception. A trivial charge, none of which would tie him to the Wardour kidnap.

The pursuit seemed to have gained manpower. Car tyres squealed in the distance behind him. Griffin spotted the traffic lights of a major junction. He ran for it as fast as he could. He went diagonally across the junction, timing his run for the moment when amber one way coincided with red the other. He was almost across when a saloon swerved out of a left-hand filter lane. The driver braked as the car's front end lifted Griffin through the air. The car danced a mad spiral across the junction, finally bouncing off two ranks of waiting traffic and coming to rest, severely buckled, against an iron bollard. The lights continued to change colour monotonously. No traffic moved. The police arrived on the scene. Griffin's unidentified body lay motionless in the road.

For Barron Odell it was a day of events. First the Englishman Hendry/Edmunds, then Stanger, and now it was the CIA coming through on StormWind's private line, which they clearly had on file, to demand an immediate meeting. In the middle of setting up a team to deal with Holly's disappearance, Odell had to suspend all activities. He asked his secretary to work late and field calls, while he received the CIA men in his office.

There were two of them, clean-cut and agelessly young, like Mormons. Odell's organisation had done one or two favours for overseas friends of the USA, so he felt relaxed about the visit.

'How can I help you boys?' he asked amiably.

Odell's relaxation was not to last long. The senior CIA officer took a deep breath and came to the point. 'We have intelligence that something serious may have happened to your daughter. Do you have knowledge of this?'

'Certainly.'

'How did you come by the information?'

'I really can't divulge that.'

'Withholding of material assistance could endanger your daughter's life.'

Odell asked, 'What's on offer here?'

The reply was not encouraging. 'We're at the coordination stage. But if you have access to information, it's in your daughter's interest that you share it with us.'

'As soon as I can, believe me, I'll come to you.'

The CIA men exchanged glances. They had prepared for this contingency and now the younger officer took over, a man with cold blue eyes. 'We'll level with you, Mr Odell. We know what business you're in. Because of other factors involved we want this case to be handled from Langley.'

'Gentlemen, I'll cooperate all I can. But my daughter's life's in the balance here. You're asking me to sit on my hands. I don't break laws, you know that. Not any more than you do.' Odell was disappointed when no guffaws of laughter greeted this, only sickly smiles.

The CIA man continued, 'Mr Odell, we are warning you off.'

Odell's face set hard, as it always did at hints of force. He said, 'I've always maintained good relations with the Agency. Who wants a beef? Why not work together on this?' He meant they should let him play it his way but the CIA men were having none of it.

'OK, you give us no choice. Sergeant Kowicki died last week.' Odell shook his head, uncomprehendingly. 'We'll help your memory. He was your station sergeant in the 5th Precinct twenty-nine years ago.'

'Long time,' Odell said.

'Sure. There was a third cop, what was his name?'

'What are you guys talking about?'

'His name was Henderson, but don't worry, he's dead too.'

'And?'

'You all three left the force together.'

This phase of Odell's life was buried so deep in his memory that he no longer had independent access to it. The reminder was like hearing about someone else. Quietly he said, 'I quit the force for business reasons.'

'The business was called murder, Mr Odell. You and the other two officers beat a man to death in a police cell.' The CIA man was calm, matter-of-fact. Beneath his ruddy cheeks Odell's skin was bloodless. 'Henderson became a junkie. They fished him out of a river somewhere. Sergeant Kowicki ended up a medical case – heart, nerves, mind. Guilt and the fear of prosecution rotted his life. In the end he confessed. Nobody wanted a scandal, just like all those years ago they didn't want a scandal. But we have the confession, the forensic reports which were conveniently not referred to at the time, and putting it simply, we've got enough to blow you out of the water.'

'What do you want?' Odell asked.

'Just keep out of this case. It's sensitive, and we don't want StormWind's wolf-pack running all over it. If you don't help us, OK, but it may be your daughter's life you're kissing good-bye. But help us or not, stay away from it. Or we go public on the truth behind Barron Odell.'

After the CIA men had left, Odell's heart thudded uncontrollably for some minutes as he struggled to get himself back on course. He had refused to humble himself by telling his side of the story. But now they had gone, he wished he had rubbed their faces in it. The man whose memory they had dredged up had raped and then murdered a child. Odell had seen both the body, a sight which still haunted him, and the smile of indifference on the face of the murderer. For Odell it had been one too many. As for Henderson and Kowicki, they had been little more than bystanders. Odell had executed a primitive justice, which ensured that the man would never kill a child again, or smile about the one he had killed already.

Many years ago Odell had successfully packaged this episode away, so it would never trouble him again. Others would not see it his way. The efficiency with which these Agency men had fixed him, convinced Odell not to test them further. They had come fully equipped. They meant it.

The lights were coming on across Boston as Odell tapped out the number which he read from Bobby Stanger's card. Stanger was out, but his recorded voice, to Odell's taste too growlingly laid-back, requested details in order for Stanger to reply as soon as possible. Odell let seconds elapse after the tone, then responded.

But Stanger was not out. The line suddenly became live. 'Oh hi, Mr Odell. Good to hear from you.'

Annoyed at being duped by technology, Odell growled, 'What's going on?'

'Sorry, I had the machine on. Sometimes people ring that I don't want to talk to. What can I do for you?'

'The Bar at the Ritz. You know it?'

'Sure.'

'Be there in half an hour.'

The bar of the Ritz hotel was like a gentleman's club – panelled in walnut, a style Odell liked to see around him, a splendid fireplace and fine views of the Public Garden, the city lights now reflected in its lake. In the background a pianist played jazz on a baby grand. Both men sipped the perfect dry martinis Odell had recommended. It was not Stanger's usual type of place. He tried not to stare.

'This Mr Hendry,' Odell asked. 'Did you have any further contact with him?'

'Yeah, we're meeting tomorrow.' Hendry, stalled by Odell's request for time, had phoned Stanger for company and because he feared that too much time on his hands in Boston would drive him back to Eileen, an encounter which he felt would not be a success second time around. Odell was pleased that Stanger was seeing Hendry again.

'And your offer to me is still on the table?'

'Always,' Stanger said.

'Finish your drink, let's go for a drive.'

In Odell's Cadillac they crossed the Charles River and took the Somerville route. Odell seemed to prefer to talk while driving. 'This man Hendry, how well do you know him?' Stanger immediately outlined the whole story of his acquaintance with the Englishman. He wanted Odell to have no misunderstanding.

Odell said, 'I'll be equally frank. I haven't checked out references on you, I don't have time. My guarantee is that if you screw up or rook me, you'll never draw easy breath in this town again. On the other hand, if you're of use to me, it could do your career some good. Do we have an interface?'

'Sure,' Stanger answered casually, guessing that too much servility would not commend him.

Odell brought Stanger up to date. The one thing he did not reveal was Hendry's use of a different name, in case Stanger let it slip. 'I'm keeping Mr Hendry hanging around for a couple of days. Not because I have any problems with the money, but for – '

'Strategic reasons,' Stanger suggested.

Odell nodded. 'Yeah, I like that. Strategic reasons. I want you to stay with him. Pick up what you can. This of course may be nothing. Above all, don't overplay your hand. Be ready to trail him back to Europe – '

'I anticipated that,' Stanger said. 'How about I try this – I find out the plane he's booked on, then take an earlier flight myself, so I'm there waiting for him.'

'That's good, Mr Stanger, real good. I begin to think I've chosen the right man. The authorities will follow me to London, or have an alert on me there. But in London I hand over to you, and from then on you liaise with my team from Storm-Wind. While all the spooks and gooks are watching me, you get my daughter back. Accept?'

'Right up my street,' Stanger said.

'You handle a weapon?' Odell asked.

'No problem.'

'My boys will fix you up over there.' Still in the freeway fast lane, Odell reached over to shake Stanger's hand.

Boston was growing on Ed Hendry, in spite of his uneasy family situation upstate. Stanger had shown him the town; ex-soldiers, treating the remainder of their lives as one long furlough, they had dined and drunk, drunk and drunk again, raking around Chinatown and the Combat Zone. Finally, as the night's sky paled into morning, they had got laid, in separate rooms of the same apartment, with a couple of girls Stanger seemed to know well. Hendry did not know that Stanger had paid them and Barron Odell had no knowledge of where his expenses were being spent.

Meanwhile, Hendry's next meeting with Odell took place on Boston Common. Since Hendry seemed unaware of Storm-Wind's function, Odell was anxious not to alert his curiosity. So they strolled the Common, Odell tossing corn grains to the

122

pigeons. 'The money will be ready tomorrow. When do we hand over?'

'Friday.'

'Where?'

Hendry said, 'On Friday, that's two days from now, be in Paris. Have the money split in two halves. At midnight be at this address.' Hendry gave Odell the prepared piece of paper. 'It's an all-night bar. You'll be called there and given two separate locations. If you're taking one half of the money, get somebody you trust for the other. Once the money's delivered and checked, your daughter will be freed.'

Odell played along, wishing only to keep Hendry pliant. 'I just want my daughter back safe, Mr Edmunds, OK? This is the only daughter I have.'

It was a sensitive nerve to touch with Hendry. He offered Odell an idea. 'When we contact you, give us the number of your Paris hotel. Then once your daughter's released she can call you.'

Odell nodded gratefully, the relieved father. 'Thanks, I'll do that.'

Ten

Weidinger summoned McDade to a meeting. Before McDade could leave the chateau, Loman phoned through the news that Griffin had gone to reconnoitre the Wardour home, and had not returned. Loman sounded like a man whose nerve was failing by the minute, a man who McDade feared might abort the mission completely and just go to ground in London. Loman wanted to return to France, to the security of the team. McDade told him to hang on in London. Loman asked if Wardour was still all right. McDade answered irritably, of course. Afterwards he wondered why Loman had asked.

Left alone at the chateau, Robin Knight promptly began to betray all the confidence McDade had placed in him. Knight now passed the time in a kind of trance. The two bound bodies upstairs, the ugly heap of garden soil which covered Nevis, the drowsy stillness of the countryside, made such a state of mind inevitable. But once McDade had left, saying only that he would be out for a few hours, Knight's unreal calm began to give way.

He noticed it himself from the number of times he checked his wristwatch. His nervous system was counting minutes till McDade returned, but with every passing second Knight's inner panic grew. The flaw in his character, which had destroyed his chances as a submarine commander – that impulse to rush to a judgment, followed by a stronger compulsion to doubt and revoke it, leading to chaotically incorrect action – now took him over completely.

Two factors in particular combined to tip Knight over the edge. The first was a strangulated coughing noise from Wardour's room. Knight had forced himself to accept Nevis's murder on the basis that nobody would be looking for the big cockney, and if his body was ever found he, Knight, had had no part in the killing. But if Wardour should die while in their keeping, he was fully implicated. Each kidnapper would face the same retribution. Hearing Wardour's agitated noises, Knight rushed up to the MP's room. The fit of coughing had shaken the first trace of colour for days into Wardour's face, but it was no more than an irritation in the chest that had cleared by the time Knight arrived.

All the same Knight asked, 'Are you OK?'

Wardour did not answer. He was staring at Knight with a look on his face that had never surfaced before – surprise, almost a hunger, the recognition of someone recalled from long ago.

Then Knight realised what it meant. He had forgotten the hood. Wardour had seen his face. Knight wheeled round and strode out of the room. One small mistake – if only he could rewind time five seconds and do it all again, this time with his face concealed.

Knight argued with himself that Wardour's state of conscious-ness was by now too feeble to retain the impression of a face glimpsed only for a few moments. But Knight had no trust in his own reassurances. He began to wish Hendry was back, to cut through the confusion and simplify the objectives. Knight decided not to tell McDade that Wardour had seen his naked face. He had no wish to join Nevis.

The second glitch was a motor engine in the distance, growing louder. McDade was early, too early, but Knight breathed easier for a minute. Then from the top floor he saw, instead of the big Nissan, a yellow van. Some kind of business call, the one thing they had feared, intrusion from the outside world. Knight hap-pened to know the EDF abbreviation, Electricité de France, but he could only guess at EDF's business here. An unpaid bill? A plan to lay cable across the estate? But why no phone call? Or had they phoned? Had McDade planned to bluff them, and kept it to himself?

The electrician, a worker rather than an official, soon disap-peared from Knight's view. A faint sound of whistling drifted up as the electrician surveyed the outside. One of the captives might hear and cry out. But even as this fear struck him, Knight had another thought which sent a blade of ice through his back.

What if the electrician was a front? If somebody was on to them, this could be an extraordinary foray under the guise of a request to check the power main. If the electrician entered the house Knight would have to tackle him. In the recruitment screening, McDade had stressed that *tolerance* of physical violence might be needed. But nothing had been said about exercising it. Apart from basic self-defence, Knight had no stomach for physical aggression. Besides, if the electrician was the advance guard for a rescue party, he was certain to outrank Knight at combat.

The ex-submariner sweated, his mind sliding from scheme to scheme, and quickly rejecting them all. He was ready to go and silence the captives if they made a sound. But at the same time Knight knew that any such attempt would itself sound the alarm. Once more indecision gripped him.

Within five minutes the electrician had returned to his van. He lit a cigarette and gazed around, but nothing in his demeanour suggested suspicion. Then, without having tried to rouse any-body in the house, he got in the van and drove away.

Knight's legs felt like rubber. Relief made his body tremble. He ran through every possible reason for the incident, from the most sinister, to the inoffensive explanation of a lazy employee getting conveniently lost for half an hour. But even skiving workers had eyes and ears, and maybe the electrician had spot-ted Nevis's grave, or been alerted by some macabre *frisson* about the place. Maybe his brother-in-law was the village *gendarme*, who over a *pastis* that evening would hear about something that had been bothering the electrician all day. Knight felt a lack of that framework with which the Navy had once provided him. Even the way they had thrown him out had been admirable in its machine-like efficiency. A protocol for every situation. Exactly what he lacked now.

Driven by instinct, Knight went outside. The stub of the electrician's cigarette still smouldered on the weed-covered gravel. Knight scrutinised every angle of the property, rabbit-anxious at every leaf that stirred. Then he walked away, faster all the time, and kept on walking.

★

McDade and Weidinger stopped on a track that led down to an old ruined watermill. Weidinger said, 'Your ransom won't work. They never do.'

Suppressing the news about Griffin, McDade answered, 'It's going like clockwork. Soft money.'

'I have to tell you,' Weidinger said, 'that in what I am about to suggest, I don't think you have an option.'

McDade bridled, welcoming no man's coercion. But things were rattling so badly at his end, worse than Weidinger knew, that he felt obliged to hear the Swiss out.

'I talked to Dermot Phelan.' Weidinger made it sound casual, everyday, but McDade was duly impressed.

'How?'

'Through a contact. The name Wardour seemed to carry some weight.'

McDade said, 'I think you better tell me what's going down.'

'Let the ransom go ahead. If you can collect the money, fine. But when one of your men decided to work for the other side, we gained a problem. By the way, how did you deal with that?'

'I dealt with it,' McDade said.

Weidinger still looked disappointed at McDade's choice of personnel. He stroked his jaw with his nail-less finger. 'Sean, I know a man who flies helicopters – anywhere, for a price, any cargo. He will airlift both your guests, plus you, out of here. A boat will be waiting off the Irish coast, to take you into the Republic. The pay-off is that the IRA get the credit for brokering Wardour's return. Wardour himself is already in all sorts of trouble, so our original objective is achieved. And the IRA and I then become like this.' Weidinger crossed the first two fingers on his left hand. 'And you – '

'There's something I better tell you,' McDade interrupted.

'The Carthy girl? I already know. I thought it wise to run your name past Phelan. He seemed well disposed towards you. As far as he's concerned you're welcome back, if you take him such a prize. They will look after you, Sean. No doubt the problem of the Carthy girl can be written off. Who was she, anyway?'

Unusually defensive, McDade said, 'A prick-teasing little colleen who liked hanging out with players. She had it coming.'

'Players?'

'It's what the Brits call the serious men.'

'Well,' Weidinger said, 'when we give them Wardour, we believe the leadership will find a way to overlook that small problem.'

McDade asked, 'What about the other guys here?'

'Unfortunately there's no place for them. I shall arrange an anonymous call to alert the French authorities that a terrorist group is holding Wardour at the chateau, armed and extremely dangerous. I will fix the timing so that as you fly out, they move in. These boys will shoot first, especially if they think your men are armed.'

'What about Wardour's girlfriend?' Barron Odell's daughter. If ever a liability had become an investment she had. For once McDade knew something that Weidinger didn't.

'She goes too, naturally.'

'So after I hand them over, what?'

'You have bought your way back in. It's what you want, isn't it?'

Since he was a teenager it was the only life McDade had known. He inclined his head in solemn agreement. 'What are the IRA supposed to do with these people?'

'The way we will set it up is like this,' Weidinger explained. 'The IRA chiefs want media acceptance and a politically cleaner smell. They will mediate the deal with the British government. On condition that no questions are asked, they will arrange the safe return of Wardour and his lady friend. Purely as a gesture of goodwill, and to raise their international standing. Smart, isn't it?'

McDade nodded, barely concealing his excitement. 'It's smart,' he agreed.

As he entered the grounds of Sous-bois, McDade caught sight of a solitary figure a quarter of a mile away, apparently heading for the house. McDade swore, slowed down, then speeded the

128

car up. As he got nearer, he recognised Knight. That was all right, then. But to McDade the encounter was heavy with apprehension.

Knight was waiting for the car to pull in. McDade peered into his face, but Knight appeared relaxed.

'What's this?' McDade asked.

Knight said, 'Trouble.' As he had approached the borders of the estate and the possibility of escape, Knight's nerve had faltered again. Suddenly the chateau had become a haven of safety, compared with taking his chance in the real world. Fear, and his serviceman's programming, had turned him back to the eerie house where decisions were made for him. But he had started checking his watch again, hoping to God that McDade returned soon.

'What trouble?' McDade was unsure whether to drive on.

'A visit. It looked like something to do with electricity. The guy went away again, didn't seem bothered.'

Knight was too offhand, less confident than he acted. McDade asked, 'Did he see anybody?'

'No.'

'For real, you reckon, or somebody sussing the place?'

'Could be either. I came out here to look for signs of activity.'

'That was stupid,' McDade said softly.

'I thought – ' Knight protested.

McDade cut in, 'You don't leave the house. Especially if somebody's casing the fucking place. It was stupid.'

'I suppose so.' Knight was shamefaced enough for McDade, who had more pressing things to think about, to accept his reason for having left Wardour and Holly unattended. But Knight had dropped a few points in McDade's estimation. Once he had ascertained that the captives were exactly as he had left them, McDade privately reflected that perhaps it was a good thing that Knight's days were numbered.

The American end of things was also bothering McDade. Hendry should be in the sky by now, or even somewhere back in Europe. McDade also feared a follow-up call to the electrician's visit. But at least it was past working hours for today.

At the phone's next ring he muttered, 'That'll be Ed.' But it was Dickie Loman. After almost a day with no contact from Griffin, Loman had cracked. While his money would still stretch to the Paris flight and a single rail fare to Angers he had run for the safety of Sous-bois.

McDade was reluctant to leave Knight alone again. But his desire to get Loman's information first was stronger. At the station the Irishman inferred half of it by sight. The City man was a person of normally impeccable appearance, in whom any strain showed by small touches of dishevelment, sweat marks and rumpled clothing, which in many others would have passed unnoticed. Tonight Loman was looking very dishevelled indeed.

As the car roared back through the dark, McDade listened coldly to Loman's tale of self-justification. Loman presented it as the only rational action he could have taken. He was certain that the police had been present when he spoke to Jessica Wardour. Against his advice, Griffin had walked into a trap.

'I had to get back here,' Loman said.

'You figure they got Griff?' McDade asked.

'We had a rendezvous fixed. Why else would he not show up?'

'So what if they got him?' Loman was outraged. Were the men on the team suddenly dispensable? But he was missing McDade's point. 'Nothing ties Griffin to us. Maybe they tailed him and he didn't want to lead them back to you. Did he have a contact number?'

'We arranged a call box and a time. He didn't ring.'

'Griffin's a clever boy,' McDade said sanguinely. 'He'll be in touch.'

'Are you saying I shouldn't have come back?'

In the car's darkness McDade almost smiled. After what Weidinger had proposed, Loman's action in returning could hardly have been more convenient. 'Now you're here, you're here,' he answered. 'How did things stand with the Wardour woman?'

'She was expecting to hear from me. Now she won't.'

130

'Well, if she's playing a little game, that'll teach her not to, won't it?'

As they neared the chateau, one nagging thought vibrated more loudly in Loman's mind. He could still hear Jessica Wardour scream the word *murderers*. 'What now?' he asked McDade. Loman prayed that the Irishman would not order him back. His lonely outpost in London had got too much.

But McDade just said, 'We still hold all the cards, Dickie. Don't forget that. Relax.'

Loman and Knight respected each other, but were held apart by the fact that in the normal run of their lives they would never have met. To add to which, Loman now resented Knight's having spent the last four days playing housemaid at the chateau. No small talk they could make would avoid the touchy subject of why Loman had returned. So their reunion, the pretence of a communal meal, was dominated by a strained silence.

Loman's difficulty in regaining his bearings was compounded by a bewilderment of which the other men had no knowledge. As soon as he had arrived at the chateau, Loman had taken the opportunity of hooding up and entering Wardour's room. The MP's appearance, the grey face of a man starved of stimulus and hope, shocked Loman, the more since he had been in daily contact with Wardour's wife and almost come to think of himself as a negotiator working on behalf of the Wardour family. But Jessica Wardour had shrieked, *murderers*. And one thing Wardour was not, was dead. Neither were there any signs of injury. Loman's rather conventional view of women came to his rescue, and he put Jessica Wardour's behaviour down to hysteria. But when he asked where Nevis was, Knight had shrugged and said, 'Ask Sean.'

To Loman's taste McDade had been too relaxed about the Wardour ransom falling apart. 'I'm asking you,' he persisted with Knight.

'Nevis tried to betray us,' Knight hedged. He had not liked the gross Londoner, but a man being pistolled in cold blood was hard to stomach. And worse, the ease with which McDade had executed Nevis gave a pointer to what might happen to others who crossed him. From that angle Knight felt relieved at Loman's unexpected return.

But Loman said speculatively: 'Nevis phoned London, didn't he?'

Knight's jaw went slack. McDade had reassured him that the call had been intercepted and neutralised. But Griffin had vanished, the ransom was off, and Loman was back. McDade had to be lying to somebody. 'How did you know?' Knight asked.

'Why do you think I'm here?'

'Then we're all – '

'Where's Nevis?' Loman asked again.

Knight swallowed hard. 'Sean killed him.'

It was Loman's turn to go pale and brush beads of moisture from his upper lip. The transaction now had blood on it. Loman could no longer dignify the nature of this business.

McDade entered the kitchen where Knight and Loman sat over half-eaten cold food which they felt too sick to finish. 'Well, lads,' he said by way of greeting. He scraped a chair on the floor and seated himself. His eyes switched between the other two faces, hunting out weakness. Before this atmosphere could break either of them, the phone came to life several rooms away. Both Knight and Loman twitched at the sound.

McDade went in the direction of the bell. The boys had shaped up well in Spain, but their inferior calibre was showing now. The only one McDade felt confident of was Hendry, the one who had sweated it out on the streets of Belfast. Hendry, he knew.

As if to prove McDade right, it was Hendry on the line. 'I'm in London. I'll be with you early tomorrow. The switch is set for Paris, tomorrow night.' Not even waiting for a compliment, Hendry hung up.

On his way back to the kitchen McDade reflected that, of all of them, Hendry was the one he would be sorry to see wasted. But so it had to be.

Giving away nothing, McDade sat down at the table. Then

132

he smashed his hand down flat on its scarred surface, with an abrupt jolting force that sent the nerves in the other men's bodies rippling. McDade bared his teeth, discoloured and misshapen apart from the uniform ones of his denture. 'The deal is on with the girl. OK, lads, time we had something to drink to!'

Tired, Ed Hendry registered at the unpretentious Fulham hotel with a sensation of relief. It was like the feeling the troops got at the end of a tour of duty in Ulster, something like disbelief at the fact that they were still alive, yielding to a euphoria which rapidly drained the emotions, and then the depressed feeling that this end was only temporary.

Yet within an hour, after cod and chips drenched in vinegar and eaten from newspaper as he walked along, Hendry was on the street again. In a pub he washed the grease from his hands, drank a quick beer, then walked the lamplit streets as a way of deflecting stress. At no point did it occur to him that he had been followed.

Ironically, the reason Hendry had not found a room at one of the soulless but convenient airport hotels was an instinctive impulse to take cover in the guts of the city. As soon as he had entered British airspace, Hendry had felt himself in the vicinity of a giant web, in which one foolish move might snare him. The darker, close-set streets of the inner districts offered a refuge. What Hendry did not know was that while he waited by the baggage carousel, Bobby Stanger had pointed him out to a recruited taxi driver who tracked Hendry through the exit areas and, just as he was searching for transport, stepped up and said, 'Taxi, guv?' Momentarily exhausted, and impressed by a promptness of service unusual this side of the Atlantic, Hendry muttered thanks and followed the driver to his cab. From a following taxi Bobby Stanger saw Hendry disappear into the fluorescent-lit foyer of the Fulham hotel.

The factor that impressed people most about Hendry – his soldier's ability to reduce his focus to the immediate task in front of him – worked against him now. By the time he went to bed, after a little more Irish whiskey than his normal regime allowed, Hendry fell gratefully asleep. On the phone McDade had sounded chipper, and Hendry felt satisfied that everything was going well. Like a good regular army man, when there was nothing left to do, he got his head down.

Stanger, meanwhile, returned to his room at the airport. He needed to be up very early, and like Hendry he felt worn out. But Stanger always found it impossible to relax in places like this. Too many planes coming and going, too much movement around him. He sipped a vodka and wondered why Hendry had taken refuge in a place which was so obviously temporary. Stanger clicked the ice cubes as if about to roll dice whose throw would answer the conundrum. Was it a ruse? Had Hendry walked into the hotel and straight out the back door? Was he already secreted away somewhere else altogether? From his years as a private investigator, Stanger could recall a dozen similar stories.

Late night nerves, he told himself, low blood sugar. Hendry was tucked up for the night, had no reason for such antics. All the same, Stanger set his wristwatch alarm for four a.m., then turned uncomfortably in the aseptic-smelling bed for some time before unconsciousness came.

But Hendry continued to have Napoleon's prime requisite for a soldier, luck. By habit he woke early, shrugged off sleep easily. The few hours' oblivion had refreshed him. Having no further need for leisure, he quit the hotel. Having paid for the room the night before, he now left his key on the desk and let himself out onto a depressing scene where the only thing to penetrate the dawn rain was the light of a trundling milk float. But Hendry wasn't here for the sights. Buoyed up by the need to keep things moving, he swung off along the street.

Not much later, Bobby Stanger was shaking himself together from a disturbed night. He had no idea how, in the broad London daylight, he was going to keep tabs on Hendry's movements. But he was sticking to the basic maxim of giving the employer value for his dollar. Stanger did not particularly trust Odell, could guarantee he was using him, but for $200 a day

Stanger didn't mind being used by anybody. It was just a pity he had to be on opposite sides of the fence from such a down-the-line character as Ed Hendry.

Stanger got someone awake enough to take him to Fulham. For the promise of an extra tip the cabby was happy to rouse the hotel clerk and announce that Mr Fotheringhay's taxi was waiting. The clerk would answer that no Mr Fotheringhay was staying at the hotel. The taxi driver would then repeat the description that Stanger had given him – Englishman, mid-thirties, thinning blond hair, moustache, carrying a single black case. The man who had arrived last night, and asked the company to send him a cab first thing this morning. Ah, the clerk would say, you mean Mr Hendry. The taxi driver would look in his pocketbook and say, sorry, you're right, mistaken name. When Hendry came down and said he had ordered no taxi, the driver would plead incomprehension, apologise, and offer the service anyway, now or later, because Stanger figured wherever Hendry was bound, he would need transport.

Stanger waited opposite the cab, unsighted from the hotel, for the driver to return, which he did within two minutes.

'He's gone,' the driver said.

'What?'

'Left his key on the desk and just vanished.'

'Christ sake!' Stanger said, immediately certain that Hendry had spotted and evaded him.

'Sorry, guv.' The driver, all sympathy, awaited his tip.

Stanger persisted. 'You got the name right?'

'Sure. Like you said, Hendry. The man checked his room. He's gone.' Stanger handed over a note. Unsure of the value of sterling, he construed the size of the tip from the cabby's unimpressed face. About to leave, Stanger was brought up by the driver saying, 'There was another thing.' Stanger got the point and handed over a £10 note with accompanying body language that said, that's all. 'Last night the clerk heard this Hendry guy phone the airport. He was asking about flights to Paris.'

Having lost Hendry, and suspecting that Odell had sent him

out to create a false trail to camouflage Odell's own activities, Stanger wondered how he could make being at a loose end in a rainy London work for him. Then he spotted the word 'kidnap' among the headlines of a tabloid. The paper had got round the news embargo by covertly snapping a haggard-faced Jessica Wardour leaving her house. The accompanying copy referred to the Wardours' residence as being off Regent's Park. It also described Roderick Wardour as an MP. Stanger knew nothing of the Wardour case, but in a small place like England two kidnaps running simultaneously was too much of a coincidence to pass up. Stanger now began to find that although London taxi drivers seemed less flamboyant than their American counter-parts, they had their uses.

Stanger took a cab to Regent's Park. On the way he mentioned the case to the driver, a man who spoke with a foreign accent and didn't seem to know anything about the kidnap. Stanger then began taking short rides in cabs. In the fourth he found an interested driver, more the stateside type of cabby who would talk about psychoanalysis or spontaneously break out into grand opera. This cabby instantly offered the information that the MP had disappeared in company with an American woman. The name he forgot, and even a generous tip couldn't bring it back. But by then Stanger was sure he had struck the scent. A government minister into the bargain – now he knew why Odell had the CIA on his back. Holly was the dolphin in the tuna net. Or maybe it was worse than that. When Stanger asked if the Wardours didn't live around here, the cabby nonchalantly named the street. Stanger acted the goggle-eyed tourist and said, 'Gee, I'd sure like to see the house.'

The driver took two short corners and a minute later was pointing out the Wardour residence. Stanger got out a short distance later. The rain had stopped and the tarmac smelt fresh. Stanger turned his collar down and whistled his way along the street, giving himself some fifty yards in which to decide exactly how he was going to handle this.

Somehow he had expected a British bobby to be on the door, like 10 Downing Street, but in reality he knew that any police

136

presence would be indoors or concealed away from the property. Five more paces, and the pressure kicked up a brilliant idea, as Stanger knew it would, in that worn-in, well-oiled psychology of his. Quickly Stanger checked himself over. He was shaved, and the bad night didn't show too much. His hair was its usual black tangled self, but the greying temples seemed right for this district, which reminded him of Boston's Beacon Hill. The suit and tie, the white raincoat, fine, he could be whoever he decided to be.

The woman at the door was either a faded elderly relative or a well turned out cleaning lady. 'I'm afraid Mrs Wardour isn't in.'

'I'm a friend of her husband's from the States, Bobby Stanger.' Stanger raised the intonation on his surname, made it like a question, as if surprised the woman didn't recognise him.

Even as the daily help was shaking her head, Stanger saw a smart but harassed blonde woman appear behind her, drawn by the unfamiliar American voice. 'It's all right, Millie.' With a narrow-eyed look at Stanger, the old woman gave way. Stanger gave his easy-charmer smile.

'You must be – ' Christ! He couldn't remember. He had read her name in that paper, but now his brain refused to recall it. ' – Rod's wife. He talked about you a lot.' The expressionless face remained unmoved. 'In Washington.' If Mrs Wardour said her husband had never been to Washington, Stanger would have to bluff it out. If she said he had never been to the USA at all, he was in real trouble. But something worked. Jessica Wardour nodded vaguely. Stanger went for the kill.

'Rod gave me the address and said if ever I was in London – I'm sorry, this is clearly inconvenient. I should have rung, but I lost the number.'

After a long moment Jessica said, 'You'd better come through.'

In the drawing room she showed him to a chair. Stanger removed his raincoat and kept it draped over his knee.

'You do know, don't you?' Jessica asked.

'I'm sorry?' Stanger looked puzzled.

137

'About my husband.'

Stanger's face became appropriately grave. 'He's not – ?'

'He's been kidnapped.'

'I don't believe it.' He feigned surprise.

'You must be the only person in the world not to have heard.' An overstatement, Stanger thought, even allowing for natural emotion.

He said, 'I've been travelling. I only arrived here last night.'

'I see.'

Stanger could feel the shock wearing thin, the numbness of Mrs Wardour's mind unclouding. His convincingness had got him in the door, but now she was thinking that the Right Honourable Roderick Wardour didn't invite ramshackle Yankees to drop in on him whenever they were passing.

'Who are the kidnappers?'

'We don't know.'

'You don't know? There are people in the business of rescuing kidnap victims. Maybe you need help. Who's working on the case?'

'It's being taken care of.'

Stanger thought she probably knew he was a liar. But she must also know he couldn't be the enemy. 'He was alone?' he asked.

'There was a woman with him.' But now Jessica Wardour's pride took over. Later she would wonder why she had ever told this to a stranger, but at the time it felt like a way of fighting back. 'A decoy. We suspect the IRA.'

Stanger got up and offered his hand, making to leave. 'This is an unfortunate time. I'm sorry to have troubled you, I truly am. Please accept my apologies.' He was in a hurry to contact Odell. The big man might like to know how they saw his daughter. Also, Stanger thought, it was time to make an impression.

Eleven

Rather than leave Knight and Loman together at the chateau, McDade sent Knight to pick up Hendry from the train. Everybody was getting edgy. McDade felt relief that it would now soon be over, although for him *over* meant something different from what the others understood. And although this was a relatively deserted part of France, their movements were bound to be noticed soon.

When Hendry arrived, even McDade, resilient though he was, realised how stale and depleted their days as jailers had made them. Hendry was like a breath of air from the outside world, nervously alert, excited even. As he blew the steam from his coffee his lips kept twitching into a smile. 'Odell's got the money. He delivers in Paris tonight.'

But even as he spoke, Hendry was sensing the lower spirits of the others. McDade whispered, 'Listen, Ed – ' and quickly cued Hendry in on what had happened to Nevis and Griffin.

'So the Wardour deal?'

'It's off.'

Suddenly Hendry looked betrayed and very mean. All the good work he had done wasted. 'Then how the hell can we trade the woman?'

McDade had rehearsed this. Flapping his hands to keep voices and tempers down, he said, 'We split the money from the Odell girl. Only a four-way split now, remember. Then we let Wardour go.' McDade's eyes flickered round the three other faces. He had wondered if they would fight him on this. But no, just as he had thought, they showed relief. McDade continued, 'We've treated him well enough. They'll be glad to get him back. Nobody's coming after us.' They'll be especially glad, McDade thought ghoulishly, when they count his fingers. He wondered if those people had a sense of humour.

Hendry wanted to see Holly Odell. Having spent days negotiating her safe return, he suddenly needed to satisfy himself of her physical well-being. He had staked his life on this human merchandise. He put on a hood and went up to the bedroom where Holly lay bound.

Two things shocked Hendry. For all his experience of life's ugly side, he was deeply shockable, especially where women were involved. The sight of Holly made Hendry feel the way he did at the sight of animal charities' advertising which used pictures of starved and tortured puppies. He had a powerful urge to get his hands on the bastards who had done this. Although Holly Odell was neither starved nor tortured, in her soul she had become both these things. From within the safety of the hood Hendry gazed at the face of a woman who no longer had any desire to live. At this moment he realised that, however smoothly the handover proceeded, they would not be giving back the woman they had seized six days earlier. In his mind Hendry saw Barron Odell's unforgiving eyes. In a flush of chill self-questioning, Hendry wondered if the big man would really kiss his money goodbye quite so easily.

The other thing that bothered Hendry was donning the black hood. Even worse now than when he had been at the chateau before, the act summoned up visions of the IRA hard men. One of life's clean-faced soldiers, Hendry had felt, since his return, disturbed, even dirtied, by the black hoods.

'You see, she's fine,' McDade said. Hendry nodded assent. But having returned from a world in which women looked the way they ought to, he thought that if this was fine, he wouldn't want to see Holly Odell when she was in a bad way.

The main phone at Sous-bois was in the small study, the dusty period piece of a room where McDade spent much of his time and which the others had come to regard as his office. Normally McDade took the messages from team members calling base, and others who were nearer waited deferentially for him to answer the phone. But soon after Hendry's arrival the phone rang and McDade was nowhere about – locked in the bathroom perhaps, or somewhere outside. Since McDade had never expressly forbidden others to take calls, Robin Knight entered the study and took the call himself.

The speaker asked for a Monsieur something or other in French, then switched to English in order to regret that he clearly had the wrong number. Knight said nothing about this. Distracted, he let it go from his mind. He would have forgotten it entirely but for the fact that days before, on an occasion when McDade was out in the car, Knight had taken a similar call and been told wrong number by a voice which he would swear was the same as this one today.

Knight took a stroll in the garden with Hendry. Their earlier relationship was still something the rest of the team had been kept in the dark about. To them also it now seemed very distant. Hendry sensed that Knight's energy and nerve were failing. He was two days unshaven and had a slight tic at the corner of one eye, both signs that he was approaching the end of his tether.

'Not long now,' Hendry said reassuringly. It was what the soldiers used to mutter to each other on the streets of Belfast and Derry, still did for all Hendry knew. It constituted their ironical way of saying, you'll only get out when they carry you out. 'It'll be OK. Sean's sending you and Loman to Paris.'

Instantly revealing what had been on his mind, Knight said, 'I'd rather go with you.'

'What the man says, he gets. That was the deal.' Knight was looking for Hendry to show one sign of vulnerability, one small opening through which he could pour his own growing despair. But both Hendry and he were ex-officers, had dealt with failure of morale in subordinates. Knight knew he had chosen the wrong man to lean on. Still, he persisted, 'They're paying to get the Odell girl back alive, aren't they?'

'That's right.'

'And if something goes wrong with the payment?'

Now Knight's hang-up was out, Hendry said, 'When you were in submarines, you worked the Polaris ships?'

'Yes.'

'You wanted to become a commander?'

'As I told you,' Knight said defensively, referring to a time that seemed a hundred years ago.

'How many missiles do they carry?'

'Sixteen.'

'You know what just one of those missiles would do.' Knight was silent. Hendry continued, 'Destroy a city, devastate hundreds of square miles, kill millions of people. You broke your back to be the man who would push one of those buttons. Let me ask you a question. Have you ever killed anybody? No? Well, I have. I don't feel good about it, but I'll tell you one thing, I couldn't launch one of those missiles. I'll kill my enemy, sure, but not the whole human race.'

Hendry looked across to where Nevis was buried. Quietly he added, as Knight looked shamefacedly down, 'Don't you become my enemy.'

When the CIA nerve-centre at Langley received intelligence that Barron Odell was booked on a Pan Am flight Boston–London, a flicker of relief like the flexing of cramped muscles went through the team handling the American end of the Holly Odell kidnap. A dormant target bore slow fruit, but once he moved, life became more interesting. Cheered to have something to put in their report, the CIA men gave no time to reflection on how willingly Odell had committed himself to their wiretap, how carefully he had repeated the time and flight code.

But they would not have been CIA if they had not taken it for granted that Odell would suspect a tail somewhere along the way. With his police and security background he would expect them, at the very least, to be waiting for him when he landed in London. The CIA now pulled a stunt which they reckoned even a Barron Odell would not be ready for.

Someone took the shuttle up to Logan International and explained to the Pan Am executive officer that they needed to vacate a seat on that morning's flight to London. They specified the seat number and requested details on its prospective occupant. Upon contact the old lady from Swampscott was not at all bothered – fairly thrilled, in fact – to help out these people she still thought of as *G-Men*. She readily accepted their offer of a seat on the next day's Concorde to make up for the inconvenience. Just wait till her daughter in Europe heard why she was a day late.

And so it happened that Dick Ginistrelli rode the Pan Am Boeing to London in the next seat to Barron Odell. As they settled into a few hours of Atlantic cloud, after a drink and a brief nap, Odell began to take an interest in the book on his neighbour's lap. Odell had never been much of a reader, but certain books read at the right time stood out like milestones along the route of his own personal development. As he got older, rather than discover new books, Odell tended to revisit these well-known monoliths. Even without seeing the jacket, he had no difficulty recognising his fellow-passenger's book.

Snatched in a rush to the airport – anything on Ireland, Ginistrelli had said, following his own flash of intuition – the book struck deeper home than anybody had the right to expect. Its title was *The Great Hunger*, its subject-matter the famines of the 1840s which had done so much to poison that country's subsequent history. Odell's own copy had been inscribed by his mother. Next to him the bespectacled, rather academic-looking young man was reading seriously. As Ginistrelli turned the pages, Odell made no secret of the fact that he was following the text in tandem. Finally it got so that Ginistrelli gave a polite look sideways before moving on.

Odell laughed. 'Sorry, I got engrossed. Hell of a book.'

'You know it?'

'I read it three times.'

Ginistrelli said, 'Really?' and introduced himself.

'From your name,' Odell said, 'I'm surprised you find this subject' – he indicated the book – 'interesting.'

'My family came through Ellis Island,' Ginistrelli said. 'I guess the new world was peopled with the outcasts of the old. We both have starving ancestors.'

Dick Ginistrelli was thirty years old and had a similar view of the world to that of a chess player – fulfilment lay in the exercise of mental skill, end of story. The Langley computer had given him the cue that Odell was passionate about the Irish problem, and his seniors had set up the seat exchange. But the book had been entirely Ginistrelli's own idea, and he felt more than satisfied with the outcome.

When they separated at Heathrow, Odell shook Ginistrelli's hand warmly and said, to conclude their long conversation, in which Ginistrelli had plausibly acted the part of Irish sympathiser, 'If you want, I could get you an interesting contact while you're over here.'

Dick Ginistrelli said, 'I'd be very happy about that.' He said he was staying with friends in London while carrying out research for a market survey organisation.

Odell reached for a pocketbook and said, 'Just give me your London number.'

Ginistrelli thumbed his own filofax. The gesture looked natural, but he had no fake number written down, and it would show. And if he invented one it wouldn't answer. Odell knew the type. A brain man with no gut feel, no buzz for coming danger. But with studied calm Ginistrelli said, 'I don't plan to be there much. Maybe it's better if I call you.'

'Sure,' Odell said blandly, and gave Ginistrelli the number of his hotel. Then they parted. Odell felt good, really smug, to have prompted that one giveaway that suddenly told him who Ginistrelli had to be. *He had no London number.* Odell was a man who every time he saw a mouse, smelt a rat. He often felt that his strongest emotion, more powerful even than love or hate, was suspicion. They had hung Ginistrelli on him for the flight, the Ireland stuff was a front, and if Ginistrelli had given him a London number, Odell would have taken the bait for a while longer. But there was no number, and the plot's convincingness was what damned it. Odell had read their cards, and all the way through the London traffic his mottled face reddened with suppressed laughter. The clowns had worked so hard to pin him down in London that their own smartness would never allow them to consider that his presence there might just be a diversion anyway. He had even given Ginistrelli the correct number for his hotel. He was happy for them to think they had

144

him tabbed. For a while the beauty of this scenario prevented Odell from thinking about his true reason for having returned to Europe.

At exactly six o'clock that evening Bobby Stanger called Odell and learnt which London hotel and which room number he was occupying. Stanger went there directly. He hardly had time to rap the door before Odell let him in.

'I got CIA round my neck here,' Odell said, 'and that's fine. I also have – ' he indicated the two leather cases on the bed. They were surprisingly small: Stanger knew what they contained but he had somehow figured half a million would take more space. A ransom as big as the Ritz. In his terms such a big whack of money deserved better than an executive's lunch-case. As he flicked through the neatly bundled fifty-dollar bills, five thousand in each case, Stanger whistled.

Odell looked impatient and snapped, 'They'll get you what you need. Apart from that, it's ninety per cent toilet paper.'

Stanger looked again. The dollar's only protection was its special blue and red fibre-flecked paper and high-quality indigo printing. Stanger knew this in theory, but his eye was not practised enough to differentiate the bills which he now riffled through his hands. He shook his head in defeat. 'How did you get them in?'

'Shanks's pony. Just walked it through.'

'What about Customs?'

Odell gave his gravelly laugh. 'With the Intelligence people on my back? My ticket through Customs was the CIA. Any problem, they'd have cleared me, after what they went through to follow me here.'

'Smart,' Stanger said.

'Sure, and what's even smarter is what you found out. What did you tell the Wardour woman?'

'I said I was a friend of her husband's. I think she bought it. But they figure the IRA are behind the kidnap, and they make Holly part of the team.'

'Did Wardour's wife know anything?'

'No. But as far as they're concerned the only one being ransomed is Wardour. They know a girl was involved, but – '

'They got her identity?'

'I didn't ask. Mrs Wardour was looking curious at me, so I got out.'

Odell's eyes grew rounder and wider as he concentrated. 'Your opinion?'

Stanger said, 'Why would they ransom Holly if she's on the team?'

'A scam?'

'You know your daughter, I don't. Would she fleece you?'

'She might.' Paternal pride made Odell say this, but he didn't want to believe it. Yet, did he know his daughter? Did any parent know their child?

'Thing is,' Stanger said, 'I get the feeling that the only people looking out for Holly are you and me. It seems like to everybody else, she's a bad girl.'

Odell nodded and asked, 'Are you ready to move?'

Before Stanger could indicate an affirmative, Odell was handing him the plane ticket to Paris, which one of the StormWind men had booked at Heathrow in Stanger's name and left at Odell's hotel reception. 'There will be two hand-overs, hence the two bags. Be at this location midnight. It's a bar, there's the address. You'll hear from this guy Hendry. Officially he's still Edmunds. He's not expecting you, so don't blow it. He'll tell you the two points at which to deliver the money. One thing I don't know is who you'll be facing at that stage. But you'll be met by three of my boys – split into pairs and follow the plan we agreed. And one thing.' Stanger's eyes, melancholy, thoughtful, looked the question. 'I want Holly alive. A-L-I-V-E. Oh yeah,' Odell gave his harsh, unmirthful laugh, 'the good money in those bags is your payoff. My boys already know that. So take good care of it.'

Evening came on. At the chateau, nerves were wearing thin. It was a relief when, with no preamble, McDade said, 'We better shift the merchandise.'

146

Hendry, to whom he was speaking, asked, 'Which?'

'Both.'

'Why both?'

McDade shrugged. 'Let them think they're staying together. Keep the girl quiet.'

Hendry persisted. 'But after Robin and Dickie leave – '

'Two of us to mind two of them? You think they'll make a run for it? Believe me, Ed, they can hardly walk. They won't be running anywhere.' McDade's words came grotesquely to life as the four hooded men ushered Roderick Wardour and Holly Odell down to the garden. The captives made their way slowly, with the faltering steps and unseeing gaze of chronic old age. Hendry felt appalled, glad it would soon be finished. In his cotton jacket he had an automatic. Just in case, McDade had said. But Hendry now felt ashamed that he had contemplated using it on these two broken individuals.

Holly and Wardour showed no emotion towards each other. They were united by the thought that perhaps their only liberation now would come from a bullet in the head. They strained to understand as McDade spoke reassuring words. But for the captives even normal English had become a mental snowstorm, in whose thickening blur normal shapes and meanings were lost.

'Listen carefully,' McDade told them. 'All this will soon be over. By the time day breaks, you'll be on your way.' Through the slits in his hood, his eyes tracked their faces for reaction. If anything, the news made them look even more dazed and tired. 'The arrangements are almost finalised. We want you to exercise a little, adjust to the idea of going back. We have to lock you up again in a minute, but this time there'll be no tying you down. We'll get you some supper. Then at the right time we'll take you to a certain place, and you'll be free.'

Silently, breaking together in a melting of emotion that was beyond words, Wardour and Holly began to cry. Their bodies shook as the tears flowed. McDade left Hendry to keep an eye on them, and returned to the house. It was time for Knight and Loman to get under way.

★

Stanger was met at Orly by one of Odell's StormWind men, who took him to a hired car in which the other two waited. They all three had that brooding quality which Stanger had found in Odell, the bearing of men who chewed on unhappiness and spent their lives trying to digest it. Their black-and-white mentality unnerved him. After they had coordinated their plans, Stanger suggested they split up for the couple of hours remaining. Their rendezvous was at midnight. The StormWind trio were amenable, keeping Stanger at a courteous distance. But they stayed together themselves, in a sort of team huddle which made Stanger glad not to be one of the kidnappers.

At midnight, while the others waited in the car, Stanger went to the public phone at the rear of a late-night bar, where he was called promptly by Ed Hendry. Stanger acted the stranger, just another of life's little ironies. He didn't even blink.

'Mr Odell?' Hendry checked.

'I'm Mr Odell's representative, working from Paris.'

This was the formula Hendry was expecting. Identifying himself as Edmunds, he got straight down to directions. The exchange was so brief, Stanger thought, there was no chance Hendry had identified him. Stanger returned to the StormWind men. 'OK, let's go.'

The hand-overs would take place some five miles apart, at the points where the Seine ran under the inner motorway ring. Paris by night, given the business in hand, could have been any city anywhere. The four men in the Hertz Citroën drove to the nearer rendezvous with no regard for the capital's illuminated splendours.

Hendry had selected both locations for their ease of recognition – in each case a Credit Lyonnais by a major crossroads. He had reasoned that the vicinity of a bank would be quiet around midnight. Apart from sporadic traffic, so it proved.

Together with the StormWind man called Redmond, Stanger got out. He had gathered by now that the StormWind operatives talked as little as possible. Like zen archers, they achieved success by concentrating on their target to the exclusion of everything else. The attaché case under one arm, Stanger surveyed the bank across the road. Although he was on time, he saw no one. One problem could be a car swooping out of the darkness, for somebody to grab the money at gunpoint, and scream back into the night. To deal with this extreme, Redmond was hidden in a nearby alley, nursing a Colt automatic, with which he would hit first the tyres, then the windshield, then anything else he had to hit to stop the car. But no such car appeared. Instead a solitary pedestrian approached along the street. He looked un-French in an indefinable way, which was what told Stanger that this was his contact. Robin Knight, in turn, had no doubt about the man with the case under his arm. Stanger crossed the road immediately, to deflect any accidental sighting of Redmond in the alley.

Stanger identified himself using the same phrase he had used with Hendry on the phone, then said, 'How do we play this?'

Knight said, 'I check the money, then I drive away. I let them know everything's correct, and when my colleagues and I arrive back, the girl will be released. When and where, you will learn later.'

'Why should we believe you?' Stanger asked.

Stiffened by the whisky he had consumed earlier, Knight said, 'If the deal's good, it's good. We haven't come all this way to ruin it now.' He was repeating what Hendry had said to him before he left the chateau.

Stanger asked, 'Where can we go check the money? I don't have a car. I came out by Metro.' Stanger knew a lack of wheels would make him sound vulnerable. 'Do you have a car?'

Knight said yes, and Stanger suggested they go there. He needed to see if this Englishman had company. But Knight's nerves told him that the American would hijack his transport. There was something he didn't like. Beneath a lamp on a quiet street Knight said, 'We'll do it here.'

If he had company, Stanger thought, I'd know about it by now. He handed over the case, then backed off a step. He felt the Englishman weakening, about to run with the money unexamined. 'Go ahead, take a look,' he prompted.

Knight, by now trembling with desperation to be in his car

and away, unclicked the catch. The batches of dollar bills looked fine. He nodded and shut the case again. Stanger, with a brief skip in the air, kicked Knight's ankle, kicked it with a savagery that meant the Englishman would not walk properly for a week. Knight yelled and went down, Stanger put fingers to his teeth and whistled. Redmond, all burning eyes and Zapata moustache, came at a clattering run along the deserted pavement. Stanger knelt over Knight and put a hand to his mouth to stop him moaning. 'It's all right, friend,' he said. 'Take us to your car, we're going to drive you home. That's after you ring Poppa.'

Meanwhile, at Charenton-le-Pont, Dickie Loman took receipt of the money and got as far as his car. Sweating with relief that the money was in order and the open road ahead of him, he revved the engine and spurted away. He had time to take one deep breath. Then another vehicle shot out of a side street and rammed him.

Loman's car, with badly crumpled off-side doors, was thrown across the road. The driver of the other car leapt out and ran across. Loman was shaken and bleeding from the impact of his head with the mirror, which had snapped from its baseplate and fallen to the floor of the car. Martin, the StormWind man, who had timed the collision perfectly so that the Hertz Citroën had nothing worse than a twisted fender, was effusive. 'Hey, I'm sorry, it was all my fault. I just wasn't looking. Hey look, do we have to get the police?'

Loman revived quickly. 'Oh my God, no. It's all right. Let's forget it.' He reached for the case on the dented passenger side. He breathed again. It was intact. 'Got to get out of here.'

Martin was all concern. 'Listen, buddy, you can't drive, the condition you're in. The car's probably got chassis damage. If you're in a hurry the least I can do is take you where you want to be. And then you don't report me to the cops. What do you say?'

As his eagerness to escape fought with the gathering inertia of shock, Loman allowed Martin to help him from the car and into the Citroën. Martin made sure the keys were left in the Nissan's ignition. In the street a few people were assembling.

But before anything had time to happen, Loman, clutching his case of money, was whisked away into Paris's southern suburbs.

Martin could not have been kinder, more apologetic. When Loman asked to stop and make a phone call – in which he carefully did not mention the accident – Martin waited patiently in the car. As soon as the Citroën had pulled away from the scene of the crash, the StormWind man who had given Loman the money – an ex-FBI agent called Brenner – had emerged from the shadows and steered the scarred but driveable Nissan after them. Soon both cars were heading into dark countryside.

Twelve

A light rain thickened the night around the chateau of Sousbois. Inside, Hendry and McDade paced the corridors, trying to fill hours that refused to pass. Hendry hung around while McDade, a hand-rolled cigarette stuck to his lip, curtly answered a phone call. 'That was Dickie. He's on his way.'

'Again?' Hendry was like a soldier about to go into combat. His nerves were almost too alert. There had been an earlier call which McDade had also said was Loman.

McDade said, 'Just confirming.'

'Why should he confirm? I thought we said one call.'

'The wee chap's a bit nervous.'

'What's gone wrong?' Hendry demanded.

McDade rushed to reassure. 'No, no, Ed. Everything's fine, Robin and Dickie both collected, no snags. They're on their way back. Once we sort the money, we're away.' McDade lit his remnant of cigarette. The earlier call had been from Lucian Weidinger, informing him of when the helicopter would arrive. Thinking quickly, McDade had said it was Loman calling in for clarification. Hendry rightly remained uneasy about this. McDade realised how lucky he had been, with Hendry so far out of the way during most of their occupation of the chateau. McDade had made a shrewd choice in removing the one man he could never have fooled for long.

They brewed some coffee, black, rank, sleep-murdering stuff, a Macbeth of a drink. Hendry asked, 'What if they're being followed?'

'Look, they both said they're clear. What more can we ask for?'

It was too good to believe. And yet Hendry's own part of the operation, as Hendry himself saw it, had gone with military precision. So why shouldn't this? But Hendry's strength was also his weakness: the regular army attitude that if the problem didn't grip him by the throat, it wasn't a problem. And the long empty hours were taking their toll. Hendry withdrew into his real talent, the British squaddie's capacity for waiting, endlessly waiting, with a cool head and a blank mind.

'Fucking rain,' he grumbled. 'I could use a walk.'

McDade had been taxing his mind with how he was to remove Holly and Wardour against Hendry's opposition. There might be no way other than a bullet. And since Hendry was armed, the shot would have to be a total surprise. Before McDade could decide if it was a good or bad thing to have Hendry wandering around outside, they both started. Beyond the shutters the rain muffled sound. Yet both men had picked up the distinct noise, somewhere in the distance, of a helicopter. For aircraft to overfly the Sous-bois estate was not unknown. But at this hour, on this night and in such weather, the buzz of a helicopter was ominous. Hendry looked at McDade. The Irishman was too relaxed for his liking. Feeling his own security at stake, Hendry flung open the nearest outside door just in time to hear rotors run down and die as the helicopter came to rest. Hendry's judgment of these things was still excellent. He estimated it had been a mile away, certainly no more.

He turned back to McDade, who was lethargically staring into nowhere. 'Didn't you hear it?'

'It's gone,' McDade said. 'I can't hear it now.'

'It came down.'

'Never.'

'I'm telling you.'

'Shut the door, Ed. You're getting jumpy. The boys will be here soon. Stay cool and wait it out now.'

Hendry obeyed, and pulled the door shut. But after a minute of failing to settle, he took his jacket, whose pocket still held the automatic, and went out. McDade followed in an effort to restrain him.

'This is crazy. What the hell are you going to do out there?'

'If somebody's around I want to know who it is.'

'You think we should both look?'

153

Hendry said, 'No, you stay here. I'll be ten minutes, most.'

'Watch for headlights. It'll be the boys returning. When you see them, get the hell back here.'

Hendry advanced. The rain had almost stopped, and up in the night sky faint stars were appearing. Hendry headed off through the unkempt gardens, towards where he believed the helicopter had landed. Dark masses of vegetation dripped water. After a few hundred yards Hendry lost any discernible path. The little time he had spent here had given him no real mental map of the chateau's surrounding area. Even Sous-bois itself, as Hendry periodically looked round for the landmark, soon disappeared, its shuttered windows merging with the night.

A fresh breeze chilled Hendry's body through the wet clothing as he pushed on into the unknown meadows and *bocage* of the estate. He had no doubt that there was a helicopter somewhere out here, and more to the point, its crew. But however urgently he listened, Hendry's ears were unable to detect any sound of movement.

He had doubts of the wisdom of what he was doing. But his only possible reaction to danger at this point was to meet it head-on. He wondered how McDade could take it so calmly. Because, Hendry replied to himself, McDade thought nerves had produced a delusion in his, Hendry's, mind. And this fuelled Hendry's determination to head off the trouble which he sensed out here, beyond this cloying darkness.

As soon as Hendry was away from the house, McDade went up to the library. Wardour and Holly had willingly accepted their incarceration in this long, musty room. The opportunity to begin reusing their limbs was all the freedom they could manage. But it had been an awkward few hours. Along with physical mobility, they had lost the simple devices of speech – words would not come, their lips and tongues formed sounds which failed to connect with the confusion in their minds. Above all, guilt restrained them, various guilts at what had brought them together for this week of captivity, and uncertainty at what would happen now they were to be returned. For Roderick Wardour in particular, the prospect of liberation was made a bitter joke by thoughts of facing Jessica, of the story coming out, of the terminal damage to his career.

Within Holly there was a greater turmoil. She resented the fact that her life had been endangered because of Wardour's status as a politician. She sensed his mind already pushing her to the margin, calculating his own political gains and losses. At least she was aware of how much he had suffered. For Wardour, however, Holly felt she no longer counted as a person, just an embarrassment. He had reverted to type, just another stuffed-shirt Englishman. Maybe this was how it would have ended all along. No doubt, Holly said to herself, no doubt. And hated him for it. Most of their reunion in the library passed in a state of depressed withdrawal, keeping the long room's space between them. Yet when the key turned in the lock they moved instinctively towards each other, and their eyes met for sustenance as McDade entered the room.

Advancing towards them, the Irishman raised his hands to damp down their air of twitching readiness. They would not be freed in quite the way they expected. McDade was keenly aware of how the prolongation of his own life would depend on the self-control of these two.

Hooded, he drew them towards him conspiratorially and said, 'Out there is a helicopter – ' Out there also was Ed Hendry, armed with an automatic. But McDade knew things Hendry didn't. He went on. 'Things may get a bit crowded round here. There may even be some shooting, but we'll be well out of all that. I have the keys to your car,' McDade pointed to Wardour and produced the keys, 'and we're going to drive out of this place to where the helicopter has put down.'

'And then?' Wardour asked.

'We're taking you back.'

'Back?' Wardour repeated.

Holly said, 'Why should there be shooting?'

McDade ignored her question. 'Are you both ready?'

'I'm sorry,' said Wardour, 'but I don't trust you.'

'If I were you,' McDade replied, 'I wouldn't trust me either.

155

But your choice is limited. You'd better believe that your only way out of here is with me.'

As they left, McDade hoped that Hendry would not reappear. McDade had his own automatic in his coat and if he saw Hendry again he would have to stop him dead. Hendry or anyone else, for that matter.

Dickie Loman's nerves were recovering from the collision, and he gave Martin directions from a map which he studied with the aid of a pen-light. Loman dwelt with relief on how everything could have gone wrong because of the accident. But as he became less shaky, his mind tuned into something about the obliging American who had offered to drive him home. Perhaps it was an over-readiness to respond every time Loman indicated a new road to take. Loman decided to retrieve himself from his fear. 'I'm feeling much better. I'll take over now,' he suggested.

'No way. That was a nasty shock you had back there.'

'Really. I must insist.'

'It's no trouble,' Martin assured him.

'But how are you going to get back to Paris?'

'I'll take a train,' Martin said.

'But it's two in the morning,' Loman persisted, distrusting the American's generosity.

'I'll wait.'

Perhaps Martin was genuine. Loman tried to convince himself. In desperation he searched the map. At the next route sign he said, 'That's it, Conches, three kilometres.'

'Fine,' Martin said, and followed the arrows for Conches. But as the village opened up, Loman began to sweat. 'Down here?' the American asked.

'Perhaps it's best if I drop you at the station.'

'I could use a coffee. Which way to your place?'

Loman's heart felt like an empty paper bag. 'Look, I really don't feel up to it. Do you mind if – '

Martin ran the car to a halt in the silent village square. Loman had ignored the car which had seemed to be following them.

But now it pulled in behind them he could ignore it no longer. Martin said, 'OK. Where is Holly Odell?'

Loman groaned, 'Oh my God.'

'Be quick, please.'

'Look,' Loman held up the case of money, 'I'm sure we can come to an arrangement.'

Martin grabbed the case and dropped it to the floor below his legs. 'The arrangement is, take me to Holly Odell, or I'm going to blow your fucking head off.'

By contrast, the return drive in Robin Knight's car was uneventful, almost so easy that Bobby Stanger began to wonder if Knight was not pulling some kind of bluff, sacrificing himself to save the others. But it didn't make sense that way. The Englishman's only hope was the ransom money, and that was firmly in Stanger's keeping. Successive kilometres of dark French road floated by. Stanger rode in front and Redmond was a silent brooding presence behind Knight's head. Knight finally revealed what was on his mind.

'If you'd cooperated with the plan, Miss Odell would be safe by now. As it is, you're risking her life for the sake of the money.'

'You're the kidnapper, pal, not me,' Stanger said. 'Just drive.' But for many more miles Stanger thought over just what they were doing here, and what his employer really wanted. Because the more he thought about Barron Odell, the less he was inspired to see a loving father.

'We're almost there,' Knight said. He tried to think up ways of bargaining for his own safety. But he had no leverage with these men, and the attempt would weaken him in their eyes. His only chance was to be as helpful as possible. 'In about half a mile there's a gateway, then the road leads to a country house. The best thing is if I turn the headlights off once we're inside the estate.'

But Stanger was suspicious of people who suddenly became so compliant. 'They're expecting you back, right?' he demanded.

'Yes, but – '

'So do everything normal. Drive to the house normally. If I want you to change it, I'll let you know.'

'Whatever you say,' Knight answered, then, 'there's somebody coming.'

A car with dipped lights rounded a bend ahead. The oncoming driver seemed to be slowing on approach. But having gauged the gap, he accelerated and forced Knight to swing sideways onto the grass verge. All three men knew this was no ordinary French motorist, but there was no time to think further. Knight stamped on the pedal as Stanger shouted at him to get going. But the rear wheel had locked in some pocket of grassy mud, which its repeated spinning only dug deeper. Knight sweated and cursed. His foot made the engine scream. But the car only canted further over, away from the road.

Stanger demanded, 'How far is this place?'

'Not far, just – '

'Let's go.'

They bundled out of the tilted car. The ransom money clutched under his arm, Stanger ordered Knight to run. But Knight's ankle, swollen from Stanger's kick, only allowed him to hobble. Stanger's gun forced Knight into a fast limp. Of the three men, only Redmond was fully fit. By the time they reached the gateway to the estate, Stanger himself was out of breath. Worse, he was burdened with the sense of a bloody great disaster about to descend on him.

Hendry decided to turn back. He had tried to use the few visible stars to keep a straight course. But the black gullies of the terrain frustrated him. Hendry had seen and heard nothing. He felt foolishly that maybe it had been overreaction after all. But it was worth it, to have proved there was no danger. Although by now he had lost any exact bearing on the chateau's position, he tried to retrace his steps.

The brick-paved path he struck was so well made, Hendry guessed it must lead somewhere towards the house. He moved at a fast marching pace, but every step increased his anger at himself for ever leaving the chateau. Then he heard a voice. It came faintly, just a snatch of human sound carried on the air, wind-borne, unrecognisable. Hendry fingered the gun in his pocket. The path he had taken was all wrong, but he found no clear way off it. He looked everywhere for a glimmer of light from the chateau, but in every direction saw total darkness.

Then Hendry heard a car approaching. At last something was happening. Two cars in fact. From their distant beams he was able to pinpoint the road to the house, a quarter of a mile away. Two cars together! Hendry's spirits rose again at the efficiency with which Knight and Loman had synchronised their returns. Things would work out now.

Confused by the absence of even the smallest light as the car drew near, Dickie Loman followed the drive up to the chateau. McDade had thrown the fusebox switch as he left, and now the full beam of Loman's car gave the shuttered, decaying house a ghostly elegance. The cars slewed to a stop on the forecourt. On the way, Martin had tried to browbeat details out of Loman, but all Loman was able to tell him was that on return he would report to the others.

'How many others?'

'Two.'

'Armed?'

'I'm not certain.'

'And then?' But Loman didn't know.

Now Martin said, 'Sound the horn.' Loman complied. 'What is this goddamn place?' Martin cursed.

'I hope you don't think I'm kidding you,' Loman said.

'Listen, creep, I think somebody's kidding *you*. This fucking place is empty.'

'That can't be,' Loman protested. 'They were here.'

'Well they're sure as fuck not here now. This leader guy – what's his name?'

'Sean.'

'Get out the car, call him.' Martin tapped his automatic on Loman's skull. 'Nothing clever.'

Loman obeyed. In the car beams he felt frighteningly

exposed. Perhaps the darkness was another ploy of McDade's. He began calling. 'Sean, Sean. It's me, Dickie.' Betrayal stared back at Loman from the dead portals of Sous-bois. Even his contingency plan, that at the first sign of trouble he could abscond with the money, had been ripped away from him. Then came voices.

At first Loman thought it must be McDade. But he listened again. The voices were French, and not directed at him. He turned back to Martin. 'There's somebody out here.'

Martin doused the headlamps. In the car behind, Brenner did likewise. With guns drawn both men got out. Martin collared Loman and dragged him along as a shield. Then they heard footsteps on the drive behind them. Loman's mind spun – McDade, Knight, Hendry? For God's sake could somebody come and explain all this to him?

There were two figures. A shred of starlight off the roof of a car brought them to a halt. Stanger and Redmond were also bemused by the blacked-out house looming ahead. Some mental antenna told the men crouched behind the cars who it was. Martin called, 'Hey Bobby, over here.'

'It's Martin,' Stanger said to Redmond. He was angry because the plan had been to join up at the main gate. But after five minutes' wait for Stanger's car to arrive, Martin had ordered Loman to drive all the way. Stanger had suspected all through that once it got to cases, the StormWind boys were going to do it their way. Now they were dug in behind a car, yelling out of the darkness. Stanger didn't like any of it. Their only strength lay in keeping together. But Redmond was already acting independently. He had got halfway to the cars when a light beamed on. The floodlight was total, a huge *son et lumière* effect in which the only sound was a harsh bullhorned voice, in a heavy French accent, demanding immediate surrender.

In the floodlight's dark hinterland men were running, taking position, running again. A whole sector of the night bristled with weaponry. Stanger watched in amazement as Martin and Brenner in concert aimed a burst of pistol fire at the floodlight in a vain attempt to shatter its source. Stanger accepted that life had its modicum of violence. But this was different. He had walked into a giant killing machine. At the first shots he plunged towards the nearest patch of dark cover. He slipped and fell, hit undergrowth, mud, rock, scrambled to regain a footing, ignored pain, ignored the bursts of automatic rifle fire behind him, and above all, kept moving.

Loman had started running as soon as the StormWind men unloosed their pistol shots. As if for security, he scuttled towards the house. A ripple of bullets sprawled him below one of the shuttered windows. Redmond never made it to the cars, but was torn apart by twenty or thirty rounds hitting simultaneously. After that the French anti-terrorist squads poured bullets into the cars, filling the air with a howling rain of heavy metal, until a petrol tank ignited and took both vehicles with it. By then both Martin and Brenner were so grievously wounded that the spectacular pyre only hastened a death already imminent.

Seconds before the gas tank explosion while machine-gun fire still clattered into the cars, Stanger came upon someone else in the darkness. This man was not escaping like himself, but standing in stupefaction at what was happening in the distance. The man was armed and went for a gun, as did Stanger. But before either of them could shoot, the cars fireballed. In the obscene glow, Ed Hendry and Bobby Stanger looked into each other's faces.

Hendry was by now too dazed to work out Stanger's role in all this. Stanger just said, 'Come on, soldier, let's get out of here.'

Hendry knew the path. That was all he knew. They ran.

Somewhere in the darkness a helicopter took off. And elsewhere on the estate, abandoned by Stanger and Redmond, Robin Knight limped impotently away from the gunfire, for all the world like the crippled boy in the Pied Piper story, on whom the mountain had closed.

Thirteen

The next day's dawn found Barron Odell in a very bad way. Fully dressed, he had managed a few hours of whisky-aided sleep in a hotel armchair. Every so often he woke and glared at the phone, as if the urgency of his longing could make it ring. At eight a.m. he had just stripped and showered. Conceding mental and physical exhaustion, he was about to climb between the sheets, when finally the phone rang.

'Mr Odell? Dick Ginistrelli.' The adrenalin whirling in Odell's veins turned to poison. His heart banged like a worn piston.

'Yeah, what?'

'I wondered if I could buy you breakfast.' There was silence. 'You remember me? We – '

'Yeah, sure. Look, I'm not feeling too well.'

'I'm sorry. Can I help at all?'

'Thanks, no. It was nice talking to you, and maybe we'll meet up again.' Odell growled a decisive 'Goodbye' before Ginistrelli could say any more.

Stanger had not phoned. Odell had not heard from Holly or his StormWind boys. His presence in London was a false trail for anyone who had an interest in the case, and because frankly he himself was out of condition for heavy work. But now Odell faced the one thing he feared most – impotence. Sexually he had entered a terminal decline years ago, but the prime substitutes for sex, power and money, had promised to see him through. Yet here he was, reduced to a hangover in a hotel room, begging a phone to restore his potency, while his money and his power lay in the hands of other men.

Odell sank into an instant sleep, a ghost-train ride through jeering dreams. His sparse sandy hair failed to stop the copious sweat of his head soaking the pillow. He woke suddenly, with one very clear thought in his mind. He had made no secret of his hotel to the CIA, if indeed that was Ginistrelli's master. So they were probably out there now, waiting for him, and probably the British security service too. All Odell had expected was to hear that Holly was free, then he could play all the games with the CIA that he wanted. But now they were in possession of all the information, while he had nothing. Odell's fists clenched at the thought that they had fooled *him*. They could have known Holly's whereabouts all along, while he was sweating it out in a hotel room.

Odell was wrong about what the CIA knew at that point. But he was correct about Ginistrelli, who after his abortive attempt to engage Odell for breakfast, had taken up a position in the Paddington street from which to observe Odell's next move.

At Sous-bois the French security forces listened to the silence for a few minutes, the dreadful blood-imbued silence after the spatter of bullets, in which the black skeletons of the cars still burned fitfully. Then at the word of command they ran forward to take the chateau. Armed men occupied the shadows while the loudhailer voice demanded no further resistance. As they kicked in doors, which opened readily, and clattered into the house, freezing into poised silence along the dark corridors, Sous-bois remained shrouded in its secrecy. With muttered directives and encouragements, fifteen or twenty men scoured the building, relying on their night-adapted vision and hearing to warn them of danger, not even offering a single flashlight target to any hidden gunman.

Within minutes they had the lights on, and now, fingers on triggers, combed every alcove. Room by room their relief increased, as they confirmed that the place was empty. For such anti-terrorist men the job contained its own justification. They had no interest in who exactly might be here. The exchange of gunfire had been the raw material of their work, and having killed for the night they relaxed in the empty rooms, lit cigarettes and made the occasional wry comment which was the only nervous release they allowed themselves.

In the rooms where Wardour and Holly had served their week's captivity no evidence remained, except items of unidentified baggage and the nylon ropes with which they had been tied up. As he had ushered the captives out of Sous-bois, McDade had meticulously returned their personal effects. In addition he had made sure to remove any name tags from things they had to leave behind.

Half a kilometre away, protected by darkness, like a blind man in a cinema, Lucian Weidinger coolly followed the sounds erupting from the chateau. They confirmed everything he knew. Apart from McDade, Weidinger was counting on the remaining kidnappers to be killed. Any that were not, would be thrown into jail, and Weidinger was satisfied that their usefulness to the police would be practically zero. For one thing, none of them had met him. The only way they could mitigate their own guilt was to finger McDade. But Weidinger's scenario painted McDade as the *rescuer* of the captives. McDade had not handled a note of the ransom money. The captives' families had never heard his voice. And he had brought Wardour and Holly Odell out in one piece.

Once Sous-bois returned to silence, Weidinger drove away, satisfied that now he could dismiss the kidnappers from his thoughts. It was, after all, the fate of dispensable people, to be dispensed with.

Hours later, at about the time Odell was being called by Ginistrelli, Robin Knight delivered himself into the custody of the French police. After hours of physical and mental pain wandering country roads, resting rarely because his ankle hurt worse than when he kept on the move, Knight saw the dawn-whitening of the sky as a sign to redeem the mess he had got his life into. He blocked off all speculation about what had happened at the chateau, to the men he had regarded as comrades, the ransom money, the hostages. He had been spared the death that had certainly come to some of the others. As if in return for this, he told himself capture was inevitable.

Entering a small town at daybreak, Knight found the humble-looking police station and asked the desk officer if anyone there spoke English. After two hours alone in an interview room, where from time to time *gendarmes* brought him coffee and viewed him with a sort of bewildered curiosity, Knight was seen by a detective who inhaled gulps of *caporal* smoke and questioned him impatiently in imperfect but rapid English. Knight explained briefly that he had been involved in events at the chateau, which he was unable to name, since the ancient title Sous-bois had remained unknown to its occupants. Knight then insisted to the bemused detective that he would only make a full confession to the British police.

More time elapsed as the detective went away and tried to disentangle this story about unspecified events at some chateau. Seeking greater leverage, the detective told Knight that he would be held indefinitely. No contact would be made with the British authorities until more information was forthcoming. At which point Knight referred curtly to the Wardour kidnap. The detective professed ignorance, but Knight knew that things would start to happen now. Short of beating the truth out of this furtive, exhausted Englishman, the detective had little option but to pass the whole thing higher up. And now machinery began to turn. Knight was given a bed in a cell, on which he found the sleep of those relieved of a great burden. And hours, precious to some, dangerous to others, began to drain away.

At Scotland Yard, Commander Mike Wiley lit a cigarette with one hand and switched on his electric shaver with the other. Three months earlier he had given up drinking alcohol and gone back to cigarettes, choosing the drug that might shorten his life but at least would not affect his ability to do his job. A serious man, Wiley did not want to end up promoted sideways as just another copper with a drink problem.

In the Scotland Yard operations room set up to deal with the Wardour case, Wiley waited for his boys to touch base on the Odell surveillance. The routine Special Branch watch at the airport had triggered off the alert that Barron Odell had returned to the United Kingdom. Having tracked him to the hotel, they now found themselves, in the early morning, sharing the vigil.

Since they had had to clutch at every strand that came their way, Wiley had ordered his team to pull in the man who appeared to be watching Odell's hotel. But until he heard from them, Wiley's mind played over his other problems. A lapsed Catholic, for a year he had been stealing occasional hours at the flat of a young policewoman, and was still failing to resolve the equation between romance and guilt. And his teenage daughter was far too active with boyfriends. Wiley conceded that he had always been an absentee father, but in his day at least parents only worried about pregnancy. But then came herpes, now Aids, and the fear of pregnancy still hadn't gone away. Wiley's solution was to immerse himself in work up to his neck. But the Wardour case was the last thing he needed. Whenever a politician was involved, the police would never know the whole truth. Inconvenient facts would be buried, important persons protected, scandal avoided 'in the national interest'. But until they could recover Roderick Wardour, dead or alive, and clear up the rumoured IRA connection, Mike Wiley was stuck with it.

The phone erupted, loud in the operations room. Wiley crushed his cigarette and snapped off his shaver.

'He's CIA, guv.'

'Oh Christ. Got proof?'

'Yeah.'

'Bring the bastard – kindly ask the gentleman to come back here for a chat with us.'

Bobby Stanger remembered about the car, which only minutes earlier he had abandoned with its wheel in a roadside ditch. Then he rejected the idea; by the time he and Hendry got it back on the road those goons with machine guns would be on top of them. If they escaped, it had to be on foot.

'What do you say?' he asked Hendry. 'We stick together?'

Hendry resembled a victim of shell shock. Nothing added up any more. He had last seen Stanger in Boston, and all Hendry could think was that Stanger had pursued him here. Hendry felt stupid, stupid and angry. For a few bitter moments he felt it would have been better to go down in that hail of gunfire. 'You conned me, you bastard.'

'Taking care of business,' Stanger said. 'If you feel sore about it, OK. But we might need each other.'

'Why should I need you?'

'There's half the ransom money in this bag,' Stanger said. 'Would a two-way split soothe your feelings? Two hundred and fifty grand between us?' Stanger would have to work out later how to identify the good bills and sort them into his own share. But in case Hendry had any other ideas, Stanger pulled his gun. Hendry's hand went to his own pocket. Stanger had been right, the Englishman was armed. 'These won't do us any good now. Right?' Hendry agreed. Wisely or not, they buried the automatics in a tangle of underbrush. Their first need was to strike a road where they could hitch a ride. Then resurface in a city, where they could get new clothes for dollars and merge with the crowds while they planned their next move.

After an hour of walking, in which he soon became aware of Hendry's superior fitness, Stanger had a thought and asked, 'Did you leave your papers behind?' Hendry never even visited the toilet without taking his passport. The question genuinely surprised him. He tapped a button-down flap on his jacket. Some paces later Stanger said, 'Now for the tricky one. What happened to Holly Odell?'

Hendry had been feeling bad about this. He grunted. 'You tell me.'

Stanger said, 'There's a lot of things I don't want to know, but I guess I have to find them out sooner or later.' For instance, he thought, the possible non-return of Barron Odell's daughter, the massacre of the StormWind men, the vapour trail where half the ransom money had been.

'What I want to know,' Hendry said, 'is who were those people back there?'

'We were set up,' Stanger said. 'You and me both.'

'A rescue attempt, or what?'

167

'What else? Was somebody cheating on you?'

Hendry remained stubbornly silent on this point.

'Was she in the house?' Stanger asked.

'She was there two hours ago. We were getting ready to release her.'

'Somebody beat us to it.'

Recalling the gunfire, Hendry said, 'Let's hope so.'

A cold dawn was spreading across the eastern sky. The French countryside slowly shook off its oblivion. Stanger looked up and whistled the opening bars of 'The Star-Spangled Banner'. Hendry didn't get the joke.

The same paling dawn saw the Alouette helicopter well over the Channel. The sky was still deep blue when, a few miles after the dark coastline of Jersey, the pilot responded to a light flashing in the wastes of grey water below.

During the whole flight from inland France none of the three passengers had attempted communication, even by signs. Their separate, still unpredictable destinies made them uncertain with each other. McDade sat near the pilot while Wardour and Holly crouched behind. He now removed his earphones and crawled back. To their disbelief he indicated with gestures that it was time to leave. The Alouette slowed, then hovered. As it hung in the air McDade, who seemed to know what he was doing, released the door and slid it open on an infinity of cold air and heaving ocean.

McDade himself had no stomach for heights. The vibration of the helicopter in the surrounding gulf made his legs buckle, his insides gape. But he held on long enough to drop the ladder towards the waiting motor launch, as the pilot eased the helicopter over the boat.

Without explanation McDade motioned the others to leave. Holly clung desperately to the Alouette's superstructure, unable to force herself out into the howling wind. Wardour had been athletic as a young man, and wanted to get this endless journey over. He screwed up his face and lowered himself stiffly onto the ladder. With McDade helping, Holly made it out. Then

McDade, crooning some inhuman dirge to siphon off his fear, climbed into space. They were not even wearing lifejackets. Blue knuckles let go the harsh rope. One by one they fell into the rocking boat, where another anonymous trafficker awaited them. Once McDade was sprawled on the boat's floor, the helicopter screamed engines and veered away. The boat kicked off into the waves as its three passengers huddled for shelter from the wind.

Almost animal-like in their silence, they again avoided the exchange of any word or signal. Only as land came in sight Holly asked Wardour, 'What's your wife's name?'

Before they brought Dick Ginistrelli in to Scotland Yard, Mike Wiley had already checked with his MI5 overlords that CIA involvement in the Wardour kidnap had not been requested, at least not to the extent of surveillance on the streets of London. The official view was still that the Odell girl was a suspect rather than a victim. Her complicity would explain, for a start, how the kidnappers had known where to snatch Wardour. To senior members of police and government, hungry for explanations, the IRA connection was the one that had stuck.

On the way to the Yard Ginistrelli prepared a speech about the defence of the rights of US nationals overseas – an American woman was a hostage, just as much as the British MP who was getting all the limelight, and American Intelligence were entitled to follow up any lead which might bring about her safe return. Ginistrelli was sure that the confidence he had established in Odell would lead to some vital slip being made. And now these London policemen, maybe figuring the same, were crowding him out.

Ginistrelli prepared for a fight, but all that happened was that they left him in a room, the sort of featureless room which is an essential part of police operations. The policeman who came to him couldn't have been nicer. There was talk of constructive cooperation, special relationships, pooling of energy: if he wouldn't mind being patient, a meeting with one of his equivalents from Five was being fixed up for later. Meanwhile, breakfast?

Relieved, Ginistrelli accepted. An intellectual rather than a policeman, he only slowly realised that they hadn't brought him to Scotland Yard for social niceties. But he was getting a buzz from being active in the field, and had little choice but to play along. Except that Barron Odell was now in the Yard's safekeeping.

Something had happened, something more momentous than Ginistrelli could have guessed. While the CIA man had been sitting in the London rush hour, Mike Wiley had taken a call from the French Sûreté. Robin Knight had got his wish, the French authorities had concluded that the only way to extract information from him was to accede to his demand to see the British police. The name Wardour was the magic link. Wiley found a graduate officer who spoke French, and by the time Ginistrelli arrived at the Yard the two Branch men were already bound for the airport.

The rocky headland seemed to come floating from the green-grey horizon, drawing with it a wake of low cliffs, a long stretch of shoreline that might be anywhere in western Britain. At Holly's question about his wife, Wardour smiled ruefully, lips thinned by the rough sea breeze. But he could not make himself speak Jessica's name. He was all too aware that she might be waiting when they disembarked. No doubt that was why Holly had asked. Wardour sipped the rum which the otherwise indifferent man at the boat controls had given them against the cold, then passed the bottle to McDade.

'Where is this?' he asked.

McDade shouted back, 'Guess. Smell the kelp.'

Wardour's heart sank. It was Ireland. The fear he had suppressed now rose like sea-sickness. They were not to be freed after all. Holly had caught that feeling too.

She yelled at McDade, 'Where are you taking us now?'

As the launch stabilised, somebody was rowing out to ferry them through the shallow water. How could McDade explain

170

that he was as much cargo as the others? And then, he had to keep reminding himself, in Belfast a faction of hard men wanted him dead. So even at this stage he half-expected a gunshot in the temple, his body dumped straight back into these deserted Irish waters. 'Don't worry,' he shouted back. 'Everything's fine.'

McDade had known that Weidinger, calculating Swiss sonofabitch that he was, excelled at organisation. But this morning's sequence of events wrung true admiration from the normally irreverent Irishman. From the rowing-boat they transferred to a car, a new Ford limousine in which, for the first time this journey, they experienced bodily comfort in the well-upholstered, warm interior. Two polite but distant Irishmen sat in front. Miles of lonely countryside slipped by. Again nobody spoke. Salvation had become an individual matter. There was no one story that would suit the three of them. And if the men in front were their new jailers, it would be stupid to give away the smallest fear or hope.

After two hours they finally left the road and turned into the grounds of a large grey house partly screened by trees. It was like Sous-bois all over again. But on arrival the Irishmen showed them in, escorted them to bedrooms with *en suite* baths, clean linen, towels, and suggested that after freshening up they made for the smell of bacon and mushrooms drifting from the kitchen. The Irishmen looked at McDade a moment longer than at the others. Even Wardour, the famous politician, didn't interest them so very much. But McDade they looked at with, it had to be said, respect.

A female cook, full-bodied and jovially Irish, but exercising the same discretion as the others, laid out breakfast, then withdrew. Wardour, his mind growing sharper by the minute, demanded of McDade, 'What now?'

McDade looked up. 'You may have gathered that I'm not in control of things here.'

But neither Wardour nor Holly could shake off the routine of the last week. McDade had been their jailer, with power of life or death over them. They could not register that he was now as helpless as themselves.

'Then what the hell's going on?'

'Things are being worked out. This stuff's real good. I'm sorry we didn't feed you better back in France.'

Deep inside Wardour an untapped well of anger was pressing for release. As he regained physical strength and took in the thought that McDade no longer controlled his destiny, Wardour began to toy with revenge. This aggression also enabled him to avoid thoughts of the embarrassment awaiting him in London.

Holly ate slowly, watching Wardour for cues, despising her dependence on him but admitting the truth, that he was the one people were interested in. She herself was only inconvenient baggage. Holly believed this was Wardour's view too. Finally she could stand it no longer and went up to her room. After some uneasy minutes Wardour pushed his plate away and also went upstairs.

Holly's door was just open, Wardour went in. She was crying, her body shaking. Wardour made no move towards her: after a week of isolated captivity, remembered sexual passion was not enough of a bridge. Tall and suddenly emanating power and self-importance, Wardour stood above a woman who had strayed into a brief amorous fling, after which nothing had made sense any more.

'What is it?' he asked.

'It's all right, I'll recover.'

Wardour sat on the bed, but kept a metre between them, all reserved Englishman now. 'Once we get back – '

'Where's *back*?'

'Look, maybe we'll have to leave it for a while, but then – I do want to see you again.'

On Holly's face slanting lines of exhaustion ran from her eye sockets the length of her cheekbones. Her long mouth was lower on one side than the other. Wardour had never noticed this before. Or he had forgotten? There was so much he had forgotten. 'And your wife?'

All along Wardour had told himself that Jessica was not the

problem – Jess would be all right. Jess would see him through. Why were women so funny about other women? 'She'll be OK.'

'You'll fix her, then you'll fix me? Then get on with your career?' she said bitterly.

'For God's sake,' Wardour protested. 'You don't blame me for this, do you?'

Holly also raised her voice. 'I had a nice life. You weren't part of it. I just want to get back to it. If you're not part of it, I won't worry.'

'Was it a nice life?' Wardour asked.

'You thought it was pathetic, didn't you? When you came to my flat, I could see it all over your face.'

Always afraid of patronising, Wardour had no way of expressing how sorry for her he had felt. He said, 'That's untrue.'

'Well, it was pathetic. Then I met you in that traffic jam. For me it couldn't have happened any other way. If I'd had time to think, I'd never have got there. And that one time brought me back to life. People are going to say it was just furtive sex in a wood. But it brought me back to life. You made me feel strong again. I'll always remember you for that.'

Wardour gazed out of the window. Ireland: green pastures, distant hills; apart from some Friesian cattle, nothing moving. A new fear began to grow in him, a fear of all the things he would not be able to do – live up to Holly, keep her, protect her from the destruction which he felt sucking him in. At the same time he understood more now of the strange power with which Holly had loved him. He was humbled by her words. 'You saved my life too,' he said.

Drawn and tired, shabby in spite of the baths they had both had, still wearing the crumpled clothes they had lived in for a week, Wardour and Holly looked at each other candidly, feelings finally overcoming fear for themselves. Wardour opened his arms. As Holly got up and came to him, tears overbrimmed his eyes. By the window Holly hugged him, sobbing silently as he stroked her still wet hair.

The one thing Robin Knight could not do was specify which

country house they had used. He had lost any sense of place and direction. All he could give the Sûreté was a vague architectural description that could have applied to dozens of grandish residences in the region. But by now the French police were themselves able to identify Sous-bois from the previous night's slaughter. The one blank they drew was the dead men. Only Loman had carried identification. The StormWind agents had left their papers in lockers in Paris. Of the original four, only Stanger would now go back to reclaim his. So the French police had three anonymous bodies in cold storage, and the firm conviction that Robin Knight could reveal who they were. But Knight refused even to give his own name until faced with a British police officer.

'Did you know Richard Loman?'

'Yes.'

'Who was he?'

'I don't know anything about him. A kidnapper.'

'Like you?'

'Yes.'

'Who were the other men?'

But however they tried it, at this point Knight was silent. Since he was not actually refusing cooperation, the Sûreté people kept the pressure light. The man was not a normal criminal, so either he would never break or a few hours' solitude would crack him. Meanwhile they waited for more information to come in.

What came their way, unexpectedly fast, was a directive from the Elysée ordering complete cooperation with the Special Branch men who were already on their way from London. Mike Wiley had made the right phone call before he left, and while he still waited at Heathrow a call had been put through from Downing Street to the President of the Republic. The French wanted to offload the case. With the unification of Europe and the linking of the British and French mainlands by tunnel, the French authorities were becoming progressively nervous about their own people being drawn into the terrorist orbit. The day the bombers hit the tunnel it would hold French as well as

British travellers, and the French government wanted to do nothing to make that black day for France any more of a certainty. So as soon as the Sous-bois affair was labelled IRA the French were only too glad to hand it over.

Hence the unexpected welcome Mike Wiley and the fresh-faced Detective Sergeant Lucas Brand received from their opposite numbers in Poitiers. Once they discovered that Brand spoke their language, the local detectives conveyed in rapid French the story of Knight's appearance. For the sake of *entente cordiale* Wiley accepted a gauloise, then muttered to Brand to get them face to face with this missing link.

The Yard men were taken to the interview room. The holstered *gendarme* withdrew on their arrival. Getting to his feet, Robin Knight displayed all the signs of an officer and a gentleman who wanted to restore his good name. 'I'm sorry to bring you all this way,' he began, 'but I couldn't trust the French police to return me to London. I'm afraid it's not very cosy.'

Wiley's button-like eyes glared. He was not impressed by this attempt to act the host, put the visiting coppers at their ease. Knight's middle-class manners were out of place here. Lucas Brand leaned in a corner while Wiley pulled up a chair and sat backwards on it, his hands praying. Or was it throttling?

'Your name?'

'Robin Knight.' Knight had intended to slip in his former submarine rank, but something in Wiley's bearing warned him off.

Tersely, Wiley introduced himself and Brand. 'I understand you have information relating to a certain matter.'

Knight smiled at the police-speak. 'They've probably told you – '

'You tell us,' Wiley interrupted.

'Now you're here I'm prepared to make a written statement.'

'Later.'

The French police had made it all too plain that, for what visual inspection was worth, the bodies at Sous-bois did not appear to include that of Roderick Wardour. Nor was there a woman among them. Wiley searched Knight's face, taking his

175

time the way he always did when he knew it was going to be a long haul. 'Do you know the whereabouts of Roderick Wardour?'

'I last saw him yesterday evening – '

'That wasn't the question,' Lucas Brand chipped in.

'He was at the house – ' From their faces Knight caught their implication; Wardour was dead! Knight's blood froze. Or were they bluffing?

'We know where the place is. Wardour was not there.'

Knight said uneasily, 'They were going to release him last night.'

Wiley shifted on the chair and breathed heavily, yielding to impatience. This French business was not a solution, it was going to be just another bloody problem. 'Let me get this straight, Mr Knight. Are you asking us to believe you were an innocent bystander?'

'No,' Knight said. 'I was involved from the beginning.' But for all his candour, Knight was getting worried. He burst out, 'It would all have gone like clockwork if it hadn't been for the Americans.'

'The Americans!'

'Wardour would have been back in England by now.'

'*What* bloody Americans?'

'Shall I start at the beginning?'

For a full minute Wiley stared into Knight's waxy, unshaven face, which during that time grew paler and more anxious. Then Wiley smiled. 'We're taking you back to London. We're grateful for the way you've come forward.'

Knight visibly relaxed. From the corner Lucas Brand watched Wiley's smile. People on the receiving end of that smile never knew it, but something bad was coming their way.

Fourteen

Two grey Vauxhalls threaded their way through the barrier of a dense Irish rain, whose wetting it felt no sun could ever dry out. They were unremarkable cars except that they were checked over weekly and sheltered their occupants behind bulletproof glass. Since the day when a Protestant paramilitary had stepped through the Belfast traffic and put three revolver slugs in the neck and shoulders of Dermot Phelan, such precautions had become commonplace.

As soon as the cars came to a halt, a clutch of raincoated men clattered up to the house. Hearing the cars approach, Roderick Wardour leapt to the window. Even through the blur of the rain he recognised Phelan, a tall man with a bush of black hair through which a white stripe, inherited down the male line of his family, ran from forehead to crown. 'Now we know,' he muttered.

Before Holly could join him at the window or ask what he meant, one of their minders was at the bedroom door, inviting Wardour downstairs to meet their visitor.

In the hall Phelan was throwing off his wet coat, wiping the rain from his moustache, clamping the familiar curled pipe between his large teeth, and laughingly greeting Wardour with an outstretched hand. Phelan was an energetic mountain of a man, who could just as instantly relapse into a bleak, brooding nihilism which would freeze the bones of those who tried to deal with him. Wardour had once been one such. But Phelan was treating this occasion as a renewal of old friendship. His handshake was firm and reassuring, his speech voluble. 'First, an apology, but not for your being here, because after all you'd rather be here than where you were before, I guess, eh? An apology anyway for what's happened to you, although in spite of what you may think, we weren't behind it.'

177

Phelan ushered Wardour into a comfortably proportioned room in which a log fire and whisky had been provided. Phelan did not share the traditional abstemiousness of the republican leadership. He poured them both a good shot and pulled up the chairs. 'Well, to unity.' Phelan smiled. 'And diversity.'

Dermot Phelan was a complex, cunning man who concealed his sharp mind behind a bluff manner and well-worn clothes of modest quality that would never upstage the ordinary people whose support had given him power. No ordinary man himself, he was one of the few politicians for whom Wardour felt respect. Even if in Phelan's shadow murderers lurked.

'I'm surprised you're involved in this, Dermot.'

'Purely as a middleman. If you asked me what all that was about, I couldn't tell you. Somebody got in a mess, and we got them out of it. In return we get to arrange your safe passage back to the bosom of your family and Her Majesty's Government.'

'As simple as that?'

'That simple.'

'With what strings attached?'

Phelan's strong teeth bared around his crusted pipe stem. 'No strings.'

'Just the oxygen of publicity?'

'No such thing as bad publicity, Roderick.'

Not even bombing the innocent? Wardour thought but refrained from saying. 'So what happens next?' he asked.

Phelan's answer hit Wardour like a heavy weight between the shoulder blades. The shock of reality. 'Maximum two days, you'll be home.'

Meanwhile, upstairs, one of the Irishmen used easy but non-committal conversation with Holly to keep an eye on her. And in the kitchen the others shared a drink and a chat with McDade. To them he was the stabber from Ardoyne, a player, a man of legend. None of them wanted to get too friendly since McDade's role here remained uncertain. But there was no denying the awe in which he was held, or the almost childlike excitement of McDade's response to it. And McDade enjoyed the one secret, the identity of Holly Odell, which as yet none of the Irishmen suspected.

Leaving Wardour to contemplate his return to London, Dermot Phelan joined McDade in the kitchen. The two men found themselves suddenly alone. They greeted each other with a hug and a long moment of searching eye-contact. They had first met as teenage petrol-bomb throwers in the Falls Road riots, in days which now carried an aristocratic pedigree in republican folklore. Since then their paths had diverged. McDade the unstable killer, Phelan the man of vision at the calm centre. The one destined for the history books, the other for an early grave in the republican plot at Milltown.

Phelan made a diffident outward-sweeping gesture which he had copied years ago from Brando in *The Godfather*. It signified contempt for anything other than the hardest of hard truths. 'Apart from surprising the shit out of everybody,' Phelan said, 'what do you want, Sean?'

McDade said simply, 'I want back.'

'You're a great guy with a bomb and a knife,' Phelan said. 'The Brits might not know your name, but they sure know *you*. You're what makes every Brit soldier sweat in the dark.'

McDade recognised the point being made. 'I've changed, Dermot.'

'How changed?' Phelan pinched McDade's cheek and gave it a playful slap. 'If men like you change, what do we become? Toothless old tossers singing songs over our beer.'

'I've done my share of the killing. I've got ideas now.'

'So has Eamonn Carthy. The word will soon be out. And then what?'

McDade chewed his lip. He had to build up a strong defence against that vengeance waiting for him in the North. 'I was hoping we could get round that.'

Phelan stared candidly through pipesmoke and matchflame. 'In exchange for what, Sean?'

'I've brought you Wardour.'

'A poisoned chalice, if we're not careful. Anyways, it was not you fixed it up. Mastermind is one thing, Sean. Errand boy is another.'

'I kept him safe. If it hadn't been for me, he'd be dead now.'

'So would you.'

'I got you his girlfriend too.' Phelan made his Godfather gesture again. McDade countered, 'You know whose daughter she is?'

Phelan's cold eyes waited for McDade to answer his own question.

'Barron Odell.'

Phelan was expert at the deadpan face, but at Odell's name the pipe froze inches short of his lips. A fascinated, calculating light entered his eyes.

In London the sun was shining. The unmarked police car swung out of the swirl of Westminster traffic into Scotland Yard. The journey had been quick – the Sûreté had laid on a helicopter to Orly – but the silence of Robin Knight's escort had triggered him into a cycle of manic-depression. As one inner voice told him that the nightmare was over, another whispered that it was only just beginning. Once they were over the landscape of southern England, Knight's guilt turned to a pathetic anxiety. The country he had once pledged himself to defend was witness-ing his return as a common criminal. It was not an experience his life had schooled him for.

The police were not on his side. They had been dismissive about his rambling account of the prelude to the kidnap, and manifested no interest in his personal background, or his remorse for the mistakes he had made. Once it was clear that Knight did not know what had happened to Wardour, Wiley and Brand verged on anger in their frustration. If the Sûreté had not been so keen to get rid of Knight, Wiley would gladly have abandoned him to the mercies of a French police cell indefinitely. As far as Mike Wiley was concerned, it was just possible that Knight was a mental case. Every major crime sucked in its troop of fantasists, weird sods whose mediocrity or self-hate forced them to confess to deeds they had never committed. Often very convincingly too, that was the trouble. But although his story was short on leads, Knight held firm wherever Wiley probed. The main thing they had from him so far was confirmation of the Irish connection.

'An Irishman called Sean? Big deal. What was his real name?'

'As far as I know, it was Sean.'

'Are you telling me you used your own names?'

'The thinking behind it,' Knight explained patiently, 'was that in a crisis people don't react to assumed names. So to the best of my knowledge his name really was Sean.'

'Well,' Wiley said sarcastically, 'that certainly narrows it down. Halfway across Europe for an Irishman called Sean.'

Back at Scotland Yard Knight was left alone, overseen by a uniformed officer, to prepare his written statement. 'How do you read him, sir?' Lucas Brand asked, as they shared a ten minute mealbreak in Wiley's office.

'He's for real. He doesn't know where Wardour is, if he's dead or alive. He doesn't know who the woman was, or how she got mixed up in it. But he's for real all right.' Wiley paused. 'What I don't like is, he's too happy.'

'Happy?'

'He likes being here. The guy was terrified in France. We've brought him home, cheered him up. He sees us as his protection.'

'So you're thinking, once he's given us all the background – '

'Judas goat,' Wiley said. 'We'll nail him out there. Then wait for the tigers.'

Wiley's last update on Barron Odell had been relayed to him in Poitiers. Odell had taken to the London streets, and was being followed. Two members of Wiley's team had earlier intercepted Barron Odell in the foyer of his hotel. Flushed from a shave and a bath, angry and worried at the total silence from the outside world, from which he could only construe a monumental foul-up, Odell was not an easy man to block. The power he exuded was part muscle, part malignant psychological energy. The two detectives barely got to the revolving doors in time.

'What's this, what's this?' Odell demanded angrily.

The senior detective hurriedly flashed his card. Odell was unimpressed. 'What do you people think you're doing? This is my hotel, I'm visiting here. You don't pull me in like some goddamn thief. What is this?' Odell's stentorian voice was attracting the wrong kind of looks from the occupants of the foyer.

'We think we may be able to help you, sir,' the detective explained. Peddle the soft line, Wiley had said. But Odell was having none of it.

'Like how?'

'We believe your daughter's been kidnapped, and that's why you're here. Can we talk privately?'

Odell's mind raced. He had been a cop once, didn't they know that? They had no proof it was Holly. Most likely they were just trying to bluff a confirmation out of him. *And*, Stanger was dead or in custody, else he would have made contact. Odell's answer was uncompromising. 'I've nothing to say. I don't know what you're talking about.'

'Mr Odell – '

'Is this an arrest?'

'No sir, but we – '

'Excuse me.' Odell was brusque, unstoppable. From a car parked on yellow lines opposite the hotel, the detectives radioed in that Odell had run loose, and they were pursuing.

For the detectives all this was a formality. Equally, Odell with his law enforcement background knew they would not simply let him go. For him the formality consisted in shaking them off. The London traffic seemed to be in permanent gridlock, so he stayed on foot. Within a half-mile stretch of under-passes, one-way streets, of entering places by one door and exiting by another, he had lost them, unless every other person on the street was an undercover cop. Odell doubted he was so very important. Nonetheless, he was careful to phone ahead to the place he was making for, a small hotel in Kilburn. The news he received was interesting. But still he took time out on the way to buy a *Sporting Life* and a bottle of Guinness, which he consumed with a cigar at a pavement table. From here he could make sure that the quiet side-street contained no more pursuers.

Two minutes was enough. Leaving the drink unfinished and the paper unread, Odell completed his journey. The hotel, nameless and distinguished only by a defective neon sign that announced 'Bed and Breakfast – No Vacancies', was a contact point for the republican cause in London. Odell's blood pressure nudged danger levels as he approached the place, whose number he had also given to Stanger as a fall-back if for some reason the Paddington hotel failed to raise him. Odell had used the contact on previous trips. The premises sometimes changed, but Seamus Maginty didn't. Trying Maginty as a last resort this morning, Odell had learnt that a call had come through for him there. It had been a call on spec, but Odell felt the strong hand of fate in force. Declining all details on the phone, he insisted on following it up in person.

The chance call had come from Dermot Phelan, who had followed Odell's deliberately clear trail to London via his Boston answer machine. Hazarding that Odell's trip might well include some republican business, Phelan had rung Maginty's Kilburn hotel and requested them, if they could get wind of Odell, to give him the Irish number. Only half an hour had separated Phelan's and Odell's calls to the Kilburn hotel. When the phone subsequently rang in the isolated house in the heart of Connacht, even Dermot Phelan's imperturbable mind had to admit that, given all life's near misses, this lucky hit had a peculiar beauty about it.

Diffidently, Phelan introduced himself and said, 'You may not know me, Mr Odell.'

But any contact with the Irish republicans brought out a boyish enthusiasm in Odell. 'Do I know you, Mr Phelan? Only like you were my brother.'

Without emotion Phelan continued, 'Mr Odell, we have your daughter. We have her safe, she's well, and we would like to reunite you.'

'But what about – '

'We took care of everything. She's fine.'

Sudden tears streamed down Odell's face. 'What – when – ?'

Phelan's soft, deep voice said, 'My boys will meet you in Dublin.'

When Holly heard the news, she also burst into tears. She ran straight to Wardour's arms. The tears were confused. This gentle sojourn in the Irish countryside was still captivity. There was no question of her leaving if she wanted. Yet she feared the return to London. She knew that life could never be normal again. Wardour did his best to comfort her, but he was equally staggered by the news. His attitude to the IRA, as it always had, swung between extremes. How had these people found Holly's father so quickly? Wardour's suspicions that, knowingly or not, Holly had been involved in his kidnap, surfaced all over again.

At a diplomatic moment Phelan asked for a word with Wardour in private. 'The question is, Roderick, how do you want to go back?'

Wardour looked down at his shabby, soiled clothes. 'Soon.'

'Security are going to grab you once you enter the UK. Do you want to see your wife first?'

Wardour bridled at the implication. 'Why?'

'I make no judgment. But if you wish, I daresay we could get her over.'

Wardour looked at the door, imagined Jessica walking in. No, impossible. 'I'll take care of all that in London.'

Phelan got his pipe billowing. 'OK. We'll hand you over at the border. Tomorrow, after we've squared the British government about our role in all this.'

'They'll believe me, not you,' Wardour said.

'So would I, in their place. And what will you tell them?'

'The truth.'

'If only your colleagues in the government did that,' Phelan said.

'And then you go on killing us, and we go on killing you. For how much longer?'

'Only till the end of time. Or till someone lifts the curse.'

'But why?' Wardour asked.

'The Irish cover everything up with a sort of sentimental whimsy,' Phelan said. 'That's how they've always dealt with oppression. The British stiffen the old upper lip and think, as long as you call a thing duty it must be all right. You ask when will it end? Only when we can all get together and admit that a pile of shit is precisely that and no more, regardless what colour flag you drape over it.' The ash in his pipe glowed. 'But don't hold your breath.'

'Well' – Roderick Wardour clapped his hands and kept them pressed together, 'this is the nicest prison I was ever in.' He smiled a smile that begged Holly to do the same, to reassure him that the nightmare was almost over. Holly tried to resist, then gave in and smiled. Some people put hurt behind them, others couldn't. Holly couldn't. The hurt lived on. She wondered if for Wardour she was now part of a hurt which he couldn't wait to discard. If she asked him, he would lie. If her suspicion was true, there was not one damn thing she could do about it.

'It looks like we go tomorrow,' Wardour said.

'Why not now? I mean, why are we here?'

'The IRA have their own way of operating.'

'Will we ever understand what this is all about?'

Stiffly Wardour said, 'I intend to.'

'Tomorrow seems like for ever away.'

'Yes. One thing I don't understand is – ' Wardour did not mention that, when he had put the question of Barron Odell directly, Phelan had declined to explain. But Holly read what he was thinking.

'I know. You mean why my father's coming here.'

'For a long time, when we were back there, I believed that you had something to do with the kidnap.'

'And now?'

'No, I don't believe it now. But others might.'

'What are you saying?'

'What's your father's connection to these people?'

185

'Would you believe me if I said I didn't know?'

Wardour thought silently for a moment. The little Irishman, McDade, was the key. And then Dermot Phelan was able to produce Holly's father out of a hat. But Wardour was sure the IRA would never have kidnapped him just to free him again. He put his arms round Holly. 'Of course I believe you.'

'How are they taking you back?'

'Oh, probably hand me over to the Army or something. Dead of night, blanket security, you know.' Wardour wanted to find out all he could about Barron Odell, but this was not the time. He had a premonition that tomorrow everything would be swept away, would once again fly out of his control. The conviction that this strange normality, of being cut off from the rest of the world, would soon end paralysed Wardour's urge to seek answers.

'So it's just one more night – ' he said.

This was the night they had never shared, the warm French night in which to explore the nakedness they had barely discovered in England. Holly knew what Wardour was thinking. She had been thinking it herself. She said, 'They don't seem too puritanical here.' Wardour laughed, slightly embarrassed, a man shy about these things being put into words. 'They'll bug the bed,' Holly said, 'and some time later make you pay for the tape.'

But Wardour was once again the reckless romantic she had fallen for on that snarled-up motorway. Their hands moved shyly on each other. In their faces emotion began to stir again. 'Until tomorrow,' Wardour said, 'I don't care.'

In the evening there was a dinner at which Wardour and Holly, but not McDade, were the honoured guests. Dermot Phelan hosted, with three other men, friends and colleagues of his, men Wardour did not know but treated, as they treated him, with the deference due to unostentatious but real power. The Irishmen had a natural gentility, and spoke in beguiling accents, their conversation light and frequently amusing. Much of the talk concerned Ireland, but was conducted as if it referred to a far-off country of which they had only read in books. Holly noted how they talked of centuries ago as if those events were their own experience, had marked their parents' or their own lives, and had already scarred their children. Holly smiled as the Irishmen politely addressed remarks to her. But something about them made her blood run cold.

Only once did the reality of the North break through the social veneer. 'Your policy,' Wardour said, reversing the usual formula, 'is still the ballot box in one hand and the Armalite in the other.' It was the first reference to the province's backdrop of killing. Phelan chewed on his unlit pipe, eyes narrowed. 'As time goes by, the ballot box will do the Armalite's work for us. After all, the British army are in Ulster to defend the democratic process, a majority who elect to be part of the United Kingdom. If we accept all the premises of that view, what will they say in a generation's time when a majority in Ulster elect to leave the aforementioned United Kingdom? If the population of the North *vote* to be reunited with Ireland? Will you British still respect the democratic process, or will it then become the colonial war which we maintain it always has been?'

Wardour interrupted, 'Yes, but – '

'There are no buts, my friend. The Protestants are a declining breed. We produce more children than they do. In two decades more, those children will be electors. When you get back to Westminster, do the same arithmetic we've done. Then think how you're going to play it when you're Prime Minister.' It was the right note to strike. Phelan grinned, and the others laughed at the gentle sadism of his remark.

Wardour tried to hide his flattered vanity by asking, 'But what if the Irish Republic don't want you?'

Phelan said, 'All over the world the trend is for the old empires to be breaking up and nations, especially small nations, to be reasserting themselves. The border is a wound in the side of Ireland, and whatever the southern Irish tell you, what they tell us is that the wound needs healing.' Phelan's tone was that of a man of reason, but his words left a silence. Holly took advantage of it to leave the room.

On the stair, Holly met Sean McDade. Since they left France it was the first moment they had been alone together. Holly fought down an impulse to turn back. She lowered her eyes, not submissively but to denote a wish to blot out McDade's existence. However, McDade flattened himself against the wall with an almost derisive politeness, waiting for Holly to pass. When she was only one step below him, McDade said, 'I hear your father's arriving tomorrow.'

With no concession to good manners Holly said, 'And?'

'I'm looking forward to meeting him. He must be quite a man.'

'Why do you say that?'

'To come all this way. He must be devoted to you.' Something wheedling and faintly mocking in the lilt of McDade's speech made Holly want to throw him down the stairs.

Intending threat, she said, 'Wait till my father finds out who you are.'

McDade answered, 'I can't wait for that moment, Miss Odell.' With which words his eyes seemed to Holly to meet her own more sharply than before. Acting submissively, McDade contrived to dominate totally. That was his technique. Inwardly Holly shuddered. It took all her strength to pass on up the stair. She felt McDade watching her every step of the way.

Fifteen

Barron Odell, now moving through events like a sleepwalker, took the Dublin flight which Phelan had suggested. He was collected at the airport and taken to a hotel where a room had already been booked, the bill to be taken care of, and invited to have a pleasant night in the fair city.

At eight o'clock the next morning the same Irishman picked Odell up and together they headed out past Phoenix Park on the N4. Two hours later Odell was shaking the hand of Dermot Phelan, whose dark hair with its white stripe he recognised before introductions were made. Odell was fulsome. 'I can't believe this, an honour to meet you, Mr Phelan.'

'We have much to talk about,' Phelan said. 'But first – ' In the doorway behind Phelan, Holly waited. As Odell's eyes met hers, she burst into tears. After a long emotional embrace, the Odells were led inside. At the tall figure of Roderick Wardour, whose whole bearing fitted perfectly with the setting of a country house, Odell started. His tunnel vision about his daughter had erased thoughts of the MP, just as for the interim he had also ceased to speculate about Bobby Stanger.

As Phelan made the introductions, Wardour briskly shook hands. On this occasion McDade was also invited to be present. Phelan introduced him almost proudly as the man who had rescued the hostages.

'A bit more complicated than that,' McDade said. 'For a while I was also the jailer, so to speak, but I kept them safe and delivered them back without, I hope, too much harm done.' McDade looked candidly at Wardour and Holly and said, 'Maybe one day I can apologise to you two properly.'

With a nervous laugh Phelan patted McDade's arm. Wardour gave a public-man smile. Holly, still pleading that she was unwell after the Dublin Bay prawns last night, which was the excuse she had given for her disappearance during dinner, looked away and ignored McDade's words.

Odell had forgotten ever meeting McDade, who for the moment left the matter unraised as they clasped hands. 'You got them both out, and in my book that makes you all right. As of now, I owe you.'

In a fleeting moment before everybody could be organised for drinks, Phelan muttered to Odell, 'Does your daughter know? About your connection with us?'

'No.'

'She'll want to know how we got you here. Given who her companion is, it might be better to make up a story.'

Such organisational acumen appealed to Odell. He nodded eagerly. Although this reunion on Irish soil had made him want Holly to know about his lifelong fund-raising for the boys in Ulster, he took the point that Wardour was a complication. And just what part his daughter and the MP were playing in each other's lives, Odell thought, would take longer than today to sort out. The two men quickly patched up something about an MI5 liaison, something Holly could never check. But this meeting in deepest, greenest Connacht had all manner of hidden trip-wires for Odell. A moment came when, very discreetly Odell reflected later, Sean McDade said to him, out of the hearing of anyone else, 'I remember you, sir, but you haven't remembered me.'

'I'm sorry,' Odell said, 'I don't – '

He peered at McDade's face. There was only one way they could have met, and Odell have forgotten.

'I had the pleasure to call on you a couple of times. In the early days,' said McDade.

'I got it,' Odell said. 'I got it, sure.' Untrue, but easy to pretend. The bagmen had always been anonymous, the connection brief. Odell hadn't even met them every time. In any case, McDade's face and Odell's memory had both aged. But for one moment they affirmed the cause which had long ago brought them together. 'And we're still in there, my boy, we're still in there.'

190

Smilingly McDade said, 'To the death, sir.'

Needing to crown the moment, Odell said, 'I want you to come and visit me. My place upstate resembles this Irish landscape. Holly's coming home, and I propose to invite Mr Wardour, to celebrate this nightmare being over. As the man that got them back, I want you to be there.'

'What can I say?' McDade answered, dwarfed in every respect by this expansive American.

Odell, uncontainable when once possessed by an idea, went in search of Wardour, clapped him on the arm and said, 'Roderick, I want you to be my guest back home. It's a small farm, I keep it mainly for pleasure, and I'd like you and Holly and Mr McDade to spend maybe a week there, after you sort out your business in London.' Wardour considered all aspects of this offer. He remained unsure exactly who Barron Odell was. But Wardour knew he was not far wrong if he guessed Odell to be an American supporter of the IRA. That was certainly a compromise he could do without. But on that basis, so was Holly. What were the security services going to make of her? And here Wardour dug his heels in. He was entitled to a life of his own. Recovered from captivity, the grandee in him said he would see them all damned before he gave Holly up. Her father's invitation was the perfect excuse. 'Inconvenient,' he would tell Jessica, 'but how could I turn the man down?' The thought of Jessica was another worry. But Wardour accepted the invitation warmly.

From media coverage Odell had picked up something about Wardour being married, and added, 'Of course, the invite includes your wife.'

Wardour was distinctly uneasy. 'Well, she has a full schedule, but I'll certainly try to persuade her.'

A smooth liar, Odell thought, but said, 'Sure, sure,' anxious to get this awkward moment over.

Wardour went to find Holly. She was sitting alone in her room, the room they had not occupied. The intensity of last night's experience had swept aside all Wardour's doubts. Used to a comfortably monogamous sex life, a pleasant if predictable extension of domestic routine, Wardour was taken aback by this first night in bed with Holly. Indelible on his mind, this sexuality of total nakedness had surprised Wardour, revealed in himself things he had not known before. One such revelation was the discovery that sex could be more than a work-out or a romp; it could flood with light every chamber of the mind, shake the axis of the self into a different tilt, so that nothing in the world could ever look the same again.

'I don't know how they're going to do it,' he said, 'but one of us could be spirited away soon.' He put an arm round Holly's shoulders. His other hand touched her breast. Jessica was not a toucher and Wardour still expected to be reproached for such a gesture at the wrong time of day. Holly moved fractionally nearer to him, and Wardour felt agreeably foolish that such a simple thing could move him so deeply. 'Well,' he said, 'we made it, I think.'

'You bet we made it,' Holly said. Then the tone of her voice changed. 'If you want to stop – '

A shade abruptly Wardour said, 'You mean if I decide never to see you again, for reasons of career, you'll understand? What kind of man do you think I am?'

'A politician,' Holly said.

'Politics is a job,' Wardour said, 'not an epitaph. Anyway, your father wants us to go to America.'

'I know. But with McDade too. Did you accept?'

'I intend to make good use of McDade.' He kissed Holly. 'Of course I accepted.'

Holly returned the kiss. 'Good.' But she knew the problem would be in London, not New England.

Wardour said, 'I don't know when I'll be able to get in touch. God knows what's going to happen when they take me back. But don't give up on me.'

'When you're ready, I'll be ready.' Wardour kissed her. 'Thanks for a hell of a weekend,' she said.

'Thanks for changing my life.'

'You're sure?'

'I'm sure. And it needed it.'

Their lips met again, as if this really might be the last time.

One of the quietly discreet Irishmen began letting everyone know the schedule for leaving the grey house, leaving Connacht, leaving this artificial serenity. Walking the grounds of the place, sunk in a reverie of his ancestors, Barron Odell was prompted by the imminence of the departures to go in search of Sean McDade. Not finding him, he asked. There was no shortage of people to ask.

A minute later McDade appeared, very much a man who had been sent for and felt honoured by it. But he saw immediately that Odell, normally a loud, ebullient man, was the more diffident of the two.

'I want you to know that my invite to visit me in the States was genuine,' Odell said.

'I took it so, Mr Odell. It's a source of great satisfaction to me.'

'You said we'd met. I've been thinking back and yes, I remember you.'

'I was just an insignificant lad,' McDade said. 'But I'm gratified to have made an impression on such a man as yourself.'

'In a certain respect,' Odell said, 'I regard you as my superior.'

'I can't believe that at all.'

'No, I mean it. You're a serious man, Mr McDade.'

'We're both committed to the same cause, sir.'

'That's true, that's true. And I hope we can both still serve it well. I'll make contact with you through Mr Phelan, if that's acceptable to you.' McDade accepted with modesty. But in fact, whatever Phelan's private thoughts about him, McDade knew that the hierarchy had to be impressed by this big American calling transatlantic, as impressed as McDade was himself. Odell offered his hand, then McDade went back inside. Cars were being got ready. McDade was to be taken away first.

Odell was for real as far as he went, and for the moment his horizon was Irish. Every life needs romance, and Odell's romantic energy had long come from the myth of a united Ireland, a

193

symbol which was only possible if he could glamorise such men as Sean McDade. But a different reality nagged at Odell's mind. If he was only dealing with the kidnap and return of his daughter, he could wipe the slate clean of all that and let the Irish cause take him over completely. But he had sent StormWind men into France, on which he did not as yet know the full story. Odell's instincts told him that he would not like the full story, so his motives for coaxing McDade into the American trip were not merely romantic, much as Odell wished they were.

None of this was understood by Holly, who had been watching from an upstairs window, unobserved by the two men outside. All she saw was her father, starry-eyed in the company of IRA men, craving the approval of vermin like McDade. The trip to America, she began to fear, would not just be a passionate interlude with Roderick Wardour. Other dreams were waiting to be played out.

'This statement,' Mike Wiley said. 'Interesting reading.' Robin Knight looked tired. The isolation of being a star witness was closing in on him. 'There are certain areas,' Wiley sniffed, 'seem a lot less clear than certain others. But OK, it's a good story.'

In spite of himself, Knight looked depressed. He had switched back completely to the simple code of honour by which he had once tried to live. According to this code, only imprisonment could wipe out what he had done. His confession was an attempt to reduce the sentence. But the police seemed less than overwhelmed. 'I'm very tired. I can't recall everything.'

'Let's understand one thing, Mr Knight. We're not making any bargains with you. You're in deep shit. If you're leaving out some tasty morsel, or shielding somebody that might pay you back one day, forget it. If Roderick Wardour winds up dead and you're all we've got, I wouldn't want to be in your shoes. We're talking about a very senior politician here. My advice to you is, don't hide anything. We want to know who was behind it.'

'I've told you I don't know that.'

194

Wiley sniffed hard again, conveying scepticism. But instead of leaving the room he paced about, as if waiting for something. Then Lucas Brand came in with a heavy file of papers under one arm. Wiley said, 'We want you to look very carefully at the faces in there. Take your time.'

The mugshots were the usual cattle-like parade of men and occasionally women, expressing their sullen resistance to the security forces the other side of the camera. Many of the photographs were years old. A fear of McDade lurked in Knight's mind, and he was nervously unsure, as he studied them, as to whether he would be able to point to McDade's picture when he saw it. But the moment did not come. McDade had never been convicted of a crime, was not even known to be a member of a proscribed organisation. The file did not have him registered.

Observing that Knight's second inspection held more relief than regret when McDade's likeness failed to appear, confirmed Wiley's view of Knight as a flaky witness. He scowled and tried not to let his frustration show. But Knight would spill more, of that Wiley was certain. If necessary they would haul him to the places covered by his story and kick him all over the relevant territory till it refreshed his memory. And Wiley still had it in mind to let Knight go, because somewhere beyond his office's grimy windows there had to be people who, to stop Robin Knight talking, would first stop him breathing. Every time he looked at Robin Knight, Wiley saw bait.

Before Lucas Brand could take the IRA file away again, the ops room got a message which made the hairs on Wiley's back crawl. 'All they said was, can you clear everything to speak to Dermot Phelan in five minutes?'

'In my office,' Wiley growled, and almost ran down a bleakly functional corridor to his equally characterless office. Wiley did not believe in making his workplace an extension of home. Such echoes only increased guilt at spending so little time there.

Wiley lit a cigarette, drummed his fingers, watched the phone. He knew Phelan only by reputation, a clever front man for terrorists, one of those slippery people they would never nail, although almost all the outrages and mutilated bodies had the seal of approval of such men. Yet clearly Phelan knew him, and as he waited Wiley had to admit that he was excited. The next thing, they'd be inviting him over to Northern Ireland to escort Roderick Wardour home.

Which was exactly what Dermot Phelan did.

After the arrangements had been settled, Wiley said, 'Just one question. Why?'

'We are simply agents in all this,' Phelan said. 'We were able to bring Mr Wardour from a situation of extreme danger to one of safety. Mr Wardour himself will substantiate the account. We wish him well, and are keen to return him to normality.'

Wiley didn't believe a word of it. The public voice of terrorism coming on like the sick animals' friend. To Wiley it smelt all wrong. But his acceptance of Phelan's plan was wholehearted.

He hardly liked to push his luck by asking, 'Is Mr Wardour alone?'

Phelan's pause was masterly. He had not been about to give this information unasked. 'You mean the young lady?'

Wiley did not enjoy the tease. 'So there's a woman, too?'

'Miss Odell came as part of the package. We'd never heard of her before. She's already free, but where she's headed for I've no idea.'

Wiley knew this was less than the truth, but the mental relief was great enough to keep him from objecting. 'One more question,' Wiley said. 'Do the media know yet?'

Phelan answered, 'No. We've promised Mr Wardour a quiet passage back. Then he can tell his story when he's ready. We'll get the credit anyway. This time we don't need to set anybody up in advance.'

Wiley returned to the ops room and asked Detective Sergeant Brand, 'What are you doing tonight, Lucas?'

'Taking a beautiful woman to the opera.'

'Even if it means missing a quick trip to Belfast?'

Brand was ambitious, reluctant to miss anything. 'Well, she's not that beautiful.'

★

Sean McDade had been driven away, with no opportunity to say goodbye to the people he had kidnapped and then, for now everybody was prepared to stretch the word, rescued. But reality had taken over, and the IRA had reclaimed its own.

On a road near the Fermanagh section of the border, Dermot Phelan signalled the car to stop. While he was relieving himself some distance from the car, the two men with McDade looked at each other, and then one of them pointed a finger to McDade's head and said, 'Bang!' Then all three laughed, McDade the loudest and most nervously of all.

Instead of getting back in the car, Phelan tapped the window for McDade to get out. Even as he did so, McDade still thought that perhaps they had brought him to this deserted stretch of road in order to finish him off. Phelan's bearing was markedly colder, but a touch too deliberate for an assassin. 'What do you want, Sean?'

'To come back.'

'You were thrown out because you were trouble. Apart from that little business with Carthy's daughter.'

'I'll follow orders from now on.'

Phelan walked a few steps and lit his pipe. 'Tell you what we're going to do with you, Sean. We'll leave you with some good friends who'll slip you over the border tonight. The action tonight is going to be somewhere else, believe me. We want you to dig in for a week.'

'A week?'

'Till we see how this Wardour thing pans out. If we've been taken advantage of, we'll find you. You know the rest of that story.'

'I swear it's straight.'

'So why did somebody give us this nice present? This Brit politician who could do us such a lot of good. Come on, McDade, what's the catch?'

'I've told you everything.'

'Come on. If you go for a ransom, at least grab a rich man. Wardour's not worth that much. Or the girl.'

'Our job was to snatch him, then pass him on. But it all changed.'

'You said the ransom was your idea.'

'Right. And if I'd come back to you with half a million quid, would you have turned me away?'

Phelan's eyes gazed mockingly at the idea that a man with so much money would willingly return to the gritty reality of Ulster. 'You know Duncastle Street, Andersonstown?' he asked.

'I delivered papers there.'

'A pub called the Penny Whistle?'

'I've taken a drink there.'

'Ask for Brian Sheedy. He'll take you to his house, you report there every day for a week. But the first day you don't show, we'll come looking for you.'

Phelan took McDade's silence for acceptance. 'The men you were with, some of them must still be on the loose, or in police hands. Who'd be you right now, Sean, tell me that. Who'd be you?'

McDade bore the slight with dignity. 'I'm back with my own people. I'm ready to take what comes.'

Phelan was suddenly more genial. 'Good lad.' He gave McDade's arm a light smack and indicated the car. 'As long as we understand each other.'

From then on it was all downhill. The reception at the isolated farmstead was warm, sentimental even, for all McDade's being a stranger. Phelan had picked the old farming couple well, pedigree republicans both. After chatting a while, Phelan left McDade to be given a good dinner. Ahead lay night, a little-used lane across the border, and Belfast.

Mike Wiley and Lucas Brand had just left Scotland Yard when the ops room fielded another call, this time from the Press. A journalist usually favourable to the police had picked up a story and wanted it confirmed. The woman DC on the desk explained that Commander Wiley was out of reach and gave the standard 'No comment'. The journalist replied that the story was hot enough to run whether the Yard chose to comment or not. He then gave an outline. The police had an hour in which to respond.

The headline would be simple, IRA HOLD MP. The paper would take the view that it was either a straightforward ransom demand, or a stunt which had misfired. Also they would be running the hypothesis that Wardour's female companion – and how dirty those words were going to sound – was herself an IRA agent. Then they would see if anybody came forward to refute this. And finally they would pursue the angle of whether Wardour, a junior minister with Northern Ireland connections, had been playing both sides of the fence.

The journalist was seeking to trade some of the innuendo for hard facts which, now the story was going public, the police might think it worth releasing. He intended to sit on it for an hour, then key it in.

The timing was lucky. Wiley was paged at Belfast Harbour airport and used the phone in the RUC office to return the call. 'Keep it twenty-four hours,' he told the journalist, 'then we'll give you something hard.'

'This is hard,' the journalist answered. 'Or are you denying it?'

Wiley himself had doubts about Wardour, too clever by half, too squeaky-clean. He didn't like being strong-armed by the Press, no policeman did. But neither would he go to the wall for a politician. 'No comment,' he said, and snapped the phone down.

The story was set for the next morning's exclusive. There had been no question of Wiley delaying it. The kidnap had been one thing, but with Wardour safe now, the news was up for grabs. Among the many things Wiley had to think about was the angry question, Who had leaked the story? Phelan had disavowed any plan to alert the Press, and since he had no particular reason to lie in this instance, Wiley believed him. But the source of the leak had to be someone who knew that the IRA were holding Wardour. His practical concerns in Ulster forced Wiley to shelve the question. But it continued to nag.

★

The Odells, father and daughter, trod English soil for the first time together. Barron Odell asked, 'Well, how does it feel?'

Holly answered, fine, although she felt a large weight of depression waiting to fall on her sooner or later. But on the flight back to London it was easier just to answer her father, fine.

Planes, airports, taxis were a numbing succession of lights and noise. Only when they climbed to Holly's flat, and her cat stretched and mewed from a window-ledge, did she return to the real world, shaking violently and sobbing as the cat purred wide-eyed in her arms.

Embarrassed, Odell said, 'Come on, baby, come on.'

He took the keys and got Holly inside. Odell was suddenly worked up by his daughter's collapse. It had been one hell of a week, all sorts of things dredged up that he needed to discuss with Holly, but could find no opportunity for. Now they were back at her flat, Holly had become a little girl who needed rest and comfort. But from the day when his wife walked out and took the child with her, Odell had missed out on the tenderer aspects of fatherhood. This was revealed now, as he stood awkwardly by while Holly made hot drinks and put herself to bed. Between the ailing child and the self-sufficient woman, Odell could find no niche for himself. Still, he sat on Holly's bed, stroking Pumpkin the cat, while his heart grew tight with an affection he could not express.

Until he heard from Stanger or the StormWind boys, Odell was unwilling to explain to anyone, including his daughter, his actions of the past week. In particular he did not want to discuss the ransom, until he learnt what had happened to that mostly forged money.

'I organised a rescue,' he said, having already told Holly that much since they met in Ireland.

'I thought you might.'

'And you say you didn't get any sign of them?' This was a puzzle Odell was constantly worrying away at. Holly shook her head sleepily. As McDade had urged them into the helicopter and the rotors had started up, she had seemed to catch the sound of gunshots. But the recent past already seemed like fantasy, and she felt she had no useful evidence to give anybody.

'No,' she said.

'Well, it'll all come out some time,' Odell said unconvincingly.

Holly asked, 'How did they find you?'

Odell produced his rehearsed explanation. 'Remember, we were meeting at Heathrow? Since you didn't show, I contacted the police. Then the security people came into it. So then I happened to be here this time, fixing up the rescue, and they got through to me with this news about my daughter being alive and well in Ireland. I didn't ask any more questions after that.'

Accepting his answer uncritically, Holly said, 'It's nothing but questions from now on.'

'Hey, come on. Get straightened out, then let's think about you and Rod Wardour coming to the farm for a week.' Odell omitted to mention the invitation extending to Wardour's wife. At a pained look in Holly's eyes he said, 'Hol, your personal life's not my concern. Live it your way. But you want somewhere to get things straight, the farm's perfect. Anyway, Rod accepted. And I asked that Irishman, McDade. Seemed the least I could do.'

Odell's excuse contained a *fait accompli*. He was not asking Holly's approval. And yet she felt how badly he wanted her to go. Weak, tired, hoping she would sleep soon, Holly nodded. Lately she was nodding at events a lot, only half understanding them.

Her father's intentions Holly preferred not to understand. Although there was nothing to prompt any mention of David's death by her father, Holly remained bitter about the bomb which had killed him, the men who had planted the bomb, and those who supported them. Barron Odell's appearance in Ireland had not been luck, or an act of charity by her captors. Once again, for no reason Holly could understand, the IRA had entered her life. She wanted to learn more, but the truth she might learn haunted her first night back in England, as it did Barron Odell's.

Geographically, the border between Northern Ireland and the Republic is devoid of logic. Farms of undulating pasture broken by blackthorn hedges straddle it, all divided by an invisible political line. Communities are split by its three hundred miles. Some three hundred roads and trackways, almost all passable to motor traffic except on routes deliberately cratered or blocked off by the army, cross it at various points. Short of barbed wire, watchtowers, minefields and dogs trained to kill, no army could seal such a frontier. Since nowhere in the bandit country of South Armagh was more than seven minutes' drive, and most of it within two minutes' drive, of the border, the main military control was weighted to the good roads that terrorists in fast cars would need to use.

The IRA escort took Roderick Wardour to one such checkpoint on the Crossmaglen road. Wardour was given no idea of where they were headed. He prematurely thought they had arrived when they came up to a waiting car and stopped. One of the IRA men got out to exchange a word, then the two cars moved on. Only a few hundred yards further on they were flagged down by soldiers of the Irish army. Flashlights swam through windows. The Irish troops waved them through. Then it was the border itself. If there were signs announcing it, Wardour missed them. But the front car pulled over for the others to go on. The road ahead unwound to a barrage of portable floodlights, behind which waited the shadowy figures of armed men. The approaches to the border had been sealed off from both sides. Only one man was going through. Wardour adjusted his tie. He was desperate for some fresh clothes.

The cars halted, and Wardour's suspicion that the other vehicle carried Dermot Phelan was confirmed. But the IRA chief kept his distance, merely observing. The men on the Republic side all withdrew. With one backward look, Wardour turned towards the harsh lights ahead. Phelan gave a brief wave, half-salute. Wardour nodded. Apprehension gripped him now. In the cool air, men's breath steamed. It had rained, and off the uneven wet tarmac the lights were glaring. Wardour could not see exactly, but guessed that they had at least a platoon there.

202

The waiting soldiers shifted about slightly, the smallest grate of boots on road, or touch of rifle on tunic metal, resounding in the taut silence.

Wardour refused to hurry. His walk down this sinister stretch of road might be the only dignity left for some time. But everybody there, himself included, feared a trick. The army would have searched the area for booby-trap wires, security forces on both sides would have scoured the border zone for hidden gunmen. All the same, as Wardour came up to them, the squad of soldiers in red berets and parachute smock hurriedly closed around him. Self-loading rifles snapped into position, aimed across the border. But the IRA men were already driving back into the Republic.

Squinting into the lights, Wardour halted, tall and erect. Car engines were starting up. Someone was shaking his hand. 'Mr Wardour, I'm Commander Michael Wiley. You're now in the United Kingdom. Welcome back, sir.'

Sixteen

From the shadows Sean McDade watched the joyriders go to work. Even before they approached the car he knew the three teenagers' game. It was himself fifteen years ago he was watching.

They knew he was there. Maybe they sensed that it was a tutorial eye he was keeping on them, or dismissed him as a harmless drunk, just another Belfast wino. If he was a decent citizen about to object, they would kick his head in. So either way they didn't care.

One boy screwdrivered the door. They piled in. Somebody hot-wired the car, which lurched away, one door still banging. They would scream up and down the Falls, maybe hit the motorway, race the car round till boredom returned, then set it ablaze. And why? Because it made them feel somebody. Because like all rituals, it had to be carried through to the end, however ridiculous, however lethal. Sometimes, when roaring around the city solitary kids would drive stolen cars into lamp-posts or walls, to crown the joyride with wreckage that might include themselves. That was recent, that despair. And never was a term less aptly used than joyride.

For himself, McDade did not despair. He had been thrown out of the Fianna, the IRA's youth section, for every form of indiscipline; a liar and cheat, a thief who stole from his own kind, a boaster who drank and gambled and beat up girls. But he had sweated it out on the fringes of violence, hanging in there for moments when they needed somebody to drive a car with no questions asked. Another Brit soldier would die, McDade would hit the pedal, drop the gunman, write off the car. Or maybe weapons needed storing, messages ferrying. McDade was always there, working off his parole.

His standing rose materially when an execution party dragged one of the Shankhill hard men, a sadistic maimer and killer of non-IRA Catholics, to a deserted spot in the city. Execution parties were training grounds for would-be Provo élite to show they could go all the way. On this occasion McDade, until now regarded as a dogsbody, stepped forward. Nobody was fighting for the job. Declining the pistol, McDade took a flick-knife from his coat. The kneeling Protestant paramilitary was hooded, stolidly silent. He awaited death at the hands of the despised Teagues with contempt. McDade ripped the hood away so they could witness the brutal man's terror. The Shankhill man spat, but his tongue was hardly back in his mouth when McDade slammed him from behind with the knife.

The frenzy of stabbing that followed paid no heed to the grisly moment of death. McDade hacked crazily at the blood-sodden clothes, the exposed flesh. Nobody knew how to stop him. More than one hardened IRA man had to turn aside and bring up his stomach at the sight. Rather than pull McDade away and cover themselves in tell-tale blood, the senior IRA officer present now pointed the execution pistol at McDade's head.

'Enough, Sean, enough. Let's go now.'

McDade got blood everywhere. The stolen car would be incinerated later, just another of the city's burnt-out wrecks. McDade himself was moved south for a year. When he returned to Ulster he was treated with a respect which life had never offered him before. Everything else was the same, the constant hassle by the occupying troops, the shifting around, the solitary monkish life, the dedication to the cause and its one-way ticket to martyrdom. But now McDade was given assignments, the occasional trip to the States to transit money or oversee consignments of Armalites.

Late in the day, the movement was concluding that McDade had character. But this improvement in his fortunes coincided with a growing rivalry between those who pressed to escalate random violence, and the more intellectual faction, returning from years of internment in Long Kesh, which they had used for self-education. The short-term had come into collision with the long. McDade himself had no political ambitions. He had grown up with the IRA old brigade from the forties and fifties, ageing men with beery breath and cloth caps, born at the wrong time. McDade had no plans to wind up like them.

So with a few others he took violence into his own hands. It was a trail ravaged by mistakes; car bombs that exploded too soon and killed innocent Catholics, shoot-outs with troops in which terrified children died, murders of the wrong people through mistaken identity or shoddy planning. Finally the hierarchy ordered the elimination of these mad dogs. In McDade's case the process was compounded by his deflowering, then badly beating up, the infatuated daughter of one of the Belfast Command.

Why McDade beat women up, he did not know. He managed to function sexually, although the act itself never did much for him. But the compulsion to commit violence on female bodies had something to do with a distant rage, with his bleak adolescence in the overcrowded Divis flats, that purgatory of concrete and damp, of RUC truncheons and demolition sites, and then the riots, the burning houses, and everywhere the visored soldiers and their gun-barrels.

After his mistreatment of Sinead Carthy, McDade was tipped off to leave Belfast in a hurry. Her father had vowed to put him to death more slowly than anyone had ever died before. Under a false identity McDade had crossed to Ardrossan, then gone south. In Spain he had managed to disappear. Now he felt strong enough to become visible again, to go for it once more. A big man on the Falls was all he had ever wanted to be.

With the sure touch of a blind man, which was what a ghettoised city made you, McDade went to the quietest place he knew, a terraced street in Ardoyne where at this time of night there would be few folk out of doors to see him. Here he skirted a back alley and climbed the wall of a narrow garden. Somewhere a car backfired, but generally Belfast seemed calm.

McDade scratched a window, the way he had always made his presence known at his grandmother's house. Knocks at the front door could never be trusted. An old face, haloed with white hair, peered out apprehensively, although the Prod hit men rarely ventured down streets like these. When she recognised McDade the old woman, moving as fast as severe arthritis allowed, let him in by the kitchen door. But she offered him no embrace. There had been too many stories. He had gone away for a bit, well, too many people went away for a bit, to spend eternity in a shameful unmarked grave. She half believed him a ghost. Belfast was full of ghosts. Folk did not embrace them.

McDade had compromised Mrs Leahy by coming here. But he also knew she would not refuse him, or ask questions. After a cup of tea he asked, 'Is Junior still around?'

Junior Keane was a distant McDade cousin, who lived opposite the grandmother. The old woman nodded. It was useless to evade. 'He is.'

'Could you ask him across?'

Mrs Leahy got her stick. Privately she thought, as she had thought for the fifteen years of Gerald Keane's life, another good youngster going off the rails. But in Belfast where else could the youngsters go?

McDade waited in the front parlour. To boys like Gerry Keane he had always been a hero figure. With quiet authority he instructed the boy to find the Penny Whistle and check the credentials of Mr Brian Sheedy. He invited Junior to think up his own pretext. They would never suspect a kid. The Keane boy was ready for anything.

As they emerged from the parlour Mrs Leahy was waiting, arms folded, mouth riveted in disapproval. She had eavesdropped enough to hear Andytown. 'For God's sake, Sean, don't send him there.'

Andersonstown itself wasn't the problem, but the big Protestant wedge of Woodvale and the Shankhill that lay between. Junior's only transport was a bike. A Protestant gang could spot a Catholic boy just by the way he cycled.

'It's dark, Gran, he'll be fine.'

'Please don't go, Gerry.'

But this was life in Belfast, men with noncommittal

expressions on their faces leaving the house at strange hours, on business from which they would return without speaking. And the women folded arms in doorways and parlours, and learnt to suffer, also without speaking.

Junior Keane went out into the night. Another unspoken detail was that McDade needed to stay at his grandmother's until he found a way of making the daily report in Andersonstown to which Phelan had ordered him. He tried to unwind in front of the TV. But what he really needed was a smoke, and his tin was empty. He cursed at not having sent Junior out for more tobacco.

McDade asked Mrs Leahy, 'Is McReady still open late?'

'He died, poor man. His heart went.'

No more than fifty, McDade thought, McReady with his daughter crippled years ago by a street bomb for which nobody admitted responsibility. Heart disease was wiping out that generation like flies. 'Anywhere else open?' he asked.

'The pubs.'

No, in a pub too many people would see him all at once. But McDade did not want to explain this. 'I'll be a few minutes. I'll come the back way again.' Mrs Leahy bolted and chained the door after him.

McDade bought his cigarette tobacco in a Crumlin Road shop whose window was all but blacked out by a heavy steel grille. Then he observed a strange thing happening to him. The self-control and cold judgment he had shown in his association with Weidinger and during the events in France, was deserting him, had already abated to the point where McDade felt he had never in his life left this city. Maybe it was the *pig*, the armoured car rumbling down the Crumlin Road, that reawoke in him the teenager whose only way of hitting back was to throw stones, petrol bombs, and then to plant the real thing. Instead of returning to Ardoyne, McDade drifted into the centre. He knew the sensation from previous returns to Belfast. The city seemed to be offering him a dare. Also, in his own mind, McDade was already back in the hierarchy of the Provisional IRA, the only place he had ever wanted to be. A man Dermot Phelan had accepted back was not going to skulk in back streets.

The windows of the Divis flats shone above the clustered rooftops of huddled, hating streets whose every alley people like McDade were trained to learn. He stared at a solitary soldier on an opposite corner, lit by orange lamplight which spilt down a wall daubed with huge political graffiti. McDade slipped away along another street. Up ahead something was going on. He saw more soldiers, and between him and the squaddies a hundred yards away there was no way out. The troopers were less provocative these days. One thing the Provos had done was teach them that the taunts and the shield-rattling, the raids when they smashed houses up before the occupants' eyes, would always be avenged. But still McDade had to avoid them.

The soldiers were knocking up several houses in a row. McDade made to turn back. The soldier he had seen on the corner was approaching now. They were all in pocket-radio contact. The whole district could be lousy with them, jumpy young troopers with rifles ready to spray the street. Hob-nailed boots on broken flagstones. Although it looked suspect, McDade returned the way he had come. If he ran they would call halt and shoot him down – maybe in that order. So he prepared to exchange a friendly word, act the Gaelic imbecile, for the benefit of this gawky boy in camouflage dress and big boots, hands gripping six pounds of kill-tech.

Many of the doors in the street were made of windowless hardboard, replacing the proper ones which had been smashed in by army boots, rifle butts, explosive, what did it matter? If the mute doorways could speak, they would all keen the same dirge. One such door was opening, opening towards McDade. A hand beckoned.

McDade's nervous system grasped it before his mind. The deathly vacuum of the street was an ambush. An anonymous call, a tip-off about hidden arms or something, had brought the squaddies here. Just as McDade ducked inside the doorway, a single shot shattered the night. The soldier, now only forty yards away, threw out an arm and keeled headlong against the nearest wall. The round that cut him down came from a vantage point that could be anything up to a quarter of a mile away in that crowded morass of buildings. The other soldiers scattered in near-panic, afraid to run, with nowhere to hide but doorways. Rifles bristled at the empty night. Behind McDade the door slammed. Anonymous arms dragged him into a darkened hallway. They hadn't wanted one of their own kind out there.

'Jesus!' McDade told his saviours. 'I didn't know, boys. Thanks!'

They bundled him along the passage. The dark smelled of piss. Broken toys littered the stairs and floor. The word had been out on the street. They wanted to know why McDade hadn't heeded it. 'Where are you from?'

'Ardoyne.' McDade's accent declared his religion.

There were three of them. A mutter about getting the hell out of there was interrupted by one of them asking, 'You called McDade?' By the light of a cheap torch they examined his face. Before he could lie about his name McDade's blood ran cold. 'Fuck if it isn't Sean McDade.'

'Great to see you, Stabber.' Could he play on their geniality? McDade wondered. But two of them pinned his arms and the third punched the arch of his ribs. Then they dragged him on collapsing legs through a rear entrance that stank of wet household rubble. From the street they heard the soldier boys firing at shadows.

A car was waiting. The driver took no notice of the extra passenger. 'One-nil to us. Let's go.'

They drove at normal speed into the mainstream traffic, making for the safety of the Falls Road. McDade tried one bid for freedom. 'Hey, boys, that was a beautiful job. A privilege to be there to see it. I got work on myself now, so how about you drop me here?'

'How about we drop you in the Lagan River?'

Everybody except McDade laughed. 'Hey, come on boys, what's it worth, huh?'

'Better ask Eamonn Carthy.'

210

Seventeen

The old port of Marseille was one place where two foreigners could stay cheaply with no questions asked. If they were unshaven and a little the worse for wear, and spent much of the time drinking away an experience they did not wish to talk about, nobody took any notice.

Eventually Stanger and Hendry had to surface again. The real world still lay out there somewhere. Stanger needed to reclaim his papers from a locker in the Gare d'Austerlitz. Lacking any other inspiration, Hendry agreed to travel to Paris too. In Paris again they could disappear for a time, but the problem lay beyond that. Without admitting as much, both men were scared of the beyond. Yet the pressure to leave France behind was intensifying.

As they collected their few personal belongings, Hendry said, 'The money.'

'The what?' Stanger asked uneasily.

'Let's split the money now.'

Stanger had kept the ransom with him everywhere, but then they had hardly been out of each other's sight. His original offer to share the quarter million was something Stanger now regretted. Once he concluded that Hendry, the criminal, needed him more than he needed Hendry, Stanger no longer perceived any advantage for which he had to pay cash.

'Sorry, Ed, the deal's off.'

Hendry took the news surprisingly calmly, not least because he had seen it coming. His blue eyes assumed a look of bleak authority. 'In that case,' he said, 'I'll take it from you.'

'Sure,' Stanger laughed.

But they both knew which of the two was fit enough to inflict the most damage. They had dodged reality, kept each other afloat, for two days. But one thing they had not done was get to know each other. Stanger could not swear that Hendry would let him leave the seedy hotel room alive, if he decided otherwise. 'Even if neither of us wins,' Hendry continued, 'we'll be in such bad shape we won't be going anywhere for a while.'

Stanger shrugged. 'OK. But you ought to know that the stuff's forged.'

'Pull the other one,' Hendry said.

'You think my client was handing over real money?'

'But we've been spending it.'

'A few bills here and there. On the basis that we'll be gone by the time somebody spots it.'

'OK,' Hendry said, 'I want you to get the money and rip it up. One note at a time. When you stop, we split it.'

'If the police pick you up walking around with all this ransom money,' Stanger said, 'it sort of tells them you're one of the kidnappers, wouldn't you say?'

'I'll take my chance,' Hendry said.

Three things: a fatalism about the whole Odell affair, a sort of affection for Hendry, and the conviction that the Englishman really would use force to obtain the money persuaded Stanger to hand it over. Hendry stuffed his pockets with wads of notes.

'I guess maybe we won't meet in Paris after all,' Stanger said, thinking that by then Hendry might have cops crawling all over him. 'But any time you're in Boston again, call me.'

'I'll do that. And sorry it fucked up back there. Maybe one day we'll know what happened.'

'I kind of hope not,' Stanger said. With a half-salute Hendry was gone, amid the traffic fumes, the grinding engines and furious car-horns of the sun-blanched street.

Once outside, Hendry fought to suppress his mounting agitation at what Stanger had said about the money. His military background had given Hendry no skill to manage finance beyond the level of the coins in his pocket. Forged money was like a stigma, something to wash away urgently. He had only insisted on his share of the ransom in case Stanger was bluffing. Settling on what he thought cunning behaviour, Hendry decided to travel across France by the most anonymous means he knew.

He took a bus to the outskirts of Marseille and looked for long-distance trucks that were likely to be making for the N7, the Rhone Valley and the route north.

Within a short time Hendry sat in the cab of a German container truck, whose driver spoke sufficient English for a rudimentary conversation, but not enough to ask awkward questions. By the time Hendry left the truck at Orly he had decided not to use the money. His soldier's simple faith in the security of real cash in his pocket refused to let him throw it away. But in his wallet he still carried Roderick Wardour's credit cards, and to Hendry this was such a piece of luck that he had to seize it as the answer to his problem. Adept at imitating the MP's signature, he had found the cards to work perfectly so far. The temptation to go on using them was irresistible and obsessed by the need to get back to England, feeling safe with the friendly piece of plastic, Hendry booked a single flight from Orly in Wardour's name.

Normally indifferent to the routines of booking clerks, even Hendry noticed the girl read something then double-check the credit card. But the moment passed, and she booked him onto a flight to leave Paris two hours later. As he walked away from the desk, Hendry glanced round. It was one of those glances provoked by subliminal awareness. What met Hendry's eye was the booking clerk talking into a phone, watching him in a manner which stated clearly that it was Hendry she was talking about.

Hendry's heart missed a beat, a long moment in which he realised he might soon die. He knew this sensation from Belfast, from the Falklands. Death, here, meant capture, a net closing around him. Keeping to an unobtrusive pace, Hendry ordered himself to sharpen up fast. There was no longer any McDade to do his thinking for him. Hendry crossed the concourse towards an exit. A bus bound for the city centre was about to leave the terminal. Hendry boarded, paying with the remnants of French currency he still carried.

Dismounting at the first stop in Paris itself, he went to a bank. Before he entered, he transferred four $50 bills to his wallet, to avoid drawing attention by flashing a wad of high-denomination American money at the cashier. Hendry had scrutinised the notes. They all looked the same, and he argued that to the average bank employee they would be acceptable. At the foreign exchange counter he traded the dollars for francs, the entire transaction passing smoothly. Then he found a travel agent and booked a train-and-boat ticket to London. An hour and a half later Hendry was on a train heading out of Paris, north towards Calais and the Channel.

Hendry's instinct had been good. He would never know quite how good. Shortly before the call from Belfast, Mike Wiley had pressed Robin Knight back to the question of how the kidnappers had financed themselves. All along Knight had stated that Sean seemed to have plenty of French money, and initially the Scotland Yard men were content to accept this. But Knight was beginning to sense a rapid decline in his value, in particular when he tried to ask them about the jail term he was likely to get. They were like blackmailers: one more item of useful information, and they might be prepared to discuss his future. Knight had no alternative but to search more widely, for things he preferred not to remember.

One such detail was that McDade and Hendry had mentioned using Wardour's credit cards, of which the MP carried a pocketful. Wiley wanted to know what they used them for. Knight had already cued Hendry in as 'Ed', claiming as with all the other kidnappers not to know his surname. Ed had been the traveller, the American link. At this news Wiley put his team on to tracing Wardour's credit cards.

First, from Jessica Wardour, they had obtained the serial numbers. Then they contacted the respective credit companies. This was after working hours and proved difficult, but the search eventually threw up a number of debits awaiting the call-in date. With few exceptions the charges originated in Paris, mostly at Orly airport.

Although Knight now had no idea if Hendry was still alive, he told the police that 'Ed' had been in France at the time of the raid on the chateau, and on the basis of this, while Wiley flew to Belfast, the team got through to Interpol at their Rue Armengaud headquarters in Paris. Credit card checks, together with Knight's physical description of Hendry, were sent out to all major travel terminals.

It was straight into this trap that Hendry had walked at Orly. Although Knight had salved his own conscience by being deliberately vague about Hendry's appearance, the use of the name Wardour and the card number was enough to spark off a series of excited phone calls, and produce a welcoming committee for Hendry at Heathrow. To avoid arousing suspicion, no further watch was kept on Hendry. But the BA flight from Paris was delayed on landing while armed police came to arrest the one passenger who, they discovered, had never boarded.

In normal circumstances this would have been a disaster, but by the time he received the news Mike Wiley had bigger fish to fry at the Irish border, and only remarked, 'So we've got a clever bastard out there.'

As for Wardour's stolen plastic, once aboard the ferry Ed Hendry went into a toilet, where he bent each card double and crammed it into an empty Coca Cola can. Then he went on deck and dropped the can into the sea. Later, recognising that the package of dollar bills would incriminate him just as much as the credit cards, Hendry changed one last $50 bill and used a six-pack of beer to weight a carrier bag stuffed with the remainder of the money. Seizing a lonely moment at the stern of the ferry, Hendry dropped the ransom money overboard. As Calais sank on the horizon, he noticed he was breathing more easily.

At the house in Regent's Park, the strain of waiting for Roderick Wardour's return was almost worse than his absence, which by now Jessica and the children had learnt to endure. Josh and Tamsin alternated between the excitement of small children on Christmas Eve, and a more adult apprehension, sombre moods in which Jessica noted that they were physically trembling. And this in spite of the fact that, spending much of their time away at school, the children were used to long separations from their father. For herself, Jessica had been dogged by the foreboding that the end of one nightmare would just turn out to be the beginning of another. Even after Wiley rang from the army base at Bessbrook, to tell her that her husband was safe and about to return to London, Jessica felt an advance distaste at the truths that were bound to emerge with his arrival.

On the phone she had asked Wiley, 'Is he all right?'

'He's in good shape,' Wiley had answered. It sounded unconvincing, and perhaps Wiley himself distrusted Wardour's brisk resumption of normality. Wiley had seen kidnap victims before. They came back as human wreckage, not with straight shoulders and winning smiles. Wiley had also momentarily forgotten, and Jessica had not liked to ask, about the finger-stump which had been sent to her. But the image of mutilation had haunted all Jessica's confused thoughts of how she should react to Rod when she saw him again.

The episode of Nevis's finger had been the one moment during the days in France when Sean McDade's brutalised instability had asserted itself. McDade had once read of a similar case in a newspaper, and at the time it had struck him as a neat way of letting the family know that they meant business. Putting Wardour's ring on a dead man's finger was for McDade a masterstroke. Only later had he admitted that the effect of the bloody package would be to stiffen vengeance against the kidnappers, even when they found that Wardour had not been harmed. But by then events had swept on, and McDade had brushed the mistake aside.

As the cars headed back from the Irish border, Wiley had questioned Wardour on his physical condition. But Wardour was suffering from no actual abuse or injury, and the detective had moved on to other things.

After another call from RAF Northolt, as they counted minutes to Rod's return, Jessica braced herself for the sight of her butchered traumatised husband. The kids, unable to keep quiet any longer, were in the street, clutching each other's hands and bodies at every car that passed.

There was no mistaking the police car, a dark Rover whose

shape and movement conveyed authority, with several men inside and another car following.

'He's here! He's here!' the children shouted.

Jessica attempted to keep Josh and Tamsin away from the cars. Mike Wiley, looking exhausted but ready for a long night, got out and held the door for the tall figure of Roderick Wardour to unfold itself from the car.

Wardour came towards his family with outstretched arms. In the light of the streetlamps he looked washed out, but there was no sign of the bandaged hand that Jessica was expecting. Even as all four members of the family hugged each other, Jessica's mind whirled back to Wardour's story of undercover work being the reason for his absence that weekend. She wondered if the kidnap had just been a security blind after all. But apart from his rumpled clothes, Wardour looked much as he did after a normal day's business at the House. One way or another, Jessica felt that she had been exploited. The reason no longer mattered.

For the moment Wardour was saying, 'Oh God, I never thought I'd see you all again.' He began to cry.

Jessica put an arm round him and led him inside. She had spent most of the evening preparing an absurdly elaborate meal for the homecoming, with all the best tableware and candles flickering off the dark wood and silver. At the sight of the familiar objects of his home, Wardour collapsed onto the leather settee, his head buried in his hands.

His head bloody and bowed beneath two pairs of leather-gloved fists, Sean McDade collapsed on the shabby carpet of the sub-urban parlour to which Carthy's men had taken him. Below a plastic crucifix, hanging awry and the wall's only adornment, bloodspots had spattered the drab emulsion. A bare bulb threw yellow light over the dreary room and its grunting brutality.

From one corner Eamonn Carthy watched. He had waited here, at these 'business premises' whose occupant had conveniently absented himself for the evening, to hear of the death of yet another British soldier. But with the news had come the surprise present of his daughter's violator. Blood was in the air that night, and the boys needed no persuading to settle Sean McDade.

Carthy was a gaunt man in his early fifties, but wasted beyond those years by bitterness and the innate asceticism of that generation of Irish republicans. His long lined face, with its thinning greasy hair and heavy unstylish glasses, stared down at McDade's helpless form like that of an inquisitor inflicting pain for the good of the sufferer's soul. The boys prepared to drag the half-conscious McDade to his feet for a resumption of the beating.

Carthy's reedy, unforgiving voice asked, 'You were saying?' But McDade could barely move a hand to indicate his inability to continue the words with which he had tried to buy his life. 'Take him upstairs and freshen him up,' Carthy ordered.

Five minutes later they brought McDade down again, the blood cleaned from his swelling face. On his clothes the stains remained, only darkened by liberal quantities of water.

'So you think you can be useful to me? You got very little time, so make it good.'

McDade pleaded for time. Through a mouth lacerated by a dislodged and splintered denture, he tried to make Carthy understand that he had a story to tell. A story in which Carthy would be interested, very interested, and from which he would realise that he, McDade, was willing and able to be a useful man again.

'Take the cringing little shite out and finish him off.'

McDade's legs buckled. He had already wet himself once, and now did so again. Strange how he had never felt fear in the presence of British soldiers, had never worried what those Protestant or army bastards might do to him. But to be in the hands of his own people filled McDade with a paralysing dread, a dread that made him shake and grovel. His voice rose to a squeal as four strong arms forced him through the doorway, almost cracking his fingers as they loosened them from the jamb. If he had been thinking, McDade would have known they would not finish him here, in the garden of a terraced house off the Falls Road. But he was not thinking, and he knew what this mixture of puritanical zeal and blind violence could do. He yelled, 'I can get you a Brit MP.'

Carthy's face, seamed with many sour years, showed not a flicker of interest. But he ordered, 'Hold him there, boys.'

Carthy was a proletarian, a one-time worker in the docks. Although he now commanded large sums of money, he still dressed in cheap, worn clothes, his breath smelt of coarse tobacco, the armpits of his clothes of rank sweat. His face, as he stared into McDade's, was like a cartoon of hate. The naked light glinted off his glasses, bleaching out the eyes. 'What fucking MP?'

Through rubber lips and gapped teeth, McDade spat the word, 'Wardour.'

The power of the politician's name was even greater than McDade could have realised. Wardour's return to the United Kingdom, still only hours old, had not yet been released to the media. So as far as Eamonn Carthy and the rest of the world knew, Roderick Wardour remained the kidnap victim, the vanished MP. Carthy repeated his name, contemptuous of McDade's devices, but curious to hear more. McDade persisted, 'I can tell you everything. And I can get you this guy.'

Calculation, the terse brutal arithmetic of the troubles, ran through Carthy's mind. He hated McDade, in the same way as he hated all those who deviated from the republican cause, whether into some soft-centred accommodation with the loyalists, or into ego-tripping lawlessness. How many wild young boys had Carthy ordered knee-capped for bringing the cause into disrepute, not to say threatening the efficiency of those who remained true? Carthy knew he could hear McDade out, then kill him. Or hear him out, use him, then kill him still.

'Get the young man a drink,' he said.

McDade was allowed an armchair with busted springs and open sides, only bare wood on which to rest his aching arms. The house itself was safe, in a street whose Catholic inhabitants saw and heard nothing, and down which nobody but Catholics ever went. Carthy sent one of his henchmen out to ask the owner to kindly stay with a friend tonight. For a while Carthy believed that McDade was feeding him a tale simply to buy time. Anybody could invent a story about the missing MP. The more fantastic the tale, the easier it was for any young punk to claim to be part of it. But McDade was giving too many hostages, too much hard core, to be lying.

'I'm telling you, they brought us to Connacht. I came over the border last night. Wardour was going back about the same time. For all I know he's back in England now.' Carthy was planning to catch the TV news later, to hear of the shooting of another British soldier. Maybe the return of Roderick Wardour too. But Carthy's eyes had narrowed at another name.

'You say Dermot Phelan was involved?'

'Seems he organised everything.'

'The kidnap too, Phelan organise that?'

'No, not that.'

'So who did?'

McDade insisted, 'I could never find out. I was just working for pay, I didn't ask questions.'

Carthy spat tobacco from his lip and let this point go. His interest lay elsewhere. 'Now tell me about Odell again.'

After hours of emotional readjustment to the fact that they were finally reunited, the Wardour family got ready for bed. Roderick had taken a long bath and put on pyjamas and a silk dressing-gown, which relaxed him but also gave him the appearance of a convalescent. This made it easier for his family to treat him with the gentle distance which he seemed to require. Significantly, Jessica herself changed into night things before the moment of truth when the Wardours shut their bedroom door, which they normally kept open at night, and faced each other alone.

They lay on top of the bed. Both tried to be casual, but were tormented by the semaphore of intimacy. Staying outside the bedclothes signalled that it might still be necessary for one of them to get up again. Which would be less painful if the marital sheets had not yet enfolded them.

They held hands, maintaining touch but unable to go any

220

further. This prompted Wardour to say, 'I'm afraid the bastards took my ring.' Sideways on, Wardour did not see the horrified pallor on Jessica's face. She had not mentioned the ring or how it had come to her.

'The police have got it,' she said.

'The police?'

'The kidnappers sent it to me. As a sign they'd really got you.'

'I'd like to get it back.'

'They're keeping it for evidence for the time being.'

'Yes, of course.' Afraid of a return to silence, Wardour went on, 'I have to go over things with the police. Also see the PM and the constituency. There has to be a press conference. And we can't have the phones off for ever – '

Jessica interrupted, 'Rod, just tell me the truth.'

'I've told you as much as I know.'

Impatient, because he was insulting her intelligence, Jessica snapped, 'About the woman.'

Of the many different fictions he had rehearsed to account for his weekend with Holly, Wardour had failed to choose one. Whichever lie he told would be exposed by what Holly told the police or the Press on her own account.

To spare them both, Jessica said, 'Look, I'll let it pass on one condition. If you tell me categorically that you'll never see her again.'

But Wardour suffered from an inability to bow to an ultimatum, even to save his marriage. 'I can't do that,' he said.

Jessica had spoken the following words to herself so many times that they came easily, although without feeling. 'All right, then. I'll go on supporting you in your career, if you have any career left after this. But once the kids go back to school, I want separate bedrooms.'

For some interminable minutes longer, they lay there, like stone carvings on a tomb. Tonight was going to be impossible. Wardour got up. There was a couch in his study. Before he left the room Jessica told him, 'You've let me down as a man. I can

221

live with that. What hurts is that you're so obviously not the politician I took you for.'

As the long sleepless first night home ebbed away into a grey London dawn, a burning and deeply raging sense of injustice took hold of Wardour. Somebody had tried to destroy him. For the time being he left aside the question of whether Holly was involved. But behind the kidnap lay something else, something more sinister than a ransom. Somebody had tried to destroy him, and there was no reason to assume that, just because he was back in London, this process had ended. Businesslike, Wardour made up his mind to the fact that nothing could ever be the same again. Jessica's reaction was only a small part of what he was going to have to face, in the coming days and months. Only through continued contact with Holly did he retain a chance of discovering the truth behind this attempt to ruin him. And if it cost his marriage, so be it.

On a shopping errand, Barron Odell let himself out onto the London street, letting the house door slam behind him. At the foot of the steps two men lounged, waiting. Odell gave them no more than a glance, but they had drawn themselves up at his approach.

'You know if a Miss Holly Odell lives here?' A reporter and photographer. How did these dirtballs get on to things so fast?

'What's it to you?'

'She's today's hot news. We wouldn't mind getting into the building.' The journalist was already fingering his wallet. Odell ripped it from his hand and threw it into the road. Then he grabbed the photographer, swung the camera off his shoulder, dropped it to the ground, and stamped all over it. The journalists backed off and waited for this demented American to go on his way. Then the photographer went to his car for another camera and they resumed their position. It was all in a day's work. They were being paid a lot of money to wait, and nothing would stop them. The crucifixion of Holly Odell had begun.

Eighteen

After no more than three hours' sleep on the couch in his study, Roderick Wardour rose early. To this former short-service Guards officer, his homecoming had the right touch of austerity about it. Today he had to face the world. All right, by God, he would face it.

Jessica had beaten him to the bathroom and to the breakfast table, maintaining the facade of normal family life for when the children came down. With an amiable, but not contrite, 'Hullo', Wardour grabbed some coffee and headed back to his study. Before he had decided who to ring first, Downing Street was on the line. After that, the rest of the day was a blur.

After a meeting with the Prime Minister, in which he stressed his desire to return to the House of Commons immediately, Wardour went to a west London hotel for the obligatory press conference. This occasion was not the success which Wardour desired. One journalist asked outright, 'Was the kidnap just a publicity stunt?'

Instead of killing this with a simple denial, Wardour rejoined, 'What kind of publicity do you think I needed?'

'The whole thing looks like an advert for the IRA,' the journalist said.

'Are you suggesting it was set up?'

'Can you deny it, Mr Wardour?'

Cameras flashed. More sinister, the blank stare of the TV cameras recorded every flicker of uncertainty, every bead of sweat, as the technicians zeroed in for the reaction shot. Wardour fought to keep a grip on himself.

'I've told the police everything I know. None of which supports the interpretation you've given.'

'How do you feel about the IRA now?'

'In their dealings with me they were impeccable. I say no more than that.'

'Even though another British soldier was killed in Belfast last night?'

'I hadn't heard. I'm sorry.'

'Do you support these murderers?'

'I support no murderers. I only say that we cannot go on decade after decade, with a futile military operation which has become little more than a vendetta.'

'Is that your message to the family of this dead hero?'

'My message to them,' Wardour said, 'is not to read your newspaper.'

As a private put-down it was excellent. But while the words still echoed, Wardour regretted them. He had lost his touch, and the knives were sharpening for retaliation.

'What is your relationship to Miss Holly Odell?'

'No comment.'

The press-hounds refused to let this go. Wardour sheltered behind the police investigation still in progress. But it was clear that his act of evasion had told them everything they wanted to know.

'Is Miss Odell your lover?'

'No comment.'

In the end Wardour rose to his feet, followed by his solicitor, who had been unable to shield him. Wardour gave them a smart, 'Thank you, gentlemen', trying to leave on a genial note. But he knew it was no good. There were days when all you learnt was how many people hated you.

At the House they were gentler with him. Members smiled, nodded or muttered greetings as Wardour strode through the cathedral-like splendour of the central lobby. His return coincided with one of the periodic debates in which members agonise over whether or not to reintroduce capital punishment. Wardour had registered his intention to speak, and took the occasion to show the House that he was back in the saddle again.

Wardour's views were punitive towards killers, but he held

back from execution on the grounds that public pressure for revenge guaranteed that sooner or later the innocent would be put to death. This stance permitted the kind of speech that Wardour was good at – appeals to common sense, mixed with idealism in a way that the House of Commons liked. But this time something failed Wardour, not his nerve or his mental grasp of the sentences issuing unprompted from his mouth. The missing factor was Wardour's domination of his audience. He felt like someone practising oratory to a mirror. They were all phantoms, or was *he* the phantom? The usual laughter, collective grunts of approval and rustles of anticipation, were all absent. On a three-line whip for this debate, the crowded chamber heard Wardour out in silence. On his feet for several minutes, he felt more devastated than if they had yelled disagreement in his face. Unable to build to a climax, he trailed off inconclusively, concerned only to maintain his dignity in this eerie silence. By the time he sat down, Wardour noticed that many of the members had averted their eyes from him altogether.

The chamber of the House of Commons is a strikingly small place. MPs make speeches from their spot on the green benches, there are no podiums, and usually the audience can be counted in dozens. The intimacy of the place is one of its most daunting features. No formality or physical distance shields the MP from hostility or ridicule. Exposed nerves are as inescapable as around a dinner table.

For this reason Jessica Wardour avoided the public gallery. She always preferred to watch her husband speak from conference platforms, to gatherings of the faithful. The naked embrace of the TV cameras also disturbed her.

It was open season on Roderick Wardour now. They would hunt him down, track his face for every flicker of emotion, ready for the parliamentary hounds to close in. Jessica had always taken a share in Wardour's triumph, and felt that she had earned it. The disgrace, she had not merited.

Her sense of injustice was not helped by callers, even the well-meaning ones. Her sister, Lucy Conefort, was not well-meaning. 'I have to say it, Jessie. We were all surprised that it was another woman.'

'Why?' Jessica asked, stonily.

'So unoriginal.'

'You mean you'd have been happier if it was a man?'

'No, dear. Would you?' Lucy was good at these verbal games. Jessica hated them.

'It's not a thing I discuss.'

'Perhaps you should,' Lucy said. 'With Roddy, I mean.'

Before Jessica could use this as an excuse to terminate the visit, Lucy added, 'The thing is, Jessie, it's like the stock market. If there's a bad smell, your shares go down. And if you refuse to discuss it, they go down further. Everybody looked to Rod as a future leader. What went wrong?'

Coldly, Jessica said, 'All Rod did was go to bed with someone else.'

'Well,' Lucy said, 'if you're sure that's all . . .'

The two women's eyes met, Lucy defying Jessica to express pain, which she would then patronise, Jessica refusing to submit, Lucy enjoying it anyway.

Before Lucy left, Tony Gwyer phoned. 'You sounded surprised,' Lucy said, as Jessica returned to the room.

'Nothing surprises me any more,' Jessica said. She looked at her watch and Lucy, taking her cue, left.

Half an hour later, Gwyer arrived. He had been to the Wardours' home before, but the Gwyers had never fitted into the dinner parties which the Wardours organised. Too much push, too little class. Tony Gwyer would not have disagreed, or been upset by the judgment. But now, as he realised that Jessica was alone, he became sheepish.

'I wanted to ask how Rod's finding things. I didn't expect an invitation,' he explained.

For Jessica, it had been easier that way, to get Gwyer off the phone before Lucy could work out the caller's identity. 'I don't know how he's finding things,' she said. 'Perhaps you can tell me.'

'He's got problems,' Gwyer said. 'A lot of people would like to get behind him, but until he comes clean, they're not willing to front up.'

'Does that include you?' Jessica asked.

'Sure.'

'I thought you hated Rod.'

Gwyer looked genuinely pained. 'We're not always eye to eye, and politically he's in a different league to me. But I don't want to see him get a raw deal. I think it's especially hard on you, and the kids.'

Gwyer's motive for contacting Jessica had been to gauge how much either of the Wardours knew about the kidnap. He also wished to hear how Jessica, a woman whose air of untapped sexuality had always aroused him, was dealing with her husband's infidelity. To find himself accepting a drink from her, one on one, was better luck than Gwyer had wished for. All he had to do now was maintain a deferential sympathy, for Jessica sooner or later to open herself up to him, confidentially, even desperately.

The Wardours and the Gwyers had only ever met through their Conefort connections, and Jessica had always regarded Tony with the over-precise revulsion that people reserve for those with whom they fear too great a kinship. In Gwyer Jessica recognised a ruthlessness which she shared but for social and personal reasons she kept well hidden. Now she had become publicly vulnerable, she found this quality more sustaining than words of comfort offered by her more civilised network of friends. And Tony Gwyer, cold-eyed in spite of his expressions of concern, knew exactly what was going on. Walls were not only collapsing in Berlin; all Jessica's objections to himself were becoming irrelevant.

Leaving Jessica two hours later, and noting how Rod's return home that night had not been mentioned, Gwyer kept an appointment with Jonah Sweetman and Herbert Conefort at the latter's Belgravia apartment.

Gwyer was in malignant high spirits. The other two men were still inclined to be nervous. As a shot of confidence, Gwyer told them, 'Look at it this way, as things are going, we're some of the best friends Roddy's got. So God help him.'

The hardliners in the Provisional IRA's Northern Command feared two things above all others: decay of their support at ground level, which was unlikely as long as the British troopers went about the streets, and senior level defections towards the softer ground of negotiation, merging with the more progressive British and southern Irish politicians to achieve a settlement of the troubles. For men of Carthy's lineage, with its martyred ancestry and indomitable taste for vengeance, almost the worst thing that could happen was for the British army to pull out. In that event, the IRA could find their *raison d'être* melting away, their popular support vanishing with it, and an armed Protestant backlash awaiting them as soon as they raised their heads. Although lost in the dirty fog of history, what the IRA wanted was a reunited Ireland in which their own organisation would hold a significant measure of power. This not being an immediate objective, their only hope lay in creating a demand for their own brand of justice. The last thing they needed was to be outflanked by clever politicians like Phelan and Wardour, sensing a change in the times and pulling the rug from under the sacrificial victims of Ulster's struggle.

Eamonn Carthy's interrogation of McDade had not let up. 'So you weren't expecting the Odell girl?'

Once again McDade confirmed this. Carthy had a narrow, acidic mind which ate into things deeply but slowly.

'He took her along for a wee bit of screw?'

Carthy seemed fascinated by the detail. McDade nodded. 'And only you and Phelan knew who her da was?'

'Wardour soon got the picture too.'

'He won't be telling. But maybes the Press would like to know.'

By now McDade had reverted completely to what he had always been, an *apparatchik* of the IRA, incapable of any viewpoint or action not dictated by them.

'You want me to tell the papers?' he asked.

228

'No, leave that to me. I want you to take up this invitation to the States. Make sure you're there when Wardour goes there. Make sure he doesn't come back.'

By the time Sean McDade had to report to Brian Sheedy at the Penny Whistle in Andersonstown, he was at least on his feet again, although walking with the painful gait of a man who had been seriously beaten. Carthy's boys had taken McDade to a stinking attic in central Belfast, where they had kept him fed and rested for a day.

McDade had succeeded in persuading Carthy of the value of keeping him alive, and of letting him keep the rendezvous that Phelan had timetabled. But McDade was now Carthy's body and soul. He would expiate his sins by a plan which he had inspired, but which Carthy's own bitter logic had shaped. His bruises, he would claim, were received through running foul of some drunken British squaddies. On McDade's home turf nothing ensured a greater welcome.

Mike Wiley had not let up for a week. His wife had hardly seen him, which, given their relationship, was no tragedy for either of them. It meant that most of Wiley's sleep had been snatched in his office; his skin looked like raw pastry, and there were alarming moments when he seemed to lose all recall of the Wardour case – what it was, why it was continuing.

Roderick Wardour himself had contributed greatly to Wiley's exhaustion. The two men did not get on. During his week's captivity Wardour had believed himself abandoned by the outside world. Only after his return had the police become involved, and by this time Wardour was less than enchanted by their attentions.

In his office at Scotland Yard, Wiley had been a little too man-to-man about Wardour's relationship with Holly. The MP exacted a silent revenge by withholding information which he knew Wiley could not discover independently. The matter of the cottage in France, for example. Wardour admitted that they had booked a place through a letting agency, but said nothing about having used Jonah Sweetman's place at St Benoit as a

229

blind. The more he thought about Sweetman, who had been among the first to greet him at the House, the more Wardour was determined to follow up that lead himself.

Wiley's own distrust of politicians convinced him that, apart from a love affair which had backfired and a kidnap which had self-destructed, the MP had been up to something. By the time Wardour left Scotland Yard, the two men had reached the end of any useful cooperation they might have achieved. By a malign coincidence Wiley felt himself going down with a bad case of flu.

They offered Holly Odell money. That was the last straw. Or was it the first straw of the next load? After days of being photographed on the street, of her home and workplace made impossible, her name used in the Press to stoke the fire under Wardour, a reporter finally tracked Holly down to the friend's flat where she was staying and offered £40,000 for her story. The sum, it was made clear, might be improved if she could provide them with red meat.

Holly slammed the phone down. She cried in the bathroom for an hour. She cried out of anger with herself for not being able to take the money, she cried because she was protecting men who didn't care about her, because she was forced to carry inside her stories that other people only wanted so they could put them in a freak show. Money from journalism was specially ironic. After all, Holly herself was a journalist. But the world of women's magazines, exciting but unstable, never quite tendered a long-term future. These people were talking money she could never save, a sum that would fund her going freelance, or pay off her flat. Holly knew that part of what they were buying was the right to put her through the mincer too. It was like pornography. Before they invaded her they wanted to buy her consent, so they would feel justified in whatever lengths they went to. They talked of giving her the opportunity to tell her side of the story. Holly wanted to take the money. A few weeks, and the episode would be forgotten. Such a sum would make a difference to her life. But instead she wept in a borrowed bathroom, and knew she would turn the offer down.

Her father had never told her the truth, any truth. What Holly had stumbled on herself now made her afraid. If the Press got hold of Barron Odell's IRA connection, the nightmare would never end. More to the point, she had determined not to betray Wardour. With each day, each hour, she forced herself to accept that she would never see him again. The police and the media were implying that she had entrapped him, forcing him into actions designed to ruin his career. Holly wanted to refute the charge. But to tell the truth would somehow hurt him more.

From some impulse to resume contact, Holly sent a one-sentence note to the House of Commons, warning Wardour that the Press were dangling money at her. It seemed tactful not to quote the sum, and she lacked the inner security to add any personal message.

When Wardour received the note he had just returned from a stroll in St James' Park with Jonah Sweetman. He had followed the old Tory specifically to catch him off guard.

'Jonah, tell me one thing. You knew I was going to France. Who else knew?'

Sweetman had already been through this with the police. 'From me, nobody. My French crone at the cottage had been forewarned, of course. But all she was told was, visitors. No names, no pack drill.'

'No chance you let it slip.'

'Verbal incontinence is definitely not my line, Roddy. Bladder occasionally, yes, but the old mouth shuts like a gin trap.' The shrewd vulpine eyes looked directly up at Wardour.

'Somebody tried to destroy me,' Wardour said. 'They may have succeeded. They may not be through yet. If I do nothing else, I'm going to find out who it was.'

'Good luck to you,' Sweetman said. 'If you want my opinion, at the end of the day you'll find those IRA bogtrotters at the back of it. Perhaps better left alone, eh?'

'I'm going to fight them, Jonah. Whoever they are.'

The two politicians went separate ways. Sweetman watched

Wardour's tall thin figure striding back towards the Palace of Westminster. The knight in shining armour as kamikaze. Well, Sweetman reflected, comfort would be hard to find. Politically, Wardour was already a corpse.

Back at the cramped office which he shared with three other MPs, Wardour took Holly's letter from his in-tray. The envelope was marked *private*, so his secretary had passed it on unopened. Although unfamiliar with Holly's handwriting, Wardour knew instantly who it was from. Fear and desire flared through his body, then died a frigid death as he read the one bald sentence. Angry that Holly should have written so little, Wardour spent the next few hours trying to shake off those too easily remembered words. 'I thought you ought to know – '

All his worst prophecies were coming true, so the interpretation Wardour placed on the letter had to be blackmail. The death knell sounded again. Holly had been part of the plot all along, and now she was squeezing him for money. Well, it was all of a piece.

On House of Commons paper, Wardour named a time and a place, requiring no confirmation but hoping that Holly would be able to be there. His brusqueness matched her own.

A day and a half elapsed before Holly returned to her flat and discovered Wardour's reply. The meeting he proposed was still two days away. Holly was depressed because he had not sent her a personal word. The headed notepaper, too, made its own brutal statement. Yet, she argued, if he didn't still feel something, he would never have answered at all.

Then Holly cursed herself for caring if he still felt for her. She had watched him on the Parliament TV programme. He hadn't been good, a man dying in front of a cold audience. At the same time she had thought that if he had the energy to resume his political activities, why couldn't he find a small spark for her? And now he had sent her what amounted to a summons.

Holly went to bed, to sleep on it, took a pill that didn't work and finally got up again. A party in the building across the street rubbed salt into the wound of her own isolation. Desperate for

232

some action to get herself back on the rails, she suddenly decided not to meet him. She took Wardour's letter to the kitchen and set a match to it, flaking the charred paper into a rubbish sack, blowing it out only when the flame almost reached her fingers.

Like a lot of policemen, Mike Wiley despised the grasses he frequently made use of. No criminal ever helped the police from the goodness of his heart. These men were invariably losers who had drifted into crime through weakness. Once the game went against them, they lost their bottle and became model citizens overnight. But given all the other twists in the Wardour story, Wiley had evolved a different hypothesis about who Robin Knight was. This theory suggested that the ex-naval officer could be performing a very special role in this impenetrable case, as spreader of disinformation. Wiley was beginning to suspect that Knight was there to muddy the water.

Wiley argued that Knight's self-deliverance into the hands of the police had been a little too perfectly timed. Just when they needed an informer, there he was. His willingness to help had been all too plausible, and he had tied up large quantities of police time at crucial moments. Furthermore, his confessions had not led to a single arrest, and the leads he had given them had all petered out. Too much for Wiley's liking, Knight had the air of a man with too clear an idea of what he was doing.

Knight was also too easy-going about being kept in a cell. They could hold him there for months on end, awaiting trial. But what would the trial be about? Was Knight's relaxation a sign that, at the last moment, influential contacts would be deployed to get him out and reward him nicely for work well done? Would the trial in fact ever take place? The question lay smouldering in Wiley's mind like a badly stubbed out cigarette butt. Behind it all lay his suspicion of politicians. If the political big cheeses decided that a trial resulting from Roderick Wardour's kidnap would be against 'the public interest', there would be no trial. And Wiley's ulcer would have ached for nothing.

To a committee attended by the Commissioner and the Home Secretary, Wiley proposed what had been in his mind almost

233

from the beginning, that they release Knight and – Wiley used the phrase again, because he liked it – 'wait for the tigers'. The Home Secretary, a faintly pompous man weary of beating off cries for the reintroduction of hanging, which he privately supported, asked, 'Do I take it, Commander, that the person in your custody would presume himself to be free of any further police attention?'

Wiley sipped at his glass of water. His throat was swelling and his eyes felt like poached eggs. 'No, sir. We release him on condition that he works for us. Knight claims not to know what happened to the rest of his team. We believe that somebody somewhere is going to want to tie up the pieces.'

'And you would trust him?'

'Not for one minute. He has an ironmongery shop in a small town. There are commercial premises opposite with the usual storage rooms above. We want to put a surveillance operation in there, to monitor who comes and goes, including Knight himself, so we can check it against what he's telling us.'

'And you would announce his release?'

'I thought not. The safer he feels, the more likely he is to make a slip.'

'No one knows you have him at the moment, is that correct?'

Wiley glanced at the Commissioner. 'A very tight secret.'

'Not even Mr Wardour?'

'No.'

'You don't think my honourable friend should be told?'

Wiley recalled Wardour's aloof, obstructive manner. 'I don't think it would be in his interest. Just yet.'

A flicker of satisfied amusement twitched the corners of the Home Secretary's mouth. 'Quite. You seem unwell, Commander.'

'A cold, sir, that's all.'

'There's a decanter of single malt over there.'

'I don't drink,' Wiley said, wishing he did.

Once the Wardour children returned to school, a silence settled over the Regent's Park house, which the busy schedules of

Roderick and Jessica were somehow no longer able to fill. Social life was going to be the problem, the one area in which they could not avoid each other. Although political colleagues were now wary of being connected with Wardour, many others in his wide social circle could not wait to have him at their dinner table. As usual the invitations came through Jessica. There were only so many she could sidestep by pleading Rod's exhaustion.

'Look,' she said, 'I don't want to lose friends. For the sake of that I'm willing to keep up a front.'

Wardour was relieved. A practical man, he soon wearied of emotional sieges. 'I'm willing to do more than keep up a front.'

Jessica took a deep breath. Her eyes did not move from his. 'I told you my condition on that. You threw it back in my face.'

Holly's note had changed Wardour's view of things. He said, 'Look, Jessie, I have to find out what somebody's doing to me. And for that I have to stay in touch with the girl.'

'She's got a name, Roderick. Why can't we say it? Holly, that's her name, isn't it? But for God's sake don't call someone you've been to bed with *the girl*. Haven't you any idea how that insults me?'

Wardour's cheeks reddened. Undaunted by the massed uproar of the Commons opposition benches, he could not deflect the force of naked female emotion. But before the conversation could die, Wardour asked, 'While I was . . . being held, did anyone phone you? I mean, one of the kidnappers.'

'You know about the two men who came for the money. You don't mean them?'

'No. Somebody phoned from France. It's astonishing, but I've literally only just remembered this. It makes me realise how much of that experience is still buried.'

Jessica's face was expressionless. If he wanted therapy, it was too late. For her, heart-to-heart meant tucked up in the connubial bed, warm and trusting. And those days were gone. 'What about this phone call?' she asked.

'I made a deal with one of the kidnappers. I sensed he was getting nervous, and said if he got through to you with the name

235

of the place where I was being held, I'd do everything I could on his behalf.'

Jessica shook her head. 'Didn't you see him again?'

'They all wore hoods, so I couldn't tell. But I don't recall hearing his voice again. And there had been a shot, so – '

'It was awful at the time,' Jessica said. 'But now I find I keep going blank about it.'

Intensely, Wardour said, 'I gave him the number to the phone in my study.'

'I'm afraid I can't help,' Jessica said, with not a tinge of regret. She reached for her filofax. She had things to do.

Within two hours Jessica was in Tony Gwyer's bed, in the Ebury Street flat where he lived as a bachelor while Parliament was sitting. His wife kept up their nouveau riche grand residence in Gwyer's constituency several hundred miles from London. Said to be good politics, it was also probably the only way the Gwyer marriage had stayed together.

Jessica fell into the category of shrewd observer of others who had no objectivity about herself. So while she was very clear about why Gwyer wanted to go to bed with her, she told herself that her own reason for letting a social occasion with Gwyer become a sexual one was to rebuild her self-esteem, rubbished by Rod's infidelity. This was not true. Jessica's self-esteem had come very well out of the Wardour affair. And sex, for Jessica, had never been either ecstatic or repulsive, a source of self-esteem or self-loathing. Sex was like everything else: power, or nothing. In Gwyer's arms she felt recharged.

'You're very efficient . . . afterwards,' Gwyer called, with the slightest trace of disappointment, as Jessica disappeared into his *en suite* shower.

'I'm very efficient all the time,' she called back.

Gwyer went after her. He wanted to start again in the shower. Jessica's reaction was simple. She went on washing. He tried to caress the curves of her body. 'Let it linger,' he said.

In her briskest crystal voice Jessica asked, 'What's so romantic about being sticky?'

236

Gwyer made some protestation about it depending on whose body the stickiness came from, but Jessica was towelling and getting dressed, her mind already on the next thing. Weakened by his tousled nudity, Gwyer pulled on a robe. 'I just want to feel that you enjoyed it.'

'Of course I enjoyed it.'

'Did you come?'

The expression on Jessica's face declared this not a question for self-respecting lovers. Gwyer knew that too much probing would only drive her away. And, above all, he wanted Jessica to return for more. He would get everything he wanted in the end. He always had. 'It was one of the great orgasms of my life,' he said.

Tightening her mouth to apply lipstick, Jessica said: 'Good.'

Gwyer consoled himself with the thought that later she would allow herself to feel flattered. His tribute was certainly true in its way. For Gwyer, like Jessica, sex was not measured as an experience in itself, but as an index of a wider potency – social, financial, political. Since the best way of screwing an enemy was to screw his wife, Gwyer was elated to have possessed Jessica. She had come there to use him, and she would continue to come to his bed as long as he fulfilled this service. And that, Gwyer was content to think, could be a very long time.

Nineteen

As she approached home, Holly was once again accosted by a reporter. She identified the Press easily now. They had all the right body language, relaxed, unthreatening. But in its own way their casualness was intimidating. The pressman had taken up his position between her and the door of her building.

'Have a few words, Miss Odell?'

'No.' Holly no longer apologised about refusing.

'There are rumours the Wardour marriage is breaking up. Any comment?'

'No.' She had also learnt not to give them the abuse they deserved.

'How will you feel if you're cited in a divorce case?'

'I'd like to get to my flat. Excuse me.'

'You don't care about destroying Roderick Wardour's career?'

He was going to persist. Holly turned away. She would go somewhere else. Then there were footsteps behind. She ducked her head instinctively. This was always the moment when the flashbulbs flared. Reaction shots, the pornography of the media. But there was no camera action. A deep well-spoken male voice which Holly did not recognise said, 'Can I help?'

Holly began, 'No, really – '

But the newcomer was already warning away the reporter, who protested, 'Hey, come on, what's this to do with you? I'm doing my job here.'

'Go and do your job somewhere else.'

'Piss off, friend. Go and save hookers in Leicester Square.'

The well-spoken man took something from his pocket and showed it to the reporter, then said, 'Goodbye.'

The reporter moved off. Holly looked again at this stranger who had emerged from the dusk. She remembered him now, the younger of the two detectives who had interviewed her on

238

several occasions. Holly felt less than relieved. The police had done her no favours.

'What do you want?' she asked.

Lucas Brand said: 'I could tell you I was just passing. But in fact I came here specially. Can I see you up to your flat?'

He admitted to having been out there in the street for a short while. He did not explain why. Above all Brand did not tell her that since the first time they had interviewed Holly at Scotland Yard, he had frequently used his off-duty hours to monitor the street where she lived, wondering if a moment like this might occur, helpless to stop himself.

At the door he was reluctant to leave. Every inch the sensitive policeman, Brand avoided any act or word that might be seen as a threat. You could never trust policemen completely, Holly thought. At the same time, up to a certain point you could trust them more than most other people. She let him through.

Lucas Brand explained immediately, perhaps a little too earnest about his intentions. 'I feel that you've been given a hard time, and I wanted you to know that, for one, I don't believe you're guilty of anything, or that you deserve the hounding you've been given. I wanted to say that if I can be of any help, I'd like to.'

'Let me get this right,' Holly said. 'You're not here on police business?'

'No, it's personal.'

'Personal?'

'I'll be honest,' Brand said. 'I've seen you before. Several years ago. I was on the Gridstone station bomb team. I was in uniform then. I remember seeing you there.' The muscles in Holly's face slackened at the reminder, and at the fact that he knew things about her that she would never have talked to him about.

'That incident decided me to go into the anti-terrorist branch.'

Incident, a police word. Holly fought to damp down her own memories.

'And as soon as I saw you at the Yard – ' The sentence remained unfinished. Holly saw now the disturbed current that had the young detective in its grip. She saw too that, whether he knew it or not, Brand was asking her for help. But right now she could hardly help herself.

'Thanks for your attention,' she said. 'But life is very complicated at the moment.'

'I'm aware of that. But given the position I occupy, I'd like to help, if I can.'

'Aren't you behaving unprofessionally?' Holly asked.

'You've committed no crime,' Brand said. 'We're all entitled to private lives.'

'Some more than others, it seems,' Holly said.

Brand was boyishly uncertain what to do next. Before either of them could get too embarrassed, he gave his number and made to leave. At the door he insisted again that he wanted to help, as if nervous that she might suspect him of other motives.

Earlier that day Lucas Brand had seen Robin Knight set free.

Mike Wiley was going down with a bad dose of flu. His eyes kept losing focus, his attention wandered, beads of sweat sprang from his temples and upper lip. He hunched into a jacket that was plainly not keeping him warm, although the interview room heater was full on. It seemed that releasing Knight was the one last thing Wiley had to do before he went sick. Knight's value, as a magnet to draw together all the messy fragments of the Wardour case, had become an obsession with Wiley. Lucas Brand was not so sure.

Brand's view was that Knight was self-pitying and unstable. If anybody deemed Knight a threat, they would kill him and disappear. More likely, Brand thought, Knight's usefulness was at an end, he was not important enough for people to go after and risk endangering themselves. But Brand exercised even more than his normal discretion. As far as he was concerned the Wardour case could run for ever, if in the process it gave him an excuse to contact Holly Odell.

Hoarsely, uncharacteristically searching for words, Mike Wiley told Knight: 'Don't misunderstand what we're putting together here. You still have charges to answer. You've signed a confession which remains on record. At the same time, if you can get us any nearer to these other people, this assistance will go well with you when the whole thing finally comes to trial.'

Even burdened by his illness, Wiley was exploiting what he saw as Knight's simple-mindedness. The naval man would return to his hardware store, and resume his life there with no idea that he was being watched. At this stage even Lucas Brand had not been told of the watch-post they had set up opposite Knight's premises.

Knight seemed nervous, but satisfied with the arrangements. 'How do I report?' he asked.

'Don't worry,' Wiley said. 'We'll be in touch with you.'

He asked Lucas Brand to release Knight from custody. As they left the room Wiley buried his head in his hands as the viruses mounted another assault on his system.

Wardour's car pulled into the gravelled area at the edge of the Surrey wood. Holly, already there, immediately got out. Two other cars were parked there, empty. Before anyone could see them, Holly and Wardour took a deserted path, a different route through the wood from the one which led to the spot where they had once made love with such abandon.

'Did it have to be here?' Holly asked.

Wardour said: 'It seemed the easiest place. All the time we were prisoners, I kept thinking about when we first came here.'

Holly didn't believe him. It was just one of those gallant remarks which formed the basis of his undoubted charm. Perhaps he needed to believe it himself. 'So how are things?' she asked.

'Not good.'

'Why did you ask me here?'

'I wanted to see you again.' Wardour had decided to keep his suspicion of blackmail to himself, let Holly raise it if that was her motive. Better not risk being wrong. And as the moment had approached, he had wanted to see her again very badly.

'I have an advantage. I can watch you on the telly.'

'There's see and *see*,' Wardour said.

He turned to her. Below the dark eyebrows his eyes now held the naked light of lust. Holly stepped back and shook her head rapidly. Too much of a gentleman to insist or sulk, Wardour continued the walk.

'How are things with your wife?'

'We don't sleep together any more.'

'Punishment?'

'More than that. She stipulated that I agree never to see you again. I wouldn't. So that's that.'

Holly said: 'Are you sure that was wise?'

'Oh, I don't know what's wise any more.'

'What about my father's invitation?'

'I intend to keep it. And you?'

'Sure.'

Their eyes met again. This time their bodies were about to follow but another couple were approaching, some fifty yards away.

'Come on.' Wardour urged Holly in the opposite direction.

She said: 'It's still a problem for you, being seen with me?' Wardour was suddenly the fussy public figure again, only concerned with getting out of sight. 'Look,' Holly said, 'why are we really here?'

Wardour attempted a laugh, but it was unconvincing. 'Everybody seems to suspect me of something now. Not you as well.'

Holly stopped herself saying that they both knew why they were there: Wardour's attraction was now tainted by his need to find out the truth about her. It was the first patch of vulnerability Holly had observed in him. She felt that proving to himself that she was innocent was perhaps the only potential happiness Wardour had left. It was sad, but touching, too. If they had been able to walk among the trees for a few hours, all that needed to be said, might be.

After some awkward minutes Wardour said, 'Look, I've got to get back to town. Let's meet in America. We can sort things out there.'

With time running out, Holly allowed her reservations to

melt. At least they had re-established contact, and the feelings were starting to flow again. 'OK,' she said softly.

They relaxed into an embrace. Part-way through, while their lips and tongues continued to explore, Holly momentarily opened her eyes. She found Wardour's staring at her, or through her. She closed her eyes again quickly and tried to go on kissing. But she would never forget the torment she had glimpsed there.

Two days later Lucas Brand phoned again. Holly's feelings about the detective sergeant were mixed. His police connection with the scene of her husband's death had touched off ripples of deep sentiment in her. She felt grateful, not offended, that Brand had mentioned it. But this conflicted with what Holly called the ratcatcher syndrome: the process by which the professional hunter always ended up having more in common with his quarry than he had with any third party. Lucas Brand's life was anti-terrorism. Take away terrorism, and for all his gifted mind and open personality, what was he?

By this time Holly had also suffered a reaction from her meeting with Wardour. She felt bad at how much she had wanted him when they were together, bad because it rubbed in how easily she could be manipulated. If Wardour realised this, he could play her like a fish. After all, she had no free access to him. She couldn't phone, they couldn't eat out or walk anywhere together. They had run from some strangers in a wood and this cast an enduring and humiliating shadow over their relationship.

Old friends were a problem too. Somehow everything had been rewritten. The connection with Wardour had taken Holly into a different league. People treated her with respect, but seemed to feel that she was no longer the person they had known before. Lucas Brand could not have picked a more favourable moment. He was personable, prepared to stand back if necessary, and oozed discretion. Holly didn't need to explain things to him.

He made no secret of his liking for her. 'I wondered if I could buy you a drink.'

The bright young detective might bring complication, but evading him would be complicated too, and this particular evening had threatened a loneliness whose advance Holly viewed with mounting depression.

'All right,' she said.

They met in a pub near Earls Court. Later Brand suggested a disco. He was fair company, a talented but slightly oddball man, a proficient disco dancer who had taken it up as a cure for shyness. He claimed to be shy still, but at least he was a very stylish dancer. They went to a west London club where Brand was a member. After a few dances, they sat in one of the cushioned alcoves at the front of the club, where the dance-floor music was audible but not oppressive.

While Brand went to the cloakroom, Holly fended off two requests for a dance, sipped Campari and began to feel that life might once again acquire a sort of normality. This thought lasted all of a moment, then she froze with a sensation she had never known before, fear programmed in below the level of consciousness, fear switched on like a machine.

Triggered by a voice.

Holly's entire body shook. The air in the club was stifling, but she had gone cold, all heat and life drained from her. She knew that voice.

Not daring to look round, she heard it again, the voice of an ordinary enough Englishman talking to someone at the bar. When she had last heard it, it had come from within a black hood. The only personal signs the kidnappers had given were their voices. Unimpeded by any other stimulus, those voices had made an indelible impression on Holly's mind.

Lucas Brand returned. Even before he sat down, the rigidity of Holly's body alarmed him. In the dimly lit alcove her face displayed a deadly pallor.

'What's wrong?' he asked, concerned.

'One of the kidnappers is here,' Holly whispered.

'Are you sure?'

'I know the voice.'

From the statements of both captives and Robin Knight,

244

Brand remembered that the kidnappers had remained hooded. He also knew that no two human voices are identical, although normally it took more than the human ear to prove it.

'You could be wrong,' he suggested.

'I'm not wrong.'

'Who is it?'

Holly indicated when she heard the voice again. Lucas Brand slowly turned his head. He found himself looking at one of the club staff, a fit-looking blond man in black jacket and bow tie, the discreet uniform of the club bouncers. Brand had never seen him before, but then the disco scene was come-and-go.

'Has he seen you?'

'I don't think so.'

The bouncer's eyes, as he chatted to the barman, were fixed indifferently on the flashing penumbra of the dance area. Brand thought fast. The worst case was that Holly was mistaken, and a promising evening was about to end in a fiasco. The best case was that she was right, and Brand, who had his police identification with him, was about to arrest one of the kidnappers. Except that he would then have to account for what he was doing socialising with a woman on whom Scotland Yard still had a live file. The fine line which Lucas Brand had arrogantly thought he could overstep had suddenly opened up in front of him like the crevasse of an earthquake. But he knew he had no choice.

'Let's confront him. Can you face it?'

'I don't know.'

Brand was allowing for Holly's possible post-kidnap trauma. In all types of crime, victims experienced a compulsion to identify their persecutors in public places. But paranoia or not, Brand realised that this might be his only chance to interest Holly in himself as something more than just an overgrown boy-scout. Close to her ear, he whispered, 'We'll just go and buy a drink and see what happens. It's all right, I can handle any trouble.'

Brand had not told Holly about his martial arts training, what he called the dark side of disco. He felt her arm shaking as he took it to lead her to the bar.

The bouncer prepared to move aside. Brand discreetly blocked his way long enough for him and Holly to come face to face. Brand knew the disadvantage she suffered: she had never set eyes on this face before, so even if she was right about the voice, there was nothing more for her to seize on for confirmation. Whereas, if she was right, the bouncer . . .

There had been no time to rehearse. Holly had to make it count first time. Brand watched for the bouncer's reactions as she stood in front of him.

Holly's tortured eyes searched for recognition, but the bouncer didn't seem to realise it was his attention she wanted. 'Do you know me?' she asked.

'Afraid not.' He met her eye, and held it, steady. He was sweating slightly, but then discos were overheated and airless.

'I know your voice.'

'Could be.'

Holly began to sound desperate. 'You know who I am, don't you?'

'No, I don't, lady. Is there something I can do for you?'

Helpless, Holly said to Brand, 'It's him, I know it. Every time he speaks I know it's him.'

This assertion was a bad tactic, particularly if she was right. But Brand was helpless to control her. The bouncer shrugged in Brand's direction and said, 'Sorry, got my job to do', and moved away into the club.

In the car Lucas Brand said, 'Look, I watched his face, and there wasn't a flicker. If he's who you say he is, surely he'd have given something away.'

'You think I'm inventing it, don't you?'

Ponderously, Lucas Brand tried to salvage something. He said, 'Well, whatever's in our minds is true, of course, and you were right to put it to the test.'

'But it failed?'

'When you looked into his eyes, did you feel you'd met them before? Did you see something I didn't?'

'What difference does it make? The more I say yes, the more it shows that I'm crazy. Isn't that right?'

In the last resort Brand was a detective, trained to form conclusions only on evidence. Someone's delusions didn't stop you being in love with them, but neither did being in love convince you that the delusions were fact. And this forensic bottom-line communicated itself. By the time they got back to Holly's flat, she wanted to be left alone.

'I'm sorry. Maybe I was wrong. But you see how all these things have got to me. Perhaps I need to talk to the right kind of person. I'm sorry, that's not meant to be a put-down. You're very nice. I'll call you some time.'

She had recoiled from him because he was a policeman. The ratcatcher syndrome stood between them. Lucas Brand understood it perfectly, and there was not a damn thing he could do about it. He went away deeply angry at the way things had turned out.

With a very modest subvention from Scotland Yard as all he had to show for the last few months, Robin Knight returned to the small country town where he had his hardware store. It was a depressing homecoming, and Knight felt that nothing lay ahead for him now. At least prison would have been a framework of sorts. Yet the naval discipline, the ability to get on with the task in hand, saw him through.

The former schoolteacher who had agreed to fill out his early retirement by running the shop in Knight's absence was not sorry to see him return. The business was too much an old-style pot-and-pan, nut-and-bolt, place, and lacked the product range and imagination required for modern DIY. Too many people came in, looked around, and went out again empty-handed. The two men wound up their arrangement quickly and amicably.

Knight took over the store again, for life, as it were. He made a tour of the familiar objects without hesitation, but equally without emotion. From the same pot he poured tea into the same mug. In the stockroom a crossword he had left unfinished lay in the same spot, the newsprint yellowed, a dead moth upturned across the clues. The boredom of the place, and the depression into which Knight settled, had at first a comfortable feeling to it. Then a deeper, darker abyss began to swallow the middle distance in his life. Knight's spell as one of McDade's mercenaries had blighted all hope of a normal life, for ever. However much he had been acting out of character, Knight had taken away one thing from his months as a lawbreaker – during that whole period he had ceased to despise himself for having failed as a submarine commander. But even as a criminal he had been found wanting. And now nothing, least of all the mundane shelves of a provincial hardware store, could ever bring him such release again.

Knight's shop had an access road that ran along the rear of the property, laid out in days when ironmongery stock came by bicycle or at most a small van. This service road provided Edmund Hendry with all the cover he needed. Since he had returned to England, it had been on Hendry's mind to attempt to tie up loose ends, if only to gauge the outstanding threat to himself. This was before the incident at the discotheque. Knight's shop was the only permanent location he had to go on. He had written Knight's name on a sealed brown envelope, so that if the wrong person opened the door Hendry could claim to be paying a long overdue bill. With this fall-back, Hendry let himself in by the none too solid gate.

'My God!' Robin Knight stared into the darkness behind Hendry, suspicious of what lay beyond.

'Are you alone?' Hendry asked.

Knight had to remind himself of what his deal with the Scotland Yard men had been. 'Yes. You'd better come in.'

They went up to the flat, two plainly furnished rooms whose spartan quality, to Hendry's eye, was not even military, just lonely and run down. After a few pleasantries, the two men began to fill in gaps. Hendry was the more persistent questioner. They both avoided identifying, either by description or name, Bobby Stanger. Knight spoke vaguely of 'Americans'. Hendry claimed to have escaped alone. Knight based his story on having been arrested by the French police, rather than having surrendered to them.

'How come Scotland Yard let you go?' Hendry enquired.

'They said lack of evidence.'

'That never stopped them holding anybody.'

Knight ignored this. 'Wardour's back, did you know that?'

'Yeah, I saw. If I never do anything else I'm going to find out the truth about that. What about Sean?'

'He may have been killed. There was a lot of shooting.'

'He was never killed. That little bastard was behind it all,' said Hendry bitterly.

'That doesn't mean he survived.'

'He survived. He must be the reason you're here. That Irishman's a player. The police must figure that eventually he'll be coming for you.'

Act simple, Wiley had told Knight. As things stood, simple was now Robin Knight's limit. 'Why would Sean come after me?'

'Because you can put him away.'

'How would he know I'm here?'

Hendry asked: 'Did it occur to you that they might spread the word around?'

'Maybe you're right, and that's why I am here. I don't care any more. What do you plan to do?'

'Survive,' Hendry said. 'And get even.'

Hendry had been telling himself that he had made it, survived, would soon be back on his feet. He spent many lonely hours working on plans for hunting McDade down. He still knew the Irishman's first name only and had no certainty if he remained alive. But the fantasy of avenging himself on McDade, and even of getting the money to which he was entitled, became the adrenalin without which Hendry was finding it impossible to live.

And when he looked at Knight hollow-eyed and beaten, Hendry knew why he himself would never accept defeat. It was better to be destroyed than defeated. Although destruction might come from anywhere, one could suffer it honourably. But defeat only ever came from within, and was always dishonourable.

Unsure why he was here now, bothered by the mention of Scotland Yard, Hendry sought an excuse to leave. Both men knew they would never meet again in circumstances that were good for them. The one useful thing Hendry took away was Knight's assurance that he had only given the police the kidnappers' first names and minimal physical descriptions.

'They'll never find you on what I told them,' Knight said.

Forty-eight hours later, after coming face to face with Holly Odell and her male escort in the disco, Hendry itched to call on Knight again. But now it was not worth the risk. Bitterly recalling Knight's weakness in France, Hendry found it hard to believe that the encounter at the club was a coincidence.

Hendry watched with relief as Holly left, with her boyfriend in tow. After a minute he went outside, to survey the street and the rear of the club premises. The area seemed clear. Hendry calmed himself with the thought that if there had been anything organised about this incident, they would have taken him by now. He went back inside to finish his night's work.

During his absence in Spain, Hendry had sublet the south London maisonette which was to have been his family's home when he left the army. Immediately on his return to London, he had put the place on the market, taken a room and found work with an agency that supplied security for all occasions from private parties to regular night-spots. Hendry was booked to this particular disco for the rest of the week. The night after the encounter with Holly Odell, he failed to show up for work.

Hendry registered with another agency, and found another room. Every change wasted money, but for the safety of new cover Hendry had no option. The disco incident had shaken him. He went to ground with the unhappy feeling that, from now on, life was going to be like this; unable to rest or make his way, waiting for another blow to fall. To a man who liked things orderly, this was a life that could not go on for long.

Hendry never knew that Holly Odell's disco companion returned the following evening. Finding the bouncer absent, Lucas Brand started to ask questions.

250

Twenty

Since his return to Boston, Bobby Stanger had debated what to do with the $125,000 which lay in the wall safe of the room that passed for his office. Stanger had taken a chance and brought it back in his suitcase and hand luggage. His quandary was how to get the good notes sorted from the forged without drawing undue attention to the money's existence. He was preoccupied with this problem as he crossed the rainy street to his Chinatown brownstone, collar up against the rain.

'Name of Stanger?' a voice behind him asked.

'Don't know it,' Stanger said automatically.

Somebody else checked a photograph. 'That's him.'

Two pairs of powerful arms closed in on Stanger, who kept his hands well away from his body. He had no gun on him, but they wouldn't know that.

'You got a phone?'

'Sure.'

'Let's go in and use it.'

Stanger assumed they would kick his apartment over for the money, but all they did was make a quick call. 'We've got him . . . Right,' was all Stanger heard.

A newish Chrysler four-door took him out to a gloomy wind-swept lot below a flyover, on which rain and traffic drummed constantly while a chilling fog drifted in from the Charles River. The headlights of another car came rocking through the gloom. The two men bundled Stanger across the lot. An electronically controlled window glided down.

'You and I have an account to settle,' Barron Odell's voice rasped.

'Listen, Mr Odell, we were set up. You want to know what happened, ask the boys you sent out there. Or maybe you didn't hear from them.'

251

'But you're here,' Odell said accusingly.

'You didn't pay for my life. The job was a fuck-up. We did everything right. I'm not apologising for anything.'

Odell ordered Stanger into the Cadillac, and it drove off. 'My daughter's safe. But you didn't rescue her. So the way I see it, you return the money.'

'The money's gone,' Stanger lied.

'Replace it.'

'Replace your guys who got shot to pieces.'

This was Odell's first hard news of the StormWind men and their fate. His knuckles whitened on the wheel as he listened to Stanger's narrative.

'I have to justify this to people. Three men dead for nothing. We work in a small world. How do you think it looks?' he said.

'Stop sounding like you blame me,' said Stanger. 'If I'd got killed you wouldn't have cared how it looked. And what do you mean, for nothing? You got your daughter back.'

Odell was not about to reveal everything. The more he thought about it, the more Odell's admiration for McDade's 'rescue' of his daughter waned. McDade had professed no knowledge of the StormWind men. Maybe that was genuine, maybe not. But the fact remained that when Odell's men went down, McDade and the captives were on a prearranged flight out. The two events had to be connected. Only that day Odell had asked Dermot Phelan to pass on to McDade a specific date to be his guest stateside. His guest and more, Odell now reflected.

'Those men were like my sons,' Odell said.

Stanger said nothing. He had been there, heard the Storm-Wind men scream. He was in no mood for an old man's sentimental guilt.

'My partners too,' Odell continued. 'In their line of business, the tops. I could send them anywhere. Word gets around.' Now Stanger understood. Bad for the image. 'You're sure none of them survived? If you made it, maybe – '

'They died,' Stanger said.

'They got families, kids. What do I tell them?'

'Dangerous work.' Stanger was off the hook, and was making it clear he knew it. But Odell was still looking to hang this disaster on somebody.

'I'm still intrigued, Mr Stanger, by the ease with which you got away.'

'It wasn't *easy*.'

'Compared to the men I employ, you're a deaf blind cripple. Yet you got out of there, and they didn't. What special knowledge weren't you sharing with them?'

'It was their training killed them,' Stanger said.

Odell bridled. 'Training?'

'They ran towards danger, I ran away from it. That's the difference.'

'The next time you're working for me and there's danger,' Odell said, the words icily crisp, 'you run towards it.'

The club manager had the sallow, badly shaved look of someone who never saw daylight. His black tuxedo had come off the peg – somebody else's peg it looked like. He submitted to Lucas Brand's questions grudgingly. The bouncer had been working under the name Bill Tanner.

'When Tanner didn't show up, what did you do?'

'Normal, phone the agency. They get us a replacement.'

'They hadn't heard from him?'

'No.'

Brand took down the sparse details. When he got to the agency, it had closed for the day. Then Brand had to wait for his next spell of duty before renewing his search. He was in a potentially embarrassing spot. The only way he would be able to declare his behind-the-scenes activities, which would reveal his involvement with Holly Odell, was by presenting his Scotland Yard superiors with a coup: find and nail the kidnapper on his own. From the agency Brand eventually obtained an address. At the lodging house in question, he learnt from the old couple who ran it that Tanner appeared to have left, with a week's rent still in hand. A search of his room yielded nothing.

Brand returned to the agency and took names of other organisations in the same line of business, on the hypothesis that Tanner might be seeking similar work elsewhere. He planned to check all new enrolments, should Tanner have used a different name.

The Wardour case was stalling. Rumours were, it would soon be closed. Mike Wiley was still down with flu. In this vacuum, Lucas Brand felt exhilarated, a sense of being on to something. He had earned another phone call to Holly Odell.

Naively, Brand expected Holly to share his excitement. But she was noncommittal. 'Don't go off the boil now,' Brand pleaded. 'I know I can get him in the end.'

'Well, I hope you do.'

'We have to find out what was behind it all.'

'I guess so.'

'Can we meet?'

'I have to go to America for a couple of weeks.'

'Call me when you get back?'

Brand was careful to make it a question. Holly felt that she would not come back the person she was now, so it was easy, if not to say yes, then at least to avoid saying no.

'It depends.'

'On me finding your kidnapper?'

'No.'

'On what then?'

'I don't know. But OK, I'll call you.'

'I'm interested in this man Edmunds,' Barron Odell said. 'Hendry, you called him. The one who came to me with the ransom demand.'

'Yeah. After London I didn't see him.'

'When all those guns went off in France, you reckon he was there?'

'I didn't count the bodies. What if he wasn't?'

'If he was, and you find him, I might just forget that money of mine you never earned.'

'Why should Hendry help you? What's in it for him?'

'Get this very clear,' Odell said. 'Somebody kidnapped my

daughter. I want to know what was behind it, what or who. What's in it for Hendry is nothing, or worse than nothing. Your standard line of work is, what, missing persons, marital evasion, so on? Well, forget all that crap. Till further notice, you work for me. Bring me Hendry, or something good, or a day will come when I want back my half million.'

In his safe Stanger had only a quarter of this sum. 'Ninety per cent forged, you said.'

'When I say half a million I mean half a million. Or I bust your business out of this town. So when you trace Hendry, make sure you find a way of getting him here. The way I see it, you got all the incentive a man could need.'

Back in his apartment, Stanger took a call.

'My name's Kunzel.'

'How can I help you, Mr Kunzel?'

'I'm calling from Burlington. Your ad in the paper – '

Stanger was about to explain that he was not taking any new work for the moment, when he realised that this was not the normal divorce or misbehaviour trade. 'Reference Edmund Hendry, is that correct?' he asked.

Kunzel sounded like a cautious man. 'Why do you wish to communicate about this person?' he asked.

Stanger said: 'I have business information for Mr Hendry, but unfortunately no point of contact. I'm willing to pay for a valid address, here or in England.'

'Can you tell me the nature of the business?'

'I'm afraid not. It's to Mr Hendry's advantage, but I can't be more specific than that.'

'You understand my position,' Kunzel said. 'Unless I know what I'm letting Mr Hendry in for, I can't feel right about handing out his address.'

'Well sure, but – '

'I'm sorry, goodbye.'

Stanger did not know what to make of this call. He guessed that Kunzel was the man Hendry's wife lived with. The deep, protective voice wanted to find out something without giving anything away. Well, too bad. Stanger's next port of call would

255

be to advertise to Hendry directly through the personal columns of the London press.

But before he could organise this, Stanger received another call from Burlington. This time it was Hendry's wife, or so Stanger inferred from the English accent. She did not declare herself immediately. 'I believe you wanted to contact a Mr Edmund Hendry. I don't suppose you've been successful?'

'If you don't mind me asking,' Stanger said, 'why are you interested?'

'I badly need to contact him myself.'

'Are you a relative?'

'His wife. We're separated.'

'Don't you have anywhere you can get in touch?'

'We haven't communicated for a while. The last time I tried there was no answer. I'm not sure where he is.'

'Why have you come to me, Mrs Hendry?'

'My daughter's had a riding accident. She wants to see her father. I was about to contact the London police. If you trace him, can you tell him to get in touch?'

'Can you give me any lead, any place in England?'

Eileen Hendry dictated an address, that of the maisonette which Hendry had bought but which, as things worked out, she had never seen. There was no phone number.

'I'll do what I can,' Stanger said. 'About the police in England, I'll take care of the enquiries with them. And I'm sorry about your daughter.'

Stanger's pen etched Hendry's London address deeper and deeper into the yellow pad.

The freelance strong-arm sector was a disorganised cash-in-hand business which operated from various low-rent premises scattered about London. At the sixth agency in the district of Beckenham Lucas Brand had drawn his usual blank. Brand was aware that the sort of men who took casual work of a muscular nature were not always life's most honest citizens, and that the agency personnel might deny knowledge and then tip off the suspect that the police were interested in him. However, Brand determined to keep grinding away. At the Beckenham firm the name of Bill Tanner inspired no recognition. Brand requested names and addresses of new applicants over the last few days, at the same time giving the physical description of the bouncer as he recalled it from the disco: a medium height man with thinning blond hair, thin face, fresh complexion, neatly turned out, could well have a military background.

It was enough. The fat, wheezing man in the greasy swivel chair unglued the cigarette from his lower lip and said, 'We don't want no ag with the law, right.'

'Tell me the truth,' Brand said, 'and I won't be back.'

'Don't put me in the frame, right.'

'Why should I?'

'Try this face.' The agency man fingernailed a name in the scrawly, dog-eared ledger. The name was Ed Hendry. The address that accompanied it was only a ten-minute drive away. Brand found a block of maisonettes above a row of shops, with a slip road offering half-hour parking for cars only. The maisonettes' doors were next to the shop entrances, and Brand was able to pinpoint Hendry's address as the window with a 'For Sale' sign. The place had an uninhabited look, but then these places often did.

Lucas Brand bought a tube of mints and asked the sweet-shop keeper if he had any acquaintance with someone called Hendry, who was likely to use the door next to the sweet-shop entrance. This time Brand kept his police identity to himself. The shopkeeper shook his head. It was a passing trade business in a suburb where people preferred not to know anybody else. Brand left.

He already had another idea. Noting the estate agent's name and number from the For Sale sign, he went to a public phone and rang for details on the maisonette. From his call Brand got the agent's Croydon address, and with the aid of his map was there in five minutes. Posing as a prospective buyer, the agents took him to the maisonette. By now the tenants had moved on, and Hendry himself was living there, although out at the moment. The few pieces of furniture, strategically set out to fill

257

space, failed to create any atmosphere of home. Brand himself was scrupulously tidy, but this barren orderliness was something else. A reasonable actor, Brand went through the motions of careful scrutiny.

'What's the story?'

The agent, a young man trying to act older, was deferential but hazy. 'Not too sure. I'm filling in from our Penge branch. Believe the vendor's away a lot. Property's hardly been lived in. Showroom condition.

Brand turned aside to conceal a smile at the description. 'I'm definitely interested. I'd like to meet the owner.'

'We can try and track him down sir. Any special time?'

Brand said he would call them again later in the day. On the way out he glanced into a small utility cupboard, and saw discarded socks and underwear awaiting the wash. Perhaps somebody was living here after all.

'I'm in a position to buy,' Brand said. 'I'd like to meet Mr – '

'Hendry.'

' – Mr Hendry this evening.'

'We'll do what we can, sir.'

'I'm quite happy to make it an unaccompanied visit, now you've shown me around.'

'Fine, sir. That's probably what we would have suggested.'

Unbelievable luck, Lucas Brand thought. At worst he might have the wrong man, in which case he was committed to nothing worse than a second viewing of these unlikeable living quarters. But he might have the right man, and although he shuddered as he left the oppressive aura of the maisonette, Brand was eager to return.

Hendry had secured the place with his pay-off from the army, for his family to live in. For most of his adult life lacking any experience of normal domestic surroundings, he had viewed it uncritically and expected Eileen and Lisa to be equally happy with it. Instead they had decamped to the USA, leaving Hendry with a bitter, empty memorial to a future that would now never happen. Hendry had put the maisonette up for sale just at a time when the property market collapsed, and this kind of featureless, basic home attracted little customer interest. The tenants' rent had not covered the latest escalation in interest rates, and the building society had written demanding the shortfall to be made up immediately, unless they were to seek repossession. Hendry's reason for giving his real name at the strong-arm agency had been to provide the building society with evidence that he was in employment, and would be able to keep up the payments.

A forced sale in a depressed market would lose him thousands. So Hendry was relieved when he returned to the maisonette and found the estate agent's note, promising an interested viewer. From a public phone Hendry confirmed that he would meet Mr Brand at eight o'clock that evening. Hendry had a job that night, a private party at a big house in the West End, but the shift didn't start till ten.

Hendry had a bad memory for faces. Not knowing this, Lucas Brand had to gamble on the darkness of the disco, and the shock of seeing Holly there, to have left Hendry with no recollection of Brand himself. The gamble was justified. Hendry watched the car pull into the slip road, in front of the fast food bar, which at this time of day was the only shop open in the row. Hendry went down to let the prospective buyer in.

He was ill at ease, not because he suspected anything, but from simple dislike of a stranger walking around his home. Brand, if anything, was the opposite. He was carried away by his confidence, once he had confirmed that Hendry was the bouncer whose trail he had followed across London for a week. The degree of uncertainty had prevented Brand from requesting police back-up. As he worked himself up to making a formal arrest, he maintained his role of house buyer.

The doorbell rang, loud and unmelodious. Both men looked apprehensive. Brand had been about to make his move. The lights were on, so whoever it was knew someone was in.

Hendry frowned and said, 'Excuse me a minute.'

Brand had no choice. Hendry went down. On the doorstep he found Bobby Stanger. It was a moment from a dream, comparable to their meeting that last night at Sous-bois. It had no

259

place in real life. But the address which Eileen Hendry had given Stanger, the one she said never answered, was answering now. The American greeted Hendry with a huge grin.

Amazed, Hendry quickly explained what was happening and let Stanger in, asking him to wait a few minutes.

Brand, meanwhile, had decided to waste no more time. As soon as Hendry returned and closed the door, he flashed his police card. 'Mr Hendry, or Tanner, whatever you call yourself, you're under arrest.'

'For what?' Hendry asked.

'You're one of the kidnappers in the Wardour case. I was with Holly Odell the other night when she identified you. I warn you that I'm expert in unarmed combat, so don't try anything stupid.'

Hendry, no amateur himself, had just decided that he had nothing to lose, when the lights in the maisonette went out. A moment faster than Brand, Hendry struck out. He caught the Scotland Yard man off balance, and hit him several times, until he judged that there was no chance of him getting up immediately. Then Hendry groped his way out of the maisonette. The light of the cheerless stairway was still on.

'Very thin doors,' Stanger said. 'I heard the lot.'

'Smart move,' Hendry said breathlessly. 'But how?'

'Outside fuse box. I forced the lock with a knife, then hit the switch.'

They were now on the street. Hendry said: 'What are you doing here?'

Stanger indicated a hired car. 'Tell you on the way to the airport.'

On one of the increasingly few occasions when they were at home together, Roderick Wardour asked Jessica, 'Can we do the diaries?' This was a routine activity of many years' tradition. Until recently it had been the focus of their lives, when they would update each other's appointment books, discuss future plans and strategies. Now the filofax pages were flicked over by resentful hands.

260

Wardour had avoided the moment as long as he could. With less than a week to go, he had to face it now.

'I'm going to America. For a week or so.' He gave the dates, matter-of-fact. Jessica was not writing. 'America?'

'An invitation I can't refuse.'

Wardour had decided that a minimum of words on this subject would give the least provocation. Jessica went further, and made no direct comment at all. She knew that the woman Wardour had been with was American. Why ask questions to be insulted by lies? After an awkward silence, she asked, 'How do you feel things are going for you now?'

'I still have friends in the House,' Wardour said.

Jessica answered: 'Friends are no substitute for power.'

Stung, Wardour said, 'Who's talking about substitutes?'

Jessica's cool eyes expressed disappointment. 'I would still do anything for your career. Except one thing.' Wardour froze, waiting. 'You think I'm going to say, put up with another woman. But I'm not, I think I'm just less romantic than you. I know you haven't found me very exciting in bed – '

'You're wonderful in bed,' Wardour insisted. Almost shouted, the words sounded trite, insincere, everything they shouldn't.

'Well,' Jessica said witheringly, 'I can't argue with such a well-informed opinion.' Deliberately brutal, she changed the subject. 'Have you read the file lately?'

This referred to another of their routines: the household took daily delivery of various newspapers and journals, from which Jessica clipped any mention of her husband. She had done this from his first day in Parliament. In a whole room of the Regent's Park house, now known as the archive, Jessica spent hours each week at an eighteenth-century desk, surrounded by neat shelves of box files, monitoring the rise of Wardour's star.

Normally her question would not have needed asking. But furtively Wardour answered, 'No.'

'Perhaps you should.'

'Why?'

'It isn't going away,' Jessica said. 'I don't know how you see it inside your head, but your adoring public are not satisfied.'

'Damn them,' Wardour said.

'You don't even realise what's happening, do you?'

'What do you mean?'

'You've become one of those stories that will never go away, where nobody believes the explanations, where the innuendo never stops, where on dead news day they'll dig you up for another going over. And years from now the vultures will still be picking over the bones of your career.'

'Damn them,' Wardour repeated.

'Well then, damn me too,' Jessica said. 'Because I never saw anybody throw away so much, so easily.'

Wardour was trembling slightly, his right hand clenched, his voice hoarse with emotion. 'I am not throwing anything away. But I demand to know the truth.'

'Whose truth?' Jessica asked. 'Your truth, or the one that matters?'

'Somebody tried to smear me. They may not have finished yet. I won't take it lying down.'

'You smeared yourself,' Jessica said contemptuously. 'Why blame others?'

Wardour took the slap, but refused to respond.

'When did you say you were going to America?' she asked.

Wardour repeated the dates. Jessica simply drew a line in her personal organiser. Then she left the room. Nobody could close an issue like Jessica.

Wardour went up to his study. After an anguished hour staring at a blank sheet of paper, he began writing to Jessica things he could not say to her face. He explained the true reason why he could not let this matter rest. He had fallen in love – he had not gone looking for it, God help him, he had been unable to exercise any power against it. He had above all not wished to hurt anybody. But he could not continue his life under the suspicion that the woman with whom he had fallen in love was one of the enemy. He would go to America, retrace whatever steps he had to, and if at the end all he did was free

262

Holly Odell from his own suspicions, that would be enough. And if Jessica did not understand this motive, Wardour wrote, she did not understand him.

Only by writing it down had Wardour made the nature of his obsession clear to himself. He had never written anything like this before in his life. Each time he read it through, he felt more vulnerable. Finally, he tore it up.

Twenty-one

'Hell, I'm no farmer,' Barron Odell told Sean McDade as he drove the Irishman around the few hundred acres he owned in New Hampshire. 'The place was a gift, from a Central American head of state whose son was taken hostage.' In a quiet voice, dourly authoritative, Odell added, 'We got him back.'

'A beautiful piece of land,' McDade said.

'Well, we raise some cattle and I syndicate trout fishing. You a fisherman, Mr McDade?'

'No, I never learnt.' McDade was respectful, the remaining bruises on his face sitting oddly with the cheap suit he had bought for the trip. 'I wish I had.'

'Maybe we'll go to the lake and I'll teach you to tie a fly. That's Dave Sherry.' Odell waved to a distance horseman. 'He and his boys manage the place for me.'

To McDade's surprise, Odell himself had met him at Boston airport. As the drove out on Route 93 Odell pointed out that they were passing first through a town called Derry, and after that another called Londonderry. It was part of Odell's compulsion to display how well versed he was in the nuances of Northern Ireland.

'What's in a name?' he demanded rhetorically. 'Well, as we all know, the answer is everything.' McDade smiled respectfully. He had things on his mind. His behaviour was subdued.

As they drove around the farm Odell said, 'Do you still kill the eldest sons on the farms?'

'I'm not clear what you're getting at, Mr Odell.'

'What I'm getting at,' Odell said, 'is the policy of removing the son and heir on Protestant farms near the border, so the family abandons the farm, which can then be taken over by a Catholic family. A cruel strategy, but wise.'

264

'I'm not sure,' McDade said. 'Being mainly a Belfast operations man.'

'You don't mind me asking?'

'Not at all.'

'I have a high regard for you,' Odell said. 'I want you to know that. The boys have always had a bad press. But some of us know what it means to do the tough things that have to be done. Goddammit, when a handful of men take on an entire government, somebody has to fight dirty. Governments do little else, isn't that right?' They were returning to the house, a residential property some distance from the farm buildings.

'There's just one thing I want to know,' Odell said. 'The kidnap in which my daughter was involved, tell me it wasn't IRA-initiated.'

'On the blood of the martyrs,' McDade said.

Pleased by the phrase, Barron Odell muttered, 'Good, good.'

Although he regarded himself as an unfussy man who made few concessions in life, Odell had planned the arrangements for his guests with great care. McDade was given a bed in a simple but adequate brick building in the farm section, which was normally used as an overspill for seasonal workers or fishing parties. Even Odell's mixture of romanticism and hardness baulked at having McDade and Holly sleep under the same roof. The roles of kidnapper and victim were not easily erased.

On the way up to New Hampshire, Holly was unsettled. The encounter with Hendry, and the information that the bouncer had promptly gone missing, had brought back traumas about the kidnap which she had thought buried. When her father mentioned that McDade, on whom he dropped the epithet 'your rescuer', had already arrived, Holly's skin chilled.

'I've put him in the bunkhouse. You and Mr Wardour will be in the lodge with me. I guess our urban guerrilla prefers it that way.'

Holly said: 'Isn't that another word for murderer?'

Odell was over-excitable on this subject. 'In a country under military occupation? Didn't they one time call them partisans? Freedom fighters?'

'What about all the broken lives?' Holly said. 'They fight their dirty little war, and for everybody they shoot or blow up, hundreds of other people never recover.'

Suddenly Holly resented the fact that her father had never known the exact circumstances of David's death. It had been her own decision to leave him unaware that an IRA bomb had killed her husband; one of the incidental victims over whom terrorists shrugged their shoulders. Yet now she almost hated Odell's romantic simple-mindedness, and felt a pressure growing inside her that could only increase when she had McDade as a fellow-guest at the farm.

Odell left the argument unpursued, saying only, 'The fact remains, Hol, Mr McDade got you back alive. I don't fully understand his motive yet, and I intend to find out more about that. But I figured I owed him something.'

Holly looked out of the window and said, 'I love the maples when they change colour.'

Odell and Holly were doing the cooking. Odell was a competent, self-taught cook. Planning and preparing meals gave father and daughter a positive and innocent distraction from the more awkward aspects of this visit. When she had met McDade again, Holly was shocked by the fading bruises on his face. McDade was letting his beard grow to cover some of the marks, but the sparse black stubble, allied to the poor quality suit and open-necked shirt, gave him a lost look, a pathos behind which Holly felt there lurked a blind, reptilian danger. But perhaps she was just projecting.

'Mr McDade got on the wrong side of some British infantry,' Odell intoned, with a look at his daughter which was intended to recall their dialogue in the car.

Holly said: 'I'm sorry.' But she looked at McDade's hands and wondered how many times they had pistolled away somebody's life or planted a bomb.

266

'Occupational hazard of being an Irishman,' McDade said. 'I hope you've recovered from that nasty trick we played on you.'

With a false laugh Odell said: 'There's a lot to discuss. All in good time. We'll have a drink, then how about we get to work on these trout? Do you cook, Mr McDade?'

'Stuff out of tins,' McDade said, 'is mostly it.'

'But you eat, right? And we can talk things out over dinner.'

But the meal and the evening passed in short conversations whose artificiality served to smother the questions that were really disturbing the three of them. Furthermore, Odell had set a fourth chair at the table, and although no place had been laid, somehow the evening was dominated by that absent guest. Roderick Wardour was due to arrive the next day.

After a brief touch-down at his apartment in Boston, Bobby Stanger drove Ed Hendry out to Burlington. Lisa Hendry had three broken bones and was mottled with bruises, but was out of concussion. A quick phone call had established that none of the breaks would have serious consequences.

In the car Hendry talked obsessively about medical bills. Personally he was broke. He kept referring to the seeming affluence of the Kunzel household, then as frequently insisted that this had nothing to do with it. If he judged it necessary Hendry insisted that he would take Lisa back to Britain, where she was entitled to free treatment. He hadn't served in his country's army for twenty years for nothing. It was all a way of beating back the guilt at the poor role he had played as a father.

Stanger concentrated on the driving, thinking uneasily about the forged ransom money. Fortunately they were at the hospital by the time Hendry was saying, 'Whatever I have to do to get money for the girl's treatment, I'll do.'

Both Eileen Hendry and Jim Kunzel were apologetic, genuinely glad that Hendry had come. The apprehension of the journey lifted, and he found in himself a reserve of grace necessary to ease the pain of the two people who had lived with every minute of Lisa's accident. Even when the doctor dealt automatically with Kunzel as Eileen's companion, Hendry behaved with restraint, waiting on events. They were all united by a silent, joyous relief that the accident had not been worse.

Lisa lay plastered and strapped up. But *alive*, Hendry thought, as tears fought against his iron self-control. Lisa smiled through the wire of a dental brace, the smile half girl, half woman, enchanting. For a full minute unable to speak, Hendry sat holding her hand as their eyes met in a gaze that declared they were father and daughter after all.

'I can get in a mess too,' Lisa said.

'You're not in a mess.'

'I never saw you cry before.'

'I'm not crying.'

'My hand's wet.'

Hendry looked up at the clinic's immaculate walls. 'Condensation,' he said, as more tears fell.

Helpless with emotion, but, strangely, feeling more happiness than he had for years, Hendry made a private vow that for the rest of his life, even if he was an absentee, he would make himself into a decent father for this dark-haired girl whose smile accepted him so completely.

'Once I'm out of plaster – ' Lisa said.

The words struck deep. Hendry had found a new motto for the badge of his life. He smiled, stroked his daughter's arm, and said, 'That's right, pet. One day we'll all be out of plaster.'

On yet another shuttle from Logan International, Holly was driving Roderick Wardour out to the farm. Referring to her father, she said: 'He's in Boston today. Some business meeting. He took McDade with him for a day's sightseeing. If not for more diplomatic motives.'

'What's he expecting with us?' Roderick Wardour asked.

'I still haven't worked out what *we're* expecting.'

A touch nervously Wardour asked: 'The . . . er . . . domestic arrangements?'

'We have separate rooms. But I've already – ' A sideways glance told Wardour that Holly had prepared Barron Odell for what might happen.

268

'And he – ?'

'On one level my father's a sort of lunatic anarchist, on another a really tight-arsed puritan. You never know which one you're going to get. The problem isn't him. It's us. Isn't it?'

'I'll put my puny cards on the table,' Wardour said. 'While I'm here I'd like to spend every minute of the day and night with you. But when we go back to London I can't say what will happen. I suspect that by this time next week a lot of things will have changed.'

'How are things with your wife?'

'For twenty years it was too perfect. Now it's not perfect any more, we don't know what to do.'

'Why did you come here?'

'To be with you.'

'Jessica knows I'm here?'

'Yes.'

'So we could be doing this in England,' Holly said. 'And I thought we went abroad for secrecy.'

It was a nice touch, but Wardour's sense of humour failed him. Holly had awakened too much guilt – at what he had got her into, at his refusal to acknowledge her publicly in London. To evade the point, he asked, 'Why did your father invite McDade?'

'Gratitude, he says. For getting us out.'

'You believe that?'

'Of course not.'

'Why do you think McDade accepted?'

'To keep my father sweet. The prospect of money and guns for the IRA.'

This made Wardour uneasy. 'You're sure of this?'

'Just the way I read it,' Holly said. 'You don't have to be a genius.'

It was a tricky subject, which Wardour wanted to avoid just as, for different reasons, Barron Odell had. Since his return to politics, Wardour had learnt the hard way how apparently healing words on the subject of Northern Ireland could soon find themselves construed as virtual treason.

'The America I've seen before,' Wardour said, 'was all airports and hotels. This is something else.' He gazed out at the multi-coloured wood on the horizon, and the hills beyond, promising an expanse which, to someone used to the compact distances of England, began to be breathtaking.

'You'll shoot your first grizzly, and abseil down the Great Stone Face,' Holly said. 'As soon as my father gets twitchy, which is soon, he'll organise everybody.'

Reticently but determined, Wardour put a hand on Holly's thigh. He was surprised when she did the same to him. The gesture was not so much one of sexual desire, as a joint reassurance that they would help each other survive the coming week, which might well not be the simple social event they were pretending to discuss.

Bobby Stanger had little qualification to deal with Ed Hendry's family problems. Although in the distant past he had left behind a failed marriage of his own, which by now was only a dim memory, Stanger lacked experience of children or the loss of them. Life's major traumas were something that came his way almost exclusively as paid employment. He cleared up the nastier side for others willing to hire a middleman to absorb the pain and guilt and confusion and call it a day's work.

Seeing his daughter in a hospital bed, even if she was certain to recover, had left Hendry shaken: for a full-time parent a child's illness was a sort of reproach, and Hendry was a no-time parent. He found the sense of failed duty hard to bear.

Stanger could only offer Hendry all the drink he could take. Drunk or sober, Hendry found the presence of water restful and since Boston was not short on water, they spent a lot of time wandering the wharves or the elegantly lit banks of the Charles by night, drifting wherever the bubble of alcoholic unreality took them.

As they came down from their cloud, sharing a fifth of bourbon in the depths of the Common, Hendry said, 'You can stop nursemaiding me now. I know you've got work to do.'

'Whenever you're ready,' Stanger said.

'It's all right. I'll make it.'

Stanger asked, 'What was that scene in London? Are the police on to you?'

Hendry shrugged. With the Atlantic between him and the police it was easy to dismiss their pursuit. But at certain moments back there, Hendry had been scared. Especially by the speed with which they had tracked him down. 'They'll never find me,' he said. 'People disappear all the time.'

It was bravado; Hendry knew it and Stanger knew it. First he had to get back into Britain. He might have been lucky in getting out, but all the odds argued that they would be checking airports when he returned.

'Ed,' Stanger mumbled, 'I have to tell you this. Right now, as far as I'm concerned, work is *you*.'

'How's that?' Hendry asked.

'You've had a rough time. But did you, maybe somewhere in there, wonder how come I was in London looking for you? Like how I knew that address?'

'I guessed I must have given it to you some time,' Hendry said.

'Mm-mm. That I got from your wife. But it wasn't your wife that sent me. You remember a man called Odell?'

Hendry stiffened. He already knew how Stanger had turned up at the chateau that night, but his daughter's accident had clouded the knowledge. Now here it was again. Stanger continued, 'Bear in mind that Odell is *big*. His operation is sort of a legend. When StormWind rescue people, those people really get rescued. So then his daughter is the victim, but this time the mission screws up all over the place. Men die, good men. Odell's real sore. He's sore at me too. If I bring him you, I'm off the hook. That's his offer.'

Hendry could not have been more obliging. He answered: 'OK, I owe you. That's it. You're off the hook.'

Stanger was uneasy. 'Ed, I can't guarantee anything about this guy. I can't work him out. On a psycho scale I'd give him definitely six, maybe seven out of ten. He keeps bad company.'

271

'Like I say,' Hendry repeated, 'you've got your deal. Don't even talk about it.'

They returned to Stanger's apartment, where Stanger phoned Odell's office. The secretary said Odell was in a meeting. An hour later he called back. During the hour of waiting, Hendry and Stanger discussed their lives and the places they were going. These places, both men admitted, were growing fewer at an alarming rate.

Stanger had lived his life on the edge of failure, but never actually failed. Now he was happy to follow a star, any star that would get him past the middle-aged crack-up he had seen so many people, including the sane and the successful, slide into. 'I guess I'm like the stretcher man in a battle. Stormed at by shot and shell, right? I scrape up the bodies, but somehow don't get hit. That's about it.'

'A year ago,' Hendry was saying, 'I had everything worked out. Then, I don't know why, it all fouled up. My problem is, how do I get the slate clean?'

Then Odell's call came through. Motionless, Hendry listened as Stanger took care of business. 'Sure, Mr Odell, I can get him to you . . . No, he's not in town right now, but say tomorrow I might be able to . . . It's your concern, of course, but fact is, my integrity's at stake to some degree, and I need to feel that our mutual friend is not walking into some slaughterhouse here . . . No, he won't know what he's heading into, and he'll be docile, believe me, but having got him this far, I can't hand the man over without some assurance . . . No, sure, Mr Odell, your personal word is all I wanted . . . Absolutely, sir. Now if you'll just let me know . . .' Eyebrows ironically raised at the silently observant Hendry, Stanger started writing. After hanging up he said, 'Get your boots on, cowboy. We're heading up country.'

When they arrived at the deserted lodge, the first thing Wardour and Holly did was strip and climb into bed. But nothing worked. Half an hour later, they sat in parallel disappointment. Aware that soon Odell and McDade would be returning, they were

272

unable to use the remaining time to retrieve an occasion which had simply, in spite of the seclusion and the moderate luxury of their new surroundings, not gone right. What had they been trying to prove? That the limitless surges of ecstasy they had discovered so easily before could be recaptured on demand elsewhere? But lacking ecstasy, Holly and Roderick seemed to have nothing to fall back on. Comfort, humour, nonchalant sensuality, were not enough. The intensity of their meetings demanded tidal waves of passion. Its failure to materialise at the New Hampshire farm threatened to throw a curse over their time there.

'After all,' Wardour said, 'if we can't make it now, when can we?' Then he corrected himself. 'Sorry, that was childish.'

Holly said: 'Maybe I am too aware of my father's presence. I've never found him conducive to easy living.'

'We both thought we were coming here for an affair,' Wardour said. 'But we both know that's not really why we're here at all.'

Holly pulled the bedclothes over her breasts. What was missing, she thought, was furtiveness. Here there was no risk, none of the danger that had flared around them in England. And somehow everything had flopped. 'Are you sorry you came?'

Holly saw, but ignored, the inadvertent joke. Wardour too.

'No,' he answered. 'As they say in the Michelin guides, worth the detour.'

'Yeah? We're about to find out.'

Holly had heard Barron Odell's car engine outside. Rapidly, trying to recompose their faces, they got dressed.

Their nervousness was not justified. Odell seemed tired, even a little intimidated, by the polish of Wardour's social manner. It had been a bad day at the offices of StormWind. Judgment day had come, and Odell's account of events in France had failed to satisfy the expressionless men around his conference table. Redmond, Brenner, and Martin, they had been friends, even heroes, to some of the men gathered in Odell's Boston office. To Odell, in his more maudlin phases, these men were the sons he had never had. Yet he had been forced to stonewall.

273

Fighting down his own embarrassment and regret, he had argued that the loss of the three men had been strictly in the line of business. Risks and rewards ran high in this game, and this time the risks had come top.

But the StormWind contract men wanted details. If the loss of a man, which might have been any one of them, was inevitable, the evidence had to be convincing. And Odell had little to offer. The involvement of his own daughter in the case only reinforced the appearance of a lousy, botched operation which could only do StormWind harm, and inspired in the operatives no confidence in any future assignment. Against his whole nature, Odell had to concede point after point, mollifying the assembly with promises of an imminent report, extensive and concealing nothing, which he claimed to have in progress at this moment. It was the worst day in Odell's entire career.

He collected McDade as arranged, but on the drive back from Boston, Odell remained bitterly silent. The Irishman and what he knew was Odell's only hope to stave off the collapse of his StormWind empire. A sense of doing things in the right order kept Odell from probing McDade too directly. Aware that, on his return, Roderick Wardour would be at the farm, Odell preferred as an opening tactic to explore the mind of the MP. But when he arrived, after a brief greeting, Odell excused himself to take a bath and think things over.

McDade had asked to be dropped off at his cabin. The reason he had given Odell was to freshen up, but his real purpose was to secrete the Colt automatic picked up at a downtown address in Boston given him by Eamonn Carthy. The storekeeper had shown no surprise at McDade's arrival, or any interest in his business there, other than to deliver the piece as requested by his contact in Ireland. The only unasked-for favour the gun-store-keeper did McDade, was to take him in the back room and strap the gun into a shoulder holster for him. It was to neither of their advantages for McDade to leave with the piece banging around in his coat pocket.

Wardour asked Odell: 'Would you mind if I went and renewed my acquaintance with McDade?'

Odell had no objection. Wardour looked to Holly for a reaction, but she pointedly gave none. Sure of the direction, wearing well-cut jeans and a leather jacket, Wardour made his way to McDade's cabin.

McDade still had his hand on the automatic as he saw Wardour approaching, his walk resembling a ceremonial slow march, languid, precise, his aquiline face fixed straight ahead. He looked like he meant business. The perfect target.

McDade was just not prepared enough. He thought about it, fully aware of the luck of getting the thing done at this opportune moment. But they would hear the shot at the lodge, and McDade had as yet no programme for his movements after the shot. And with every elegant stride towards him McDade's opportunity slipped further away. Cursing, he hid gun and holster inside his bedding, and waited for the MP to knock. Affecting surprise, he let Wardour into the cabin.

'I have instant coffee, that's about the strength of it. But you're welcome.'

'Thanks, no,' Wardour said. 'It's not really a social call. I'll come to the point. I need answers.'

'Answers,' McDade repeated meditatively.

'You returned Miss Odell and me to freedom. At first I felt grateful to you for that. Now it's all in the past, I find I'm not feeling quite so tolerant towards you.'

'Is that so?'

'Getting us out of France was not an act of heroism on your part. It was organised. And judging from the gunfire as we left, not everybody was invited to the party. I intend to establish the truth, and you're the man that knows it.'

'What if I don't play along?'

'We're guests here,' Wardour said, 'and we're obliged to behave accordingly. But I've already provided for this, and once we leave here I can have you run into the ground.'

'As you see from my appearance, I don't threaten easy.'

'In Ireland, I deal with people a hundred times more powerful than you. For a favour to them, I can reach you any time I like.'

'Has it occurred to you,' McDade asked, 'that you may be looking for information you won't want to hear?'

'I don't fear the truth,' Wardour replied. 'And whatever I have to do to get it, I'm prepared for.'

The idea flashed across McDade's mind of going for the gun, shooting Wardour on the spot, and claiming that there had been a struggle, ending in an accidental discharge. As a plan it was desperately weak, but McDade's reaction to menace was always to escalate. Then, simultaneously, he had a better idea. He feigned submission.

'OK, OK. Look, let me think it over. I've got a lot of stuff to clear from my head. I'll do what I can to help you.'

Wardour, the gentleman, took these words at face value and responded in kind. 'Excellent. I could be very useful to you, you know.'

'I'll try to deserve that,' McDade said.

Twenty-two

Holly thought, I'm sitting here at dinner, at this dinner which I have largely cooked myself, with a member of the British government, a probable IRA assassin, and my father, who as far as I can tell raises money for the Irish republican movement when he's not living out some menopausal Rambo fantasy. Then she thought, my God! The scene both frightened her and made her want to laugh, laugh nervously and in disbelief. Holly had come here because she wanted to spend a week sleeping with Wardour. She had no other reason. But Wardour, like her father and McDade, had other reasons, which lurked beneath the surface attempt at dinner-table talk. And how many of them would survive, she wondered, when these reasons came to the surface?

Wardour had retreated into his role of public man, an agreeable social medium. His conversation flowed in perfectly formed sentences, which said nothing, with great authority. McDade kept grinning, nervously baring those unpleasant teeth and compulsively cracking jokes that were unfunny. Barron Odell growled, grunted, frowned, laughed at things with no humour in them. With good editing, Holly thought, it would make a great one-act production in Hampstead or off-Broadway.

But Odell was successfully concealing his own dilemma: how to get through dinner without alerting McDade to what had to happen before that night was over. After his roasting at StormWind, Odell had vowed to get the truth from McDade, if he had to cajole or beat it from him. Today Odell had been forced to jettison his romanticism about the Irish struggle, because nobody worth employing would work for StormWind again, unless he went back with quick and persuasive answers. The bitterness of this prospect gave Odell the motivation to

277

wring McDade dry. He would walk him back to his cabin, and then the night could be just as long as the little Irishman wanted.

During the meal, the phone rang. Odell excused himself and went to his den. When he heard Bobby Stanger identifying himself, for a moment Odell could not even recall giving Stanger the number. But Stanger was saying that he had Hendry/ Edmunds, could bring him out now, since Odell had said that accommodation would be a possibility. Hendry, Stanger asserted, was inclined to be cooperative, but the next day who could tell? Stanger recommended they be OK'd to make the trip tonight.

After a moment's thought Odell agreed.

'A couple of guys coming out on business,' was Odell's laconic explanation of the call. 'I said I'd put them up for the night, but you don't need to worry. OK with you, Mr McDade, if one of them rooms with you?'

'Fine,' McDade said. 'Appreciate the company.'

Bedtime refused to come. They played simple card games, but as time passed Odell became increasingly excitable, fumbling cards, losing track of what had been played, jumpy at the slightest noise. The wait lasted just two hours. When the car pulled up Odell was demonstrating the action on one of his sporting rifles. He put the gun down and went outside. In the beam of an external lamp which threw a searchlight along the drive, Odell scrutinised the faces of the arrivals.

'Mr Hendry, I believe?'

'That's the name,' Hendry said.

'You have cost me a great deal of money and trouble.'

Hendry inhaled slowly, then audibly exhaled. That was all the answer he proposed to make. It had cost him, too. And he could take any amount of tough eyeballing, from Odell or anybody.

To avert bad chemistry, Stanger assured Odell, 'He'll do everything he can to help, Mr Odell. Let's keep cool and see what we can produce.'

'You're right,' Odell said. His shirt was letting in the night

278

chill. 'My hospitality is at your disposal. But let's don't forget we have business to do.'

Odell led them in. Stanger went first, and his appearance was what the three guests expected, someone they had never met before. It did nothing to prepare them for the sight of Ed Hendry.

Holly reacted first. The blood drained from her face and she said, 'I don't believe it.'

Wardour watched Holly's reaction with concern. But at first sight Hendry meant nothing to him. Odell, silently replacing the sporting rifle in the cabinet, was watching them all.

McDade maintained the blankly expectant expression of someone about to be introduced to a complete stranger. Hendry waited for Odell's unceremonious introduction, hearing McDade's surname for the first time, then nodded. But Hendry's shock stayed with him. Sean, here! It had to be a trap. But Hendry managed to remind himself that it was his own choice to be here now. If it was a trap, he had constructed it himself. Yet Odell had got his hands on McDade, had him here. If ever Hendry thought Odell dangerous, it was now.

McDade's genial composure gave away nothing. Hendry now, as so many times before, profited from all those years on parade grounds where the one thing the soldier learnt above all others was how to go on through *any* experience without so much as blinking. But Holly Odell, Hendry could not ignore. The instant he set eyes on her, he decided not to try. He met her eye and nodded. The nod carried the faintest trace of sardonic humour, even apology.

Holly whispered to Wardour that this was the kidnapper she had identified in London. Then she realised that Wardour had no idea what she was talking about. Sensitive at being out with Lucas Brand, she had kept quiet about the entire episode. Confused, Wardour felt the situation slipping out of his control. To Odell he said, 'I think we need an explanation.'

A little bewildered, in particular by the apparent unfamiliarity between Hendry and McDade, Odell moved to break things up. Quickly pulling on a coat, he whisked Hendry out. He asked

Holly to take Stanger to the den and give him a drink. Holly obliged and then disappeared.

Wardour followed her upstairs, to learn what her reaction to Hendry meant. McDade drummed his fingers till Odell returned, then met him at the door and made signs of turning in for the night. To his surprise, Odell wished him a pleasant rest, and made no attempt to detain him – surprise, because McDade knew that the big American had not brought him, or Hendry, here for social reasons. Yet Odell accepted McDade's goodnight amiably. As he walked back to the cabin the Irishman regretted that he hadn't killed Wardour earlier and got the hell out of this place, before all these other glitches came falling from the sky.

Hands under neck, Ed Hendry lay stretched out in the small bedroom to which Odell had shown him. Overtaken by a profound tiredness, he lacked the energy even to make the normal exploration of his new surroundings. So McDade's most immediate anxiety, that Hendry would discover the gun, did not materialise.

Hearing the door click, Hendry swung off the bed. He was in a state of readiness as McDade gently shut the door and entered, still half expecting to see a gun facing him.

'I thought you were dead,' Hendry began. He didn't seem glad that things were otherwise.

'And why would that be?'

'A lot of other people are.'

Hendry didn't know he was standing between McDade and the room where the gun was hidden. McDade moved forward, but Hendry was not letting him go anywhere. 'You little bastard.'

'Come on, Ed. We got to know each other pretty well in France. Let's move on.'

Hendry's eyes blazed. Weeks of suppressed fury erupted. 'There *was* a helicopter. You knew there was a fucking helicopter. And when it took off, you were in it. The MP and the girl too. I ought to kick your fucking head in.'

280

'As you see,' McDade answered with icy self-possession, 'somebody already tried.'

Just in case this remark contained mockery, Hendry lunged forward and all but lifted McDade from the floor. Ignoring the Irishman wincing at the blows, Hendry slammed fist after fist into his body and drove him back against the wall. Even when uninjured, McDade had no gift for unarmed combat; he protected himself as best he could. Hendry stood back, sweating and breathing hard, hands still clenched. Then he took McDade by the lapels and threw him into the room's one armchair. Hendry sat on a table, looming over the Irishman.

'When you let me go out into the night, you knew there were guns out there.' McDade shook his head. Spittle flying everywhere, Hendry roared into his face, 'You knew! Right?'

McDade looked down. He had blanked all this from his mind.

'Right?' Hendry screamed. He slapped McDade's face.

'No, I'd no idea.'

'The helicopter was a coincidence? It took off just when some machine guns got to work.' Hendry lowered his voice. 'Tell me again that you didn't know, and I'll tear you apart.'

'Why has Odell got you here, Ed?'

'In that gunfire that was meant to kill me, some of Odell's Americans died. I don't know how he got you here, but my guess is he's going to nail you to a tree.'

McDade tried not to look stunned, but the mental impact showed. This was the first he had heard of Odell's employees. And like Hendry earlier, McDade now had cause to realise that, beneath the bonhomie, Odell was a man to be feared. 'If that's the case,' McDade said, 'Odell should have known better than to get involved. If he played cowboys and Indians, that's his problem. Anyways, it was your job to keep him happy. You, the contact man. Did you screw it up, or were you working some little dodge of your own?'

'The only dodge I'm working, you little paddy shit, is I'm going to tell Odell everything, the way it happened. I was there, remember. So whatever lies you tell him, he can check at source.'

'I got him his daughter back. That's all he cares about. You seen the way he looks at her?'

'He'd have got her back anyway. But you were screwing us, and in the process Odell's boys got killed. And you weren't doing all that alone.'

'Leave the thinking to me, Ed. That's how it was, right? Let's keep it that way.'

As the two men, refusing to waste further energy, but watching each other with hostile suspicion, went to their separate rooms, Hendry said, 'I wasn't sure why I came here till I saw you. Now I know exactly why I'm here.'

McDade met Hendry's eye and quietly, contemptuously, spat.

At the lodge everybody lay awake.

Bobby Stanger was thinking of Odell's money, although adulterated with dummy notes, nestling in his safe back in Boston. His debt to Odell now worked off, he was free to leave the next morning. Hendry, it seemed, might be here a long time. But before he slid into a heavy, satisfied sleep, the nose for corruption by which he lived had persuaded Stanger, unless commanded otherwise, to stick around.

Whispering because of the thinness of the walls, Holly explained to Wardour the story of her previous encounter with Hendry. She was open about Lucas Brand. Defensively she said, 'I went out with him to shut him up', but still Wardour got jealous. With a muttered 'I see', he maintained a long silence. Coolly but reasonably Holly told him, 'I'm not going to sit on my ass in London waiting till the Honourable Roderick Wardour finds time to sneak away from the House and offer me a wonderful but rather brief bonk in a place of scenic beauty.'

Wardour accepted the reproof, then found himself unable to return to speculation about the course of events at the farm. Instead he let his body turn towards Holly. Gradually they refound each other. What had refused to work for them before, now softly, magically, happened.

As only a man can do whose system in life is never to trust

282

anyone or anything, Barron Odell exhaustively thought back over the confrontation between Hendry and McDade. It was remotely possible that the two men, as they had acted, if it was an act, had never met before. But for Hendry, the emissary, and McDade, the kidnapper, to have been so perfectly coordinated without any direct contact, argued an even bigger organisation behind the kidnap than Odell had suspected. This gave his already sharp appetite for the truth an unbearable edge. Days before any of the guests arrived Odell had had an ex-FBI friend come out here and wire the cabin. His intention had been to tape the conversations he planned to have there with McDade. But the fate that had thrown Hendry here at this time was an improvement. Every word they spoke would be recorded on a machine inside the roof, which early the next day Odell would retrieve and listen in to.

McDade slept least, but stayed in bed long after daylight. Inactivity came easily to him. He had spent much of his life staring at walls, waiting. He continued to lie there, the bulk of the automatic and its holster reassuring beneath him, long after he heard Hendry get up and go out. For McDade that day was going to be long enough. What he had learnt from Hendry clarified something he had never quite understood: why Odell had brought him here. A stark realism about himself made McDade admit that he was no social asset. The information about the slaughter of Odell's agents left him no choice but to execute his task, and run. The open space, the sheer distances, of America, intimidated him. Used to warrens of back streets and alleys down which to disappear, he could see no alternative to stealing one of the cars, maybe disabling the others, and hitting the nearest freeway. For that he would need time between killing Wardour and someone finding the body. An idea began to form. McDade shook himself out of bed.

Hendry walked a mile or two, working off the restlessness of someone physically fit but underexercised. Cattle grazed behind wire fences. Visually there was no temptation to explore the farm further. At the lodge Hendry found Stanger washing the dirt of yesterday's journey from his car.

Dispensing with small talk, Stanger asked, 'Who's the Irishman?'

'He put together the team for the kidnap. And he's a killer.'

'Yeah?'

Hendry was thinking of the mound of earth that covered Nevis's corpse at the chateau. 'Yeah.'

'Don't look now, but the killer's coming your way.'

McDade strolled up, with his shambling city-sidewalk gait. He gestured at the patchy blue sky. 'Morning, gents. The joys of living, eh?'

Hendry ignored him. Stanger nodded. McDade looked away, to deter conversation. The door opened. Wardour was on his way out. McDade stopped him and asked for a word. They stepped back into the house.

McDade said in a hushed tone, 'I'll tell you everything I can. But not here. There's a lake – '

'I know it.' Wardour had been given the tour, too.

'Sort of little landing stage for boats.'

'Yes.'

'Can we meet there in an hour?'

'All right.'

McDade went to say hello to the Odells, and swallow a quick breakfast. Wardour stayed outside. His patrician eye stared at Hendry now with the full knowledge that he was one of his ex-captors. Reading Wardour's gaze accurately, Hendry was both too proud and too unsure of his ground to seek a conciliation. He took Stanger's advice and went into the house.

'And how are you involved in all this?' Wardour asked.

'I'm just the hired help,' Stanger said. 'Messenger boy, that's all.'

Like to your house in London while you were being held captive, Stanger almost said, then thought better of it.

'You work for Mr Odell?'

'For anybody that pays me.'

'What kind of work?'

'Anything reasonable considered.'

'Could you drive me somewhere within the hour?'

284

Stanger pretended to think about it. 'Sure.'

'But don't tell anybody.'

Stanger nodded assent. Awkwardly, Wardour took out some American money. Stanger waved it aside. 'Wait till I earn it.'

Wardour returned indoors and beckoned Holly upstairs, where he told her that soon he would be gone from the house for a while. 'I'm going to the lake with McDade. He's going to tell me the truth behind the kidnap.'

'But he's a – '

Wardour placed fingers to her lips. 'It was me they were kidnapping, not you. This is the only way I can find out why.'

Wardour's mixture of enthusiasm and abruptness nullified Holly's objections. For herself, she would be happy never to hear about the kidnap again. She accepted that for Wardour it was different. She had just seen McDade downstairs. He had been easy-going, shy even. So she said nothing, realising that whatever she said, Wardour was going to brush it aside.

Odell disappeared for twenty minutes, to check something over at the farm buildings. In fact, he let himself into the cabin, released trapdoor and ladder, and in the roof cavity removed and replaced the tape reel. It ran for three hours on an electronic timer which Odell set for late in the evening. As host and master of ceremonies, he could make sure that Hendry and McDade were together in the cabin at the time that suited him.

On his way back along the narrow black-top road, Odell saw McDade walking to the cabin by the footpath that led through pasture between the two buildings. Both men waved, a greeting which declared that neither of them wanted to stop.

A nimble walker when he put his mind to it, McDade was at the lake half an hour later. The lake was a substantial stretch of water whose further shores could not be seen from where he stood. A few acres of woodland shielded the lakeside area from any fishing parties which put out. McDade used every second to refine the place and positioning, even the way he and Wardour would both be facing when the moment came. The trees would muffle the shot. The water would hide the body indefinitely. McDade was unsure what to do after disposing of Wardour.

Used to the rat-runs of cities, he was only now realising how difficult it would be to escape in the space of New Hampshire.

Wardour slipped away from the house. Let them see the car drive away, let them take offence if necessary, he was too close to the truth now to start justifying himself to people. Stanger was waiting as arranged. Off the black-top they took a side-track, down which cars regularly towed fishing dinghies. Stanger set his old Chevrolet in the dried-out ruts, and let the car almost freewheel in the direction of the lake, one of whose silver reaches crept into view round a plunging hillside.

'Apart from the ride,' Stanger said, 'how do you want to use me?'

'I don't want McDade to see you. Do you mind if I drive?'

Stanger stopped the car, and they changed over. Stanger began to point out the controls, but Wardour said, 'Oh, I'll master it. What I need is for you to keep out of sight. I want to let you out somewhere in those trees before I meet McDade.'

'Can do.' The Chevvy was roomy. Stanger slid down.

'Are you armed?'

From his crumpled posture Stanger said, 'Never travel without it.'

This was not the right answer. Wardour said: 'Leave it. You're there in case McDade tries anything funny. But I don't want him killed.'

'The gun's in the trunk,' Stanger said. 'You're the boss.'

As the dirt road entered the treeline, Wardour idled the car for Stanger to get out and take cover. A few more bumpy yards, and the water gleamed through the trees. McDade had hidden when he heard a car, but seeing Wardour inside, apparently alone, the Irishman blessed his fortune. In spite of the work he was about to do, his face broke into an irrepressible grin. His escape problem was solved. Wardour himself had delivered the getaway vehicle, brought it to the spot. McDade already had money and passport with him. This was no accident – with a hostile house-partner like Hendry, McDade had left nothing of value lying around. So, luck of the devil, he was ready to go.

286

Wardour stopped short of the jetty on a patch of ground worn hard by automobile wheels. McDade showed himself.

'I expected you on foot,' he commented.

'I don't walk when I can avoid it.'

'Nice motor.' McDade was carefully looking it over.

'Let's get on.'

McDade suggested a direction. He had already selected the spot where he would strip his lower half, wade into the shallows, and drag Wardour's body under a tangle of tree roots, to pin it there for a very long time. But first he had to gain the MP's confidence by giving him some of what he wanted. A gift before dying.

'For starters,' McDade said, 'let me tell you what I don't know. I don't know why they wanted to fix you. For me it was a job, I didn't care about the reasons.'

Impatient, Wardour demanded: 'They? Who are they?'

'My contact was a Swiss. Don't ask me his name. I don't know it. As for who was behind him – ' McDade shrugged.

'What was the kidnap all about?'

'There I can help. The original idea was for us to grab you, then pass you on. The young lady of course was extra. We weren't expecting her. Your private life got tangled up in this.'

Wardour was frostily disdainful. 'How did you know where to meet me?'

'We were told. Think about it, the information had to come from you, somewhere way back.'

Sweetman, Wardour thought, as he had a number of times. But deliberate, or unintentional? And even if deliberate, it could not be Jonah alone.

'Anyways, our brief was to lift you, dope you, and pass you on. Then the instructions were cancelled. So we decided to return you, at a price. To cover expenses.'

'But as I understood it,' Wardour said, 'the ransom was never paid. You flew us out before. Why did you do that?'

'I reckoned a lot of people – maybe me, maybe you – might get killed in the process. I saw I could do myself a lot more good if I set up a rescue.'

287

'From that place in France you organised a helicopter, a boat, and people waiting for us in Ireland. How?'

'Gift of the gab,' McDade said.

'You can't have done it alone. Who was behind it?'

'The same people.'

'The Swiss you mentioned?'

'Uh – huh.'

'The same people that wanted to destroy me helped you get me back?'

'That's about the strength of it.'

'Why?'

'Maybe it had got too hot for them.'

'As we left, there was a lot of gunfire. Why?'

'That, Mr Wardour, was to take out the awkward bastards. So is this.'

In a swift movement which he had practised many times McDade drew the automatic from inside his coat.

Wardour looked at the gun without fear. 'Don't be a bloody fool.'

'Over there. Now,' McDade ordered.

Wardour began to shake. But he still managed to say, 'You can kill me, but you're bloody well not going to order me about.'

'Turn round.'

'You're not in Belfast now, you bloody little coward. Look at your victim's face for once.'

McDade's bruised features traced a wry smile, the blood in his veins as cold as a subterranean river. The Englishman was thinking he could face him down. McDade had no use for heroics. They were near enough where he had planned. He thumbed the safety and raised the pistol to fire.

Wardour stared frantically as the barrel came level with his chest. His eyes rolled wildly in a search for somewhere to run, to hide, for some protection. Where was Stanger? Wardour shook uncontrollably. Even his voice was reedy, broken now. 'Look, what do you want? I can be useful to you.'

'You will be,' McDade said.

He steadied the pistol grip with his left hand. His skinny

index finger squeezed the trigger. The crack of the shot rang out over the grey water.

Wardour clenched his eyes and his jaw tight. He hugged himself with arms that quaked. Deep shuddering waves racked his body. But as the gunshot echo died away, Wardour realised he was still there. For a moment he thought McDade had bungled it, all Wardour knew was that he was still standing, unaware of physical pain or shock. As he opened his eyes again, tremors of nervous release continued to pulse through him. But he felt no pain.

Wardour recoiled at the sight of blood on his jacket. He had been hit after all. McDade lay in the lakeside mud. The bullet that had thrown him there had jetted blood over Wardour's clothing. Wardour had seen dead bodies before, bodies that had suffered violent deaths. But he superstitiously backed away from the dead Irishman.

Then Stanger came out of the trees. The gun in his hand told Wardour that he had lied, he had been armed all along. Doing his job. It was just as well.

Stanger looked dazed, almost in shock himself. Without a word he drew out the ammunition clip. Wardour stared in mute puzzlement as he grasped Stanger's message. Not a solitary shell had gone. The clip was still full.

Twenty-three

In his den, Barron Odell played the tape which he had taken from McDade's cabin. He was satisfied to find his suspicions confirmed. Their pretence at never having met had been a consummate performance. If anything, Odell admired it. It showed the right sort of nerve. The rest of the tape was equally interesting. The more he heard of McDade, the less Odell liked him. He ran the tape repeatedly, till the dialogue was etched in his mind and he felt he could take it up where Hendry had left off. When they had met in Boston on opposite sides of the kidnap, Hendry had impressed Odell. He continued to impress him now. For McDade, on the other hand, Odell's feelings had been transformed. Whatever services McDade had rendered the cause of Irish unity, dear though it was to Odell's heart, made little impact once his business interests and his personal standing were under threat. Sentiment gave way to a cold destructiveness that fed through every fibre of his being. Eventually Odell left his den and went to seek coffee and company.

The house was empty.

Stanger picked up the gun, which McDade's fall had caused to spin some yards away. Stanger hurled it out, parallel to the lake's surface, to sink in deeper water.

Wardour protested, 'Why?'

'You want anybody to know you were here with that guy?'

No other option had occurred to Wardour. He considered.

Stanger continued, 'That was a rifle shot. Maybe a hunting accident. Not our problem. You had motive to kill McDade. But I'm your alibi. We were nowhere near here. Never even saw the guy. Let's get the car moved fast. And take that jacket off. We'll wrap it in the trunk of my car. I'll lose it later.'

'Why don't I just tell the truth?' Wardour asked.

'Because you don't know what it is,' Stanger said. 'And it always pays to have insurance.'

Odell's strategy was simple. Hendry was the hammer, McDade the nail.

Odell drove across the farm. Before he reached the cabin he met Dave Sherry, his manager. Briefly they talked business. Odell was a tolerant boss, so long as the accounts tallied.

'See anybody around?' he asked Sherry.

'Holly borrowed the jeep. I guessed you knew.'

Odell didn't, but nodded. He had noted the absence of Stanger's car. 'Anybody in the cabin?'

'Not that I know of.'

'Some house party,' Odell said. 'Breakfast, then everybody gets the hell out.'

'Sounds like hunters in the woods.'

'Yeah?'

'I was in the south pasture. Heard a shot.'

'Somebody after deer?'

'Guess so.'

'OK, Dave. Have a good day.'

'You too, Mr Odell.'

Odell knocked at the cabin. No response. He used his own key, but found the door unlocked. The low brick building was empty. Odell rattled his fingers tetchily against the nearest surface. He wondered if Hendry's verbal attack had scared the Irishman away, forced him to run. Displeased at this possibility, Odell drew the quick shallow breaths of a man with a problem whose solution lay outside his own control. The stony faces of the men around the table at StormWind kept returning to haunt him.

Roderick Wardour had seen dead bodies, but never this close, and never when he had believed till a second before that the body was meant to be his. Hysterical spasms shook his limbs, and he slowly became aware that his pants were wet. Stanger turned him away from the sight of McDade. For some minutes Wardour was willing to let the American shepherd him along.

Then, as his rational self began to recover, Wardour said, 'We have to get away from here.'

Stanger was uncompromising. 'No, we stay out here to establish credibility, that we have nothing to hide.'

'That shot was no accident,' Wardour said.

'Forget it. You don't know about it.'

'Then why are we here?'

'You wanted to see over the place. I drove. Simple. Stick to it.'

'You don't seem to understand,' Wardour said. 'There were things only McDade could tell me. Now I'll never know.'

'Have you thought why McDade wanted to kill you? This was the guy who saved your bacon. Now he comes all the way to New Hampshire to stiff you. Why?'

Wardour had asked himself the same. 'I'll never understand that.'

Stanger said: 'Some cop is going to think you got McDade to that place so a third party could line up a shot. And you brought me along just to say you had nothing to do with it. And for all I know, that's exactly the way I *was* being used.'

'You suspect me?' Wardour said.

'No, I don't. But if I was somebody else I would.'

'What, then?'

'Play it my way,' Stanger said.

Everybody had melted away. There was something Odell always thought of as his own private law: according to that law, the first abnormal fact he encountered would set him right on the path to the solution.

Prowling the lodge, Odell discovered that his Ruger hunting rifle was missing. Although no sportsman, he liked to have good shooting and fishing equipment to hand for when he entertained better qualified guests. Technological finesse more than half made up for his own lack of prowess.

The case was unlocked, the ammunition box too. The keys

292

were on the bureau, where Odell always left them when he was in residence. Dave Sherry had mentioned something about a shot. Odell tried to disregard it, but for him innocent explanations came at the end of a long line. As he took the dirt track lakewards, rain began to fall. Within minutes visibility was reduced to yards. Half a mile on Odell recognised the farm jeep, a Cherokee Pioneer 4-door, heading towards him on the single track. He sounded his horn and pulled half onto the grass. As the jeep passed, Odell waved to its occupants – Holly and Ed Hendry, Holly driving. There was no point stopping in the downpour. Seeing no let-up in the weather, Odell manoeuvred the car round and followed them.

They all arrived together. As they got out in the triple garage, Odell saw that Hendry's clothes were soaked, Holly's not at all. He made no comment, but tried to get them inside for drinks, coffee, cookies, whatever anybody wanted. But Hendry needed a change of clothes. Odell ordered Holly into the dry, and offered to take Hendry to the cabin in his own car.

Odell wanted to look inside the jeep for his missing rifle, but Holly was in no hurry to leave the garage. Odell did not want to panic her, to insist on taking Hendry back. If that happened, Odell would never know about the rifle. And he would lose his chance with Hendry. This way, he expected the rifle to reappear in its case, since Holly would not know he had noticed its absence. Then Odell would know who had put it there.

In the car he asked Hendry, 'What happened to our Irish friend?'

Hendry claimed not to have seen McDade.

'You know,' Odell said, 'it amazes me that the two of you, working for the same organisation, never met.'

Hendry had a furtiveness about him which could not be accounted for just by his miserably wet condition. 'How do you know we never met?'

'You acted that way last night. Are you now saying you were more than just an intermediary?'

'Yes, I admit it,' Hendry said.

Odell did not want to reveal the tape he had in his possession, but its contents gave him the confidence to say, 'Look, I'll come clean. I don't trust the little Irish bastard. My feeling is that you don't either. I think you can help me.'

There was still the question of the vanished rifle. But for the moment Odell was satisfied when Hendry agreed. He followed Hendry into the cabin. While the rain beat down outside, and Hendry got changed, Odell plied him with questions. He found the Englishman surprisingly willing to talk.

Hendry emerged from the bedroom in dry clothes, saying, 'McDade betrayed me and the others. I don't owe him anything.'

'Except revenge?' Odell liked nothing better than stoking up a fight.

Hendry answered, 'Sometimes revenge is all you have left.'

Odell said, 'I last saw McDade walking over here a couple of hours ago.'

It was a lead, but Hendry couldn't, or wouldn't, take it. 'I haven't seen him since he left your house.'

Odell feigned indifference and suggested going over to the lodge. As they drove back he said, 'I was surprised to see you and Holly together.'

'Why's that?' Hendry asked.

'You kept her tied up for a week. And if I've learnt one thing about my daughter, it's that she doesn't have a forgiving nature.'

Ill at ease with the language of personal relationships, Hendry said, 'We've talked it through.'

'Well, maybe she's matured. She always used to yell first and talk later.'

'She didn't yell,' Hendry said.

'No? Listen, Mr Hendry. I trust you and I want you to trust me. My years of experience have taught me when a man is biting something back. Every time I mention Holly, you bite back. Why?'

With great presence of mind, Hendry avoided mentioning the events of that afternoon by explaining how Holly had identified him by voice in a London discotheque. The experience, he said, had left him unnerved by her. Odell was highly amused.

'You don't say. You know, I always said she should become a cop.' He brought the car to a halt. 'Maybe I said it too many times. But I was right.'

Some time later, Wardour and Stanger returned to the lodge. A collective unease hung over the open-plan sitting room, with its large stone chimney-piece, pictures of early New England, and hunting trophies installed by the decor consultants. Odell had felt himself to be the master of events, but suddenly had lost the initiative, as if the other four shared a secret from which he was excluded. Unsure who to address his words to, he burst out, 'Can we please discuss what's happened to Mr McDade?'

Hendry was prompt. 'From what you said, you were the last to see him.'

Odell had verified that time as nearly as possible. 'Anything between a quarter to nine and nine-fifteen – for God's sake somebody must have seen him. A man doesn't vanish.' But as Odell looked from one to the other they all indicated with blank faces or shakes of the head that they couldn't help.

Wardour made a suggestion. 'McDade knew I was going to put a lot of pressure on him. Perhaps he decided to leave.'

Stanger met the MP's eye fleetingly, enough to signal that this was a smart idea and nice delivery.

Odell refused to be pacified. 'OK, next question. A rifle plus several rounds of ammunition has been taken from the case over there.'

'Was it broken into?' Wardour asked.

'It was left open. I trust my guests.'

The ensuing silence was accusatory.

Stanger said: 'Mr Odell, your two questions may be one question. How about, McDade took the rifle?'

Odell reacted aggressively. 'You think I hadn't considered that? I tell you, I saw McDade. He had no rifle.'

Hendry asked: 'For how long did you see him, and how close?'

'OK,' Odell admitted, 'a few seconds, and maybe fifty yards away. So what are you saying?'

'He could have seen you first, dropped the rifle, then gone back for it,' Hendry said.

'But why? Why any of it?'

'When two things disappear simultaneously,' Stanger said, 'often they disappear in company.'

Odell demanded: 'You reckon what, his target is . . . *us*?'

Holly spoke for the first time. 'What reason could he have for killing us?'

'Each of you,' Stanger said, 'seems to have represented some kind of threat to McDade.' Stanger had used the wrong tense. His words suggested that he knew McDade was no longer alive. Three pairs of eyes remained fixed on objects in the room, careful not to meet. Odell appeared not to have noticed.

Stanger, staying cool, added, 'While he was here. Maybe that was why he left.'

Odell said: 'McDade knew exactly what he was coming into.'

Hendry said: 'He didn't know about me.'

'You figure he ran from you?'

'Could be.'

'With a hunting rifle?'

'Maybe he's just gone out to shoot something,' Stanger suggested.

'I'd have lent him the gun,' Odell said. 'I'd have gone with him myself. Why should he steal it?'

'He's got his own way of doing things,' Hendry commented.

'I think we go look for him,' Odell replied. 'If he's on my property with a gun, I want to know. If he's gone, I report the theft to the police.'

'On the assumption that he's dangerous,' Wardour said. 'I'd rather not go in search of him. After all, do we really care where he is?'

'I don't want to put anybody on the line,' Odell told them, 'but I for one don't intend to sit here and wait for him.'

He unpacked another rifle from the case. Stanger offered to drive, Hendry shifted in his chair, then got up. Holly and Wardour, without any overt communication, were clearly deter-

296

mined to be alone together as soon as possible. Pausing only to check that the rain had slackened, the three men left.

Holly said: 'Could you use a drink?'

Wardour nodded. She poured them both scotch. Getting ice in the kitchen, she called, 'I thought you were going to meet McDade.'

'Yes, I was.'

'And?'

Holly returned with the ice. Wardour ignored her question. 'I was surprised to hear that you came back with Hendry. I thought he was the man you recognised in the nightclub.'

'I was driving back in the rain. I met him and gave him a lift.'

'Where had he been?'

'You mean where had *I* been.'

'Whichever.'

'Is McDade dead?' Holly asked.

'I suppose it's possible,' Wardour answered.

'If he is, how do we feel?'

'Meaning what?'

Holly said, 'Is it such a bad thing? Wasn't he just a loathsome little rat, in the end?'

'He knew a lot of things I can't find out from anywhere else.'

'Can't you just let it all go?'

'Your father needs McDade too.'

'Don't make my father's problems yours. Once you do that, you'll never get out from under.'

'Where *did* you go?' Wardour asked.

'McDade's a murderer, isn't he?'

Avoiding her eye, Wardour said, 'Well, technically you can say that. But Hendry was a soldier, and has no doubt done his share of killing. But a paratrooper's a machine who kills to order. At least people like McDade believe they're taking life for a cause.'

'Don't give me this bullshit about Ireland,' Holly said. 'I hear enough of that from my father. When you said you were meeting

McDade, I was afraid for you. I saw somebody I loved being killed again.'

His voice soft with emotion, Wardour asked, 'Where were you?'

'I know this place fairly well. There's another road across the ridge,' Holly pointed, 'which brings you to a different branch of the lake. I don't know why I went there. I just couldn't stay here. That man was *evil*.'

His voice now a grave whisper, Wardour asked, 'What did you see?'

Holly stared at the ice in her scotch. 'Why did he want to kill you?'

'I don't know.'

'But he was about to.'

Wardour looked at Holly with the steady gaze of someone watching as layers of age-brown varnish on a picture peel away to reveal the fresh, original colours beneath. Only his voice, awe-struck and tremulous, revealed the turmoil inside him. 'How did you know what was going on?'

Holly remained matter-of-fact. 'I knew you had fixed a private meeting with McDade. I didn't think any more about that. I'd gone over to the cabin to talk to him about my father. I intended to warn him off – enjoy his holiday, then go home and keep out of my father's life.'

'Or else – '

'Good question.'

'Department of Empty Threats,' Wardour said.

Holly admitted ruefully, 'I guess. Anyway, I went on foot. McDade can't have seen or heard me coming, because I looked in a side window and saw him with a gun – an automatic. He was checking it over and practising with it. I got out of sight of the cabin. I thought I might get back here and warn you. I ran, but you'd gone. I took one of Dad's rifles and drove round the head of the lake. Nobody saw me.'

'From your position, you can only have seen the gun,' Wardour said. 'You can't have known if he was going to use it.'

'I didn't have time to agonise.'

'Well, you were right. I've never been so scared. Where did you learn to shoot?'

'Years ago I used to go target shooting. It's one of those parts of my life that seems like it was somebody else now. But once you've handled guns, you don't forget.'

'What did you do with the gun?'

'It's upstairs.'

'*Upstairs!*'

'You have a better idea?'

'Oh my God,' Wardour protested. 'I don't have any ideas. But of all the stupid places – '

Holly was more controlled than he had ever seen her. 'Not necessarily.'

'You realise that the police have to be dragged into this. And whatever story we all tell, they'll crack it wide open. And meanwhile we're stuck here, we could be arrested and charged with murder! I don't believe this.'

'Thanks,' Holly said. 'It could have been your body lying by the lake, right now. But at least your career wouldn't have suffered.'

Embarrassed that she knew what he was thinking, Wardour said hurriedly, 'You saved my life, and I'll always be grateful for that. But we have to avoid further complications.'

'I think it's my problem, don't you?'

Ashamed, Wardour said: 'Look, once I tell my side of the story, you'll be out of trouble.'

'Oh sure, I just happened to be there with a rifle. What happened to McDade's gun?'

Shutting his eyes in despair, Wardour recalled what Stanger had done. *Why* had he done that? Once different people had different good ideas, everybody got screwed up. 'We threw it away.'

'*We?*'

'Stanger was there.'

From her hiding place across the arm of the lake, Holly had not seen Stanger. She pondered on this complication.

Wardour asked, 'At what point did you meet Hendry?'

'On my way back. At least that was no lie. He'd gone for some exercise. He seems none too comfortable here.'

'How much does he know?'

'That depends how intelligent he is.'

'Meaning what?'

'I said I'd forget the past if he agreed he'd been with me all the time we'd been out of the house, and back me whatever I said. He agreed.'

'You think he worked out the rest?'

'I told him I had a gun in the car and might need his help to hide it. As it happened, I didn't.'

'You took a hell of a risk.'

'I'm not so sure. He hated McDade. You only had to be in the room with them for ten seconds to feel it. Hendry's afraid of the police in England. I think he'll come across.'

'You sound like your father,' Wardour observed drily.

'The style rubs off.'

'Meanwhile, he's out there looking for his missing rifle. Or did you have an idea about that too?'

'Let's put it back.'

'Put it back,' Wardour repeated, as if nothing could be more normal.

'My father has to be brought in on this.'

'He's a respected citizen – '

'Who plays both sides of the fence.'

'What you're proposing,' Wardour said, 'is a kind of package alibi.'

'Package alibi. That's exactly it. Well said.'

Wardour suppressed his foreboding. Holly's eyes were bright, manic. The last thing she needed on a day like this was to feel isolated or undermined. Until the others returned from their search, the least Wardour could do was let Holly cling to her fragments of hope.

'What do you say, Mr Stanger, we try the lake?'

'Whatever you think,' Stanger answered. He felt that Odell

300

kept probing him and tried to act his way out of the older man's suspicion.

'Let's go to where you and Mr Wardour say you were.'

Stanger let the hint of disbelief pass. They had left McDade's body near the boat jetty. Now Stanger stopped some distance away from it, where the usable track ran out. The three men got out of the car to confront a tract of swampy ground leading to the reed-infested lakeside, over which a raw wind was now blowing.

'Strange place to come,' Odell grunted. He slotted a round into the breech of his rifle.

'The road stopped, so we did,' Stanger said.

'OK, let's take a look.'

Odell had dressed the part, in hunting cap and boots and quilted jacket. Stanger and Hendry, left to their own devices, wore more everyday clothes and were already feeling the cold. They let Odell wander away, hunched and intense, clutching the rifle, like a city vacationer in pursuit of duck or deer.

Hendry muttered, 'Do you know where he is?'

That Hendry had killed McDade was a possibility Stanger had not dismissed. Unsure how to take the question, he nodded affirmative.

'Is the idea that we find him, or not?'

As far as Stanger could see, the only thing they had on their side was time. 'Better not.'

'OK,' Hendry said. 'Take me to where he is.' Hendry had no wish to name McDade, no sentimental respect for his remains.

Stanger whispered, 'Why?'

'To make sure we don't see him. We walk right by and don't see him. And with luck Davy Crockett over there will be looking somewhere else.'

Odell gestured with the rifle. He called, 'Hey, come on. Let's fan out a little.' Hendry winced as he saw how near Odell's finger was to the trigger.

The swamp gave way to scrub, then woodland. 'In there,' Stanger said. 'Near the landing stage.'

301

Hendry joined Odell for a minute. 'You think we're looking for a dead body?'

'Starts to feel that way,' Odell said.

'Suicide,' Hendry said. 'Maybe.'

Odell's pinhead eyes were hard in his wind-reddened face. 'I covered all the possibilities. Not one of them stands out.'

Stanger had gone in front. Hendry indicated a section of the wood. Odell directed him to explore it. In the trees it was less easy to see who went where. After a few minutes Hendry caught Stanger up.

'Here?'

'Yeah, here somewhere.' Stanger was unsure. He was no countryman. Tracks in the mud meant nothing to him. Once the jetty, the only real landmark, was in view, there were not many spots where McDade's body could be. Stanger looked and acted bewildered. Hendry's face silently asked all the questions. Also without speaking, Stanger conveyed that he had no answers. 'It has to be here,' he said. 'This was the place.'

'The dead don't walk,' Hendry said.

Odell, who suspected the two men of excluding him from a shared secret, had waited for them to join up, precisely as they had done. He was now heading towards them. They had pulled exactly the ruse he would have pulled himself, and he took great satisfaction in exploiting it. Odell took the apprehension on their faces as a reaction to his own ingenuity. But before any of them could speak, their heads swung towards a noise of movement in the trees.

A scream like a chainsaw tore through the wood, but its origin was human. Every hair on their bodies writhed as the three men saw Sean McDade claw his way towards them. His face was a tortured death-mask. He held one hand clamped to the centre of a giant bloodstain that had spread through his clothes. In fright and fear, Odell levelled the rifle at McDade's anguished, advancing figure. At the sight of the weapon, McDade's face, smeared with soil and blood, begged incoherently for mercy. But then, as surely as if Odell had put a bullet into him point-

302

blank, McDade's legs buckled under him, and his body once again hit the ground.

This time he would not get up. But the three men remained still for some time. Like some savage apparition from another world, McDade had sent pure terror through each of them.

Twenty-four

It was dark by the time Odell, followed by Stanger, reappeared at the lodge. Holly, Hendry and Wardour had toyed with food and drink while they waited in conspiratorial silence for news from the hospital.

Odell sank into a chair, sighed and stared about the room, uncertain whether he had just left behind a solution or an even bigger problem. Grimacing wryly, Stanger had already nodded confirmation that, against all the odds, the medical team had pulled McDade through.

'One lung is out of action,' Odell told them, 'and he's lost a lot of blood. But they stabilised him. Looks like he'll live.'

'Good news,' Hendry said, with blank face and a total absence of inflexion.

Wardour looked at Holly, who was biting her lip. The day's events had drained everybody. Wardour, who had always been good at such moments, took control. 'When do we have to face the police, and what do we tell them? May I suggest – '

Anger lurking dangerously behind his weariness, Odell growled, 'Would somebody get me a drink? Yeah,' he said as Holly held up the whisky decanter. 'Right, now I've got my drink, let me tell you, Mr Member of Parliament and all you other would-be movie actors, everything goes through me from now on. Put your cards on the table, or go. What bothers me about McDade is not that he was nearly killed, but that it happened on my property, and one of you did it with a firearm belonging to me. So please, no more crap.'

Wardour said, 'The weapon appears to have returned.'

Odell's eyes moved slowly to the gun case. He took the sight more calmly than his normal demeanour would have suggested. Then he studied the other four people in the room. 'If anybody wants to leave, now's the time.'

'Or what?' Hendry asked.

'Or don't complain afterwards.'

Nobody left.

'OK,' Odell said. 'If anybody in this room wants me to lie for them, they better tell me the truth fast.'

'I shot McDade.' Holly's lips were the one place from which Odell had not expected to hear these words.

Ghost-voiced, he asked, 'Why?'

'McDade was about to kill me,' Wardour said.

'If McDade makes it, what's he likely to say to the police?' Odell asked. 'Because as soon as he's talking, that's who he's talking to.'

'He'll know nothing,' Wardour said. 'He'll never tell them what really happened.'

'And the weapon?' Odell asked.

'The gun's in the lake,' Stanger said. 'They won't find it if they don't look for it.'

A hard-edged silence gripped the room. Four people were now completely in the snare of Odell's power. In a tone that brooked no further discussion he outlined his own solution.

'OK, how do we get out from under this? For the whole time McDade was away from the house, we alibi each other. Nobody was with him, nobody went anywhere near that place while he was there. If McDade doesn't press it, the file will just show an unexplained accident. Hell, the world's full of them.'

At Langley, unknown to him, the file on Odell was still very much alive.

In West Germany, only days before, two American servicemen had accepted a ride in a car belonging to a British soldier, and died in the subsequent explosion. Reacting in its usual way when a terror attack went wrong, the IRA neither confirmed nor denied its responsibility, but stated its regret that these things had to happen.

In the USA the outcry led to pressure on those authorities charged with monitoring the US–IRA connection, to show proof that they were doing something to earn the taxpayers' money.

The names thrown out by the computer included that of Barron Odell.

Coincidentally, the StormWind affair had also drawn the attention of the CIA. Langley's interest in Odell was constant and generally favourable, since the interventions he organised often struck within Central American or Middle Eastern territories with which Washington's relations were sensitive. In addition, the CIA had, on occasion, commissioned Odell's services themselves. Although the kidnap of Holly Odell was a mystery already sinking beneath the dead leaves of time, the Irish connection remained sensitive. So when a disgruntled ex-marine, one of those at StormWind's latest troubled meeting, described to his CIA contact both the fiasco which had overtaken Odell's men in France, and the resultant rocky condition of the StormWind organisation, the file on Odell went into spasm again. On top of which Scotland Yard, perhaps to make up for their scant hospitality to the CIA's Dick Ginistrelli, wired Langley details of how Wardour and Holly had been brought out through Ireland, courtesy of the Irish Republican Army's public relations section.

It was known that Odell had property in New Hampshire, so the Sherwood County police were given a watching brief to report on Odell's movements in the area. A perfunctory instruction not expected to yield anything, this bore rapid fruit in the form of a surprise call from Bouverie, New Hampshire, to CIA Langley, giving notification that Odell had reported an apparent hunting accident on his property, the victim of which was Irish. Everything they had against Odell was circumstantial. And as every policeman and some wronged citizens know, circumstantial evidence can prove Santa Claus to be the Boston Strangler. But what if he *is*?

The complications of McDade being alive were almost as bad as the complications of him being dead. The important thing was to gain access to the Irishman as soon as he recovered sufficiently to understand what was being said to him. But enquiries to the Bouverie hospital the next day received the answer that McDade was still seriously ill. There was no immediate prospect of seeing him. On the phone, Odell sensed in the doctor's replies an evasiveness which was not simply concern for the patient. Odell knew a run-around when he was being given it.

The next day, Odell went to the hospital. When the receptionist paged McDade's doctor, Odell thought he detected a tremor of apprehension in the woman's face. When the young male doctor arrived, Odell knew there was something going on: the message was the same, McDade could not be disturbed.

'I reported the accident to the police,' Odell said. 'Have they been here?'

'The police have to wait too, Mr McDade's very sick.'

'He's a close personal friend. Can I just see him?'

'I'm afraid not.'

Odell was about to protest – he would be paying the bills, so he was entitled, goddammit. Then he realised that he himself was the problem. On this stroke of intuition, he gave surly thanks and went out. Unwilling to leave the premises, he sat in his car for some time. He had expected the police to be crawling all over the farm by now. His guests had spent many hours fine-tuning their stories for the inevitable enquiries. But not one cop had appeared. Yet every so often Odell had the feeling he was colliding with a thick glass wall.

Two men who might have been medical consultants appeared in the hospital's main entrance. Well groomed, discreetly suited anonymous men, they talked for a minute, then went to a car and drove away. Odell's bladder, unreliable at the best of times, loosened alarmingly with the excitement of what had just been revealed to him. The younger of the two men had been Odell's fellow-passenger on a flight to London some weeks ago. This young wop Ginistrelli was CIA. Or Barron Odell was Whoopi Goldberg.

Barely considering how they had come to be here, Odell strode back through the car park and re-entered the hospital. After a quick visit to relieve himself, he went to a public phone and called the farm.

'Hol, put Rod on.' Odell drummed his fingers, waiting. 'Mr Wardour, can you get into Bouverie immediately and meet me in front of the hospital. Bring Mr Hendry too.'

Half an hour later they arrived. Stanger had driven them in. Odell waved him on, and took the two Englishmen to his car. They got inside.

'Looks like the CIA, or *somebody*, are in on this,' he told them. 'They're crowding me out. If we want to get to McDade, my guess is it has to be soon, and it has to be you. Any suggestions?'

'Would they be impressed by a member of Her Majesty's government?' Wardour asked diffidently. 'I don't mind trying.'

Hendry had no wish to enter a hospital again so soon after Lisa's accident, but he said, 'I can do accents. I'll play an Irishman if it'll achieve anything.'

'You could be a relative of McDade,' Wardour suggested.

'Before you get in the room,' Odell said, 'let's think what you do when you get there.'

Minutes later, Wardour and Hendry were looking at the receptionist's patient, slightly strained face. Hendry gave her a quiet, sincere smile and in a tolerable southern Irish accent said, 'My cousin Sean McDade's a patient here, I believe.'

Without replying, the receptionist looked from Hendry to Wardour, who smiled and said, 'My name is Roderick Wardour, I'm a minister in the British government. We're here to see Mr McDade.'

'He's not being allowed visitors yet.'

'That's not what I was told. Who's the doctor dealing with this case?'

'Dr Edelstein, but – '

'Can you find him for me?'

Eager to get rid of a problem, the receptionist paged the doctor. Five minutes later Edelstein appeared.

'Doctor, these two men – ' the receptionist began.

Wardour introduced himself. 'We're here to see Mr McDade. It's been arranged.'

'That's out of the question.'

308

'We're expecting to meet Mr Ginistrelli here.' The gamble worked. Edelstein knew the name. Lowering his voice, Wardour pressed the point. 'Mr Ginistrelli of the CIA. Has he arrived yet? Do you know him?'

Edelstein's eyes roved nervously. 'Yes, yes. Who did you say you were again?'

Wardour flashed his House of Commons parking permit. 'Mr Ginistrelli was specific about meeting us here.'

Edelstein said, 'Look . . . uh . . . the person you've just named was here. But he left. Maybe an hour ago. He didn't say anything – '

Wardour interrupted. 'Why should he? We're here to identify Mr McDade. That's why I've brought his cousin.'

'How do you do, sir,' Hendry said, bobbing his head respectfully to Edelstein.

'It's a political matter. You understand,' Wardour said. 'If you have any suspicions about our visit, we don't object to being searched.'

Edelstein's good manners and a sense of his professional status took over. Anyway, he hadn't liked the way that those CIA men had hustled him. 'He's on a couple of drips, and he's very weak,' he said. 'But you might get a few minutes. It's along here.'

He led the Englishmen down a corridor. After ascertaining that McDade was conscious and not distressed by the visitors, he left them alone together, with the comment that he would send a nurse along in a couple of minutes.

McDade did not look so bad for the simple reason that the rest of the time he did not look so good. The clinical apparatus and clean bed-linen gave him an uncharacteristic aura of health. The hospital staff had removed his dentures, so the smile he attempted was an unhandsome baring of gums and uneven stumps. In spite of everything, McDade seemed relieved at the familiar faces.

'Hello, boys.' His voice was faint.

Wardour told Hendry to shut the door. 'Sean,' Wardour said, 'you're going to make it. You'll be all right.'

McDade was unsure how to react. Great joy and despair seemed to wrestle darkly below the film of shock or drugs which had formed over his mind. He smiled and nodded, but his eyes were dark with the sadness of failure.

Wardour continued, 'Everything's fine, Odell's cleared everything with the police. There won't be any charges.'

Indistinctly through the gaps in his teeth McDade whispered, 'I was going to kill you.'

Wardour came in close. 'All forgotten, Sean. I want you to help me. Would you like to go back to Ireland?' Wardour only suggested this as a token show of concern for McDade's future, for which, in fact, he cared nothing. He was not prepared for the childlike panic that contorted the Irishman's face.

'Never go back to Ireland.'

'Why not?'

'They'll kill me.'

Now Hendry leaned down beside McDade's head. 'If you don't help Mr Wardour, *I*'m going to kill you.' It was like a good cop/bad cop routine. Wardour did not object. His only feeling towards McDade was a ruthless desire to keep him useful.

'Sean, I'll do whatever I can to help you. Mr Odell and I are very powerful. Wherever you want to go, we can fix it. Job, false identity, name it. All we want is your help.'

McDade's eyes closed as he weakly nodded assent.

Aware that time was short, Wardour asked, 'Have some men been here to talk to you?'

McDade repeated, 'Men,' and nodded.

'They want to hurt Mr Odell. Don't tell them anything.'

McDade's eyes flared open. Suddenly, in his mind he was once again a raw kid, a teenager, running errands across Belfast and enjoying his first brushes with the Protestant police and the British soldiers. In his mind he once again stood before his brigade commander and proudly reported that, for all the enemy's threats and blows, he had given nothing away. Wardour had to lean very close to catch McDade's gap-toothed whisper. 'I didn't tell the fuckers nothing.'

310

'Someone will be in touch, Sean,' Wardour said.

Hendry still felt vindictive towards McDade. He had seen enough fellow-soldiers, whose only crime was to be on the streets of Belfast, where they had been *invited*, suddenly mangled by explosions or soft-nosed bullets, condemned to live on as half-human debris. So for McDade's clean, curable wound, Hendry had no compassion. After the Irishman was through assisting Odell and Wardour, Hendry figured, McDade still owed *him*.

The two men left, briskly alert, both conscious that after talking to them Edelstein might have gone straight to a phone.

For privacy, Holly and Wardour went for one last drive. The headlights ate up the New Hampshire darkness. They were almost back at the farm. Somebody had to say it.

'One more night.'

'Yes,' Wardour said. He clasped Holly's hand on the steering wheel. This, alone, was not what she was looking for.

The words that came were stumbling. 'Rod, if I don't say this before we get out of the car, I'll never say it, and I have to say it. Leave Jessica.'

'What?'

'I want you to leave Jessica. Your kids are away at school anyway – '

'Are you – ?'

'I'll be everything I can for you.'

'Can I think about it?'

'No. Say yes now, just say yes. Then everything else will follow from there.'

'I can't, Holly, I can't. Oh God. I can't – '

'In bed you say you love me. Out of bed you never say it. What does love mean?'

'I don't know. Listen, Holly, there's something out there like a gigantic snake. Every time I cut its head off it grows another, and continues to lie in wait. Unless I find it and root it out, I haven't got any life to offer Jessica, myself, or you.' The remainder of the journey passed in a steely silence. When they got out of the car Holly said, 'Well, at least you didn't say, can't we just be friends.'

Sparing the others a scene, and themselves a conflict which they now had too little time to recover from, they spent their final night at the Odell farm apart.

'I don't give a damn what McDade wants,' Barron Odell said the next morning. 'He stays here till he can sit down in front of the people I work with, and give an account of things that gets me out of the shit. After that he's yours. Anything I learn that might be of use to you, I'll be glad to pass on. In the Irish cause, naturally.'

'Fine,' Wardour said, although Odell was a man you would never depend on for a favour. 'Thanks.'

'But if there's nothing left after I spit him out, don't blame me.'

'Of course not,' Wardour said. 'But what about the CIA?'

'In the end the CIA need me *in* business rather than out. I'm not J. Edgar Hoover but if I go down I can take a few people with me. They'll write their reports, then give me a green light. The day after that, they'll be requesting my assistance again.'

'Well,' Wardour said, 'I hope I never need your services again. But I've enjoyed your hospitality, and you greatly impress me.'

Enjoying the flattery, Odell pretended to scorn it. 'Sure,' he growled, 'sure. I'm like the pest control man: people don't like me, but there's always a living to be made.'

'And are you happy?' Wardour asked.

Odell said, 'This world is hell. Those of us who know that, don't expect to be happy. God gave us better things to do than be happy.'

Wardour smiled, looked down, and prayed that Odell would not mention Holly. To deflect the conversation, he said, 'This man Stanger . . . I might be able to use him.'

'Be my guest,' Odell answered. 'I'm not giving him any references, but he has a certain talent.'

'And Hendry? You're finished with him?'

312

'He's yours.'

Wardour made an opportunity to speak to Hendry alone. 'I'm offering you an amnesty. I'll clear you with the police, providing you help me.'

'That's fine,' Hendry said, 'but the police will want to use me as well.'

'Whatever you have to do. But you work for me. Understood?'

'On one condition.'

Wardour was unreceptive. 'That depends.'

'Your amnesty has to include somebody else.'

'Who?'

'Another kidnapper survived.'

'What?'

'He's no more danger to you. You have to clear him as well.'

Wardour thought, then said decisively, 'All right.'

The arrangements were made. But before Wardour could leave, a phone call came through from England. Coolly, Holly held out the phone. Although he had said nothing about it, Wardour had left the New Hampshire number with Jessica, in case of anything concerning the children. Fear that it was Jessica showed on his face as he took the receiver. But bewilderingly, instead of his wife's voice, Wardour heard a man, apparently suffering with bad catarrh, whose name he had all but forgotten.

'Commander Wiley.' Jessica had given Scotland Yard the number. Wardour's heart turned to rock.

'I understand you're due home shortly. I'd like to meet you off the plane.'

'Any particular reason?' Wardour asked.

'Did you know a man called Robin Knight?'

'No.'

'If you could give me the flight details – '

Wardour left the phone, and came back with the information. 'What's this about, Commander?'

'If it's all the same to you, sir, I'll explain at the airport.'

The return to London was making Wardour edgier all the

time. He sought out Hendry. 'The man you mentioned earlier, was his name Robin Knight?'

Startled, Hendry asked, 'How do you know?'

Briefly Wardour explained about the call. 'It sounds as if Knight is dead. Why else mention his name?'

'I hope those police bastards think it was worth it,' Hendry said bitterly.

Engrossed in his own thoughts, Wardour did not ask what Hendry meant. 'I can protect you from the police,' he said, 'but not from the others.'

Hendry was stunned, appalled that Knight, basically decent, dignified, confused, humiliated by what the world had done to him, might now be dead. His reaction obliterated any fear for himself. In any case, fear was an emotion it was useless to feel in advance.

Wardour said: 'Perhaps you'd better watch out.'

Hendry replied: 'You think people like me ever stop?'

Wardour and Holly avoided saying goodbye until the last moment. Holly had not put a time on her own departure. She had been talking of perhaps trying to work in, or from, the USA again. In Holly's mind this move was largely to overcome the long aftermath of bereavement, but Wardour naturally took it as a solution to the question of their own relationship. They left it, for now, undiscussed.

When there were only minutes left and they had to concentrate all they had ever meant to each other into fleeting physical contact, Wardour said, 'Is this the end?'

'An end, maybe. Not *the* end.'

Wardour breathed deeply. It was a relief to have something ended and something else continuing, even if it remained uncertain what.

'I love you,' he said. 'Don't lose me!'

'I love you too. Don't get stuck in the traffic.'

Nobody told Sean McDade that Wardour had left, but almost immediately the Irishman began to regain strength. Odell was constantly at his bedside, questioning. But for Odell too things were changing. A succession of troubled nights had left him sick with the suspicion that the StormWind fiasco in France was in fact a notice to quit. He was rich, retirement was no problem, and his reputation would generate invitations to lecture or guest on the security circuit. The tired man's need for fantasy expanded into book and film rights on his life, perpetuating his name by funding a professorship in Irish history . . .

StormWind had no stockholders, no market quotation, nothing but the office to wind up. StormWind was Odell or nothing, and as a private individual Odell would remain Storm-Wind till the day he died. He no longer sought revenge on McDade, but a tidying up, an exoneration of his own part in the Wardour affair, and an excuse for retirement.

Not adept at hiding what prompted him emotionally, Odell conveyed enough of his changed mood for McDade to start providing the desired answers with all the considerable glibness he could muster. The Irishman emphasised that from his position at the chateau some things had remained unclear, but even to him it had been fairly obvious that Odell's representatives had gone in with big feet and guns blazing. The confirmation calls he had received from his handover boys in Paris, he claimed, had been coded to alert him, and from this McDade had got the impression that the men coming at him were cowboys. McDade knew he could bend the truth considerably. On this occasion, Odell was buying. No disrespect, McDade was careful to add. It was a phrase he used a lot when speaking to Odell. But what he said mattered little, providing it tarred the StormWind agents and left Odell feeling personally in the clear. Well, the StormWind guys were dead, and Odell needed a reason to go on living. To a man of McDade's mental agility this was an easy formula to master.

Hendry and Stanger had gone back down to Boston, and now Odell decided that the farm was making him tense. McDade could be moved, so Odell offered him a room in his duplex in the city, where he could have his own physician come in to keep an eye. McDade humbly accepted the suggestion. His suspicions

315

of Odell remained, but he could see that Odell was an old bull who had lost his urge to hurt. Mentally, Odell was out to grass already. Once again McDade blessed his luck.

The problem for Holly was that she had fixed up various appointments in Boston and was planning to use her father's apartment. Her personal contacts in the city had lapsed, and anyway she refused to find somewhere else to stay just because of McDade. And although she was the person least able to offer it, she felt that what her father needed now, above all else, was protecting. Every time she thought of Sean McDade, Holly felt this more strongly.

Twenty-five

In the grounds of Sous-bois, having cleared up the wreckage, the French police had discovered the body of Nevis. The partially decayed remains still clearly showed a bullet hole in the back. When this information was relayed to Scotland Yard, Mike Wiley had no choice but to pull in Robin Knight once more.

Nevis's killing had been one of the things Knight had neglected to mention. He covered up now by pleading ignorance. Nevis, he said, had disappeared one day while he, Knight, was out. He had not suspected murder. Wiley thought he could stampede Knight with talk of an accessory charge, but this threat only reinforced Knight in his lie. Knight was a poor liar, Wiley knew he was lying, and Knight knew that Wiley knew. But the ex-submariner no longer cared. Wiley pointed out that Knight could be rearrested again at any moment for withholding evidence. But Knight was becoming the most intractable case a policeman can be faced with: a man indifferent to his fate.

Oscillating between sick-bed and office, Wiley tried another idea. Roderick Wardour still did not know of Knight's existence. Wiley took advantage of the MP's absence from Britain to leak to the Press that one of the Wardour kidnappers was helping the police with their enquiries. No personal information on the kidnapper was disclosed. But Wiley was able to use Interpol to get the item on all the major European news programmes that evening.

Coinciding with these events, Lucian Weidinger was doing his homework. From the initial formation of the kidnap group, he had had the names and contact numbers the group members had given McDade. From Zurich, Weidinger now began ringing the numbers. He got dead lines, or cautious voices unwilling to talk, or the name he was seeking had never been heard of.

Only in the case of Robin Knight did Weidinger get a positive reaction. Anglicising his accent as finely as possible, Weidinger posed as an insurance salesman, and talked for long enough to make the call sound authentic and to ascertain that he had the right man. Once he hung up, Weidinger became puzzled. Surely Knight had not simply returned to his former life? For some hours this question tormented Weidinger. Then he saw the TV news item which Wiley had planted across Europe, and it all fell into place. Within minutes Weidinger had decided what to do. He took the first flight to London the next morning, booked into a hotel, and found a reference library which stored provincial telephone directories. It was a straightforward matter to locate the town in which Knight lived from the number Weidinger already possessed. It was only a short step further to match the number to an address.

Weidinger hired a car. A couple of hours' drive out of London brought him to the town where Knight lived. Weidinger cruised the dull main street. The address led him to a hardware shop. A Do-It-Yourself supercentre had opened in the next town, and taking someone's advice, Knight had put a sign in the window advertising that his shop now stayed open till eight every evening. Weidinger saw this notice, digested the fact, then sped away. He assumed a police presence somewhere, but by eight o'clock it would be dark and it was already mid-afternoon.

Weidinger drove to another, larger town, where he bought a strip of steel cable for a cycle gear. He shopped in a self-service store, where there was no need to speak to anybody. By the time he returned, Weidinger had changed into a track-suit, a woollen hat and a scarf that hid his jaw. He kept his face well down. If anybody was going to see him, he wanted them to report a jogger. In the event of a photograph, he was giving them nothing to go on.

Parking some distance from Knight's shop, Weidinger approached on foot. It was almost closing time. In case there were other customers, Weidinger hung around off the main street, then at one minute to eight, approached the shop. Not until he saw the shopkeeper about to turn the Open/Closed sign round the door did Weidinger go nearer. A surge of adrenalin

318

hit his system, then levelled out again to a serene purposefulness, the confidence of the criminal maniac that nothing can go wrong, providing he does not falter or stop to think.

Weidinger gripped the door handle. Behind the glass Knight paused in his action. Weidinger had guessed accurately that Knight was in business, not a bureaucrat who stopped on the dot of the hour. The door opened.

'Sorry about the panic,' Weidinger exclaimed desperately. 'You do sell plumbing components, don't you?'

'Well,' Knight said, 'it depends what – '

'A broken valve on a tank . . . water pouring all over the bloody house.'

'Have you turned off the mains?' Knight asked.

'Yes, but the tap jammed. If I can get a valve, I can do it – '

'They're over here,' Knight said.

Too near the window. Expressing relief, Weidinger accepted the chunk of brass that Knight handed him, then looked immediately further into the store. 'That's great. And while I'm here . . .' By the counter at the back of the shop, Weidinger pretended to need something on a high shelf. Simultaneously he located the position of the light switches. 'One of those – would you mind?' Grinding wheels for tap reseaters, the box said.

Pushing along a step unit that ran on castors, Knight got up to reach the highest shelf. Weidinger took the gear cable from his pocket and with one sweep of his arm, he deadened the lights. Knight gave a short-lived exclamation, surprise and fear in one. But it was already too late. Weidinger swung the cable.

Its effect was instant and devastating. Knight overbalanced and fell. The mobile step skidded away from under him. Weidinger dodged Knight's body, contriving to arch his arms with its fall in such a way as to keep the cable taut. Knight landed face down, which made it easier. Weidinger sweated heavily and gripped the cable till it bit into his own hands, until he was certain it was all over.

The hardware store occupied old premises. From outside Weidinger had noticed the cellar grille. Having first put on

319

gloves, he found the door and slid Knight's body down the rickety stairs into the dimly-lit, mildewed underground recess. The cellar door had a key. Weidinger locked it, and hid the key among the stock on a high shelf. He switched off all the lights in the shop, then removed his track suit, which covered ordinary casual clothes. He rolled the track suit up in a paper bag and left by the back way. The small walled garden sheltered him, and the service road, little more than an alley, was badly served by street lamps. Satisfied that nobody had seen him, Weidinger returned to his car. In London he had a supper engagement with Tony Gwyer and Herbert Conefort. Gwyer had sounded nervous on the phone, but Weidinger would soothe away their nerves. And if he ever needed an alibi for the earlier part of this evening, they were his men.

To those returning to Britain from the USA, at least the language was the same. To Roderick Wardour everything else felt different. He found things grating on him after New Hampshire – the squalor and bad temper of public places, the noise, the pressure of crowds. The life he was returning to made him uncomfortable, as if it was not entirely his own. He had always loved being a public figure, the stares of people in the street had given life an addictive sparkle. But now he resented the phenomenon and forced himself to ignore it.

When Mike Wiley failed to make his presence known immediately, Wardour's impatience increased. He did not make a habit of waiting for people, at airports or anywhere else. Instead a young man, whose face Wardour only vaguely recollected, stepped forward.

'Mr Wardour, I'm Detective Sergeant Lucas Brand. Commander Wiley sends his apologies. He got tied up at the Yard. I'll drive you home if I may.'

The bruise on his face was the only external sign of what had been a bad week for Lucas Brand. After his successful tracking down of Hendry and its inglorious end with the kidnapper's escape, Brand had confessed the truth. Rather than go to another officer and give mortal offence to the sometimes very

320

sensitive Wiley, Brand had visited the Commander's home, where he found Wiley still feverish and in bed. Mrs Wiley was in the house, but Brand soon detected ripples of a hostile atmosphere. Silence, like cold or damp, had penetrated the walls: Mrs Wiley's suspicions of her husband's misconduct with a young policewoman had become more than suspicions recently. Policemen rarely made competent criminals.

With a pallid, stony face Wiley listened to Brand's apologetic account of his private detective work, nursing the whisky which he claimed was curing his flu.

'Is that it? Listen, Lucas, when you run around being brilliant it just shows up what dull arseholes the rest of us are. We might be slower, but we'd have collared the guy. I've got half a mind to put you back in uniform. Spend the rest of your career doing Oxford Street for pickpockets. Who were you trying to impress, for God's sake, me, or the Odell woman?'

'Both,' Lucas Brand confessed.

'Well, the answer is neither. And keep away from her. You want a private life, leave the police force. Chase your skirt well away from the job. And no, you won't bloody resign. You wait till I think it over and decide whether or not to throw you out.'

Brand's visit left Wiley exhausted and depressed. He had reacted with professional correctness. But after the young police-man left, Wiley felt very alone, as if he had rejected his own son. A policeman's life was lonely. The reason so many were tolerant of corruption when it came their way was that few of them could face the isolation of righteousness. Only a policeman understood a policeman, and without colleagues they had nowhere to go.

Later in the day Wiley rang Brand. After a reprise of his strictures, he added that he thought, had always thought, that Brand would make a terrific detective. So by the time Wiley returned to work he was ready for Brand to substitute for him at Heathrow, but only as chauffeur. Although Brand knew the story on Robin Knight, he told Wardour nothing, resisting the MP's questions and driving him to Regent's Park with the assurance that Wiley would be in touch later in the evening.

Wardour found the house dark as he let himself in. He had not given Jessica the exact time of his return. Knowing which day, she had obviously taken no chances on him finding her there. Dropping his luggage, switching on a light, Wardour casually looked for an explanatory note. He scanned his normal mail below the ornate mirror in the hall. Nothing. Before he could look further, Wardour heard movement upstairs. At the top of the spiralling banister he saw light from one of the back rooms.

Jessica, Wardour hoped, then felt annoyed at himself for hoping that she was in the house after all. More likely a burglar. Wardour did not admit fear, especially on his own territory. The readiest weapon to hand was an empty wine bottle, kept around for its label – the vintage date and the signatures of the special dinner guests who had shared it. Wardour stepped carefully over the one tread in the oak which was liable to creak. Clutching the bottle, he climbed the stairs.

The light came from one of the children's rooms. A sound made Wardour hesitate. It didn't feel like burglars. In houses like this the valuables weren't stored on second floors and the sound had been too domestic, something like the clink of cup on saucer. Wardour approached the open door.

'Josh?'

'Hi, Dad.'

For a moment Wardour found his son's appearance strange, the effect of a new hairstyle, a fashionable centre-parted cut with hair flopping either side of the face, shaved clean above the ears. Also Josh had grown. Uneasy manhood had displaced the little boy Wardour still liked to remember.

'Why are you here?'

'Taking a break from school.'

'Any reason?'

'Things got a bit much.'

'Things?'

'Yeah, things.'

Wardour entered the room. Sprawled on his bed, Josh clicked off his personal stereo and pulled the headset from his neck.

322

Wardour shifted some clothes from a chair and sat down. 'Where's Mum?'

'Said she'd be back late.'

'School going well?'

'All right.'

'Then what's the problem?'

Josh Wardour looked directly at his father, a man he knew better from the media than person-to-person. 'You.'

Wardour affected amusement, a brief cynical laugh. 'Me?'

'I'm taking a lot of stick because of you.'

'Stick?'

'From all the other people. They say you're an IRA stooge. Look at this.' Josh threw one of his textbooks. On the flyleaf was written, *Roderick Wardour, Had a screw across the border.* 'Every time I go to the toilet I have to read that on the wall.'

Wardour tried to joke. 'I've seen worse things in toilets. Anyway, sometimes we have to sweat these things out.'

'Not if I don't know what's going on. Seems everybody knows about you except me.'

'OK,' Wardour said. 'I suppose I owe you an explanation.' He began a rapid calculation of how little he could get away with telling Josh. The phone rang downstairs. 'Oh God!'

More wound up than he was showing, Josh said, 'Let it ring.'

But Wardour was already on his way down. The caller was Mike Wiley, who wanted to meet so urgently that he was willing to come out to Regent's Park, if Wardour preferred that to convening at the Yard. Although rattled by his family predicament, Wardour invited Wiley to the house. As he hung up he had second thoughts too late. During his brief conversation with Wiley, Wardour's other line had rung, direct to his study. Josh went down to take it. Once off the line Wardour ran upstairs. Calls on his private line were always significant. He and Josh met halfway.

'Who – ?'

'Mum.'

'What's up?'

'She'll be late.'

'Nice of her to ring.' But the message had not been for him.

Josh said: 'She told me to get myself some dinner. Do you want some?'

'No,' Wardour said. 'Thanks. I'm about to have company.'

Josh disappeared into the kitchen, not asking who the company was.

Still worn from his illness, Mike Wiley followed Wardour up to his study, where his practised eye immediately told him that the MP also did not always sleep with his wife.

Wardour was avid for information. 'Tell me about this man Knight. Who was he?'

'He was a former naval officer – '

'Ah,' Wardour said, recalling the voices and physical mannerisms of the kidnappers. 'I know the one.'

Wiley explained his strategy with Knight. Wardour was not pleased to learn that one of the kidnappers had been in police custody all that time and had been released, without himself being told.

'And all you achieved,' Wardour observed, 'was to get him murdered.'

Wiley acted gruffly unconcerned. 'We took a risk.'

Wardour knew that in order to pursue activities on his own behalf, he would eventually need the cooperation of the police, so he refrained from pressing Wiley on this embarrassing point.

'We have a solid lead on another kidnapper. It shouldn't be long before we haul him in.'

Wardour asked: 'Could you tell me the name of this man?' But Wiley was not about to divulge. With some satisfaction, Wardour added, 'Would it be Hendry?' Before Wiley could show how upstaged he felt, the MP continued, 'I only know him because he made himself known to me.'

Wardour offered Wiley a strategic brandy from the supply he kept in the study for his own use, and asked, 'Cards on the table?'

Wiley, who had started drinking again during his bout of flu,

324

accepted the brandy and said, 'Are you bargaining with me, sir?'

'Of course not. But – and I speak for Miss Odell when I say this – we want Hendry to feel free from pressure, pressure from you. He's willing to help, providing he's not going to be pulled off the street and banged away by your boys.'

'You're saying you don't want us to pursue the case?'

'No. I'm saying that Hendry is our best lead, but he won't talk to you. He'll feed you through me. But you have to drop the case against him.'

Wiley pretended to consider. In fact their case against Hendry was weak: since Lucas Brand had located his flat they had wasted hours of surveillance time in a fruitless attempt to trap Hendry on his return. And Wiley could hardly charge Wardour with harbouring a known felon, since it was Wardour's evidence that made Hendry a felon in the first place. 'We can play it that way if you want,' he conceded.

Soon after, Wiley left, feeling vindictive towards the MP, this arch-manipulator. He was also feeling professionally sore about the discovery of Knight's body. After a week in which nothing seemed to happen in the life of Robin Knight, manpower requirements had forced Wiley to substitute a video camera for actual police presence, for ten hours out of the twenty-four. There was little doubt that the shadowy figure they had caught on film was the murderer, but for identification purposes the evidence was all but worthless. Irrationally, Wiley seemed to be holding Wardour responsible. His own phrase about waiting for the tigers was beginning to haunt him. The tiger had called, killed, and vanished. Wiley was no longer interested in salvaging Roderick Wardour's reputation. He would settle for coming out of all this with his professional self-respect intact.

Jessica came home soon after Wiley's departure. Wardour had devoted a great deal of thought to where he should be when she entered the house, even to what clothes he should be wearing, what activity he should plan to be in the middle of. And most of all, what kind of reunion he should try to bring about between them. As soon as he heard Jessica moving about downstairs, all his plans were obliterated by the vulnerability of his position. At this moment, only Jessica had the power to make or unmake, do or undo, and as he went slowly downstairs, trying to strike the right balance between casualness and welcome, Wardour knew he was at her mercy.

At least she had not changed the locks on the house, or had a solicitor's letter waiting for him. But Wardour's attempt to see this as a good omen died quickly once he and Jessica came face to face. As though mentally ticking off all the things it was impossible to say, they looked at each other for a long moment, their faces unsmiling, their eyes gradually revealing less and hiding more.

'Good trip?' Jessica asked.

Wardour answered, 'Interesting, yes.'

Jessica called, 'Hello, Josh!'

As his son responded, Wardour accepted that this stage of the game had been declared over.

Sadly, he returned to his study. Sad, because he very much wanted, for reasons he could not analyse or justify, to give Jessica just one kiss, to touch his lips to hers, in humility and reconciliation. And, perhaps, to reassert right of possession too. But Jessica would not want to be kissed by lips which had so recently been pressed to those of another woman. Wardour understood this all too well. The gentleman and realist in him on this occasion defeated the romantic. It did not occur to him that Jessica had just come from the bed of one of his fellow MPs.

Some time later Wardour went to watch the late news. At what he saw, he didn't know whether to laugh or cry.

Like any other large city, London possesses a network of discreet sexual services. Why eminent figures from Westminster and the City, men at the peak of careers founded on rectitude and power, should seek private humiliation and risk public ridicule in pursuit of an orgasm, journalists would speculate about each time an accident forced the phenomenon into public view. Accident, because society had an interest in maintaining discretion among its leading class. If the police broke up a kinky

326

brothel in the suburbs it was of no concern, unless the clientele they netted happened to include a well-known member of Parliament. At which point, the machinery of discretion could offer the exposed victim no further protection.

Jonah Sweetman, although priding himself on the width of his sexual repertoire, was no fishnet and high heels man. But the more upmarket situation in which he had been caught would prove at least as damaging. The West End gambling club for wealthy Middle Easterners which the police had just raided for drugs also had high-class call girls on tap, and although Sweetman was not one of the clients charged with possession of cocaine, he had been found in a room with two naked women and a Turkish multi-millionaire. This was enough for the tabloid press. The fact that the two men were also naked took second place to the moment when, being hurriedly escorted outside, Sweetman lost control of his wig. The more serious news channels focused on the drug connection and the possibility that the club was used to launder suspect Middle-Eastern money into London. Everybody else contented themselves with innuendo about white girls being supplied for the squalid pleasures of dark men. Either way, Sweetman was caught.

An MP taken red-handed was in no position to mutter to the police that he knew he could count on their cooperation, although Sweetman tried. Comedy, like tragedy, had to be acted out to the end. When first faced with a barrage of pressmen, Sweetman had tried to shrug it off by saying, 'I guess I went a bitch too far.' Everybody laughed. Old Jonah was always good for a quote. The next day they shredded him. Sweetman's comeuppance was to see himself splashed all over a media which could gloat on its own righteousness and enjoy every juicy minute.

Roderick Wardour tried a number of times, but Sweetman's phone was engaged. At first Wardour had felt horror, as if the news threatened him personally. Certainly it muddied the water. He needed to talk to Sweetman in private. But nothing and nowhere seemed to be private any more. He dropped the receiver again, brooding on what to do about Sweetman, vaguely aware of Jessica taking a call downstairs. Then she appeared in the doorway of his study.

'It's Jonah. Something terrible's happened – '

'I know. I saw the news.'

'His flat's under siege. He's asking if he can stay here. Is it all right with you?'

'Of course. But they'll follow him. You'll have an army camped out in the front garden.'

'I've got an idea for rescuing him. You don't mind?'

'Jonah's always welcome here,' Wardour said.

Jessica gave Sweetman directions to a Soho cul-de-sac which he could enter by an alley. It was unlikely anyone would tail him so closely as to spot the waiting car in which he would speed away.

As she was leaving Jessica said, 'I didn't tell him you'd just arrived back, or he might have felt he couldn't come.'

'That's fine,' Wardour said. 'Don't tell him I'm back. Give him a surprise.'

An hour later Wardour was exclaiming, 'Jonah, hullo!'

'Roddy, old friend – '

In the car Sweetman had spent all the time complaining about how, since the story had leaked, he had been hounded from place to place across London. The 'bitch too far' remark had not gone down well in the party. It sat badly with the new, more caring image. His discovery was a tip-off, he didn't doubt. One of his many well-wishers. He asked, 'When did you get back?'

'This evening.'

'I assumed . . . look, if I'm in the way . . .'

'You'll be safe here,' Wardour said, and to Jessica, 'How was your getaway?'

'Perfect. I think.'

'I've already made up a bed.'

Sweetman put on a display of mock-embarrassment, spluttered with excessive gratitude and called the Wardours the only friends he had left in London.

328

Wardour said, 'If nobody else is hungry, I'll make Jonah and me a little supper.'

'I don't mind,' Jessica said.

'Are you sure?'

'Yes.'

For both the Wardours the atmosphere was relieved by Sweetman being there. His own bizarre problems were a buffer between them, prevented them focusing on themselves.

Over a drink, a defensive but brazen figure, Sweetman said, 'Well, Roddy, us naughty boys have to take our medicine, eh?' Wardour gave a thin-lipped smile. 'Those bloody press reptiles, though. A bit of hanky panky, and they're all over the place. And for what? A man has – tastes, after all. Only normal to want to satisfy them.'

'For them it's a meal ticket,' Wardour said.

'Bloody nuisances,' Sweetman protested. 'Crowd a man's front door. I had to leave by the bloody fire escape. What I need is a minder, somebody to sweep my path as I pursue life's weary trail.'

Wardour concealed his excitement behind an offhand, indifferent front. 'If you're serious,' he said, 'I think I know just the man.'

Twenty-six

No other word affects members of the government like 'reshuffle'. For some it spells the end of ambition, a long-warranted political death, for others a leap from obscurity, the receipt of an expected reward. For a smaller number the reshuffle comes as an unforeseen blow, an unjust act of slaughter from which their career will probably never recover.

Wardour was out.

Government reshuffles follow no timetable. Their inspiration may be unrest among the electorate or the media, pressure from within the party organisation, or the autocratic whim of a Prime Minister demonstrating the exercise of real power. This particular reshuffle possessed all three strands, but to Roderick Wardour the final analysis did not matter a drop of spit. He was out.

Neither was there any formal machinery through which those affected learnt their fate. Men climbing the ladder were phoned and interviewed by the Prime Minister, and another link was forged in the chain of loyalty. For those going the other way the news could be as gentle or harsh as chance dictated.

Wardour had become used to the process by which a public figure becomes an unperson. Ostensibly nothing changes, but the man concerned senses details, mostly too small to react to, melting away from his daily existence – the conversation avoided, the opinion unsought, the confidence unreciprocated – and begins to feel like a ghost. Wardour had seen this coming, felt that he had adapted to it well, and was determined to fight his way out of it. But none of this prepared him for the mealy-mouthed language with which the chief whip, an old friend, notified Wardour of his dismissal. With icy rage he strode out of the neo-Gothic magnificence of the Palace of Westminster.

By the time he reached home, Wardour could not even recall

how he had filled the intervening hours. The bitterest feature of all was that they had offered him nothing else, not even a niche in one of the low-profile departments to save his face. The cold truth was that politicians had no face, only masks which the wrong combination of circumstances could rip away. He made sure that for the sake of his family he had shaken off all outer display of self-pity, or the kind of embitterment that sucks everybody into its angry vortex. Above all, at this moment, it was important to maintain an image. He still had to live with himself.

The house was empty. Wardour was used to being out all the time, finding Jessica there when he got back. That had been a sign of how well she had patterned herself to his movements. Wardour had looked on calmly while Jessica sacrificed herself to his ambition. They had both known why. Now the rewards would not come. Life would go on, as it did, but somehow, Wardour thought, not here.

When Jessica returned it was with Jonah Sweetman. 'I took Jonah for a drive – '

'Going stir crazy, old boy. No disrespect to your wonderful home. What's happened?'

Wardour met Jessica's eyes and held the look for a long time. 'I've been sacked.'

'Can't believe it. Absolutely can't bloody believe it,' Sweetman exclaimed.

Softer, but more violent, Jessica said, 'Oh my God.'

Wardour had already decided to play it jaunty, at least in Sweetman's presence. 'I'm having a drink. Join me.'

They sat and talked. Wardour made light of everything. He felt sorrier for Jessica than for himself. He was entitled to wreck his own life, but everything Jessica had worked for was turning to dust. Her face had become almost ugly with incomprehension and dismay. She seemed relieved to get up and answer the phone.

'Holly.' Jessica had called her *Holly*. Instead of putting the receiver down she waited for Wardour to take it from her. She hung around, refusing to go somewhere in the house out of earshot. Wardour's blood had gone cold. Assuming a look of displeasure for Jessica's benefit, he said a grave hullo.

'Hi. It's all right, I'm still in Boston.'

'Is something wrong?'

'Was that Jessica?'

'Yes.'

'Can she hear you?'

Wardour searched for words that would give nothing away. 'Probably.'

'How have things been since you got back?'

'OK.' Each time Holly waited for more, but realised that he was not going to improve on the monosyllables.

'Listen, I've got news.'

'Oh?'

'I'm not coming back.'

'Ah.'

'Or rather . . . well, I met an old friend. He offered me a job.'

'Oh, that's good.' Wardour's voice was flat and depressed.

'Working in Europe for an American syndicate.'

Wardour pulled himself together. 'Wonderful news. Congratulations!'

'You mean it?'

'Of course.'

'I'll still be around. Don't think you're getting rid of me.'

'Unthinkable.' But there could be no endearments, no trailers for the future. And not because Jessica might be listening, but because suddenly the future was different from what either of them had imagined.

'Oh, and by the way, your two goons left for London.'

Wardour said, 'Good. Anyway, I'm really glad.'

'I hoped you would be. Thanks.'

Their goodbye was subdued, almost formal. When Wardour explained the content of the call Jessica asked, although she knew the answer, 'Did you tell her about you?'

'No.'

'Sparing her feelings?' Jessica said, with the contemptuous irony of someone whose feelings had not been spared.

'No,' Wardour said grimly, 'mine.'

On the couch in his study Wardour lay awake, more hurt and angry as the dark hours wore on. The bastards had assessed him with sickening accuracy; they knew his pride would keep him from fighting. He would submit, not because he was a party man, but because he was his own man. He also felt strangely robbed of something by Holly's change of career. He realised that he had never thought of her as anything but a powerful and mysterious presence on the fringe of his own life. The violence that had widowed her, its long sad aftermath, had allowed Wardour to take her dependence on him for granted. But now Holly was demonstrating that she was in the market like everybody else. From being widely regarded as a future leader of his country, Wardour now felt like the most naive man in London. It had been such a short fall.

After a while he got up and went to the bathroom. Seeing a light on in the master bedroom, he went towards it. The door was not quite closed. Wardour looked in. Propped up on a pillow, Jessica was asleep. An open book lay on the duvet. It was the rest of someone who, once lying down with the light out, would sleep badly. Wardour no longer knew what he wanted of his wife. The loss of his ministerial post was the one blow he would never willingly have had strike Jessica. In comparison, going to bed with another woman hardly seemed important. But his political demotion was already sending out waves of depression that would not stop until they reached the furthest shores of his and Jessica's joint existence.

As Wardour stood there, helplessly asking forgiveness of her sleeping form, Jessica stirred. She had always been quick to wake up. 'What is it?'

'Nothing,' Wardour said. 'I just – ' Jessica looked away, thinking he wanted some personal item he had not yet cleared out of the room. 'I came to talk.'

Jessica said, 'I'm sorry, I don't want to.'

333

Ignoring this, Wardour sat down on the bed. He left plenty of space between them. 'I'm sorry about getting fired. Sorry on your account.'

'Oh, don't worry about me. I'll survive. I'm already working on the rest of my life.'

'Excluding me, I suppose?'

'I don't know. Who are you, Rod? I don't know that either.'

'The next part of my life is to find out,' Wardour said. But the touch of melodrama no longer had the right ring to it.

Jessica said, 'I hope you like what you find.'

'Do you want to be there?' Wardour asked.

'I don't know. I'd like to sleep now.'

Wardour stroked the bed which they had shared for so many years. 'Shall I stay?'

Jessica did not even consider. 'We're not the people we were. Don't let's pretend we can go back. Everything I took for granted has fallen apart. I've got to start again.'

'I'm sorry,' Wardour said again. He was choked with a guilt which Jessica had seen coming a long way off, and doggedly refused to relieve for him.

'I gather these things are normal for people of our age,' Jessica said. 'I'm only sorry I spent so much of my life believing otherwise.'

Wardour went away sobered, yet feeling that in a strange way Jessica had freed him for action.

'I like the cut of that young man,' Jonah Sweetman said, after he had been introduced to Ed Hendry.

'Ex Parachute Regiment,' Wardour said. 'I've used him several times. Very competent, discretion one hundred per cent. Try him.' Wardour had wrung from Scotland Yard the assurance that Hendry's flat in outer London, and Hendry himself, would be left alone by the police, to clear the way for his own exploitation of the ex-soldier.

'I'll try anything,' Sweetman said. 'Can't live like a bloody fugitive for ever.' And Sweetman launched into another encomium of the Wardours' hospitality. But he still had to brave

334

the public eye, even if only around the streets of Knightsbridge, Piccadilly and Westminster. The piranhas of the tabloids would be lurking, and God knew who else. So Sweetman hired Hendry.

The value of the investment soon emerged when Sweetman returned home. Hendry was already waiting outside. Two reporters had also taken up position there. Hendry stepped towards the taxi a moment before the journalists. But then a fourth man beat them all to it, accosting Sweetman directly.

'Hey, Mr Sweetman, Don Brady, *International News*. Don't you think old degenerates like you are unfit to govern a country? What other filthy perversions are we going to dig up on you, Mr Sweetman? I'm talking to you, Mr Sweetman – '

Head down, Sweetman thrust forward, but the reporter barred his way, even grabbed Sweetman's jacket. Hendry stepped in, his hand on the reporter's shoulder. 'OK, friend, that's it.'

'Who asked you, pinhead?' The reporter shoved Hendry away. Hendry pushed back and followed through. He took the reporter off balance, twisted his arm behind his back, ran him against the side of a parked van, then aimed a blow at the region of his kidneys which made the reporter's knees buckle.

'From now on, respect Mr Sweetman's privacy,' he growled.

But Bobby Stanger was already hobbling away down the street. His pose as a nuisance journalist had been designed to give Hendry a good start as bodyguard. The other two newspapermen were already backing off. Hendry said, 'When Mr Sweetman tells you no comment, that's it, boys. No comment. Got it?' The journalists looked eager to understand.

Up in his flat, Sweetman bubbled with admiration. 'I'm not sure about the physical bit, but, my God, it was worth a summons to see the look on those reptiles' faces. Thanks, dear boy. Drink?'

Hendry accepted a beer, surprised that Sweetman carried such a thing. It turned out to be a bottled German lager, rare and very strong. Hendry drank appreciatively while Sweetman, an affable man who liked the sound of his own voice, rattled

335

away. The longer Hendry was in the flat, the better. His current task was to pave the way for Stanger to break in and turn the place over. Then after that, Wardour had mentioned *something else*, but had deferred on the specifics.

Lunch with Mike Wiley was often a diverting event, but on this occasion, Lucas Brand reflected, it smacked of an exercise in sado-masochism. They were in the usual Chinese place off Victoria Street, and Brand had taken the invitation as a sign that he was on Wiley's good side again. But over the food the Commander punctuated his brooding with little more than sporadic snorts of frustration. Trying to earn his lunch, Brand said, 'Dare I ask if we care any more?'

'About what?' Wiley demanded.

'Doesn't this Knight business make it the murder boys' territory now?' Brand had touched a nerve. Apart from the insubordination of tacitly reminding Wiley that their business was anti-terrorism, Brand had voiced Wiley's own worst fear.

'This is not a murder case. Or, in the ordinary sense, a kidnap. And I'm buggered if I'm handing it over to anybody. I haven't wasted all this time just to – '

Lucas Brand's eyes had begun to swivel, focused somewhere beyond Wiley's head. He muttered, 'Can we change places, sir?' In restaurants Wiley always sat with his back to the clientele. This allowed him to enjoy his food, rather than be forced to observe the other diners. He answered Brand's request with a look of incredulity.

'Why?'

But Brand was already on his feet, and Wiley knew well enough how to act first and ask questions later. Once they had exchanged places he demanded, 'What the bloody hell – ?'

'The two men that just came in,' Brand said. 'The younger one did this to me.' Brand indicated the bruise that remained on his right cheekbone.

In an intent whisper Wiley asked, 'That's Hendry?'

As Brand nodded confirmation, Wiley peered along the restaurant's narrow interior at the slim neat man with thinning blond hair and trim moustache, dark blazer and grey trousers. On appearance alone, Hendry could have been a policeman. This kidnapper intrigued Wiley. So did his presence here, although the coincidence became less marked when Wiley learnt who Hendry's companion was.

'Who's the old ponce?'

'Name's Sweetman.' Brand was an avid watcher of TV news, and had a photographic memory. He added, 'The MP who's just been – '

Wiley interrupted, 'Yeah, sure. But what is this Hendry guy, some kind of politician groupie?'

Midway between New Scotland Yard and the Palace of Westminster, the restaurant was regular grazing territory for policemen and Members of Parliament. Wiley leaned closer. 'The question is, why, and what now? Do they know you here?'

'I think so,' Brand said.

'Go out the staff door. Flash your card if necessary. Tell them you have to leave the back way. When you stand up, don't show them your face.' Brand looked disconsolately at his Peking duck. Wiley grinned. 'Sorry, Lucas. See you back at the factory.'

Wiley finished his own meal at leisure and left by the front entrance, passing Sweetman's table as he went. The MP was one of those men whose voices blare in public places. He was in the middle of an anecdote which looked as if it could take up the afternoon. Hendry was listening respectfully. But by this time Wiley was not concerned to hang around for clues. The connection was already strong enough to warrant his next action. On his return to Scotland Yard, Wiley ordered a tap on Sweetman's phone.

If there was one sophistication Jessica Wardour lacked, it was sexual. When she met Tony Gwyer in Harrods, and he made no overt reference to the several times they had been to bed together, mostly during Roderick Wardour's absence in America, Jessica experienced a number of feelings – she was relieved, touched, even a little hurt. Afterwards, she realised that of course she should have experienced no feelings whatever. And

337

Gwyer had not been surprisingly gentlemanly, for someone she considered so badly socialised. He had just been playing the game.

After a few words, they had gone their separate ways. Then Jessica felt herself getting hot with discomfort at how easy it had been. She had accepted sex with Gwyer because he had seemed to know what she was looking for, better than she did herself. He had offered himself reticently, and let her make the decision. He had no more wanted a scandal than she did. If her motive had been revenge for Holly Odell, Gwyer had been its willing instrument. But the knot of things needing to be said between the Wardours was growing tighter by the day, and Jessica was learning that affairs are easier to have than to talk about. She learnt too that the world's machinery took no account of private disaster, and that, as life became more complicated, other people's motives became harder to discern.

Lucy Conefort, Jessica's sister, called to say that Archie, Lucy's father-in-law Lord Conefort, now in poor health, was about to arrive back from the West Indies. The family were organising a party at Shearwater. Rod and Jessie would want to be there, of course? Jessica had to accept, but self-doubts now flooded in, mixed with speculation about the real reason behind Lucy's eagerness to invite them.

'Sadism,' Roderick Wardour said flatly. But in the gap between the invitation and their discussion of it, Jessica had decided to take a more positive view.

'Why should it be?'

'They want to gloat. Well, I won't give them the pleasure.'

'You think Herbert has set this whole thing up for people to laugh at us?'

'Of course not. But all the more reason for not going. We won't be missed.'

'You're not interested, then, in keeping up appearances?'

Killingly, Wardour answered, 'Appearances of what?'

In spite of herself, Jessica made one more attempt. 'There is another way of taking it.'

'You mean that they're letting me know I'm still *persona*

338

grata? I think not. More likely they just don't want to offend you.'

'It's still an opportunity to re-establish yourself.'

'I can't face it,' Wardour said. 'That's the truth. Every day I go to the House, I find it harder. I don't need social occasions. I need to get away.'

Sensing another pretext for a trip with Holly, Jessica was iron-faced and unsympathetic. At the same time, if Rod was about to crack up, it was better if it happened away from the family doorstep. His next question surprised her.

'How well are you getting on with Lucy these days?'

'We bitch together occasionally. Why?'

'Will you do one thing for me, if I never ask anything else?'

'What is it?'

'Arrange for me to borrow the place at Robleda. Say for a week. Exact date to be decided.'

As if speaking an epitaph, Jessica said, 'If that's what you want.'

Jessica believed in maximum choice for the consumer. If Rod had chosen to consume his career, much as it devastated her own wishes, Jessica felt helpless to interfere. Protecting people from their own folly was something she found, politically and personally, a waste of time, her own husband not excepted. In fact, whatever self-destructive journey he was bent on now, the sooner she knew the extent of it the better.

'There is just one thing,' Jessica said. 'I have as much against the Coneforts as you do, but the *cortijo* holds a lot of memories for me. I don't want you using it as a love-nest.'

'I guarantee it,' Wardour said. He tried to put on the old integrity. But Jessica's demand had been self-defeating. She never really believed anything he said any more.

'Why do you want to go there?' she asked.

She took his answer as a sign that the breakdown was not far off. Wardour said: 'I need a battleground.'

In Herbert Conefort's Belgravia flat, the three MPs were ill at ease. Lucian Weidinger, on the other hand, was very relaxed, and left them in no doubt as to who was in command of the situation.

Sweetman raised the question of Robin Knight, which had been nagging at him. 'Now their prize witness is dead,' Sweetman said, 'they're bound to step up the investigation.'

'Using that man was a sign of desperation,' Weidinger said. 'When the ratcatcher starts employing the rats, you know he's in trouble.'

'He might leave a dead rat as bait for a bigger animal,' Gwyer said.

Weidinger remained supercilious. 'I don't see the analogy. If anybody was likely to go after Knight, it was his own kind. The police did that man no favours.'

Sweetman and Conefort both had problems meeting Weidinger's eye. Only Gwyer could hold his stare. Weidinger suspected that Gwyer had guessed the truth about Knight's murder, had guessed and was favourably impressed by it. Not that Weidinger cared, because they were all in his grip now, exactly where he had always intended them to be. Apart from the immediate money, which strictly speaking Weidinger did not need, there was no telling, in years to come, what the dividends of such a position might be.

'Meanwhile,' he said, 'what of friend Wardour? Are you gentlemen happy?'

'He's out of the government,' Sweetman said. 'That was what we wanted to achieve.'

'I also hear,' Conefort said, 'that he won't be at Dad's homecoming party.'

'Couldn't face it,' Gwyer said. 'What about Jessie?'

'She won't come alone.'

'Time she went freelance,' Gwyer said. 'Ask her again.'

'Well, I don't know – '

'Get to work on her.' Gwyer scented a kill. 'Roddy's got to learn that the world won't stop just because he's decided to get off.'

Weidinger found the British MPs an amusing trio. But he had long ago read correctly that the one with sensitive antennae was Sweetman. He, Weidinger observed, was troubled. Some of this was no doubt the result of his personal scandal, which was still very much around. But Weidinger divined more. 'And you, Mr Sweetman, what do you think?'

Sweetman was not prepared to express any view until he had emptied half a glass of gin. 'What do we do if Wardour decides to fight?'

'How should he fight?' Weidinger was courteous. The other two MPs looked displeased. They wanted to triumph at this stage, not to have new fears raised.

'I hear he's a broken man,' Conefort said. 'There's some talk of him borrowing our place in Spain. Sounds like a breakdown.'

'Or running away,' Gwyer suggested.

'I just wonder,' Sweetman said, 'if we haven't done too good a job. If you leave a man something, he'll take the bad patches as the price of life. But if you strip him of everything, he's got nothing to lose by declaring war.'

'Well,' Weidinger held up an admonitory finger to the other MPs' derision, 'Mr Sweetman has a point. What do we do if Mr Wardour declares war?' Nobody had an answer. All the truths were unpalatable. Weidinger continued, 'I tell you what we do. We assess the damage he can inflict. Then we remove his power to inflict that damage. Simple, isn't it?'

Gwyer said, 'That could include Roddy himself.'

Weidinger smiled. 'It's possible. But frankly, I don't think it would need to go that far. Once Mr Wardour finds he has the devil by the tail, he'll soon let go.'

As he was leaving, Weidinger gave Gwyer a number on which to call him in Switzerland, a call which only the most urgent circumstances would justify. Gwyer pretended to be flattered by Weidinger's confidence, but he knew that Weidinger did nothing for personal reasons. It was a sign, if sign was needed, of how serious things might yet become.

Twenty-seven

After two days in Jonah Sweetman's company it was easy work for Hendry to become expert on the MP's lax habits and abduct his spare keys to get copies made in a while-u-wait bar. These he passed to Stanger. The next part of their programme was for Hendry to call the American when he knew Sweetman was certain to be out of his apartment for several hours, so Stanger could strip it of any information that promised to be useful.

Before this could happen, Hendry was summoned to Regent's Park. 'Jonah's very happy with you,' Wardour said.

Hendry inclined his head but did not reply. The two men never referred to their army careers – Wardour the short-service officer who had known a good credential for politics when he saw it, Hendry the long-term professional who had sought escape from a lifetime of dead-end jobs – but somehow the military's invisible array of signals continued to govern them, gave them both an instant view of each other's minds.

Wardour asked, 'Are you ready for what I'm about to propose?'

'Certainly.'

'I trust you completely, you understand that?'

'Yes.'

'He's asked you to call him Jonah. Am I right?'

'Except in public.'

'Then we'll call him Jonah. I'd better explain that I have reason to believe that our friend Jonah was somehow involved in the plot against me. I know that sounds paranoid, but *plot* is the only word for it. He has no idea of your part in that.' Hendry steadily met Wardour's eye, too socially unsure of himself to comment on this. He felt he owed Wardour some recompense. But the game had moved on.

Wardour continued, 'I want you to pass him some infor-

342

mation. Be as indiscreet about me as you like. Anything to sharpen his appetite. By the way, how friendly were you with McDade?'

'Not very.'

'Good. Then you'll find this easy.'

As the evening wore on, eased by a drink or two, Wardour and Hendry improvised a dialogue. Wardour took the part of Sweetman. Hendry showed more cunning than Wardour would have credited him with. Satisfaction and enhanced respect marked their parting. The only imperative now was to get the story to Sweetman soon.

Apart from occasional meetings with his stockbroker or the firm that dealt in property on his behalf, Sweetman was never socially active much before the Westminster day's business began in the early afternoon. The MP's name was still being bandied about in the Press, and on his way to Sweetman's Knightsbridge flat, Hendry picked up a few of the tabloids which the MP was unlikely to get delivered. On the previous day, Hendry had smashed the equipment of one of their photographers, telling the enraged pressman 'Invasion of privacy'. The paper in question had not run the story, but Hendry could see that soon they would drop their interest in Sweetman and come after *him*.

Hendry took the precaution of breakfasting first, because Sweetman was a late-night eater and started the day with no more than coffee and dry toast. Offered the choice of coffee or mineral water, Hendry took water, as Sweetman outlined his programme for the day. Wait till he mentions my name, Wardour had suggested, rather than fabricate a moment and risk giving something away.

Sweetman, chuckling over the memory of Hendry bringing his foot down on the press vermin's camera, said, 'I must say, putting me on to you was one of the best things Roddy Wardour's ever done in his life.'

Hendry paused, then said, 'I think Mr Wardour's in trouble.'

'Really? How?'

'When I was at his house fixing up to come and work for you,

I overheard something. I wouldn't normally mention it, but I think he needs help.'

'The Wardour family are very dear to me. Perhaps you'd better go on.'

'Something to do with the people who kidnapped him.'

'Oh?'

'An Irishman called McDade, and I think one of the others . . . he's still in touch with them. It sounded like they're working for him now.'

Solemnly Sweetman asked, 'What work would that be?'

'He wants to find out who was behind it all. I think he's got them an amnesty with the law. They're on his side now.'

'One of them was killed, of course,' Sweetman said.

While in the USA, Wardour had speculated that Knight was dead. With all the complications of his return to Britain, Hendry had missed the news about the murder. After the initial release, the police had shut down further reports. A mental block on the subject had kept Hendry from pursuing it further. He realised now that he had discounted Wardour's opinion, had privately gone on believing that Knight was still alive.

'I didn't know,' Hendry said. Now the story was rearing its head again, he was anxious to learn more. But he was afraid now of what his curiosity would reveal.

Sweetman resumed, 'This was a telephone call you overheard?'

'That's right.'

Sounding more than ever like a family doctor, Sweetman said, 'You thought he needed help.'

'I heard him say, keep the police out of it.'

'He was not talking to the police, then?'

'It didn't sound like it.'

'What help, do you think?'

Hendry said, 'Maybe somebody should tell the police.'

'Against Mr Wardour's own wishes?'

'I don't think he knows what he's doing.'

'He has been through a very bad time. You think it's affected his judgment?'

344

'I don't know him personally, obviously,' Hendry said, 'but from what I heard, I'd say he's pretty disturbed.'

'Where are the kidnappers now? Did you gather that?' Sweetman asked.

'In hiding somewhere, I'd guess.'

'Presumably he has to bring them out of hiding.'

'I think that's what he was setting up,' Hendry replied.

'Who would you say he was talking to?'

'I couldn't say. It might have been the woman he was involved with.'

'Ah, Holly something,' Sweetman said, with false vagueness.

'The American woman,' Hendry answered dismissively.

'So that's still on. I'm surprised. Or perhaps not. Ed, you've done the right thing. Let me mull over the best course of action to take. You didn't pick up anything else?'

'I got the feeling that wherever he was going, McDade was already there.'

'And do you have any idea where this is?'

'I reckon Spain,' Hendry said. 'I heard him and his wife discussing it. I didn't catch the name, but I think it's his wife's sister's house.'

'Spain,' Sweetman repeated, with pretend incredulity, as if this was a country he had barely heard of.

Later that day Sweetman called the foreign contact number, which was always on answerphone. Without identifying himself, he said briefly that Wardour and his associates would be meeting in Spain. He gave the probable location of Robleda. More to the point, Sweetman mentioned the name McDade.

On the verge of hysteria, Sweetman's motive was simple now. If Wardour persisted, the trails he uncovered would lead all the way back to Westminster. This thing had gone on far too long and had to be terminated. The last meeting with Weidinger had scared Sweetman. With so many other problems, he obeyed his nature and bowed to the stronger personality. Weidinger had the strength of evil in him, and Sweetman was in no state to cross such a man.

★

345

As luck, or bad luck, would have it, the police tap on Sweetman's phone began the following morning. The observation van had been in position only a couple of hours when Sweetman and Hendry emerged onto the street and flagged down a taxi. Just as Sweetman got in, Hendry discovered that his wallet was missing.

'I had it earlier. It may have fallen out.' Hendry had taken his jacket off in the flat, and draped it loosely over a chair. He looked embarrassed. Sweetman handed him the keys.

'Probably somewhere in there, dear boy. Go and have a look.'

There was never any guarantee with Sweetman's timing, so for Stanger to hang around on the street would have been impracticable. To give Stanger maximum time in the flat, Hendry wanted to phone immediately rather than wait to be free of Sweetman's company. By Hendry's standards it was a neatly executed manoeuvre. But on this occasion military precision was not enough.

Hendry went back indoors and retrieved the wallet from where he had hidden it, under a carpet. Then he rapidly tapped in the number of his flat, where Stanger was waiting. 'He's out now. You should have at least three hours.'

Hendry hung up, and was promptly out on the street again, brandishing his wallet and smiling.

For purposes of realism, the police had let their unmarked observation van collect one parking ticket, which remained on the windscreen. Then they had warned the traffic wardens on that beat to take no further action, although the van might be there for some time, and men of no particular description might occasionally be seen coming and going around the spot.

They had taped one or two innocuous calls by Sweetman. But now they got the brief message sent by Hendry. From the mobile telecommunications centre, the duty officer now replayed what he had just heard to Mike Wiley at Scotland Yard.

'Somebody's about to turn the place over,' Wiley said. 'Don't move till I get there.'

By the time Wiley arrived and entered the van for a briefing, Stanger was already inside Sweetman's apartment. 'Nobody else

346

entered the place, and we haven't seen him before. He's been in there ten minutes.'

'OK, let's go.'

Detailing a detective constable to cover the rear of the property, Wiley contemplated the solid Victorian door. He was prepared to lever it open, but first he rang all the bells except Sweetman's. The ground floor answered, and into the security phone Wiley gently said, 'Sorry, madam, this is the police. Do you think you could let us in?' Wiley cursed impatiently when the expected buzz refused to come. Instead, a desiccated, very small old lady with a fox fur, head, claws and all, about her shoulders, opened the door to them. The realm of faded duchesses, Wiley thought, as the bright, beady eyes of fox and ancient lady peered at him glassily.

'Good morning, officer, can I assist you?'

Wiley gave a big smile to cover the brevity of his explanation. The old lady blinked in bemusement as a detective ushered her back to the stale opulence of her apartment.

Wiley knocked on Sweetman's door. There was no answer, no sound of movement. He called, 'Police. We know you're in there. Don't give us a hard time. We've got men outside, so don't go out the window.' Wiley tried the door. To his disbelief it was open. A stupid or a very confident man was inside.

'He might have a gun, sir,' Lucas Brand said.

'Oh, sod all that,' Wiley answered.

There were days for policemen, as for soldiers, when danger became just another boredom to shrug off. You developed a feel about these things. Wiley entered the flat.

Caught going through one of the antique bureaux, the keys to which Sweetman always left in an oriental vase, as Hendry had noted and reported, Bobby Stanger looked pissed off, *really* pissed off. He had already decided that to run or fight wouldn't help him at all. So docilely, although with extreme bad grace, he surrendered.

'Pull in Hendry,' Mike Wiley said. 'Your chance to redeem yourself, Lucas. But there's a catch.'

347

'Catch?' Lucas Brand asked.

'You've got to find him so this MP Sweetman doesn't know we're on to them. Tell Hendry we've got him on conspiracy, and his pal Stanger is banged away in one of our cells. And then you invite Hendry to come and talk to us as soon as he can do it without Sweetman knowing. Providing it's within the next eight hours. Otherwise we're going to hit him like a ton of fucking bricks. And don't say fucking, it's uncouth.'

Buoyed up by his chief's new-found high spirits, Lucas Brand had an idea. From the address Stanger had given, it was clear that he was staying at Hendry's place. Brand drove out there, used Stanger's confiscated key to let himself in, and waited. Brand occupied himself with a *Times* crossword compendium which he always kept in his car. His assumption was right; within two hours Hendry made telephone contact. At the unexpected voice he said, 'Bobby?'

Brand answered, 'Mr Hendry? Don't hang up. I'm a police officer.'

More than half certain that Hendry would drop the receiver and run, Brand waited. But the line stayed open. Brand continued, 'Stanger is under arrest. Unless you want to join him, it would be a good idea to cooperate. We want you to come to Scotland Yard, as soon as you can without Jonah Sweetman knowing. It's absolutely essential he has no knowledge of this. When you get to the Yard, walk into the reception and ask for me, Detective Sergeant Lucas Brand. I'm going straight back there now, and I hope we'll meet soon.'

Across the telephonic space of London, Brand could feel Hendry thinking. The few seconds of intense silence were terminated by a click. But the silence was enough for Brand to tell Wiley, on his return to the Yard, 'He'll be here.' And within the hour Wiley was alone with Hendry in an interview room.

Hendry was in the filthy temper of a man who has been forced to do something he knows to be bad strategy, forced because the only alternative was to face an unknown which might turn out to be worse. The only strength he had in reserve was Wardour, but Wardour's was the one name Hendry refused to use.

'Why did you and Stanger burgle Sweetman?'

Hendry fell back on the contingency story. 'Blackmail.'

'For what?'

Hendry shrugged. 'After this sex orgy thing, we thought we might get something useful on him.' The explanation stank, but was just plausible enough to deflect the spotlight from Wardour's involvement. Hendry relapsed into a brooding silence. Wiley's irritation showed in his next line of questions, in which he used a piece of information he had gleaned when Wardour bargained for Hendry's immunity, an immunity which Wiley was glad to have an excuse for rescinding now.

'You're ex-army, correct?'

'That's right.'

'Served in Northern Ireland?'

'Five tours.'

'Paras?'

'Yes.'

'Tough guys, eh?'

'Just soldiers.'

'Loyal? Were you?'

'What do you mean?'

'A simple question for a soldier, I would have thought.'

'Read my record if you're interested.'

'I don't need references, lieutenant,' Wiley answered. The designation of rank revealed that he had indeed read Hendry's record. 'I've got you here to offer a deal. And believe me, this is the last chance you get.'

'What about Stanger?' Hendry asked.

Wiley ignored the question and said: 'This is what you are going to do. If you're successful we'll overlook your latest misbehaviour. Otherwise, you and your American friend can look at bars for a while.'

'What deal?'

'You give Sweetman a simple message.'

'He'll want to know where I got it.'

'Tell him somebody who couldn't identify himself gave it to

349

you. My guess is, Sweetman's so edgy he'll swallow anything you tell him.'

'What message?'

'Just this. We've got Knight's killer on film.'

All Hendry's suppressed fears about Robin Knight now struggled to burst into the open. Wiley's watching eyes were those of the perfect policeman – cold, compassionate, and businesslike at the same time. He knew the size of the blow he had just struck Hendry. But Wiley demonstrated his control of the situation by refusing to acknowledge that Hendry and Knight had once been 'colleagues'. There was work to do. Still, Wiley respected Hendry for the composure which he managed to maintain. 'You tell him that, and then you resign.'

'What?'

'You're working for Sweetman?' Wiley had deduced this from seeing them together in the restaurant.

'Yes.'

'Quit the job. You've already done what Wardour wanted, haven't you?' Wiley's smile was brutally candid. But it was not a smile between equals. Hendry knew better than to reciprocate. Once again he was being wound up to carry out the dictates of others, the Army all over again. At least in the Army it was all about survival, man and officer alike. Always a pawn, he had wanted to be at the centre of things. But so far in civilian life Hendry felt at the centre of things the way the model duck is at the centre of the shooting gallery.

'Agreed, then?' Wiley said.

Hendry answered: 'You're the boss.'

Later, as it was getting dark, Wiley took a stroll on the Victoria Embankment. The Thames had once been London's largest sewer, and even now it remained a dirty, unglamorous river. But its openness was a relief from the crowded, dirtier streets of the city.

Space helped Wiley think. Something troubled him, and the nearest he could get to it was his own cleverness. If three decades as a policeman had taught Wiley one thing, it was that at moments like this, when all the pieces seem to be fitting together with gratifying neatness, the one per cent margin of error in even the best judgments can prove fatal. To Wiley's mind, unless he took care of that one per cent soon, all the ground he had covered would simply lead back into the quicksand in which most of the Wardour case had foundered all along.

The one per cent had walked away from Scotland Yard when he had released Hendry. Wiley had skated over the reasons for the burglary of Sweetman's flat. Hendry and Stanger had both claimed to be a team working independently. The blackmail angle was an unbreakable lie and Wiley had to accept it. The one thing Hendry would not do was suck Wardour into a conspiracy charge. He knew which side his bread was buttered.

In Sweetman's flat the police had left everything tidy, with no sign of anyone having been there. But they had overlooked two things. One, Stanger's indifference, having been caught in the act, as to whether he had replaced the papers exactly as he had found them. And two, the fact that beneath his louche exterior Jonah Sweetman had a calculating and obsessively observant mind, which effortlessly retained detail such as the precise position in which he had left things in his own living space.

The routine of Hendry's job was for him to phone Sweetman at home mid-way through the evening. If there was no answer, it meant that business had detained him at the House. Otherwise, if Sweetman proposed to go out, which he invariably did, Hendry would go along. Although the media fuss had died down, Sweetman had quickly become dependent on Hendry's company. Today, as usual, he asked him to come to the flat.

When Hendry arrived, inwardly nervous at the assignment Wiley had given him, he found Sweetman still dressed in his formal House of Commons clothes, standing unrelaxed and accusing in the centre of his exquisitely tasteful living room. The customary drink was not offered.

'I'll come straight to the point,' Sweetman said. 'Somebody's been in here today. Do you know anything about it?'

Hendry looked round, acting shocked. 'No.'

'A very clever job. Nothing seems to have been taken. But

351

things have been disturbed.' Sweetman seemed almost distraught. 'You came back in here this morning while I was in the taxi. You could have left the door open for somebody.'

'I didn't do that.'

'I don't wish to argue. The money I owe you is on the sideboard over there.'

Hendry protested, 'You've got this completely wrong – ' But Sweetman had also been reflecting on the ease with which Hendry had passed on the information about Wardour. Everything seemed to fit Sweetman's recently developed conclusion that Hendry was an undercover policeman.

He turned his back. 'Please leave.'

'There's something you ought to – '

'I trusted you, and I no longer do so. Leave immediately or I'm calling the police.' A stupidly ironic thing to say, but Sweetman could think of nothing else.

Hendry asked, 'Are you sure that's wise?'

Sweetman erupted with rage. 'What do you mean? How dare you?' He spun round, his jowly face purple beneath the unnatural straw-colour of his hairpiece. Shaking, he screamed, 'Get out!'

Hendry didn't know what to do. If Sweetman called in the police, it would be local coppers who had no knowledge of Wiley or the Scotland Yard operation. This time round Hendry would find himself under real arrest. He backed away, collecting Sweetman's money as he went. At the door, gauchely keeping his bargain, Hendry muttered, 'They've got Knight's murderer on film.' That was it. The job was done. Hendry left before Sweetman, wild-eyed and furious, flew completely out of control.

Later in the evening Hendry rang Wiley's direct number and confirmed that he had communicated as ordered.

Wiley sounded tired. 'How did Sweetman take it?'

'Pretty cool, really.'

'When you gave him the message?'

'Didn't bat an eyelid.'

'Good.'

352

'What about Stanger?'

'Don't worry. But if either of you cross my path again, you'll go down for a few years. Got it?'

'I'll bear it in mind,' Hendry said, and hung up.

For Jonah Sweetman the night was long and unbearable.

The political aspect of his part in the Wardour affair had always been ice-clear. It had been an act of faith to scupper Wardour the politician, not the man. To Sweetman the distinction was a simple one, without which democratic politics would be impossible. Sweetman's practical role had not troubled him, either. Life on the back-benches had left him very much aware that real power was exercised in closed rooms far removed from the green leather and braying voices of the Commons chamber. The same urge that periodically drove him to unorthodox sexual gatherings had been gratified by the bizarre yet potent activity of passing Wardour-gossip to a foreign phone number which never replied. Roddy had been successfully discredited. That should have been the end of the story. But just when Sweetman was feeling sated and bored by the episode, things had begun to pile up in a frightening conjunction.

Somebody had been searching his flat. Sweetman had the intriguer's grasp of these things. They had entered his flat, taken nothing, determined that he should remain ignorant of the fact. Only the security people behaved like that. Although Sweetman had blown his top at the immediate target, the long night hours persuaded him that Hendry was not the main culprit. Sweetman felt at the mercy of all the invisible apparatus of state control, of which he was such a staunch supporter when it was applied to others – hidden cameras, surveillance, bugs. Every step he took would lead him into a trap they had set for him. Added to which they had caught him bare-arsed in that west end club, where plainly they had known he was a client. They had just been waiting their moment to pounce. And then Hendry had produced this key information about Wardour. And at the back of it all, putrefying slowly in Sweetman's consciousness, was the Knight murder.

353

In a cold sweat, racked with guilt and fear, Sweetman picked up the phone. But Tony Gwyer's number was engaged. Sweetman snapped the receiver down, suddenly aware that if they had broken in here, they would certainly be taping his calls. Sweetman slipped out of his flat, and with constant glances at the empty pavements behind him, walked to Gwyer's Ebury Street address.

Gwyer opened the door wearing a silk dressing gown over striped trousers, a gleaming white shirt and spotted silk tie. Sweetman by contrast felt shabby and old.

'You look bad, Jonah.' Gwyer spoke the words with relish. He had one of those voices that even exhaustion never dulls, the voice of a man who will do business at any hour.

'I think we could be in trouble.'

'*We?*'

'They may be on to me.'

'*They?*'

'Somebody's been in my flat.'

'*Somebody?*' Gwyer showed no sympathy. His self-made-man scorn had no room for the dithery finesse of Sweetman, whose twitching was like an infection he had to repel. 'Let me get this straight, Jonah. Have you been doing something *wrong?*'

Too shaky for anger, Sweetman said in an injured tone, 'You know what I've been doing.'

'Do I?' Then Gwyer dropped the pretence. 'OK, Jonah. Take a break. You've done your bit. But don't forget that you're involved. We wouldn't want our Swiss friend to lose confidence, would we?'

'They're on to me,' Sweetman repeated. 'I can feel them everywhere.'

Gwyer whispered, 'We are not having this conversation, Jonah.'

'But – '

'We are not having this conversation!' Gwyer shouted.

'If they get their hands on me, they'll break me. I know they will.'

'You've been watching too many Gestapo movies,' Gwyer

said. 'Go home and take some valium, for God's sake. Come on, I'll walk you back. You need some fresh air.'

On their way to Knightsbridge, Gwyer said, 'The thing is, Jonah, take it from me, whoever lets our Swiss associate down, I wouldn't want to be that person. You get my drift?'

Twenty-eight

Sweetman needed a day. One day, that was all, a blank space between the disasters that were caving in on him and the rest of his life. But the one last appointment he tried to cancel proved intractable. The tone of his constituency secretary's voice conveyed the intimation that only a deathbed scenario would be sufficient to prevent the meeting they had scheduled for that day. Sweetman always flattered his constituency secretary, an earnest financier who had eyes on a seat for himself, with regular visits to London, lunch at the House, a conspiratorial exposure to Westminster's unique atmosphere. The illness which Sweetman had pleaded was conveniently forgotten and he braced himself for the slap on the wrist which he guessed was coming. But it was worse than that.

The secretary had his free lunch first, then suggested a walk in the park. What worried Sweetman was the power which the secretary clearly felt free to wield, and his own weakness against it.

'The association feel that you've served the party honourably for a long time – ' Sweetman looked at him uneasily. 'With great distinction,' the secretary added.

'And what of that?' Sweetman asked.

'Your plans for the next general election were the subject of some discussion.'

'I have no plans.'

'Ah, really? You mean – ?'

'No plans other than my normal course.'

'In that case,' the secretary said, 'I've been delegated to inform you – '

'Resign or get the chop,' Sweetman finished the sentence. 'That it, eh? What was it, that business at the club?'

'Don't misunderstand,' the secretary said. 'The constituency

356

likes to have a high profile member. It just depends on what sort of profile we're talking about.'

'So I'm going to be deselected.'

'It would save the party a lot of embarrassment if that wasn't necessary.'

'How long have I got?'

'To do what?'

'Decide.'

'What decision do you have in mind?'

Sweetman came close to losing his temper. 'I don't have to stand down, you know. I can fight the seat as an independent. I might win. Or I'd split your vote and let someone else through.'

'You could, and you might. But you won't. If you did stand against the party, of course, we'd have to mobilise everything against you that we could lay our hands on.'

'Such as?'

'Jonah, we've been friends for a long time. A lot of what I'm doing now, I learnt from you. I'm hardly going to reveal weapons you might force us to use one day, am I?'

'How did they know about the brothel?' Sweetman demanded. 'Who was really behind all that?'

'A case of bad luck, surely. And poor judgment on your part.'

'That's not the truth,' Sweetman said. 'And you bloody well know it.'

But the constituency secretary refused to admit more, and Sweetman returned to Knightsbridge feeling old age, declining health and social disgrace crowding his horizon like invading armies. He began to wonder if somewhere behind this lurked Roderick Wardour, the one man with a motive for making Sweetman pay. As he settled into a dismal, alcohol-blurred day, he tried to dignify the mess he had got into, by believing it the fruit of another man's revenge.

Later, a desolate man as he reflected that by now the Whips' office, and God knew who else on the Westminster grapevine, would know about the deselection, Sweetman drifted back to the Commons. He half hoped, half feared that he would run into Roderick Wardour. He felt about Wardour the way a man

357

who has lied in the confessional feels about meeting his priest in the street. There was no single point at which Sweetman made any of the decisions which were to guide his conduct in the next twelve hours. But as he sat in his office writing a note to Tony Gwyer, Sweetman knew that he was setting in train a sequence of events which he would not be able to put into reverse. The note to Gwyer was intended to make going back an impossibility.

Sweetman told Gwyer one simple thing: he had left a document which gave the facts behind the Wardour case. Sweetman was no more specific than that. He did not tell Gwyer why he had done this, to whom the document was addressed, or to whom it had been despatched. In fact, at that moment the document did not exist. He sent the note to Gwyer in the Commons internal mail system, which, from the lateness of the hour, meant that Gwyer would not receive it until he arrived at the House the next day. By then the confession to which Sweetman had referred would be complete, and further points of no return would have been passed.

Sweetman had not written these words out of any regard for his fellow MP, or even to make Gwyer sweat with fear, although he knew the letter would have that effect. It was purely a selfish tactic, demanded by his own psychology. To state that he had written a confession was the only way Sweetman could be sure, as he returned to Knightsbridge, that he *would* write it.

Stanger arrived back at Hendry's place at daylight. After a bad night, during which the skill of others at manipulating him preyed on his mind, Hendry had spent a couple of hours in a dead sleep. Stanger's ring on the doorbell was a disagreeable awakening. There was no doorphone. Pulling on shirt and trousers Hendry lumbered down to street level. Stanger's unshaven, puzzled face was a relief. Hendry had bet himself it would be the police again.

Neither man was in a mood for civilised dialogue, but they knew each other's flashpoints well enough to let the heavy silence of the occasion defuse some of their temper. Hendry made instant coffee, sludgy and metallic. Ignoring the taste provided a necessary diversion.

Eventually Stanger said, 'What the fuck was all that?'

Hendry explained everything.

'Do you plan to tell Wardour all this?'

'No.'

'You don't trust that guy either?'

'I trust him. I just don't want him to know we screwed up.'

'*We* screwed up?' Stanger was still sore at his night in the cells, followed by a brusque and unapologetic release into London's unwelcoming daylight.

'We got caught,' Hendry said.

But Stanger had spent the night refining solutions, and Hendry's squaddie logic, his instinct for the cut-and-dried answer, now irritated the American. 'They're tapping Sweetman's phone,' Stanger said. 'It has to be. That's how they were ready for the break-in, and how they connected me to you.'

'Why should they tap Sweetman's phone?'

'Why should Wardour want us to break into the goddamn place?'

Hendry asked: 'Did you find anything before the police got you?'

'Things don't come with labels on, saying, *incriminating evidence*.'

'Sweetman knew the place had been turned over.'

Stanger shrugged. 'The police were the last ones out. If they left footprints, what can I do?'

'Maybe they wanted Sweetman to know. Why is everybody so interested in that guy?'

'It's one of those cases,' Stanger said. 'Like there's a drain cover in the road, and every so often it lifts off and shows you a burning pit below. Then somebody tamps it down again, but it just lifts off again someplace else.'

'You can always walk away,' Hendry said.

'Yeah, sure.'

'What do you want?'

Stanger said, 'I want the same as the next guy, career enhancement. In my case that points at Barron Odell. I want to come out of this case shiny enough for him to employ me. How about you?'

'Wardour is a possible meal ticket,' Hendry conceded. 'But most of all I want to get McDade. He threw me to the wolves, and once I'm even with the wolves, I'm ready for him.'

Later, Hendry said, 'I have a feeling Wardour will want us both to go to Spain. How do you feel about that?'

Stanger's mood had improved by now. 'Wouldn't miss it.'

As if he overheard their conversation, Roderick Wardour came on the phone and said, 'We've got Jonah booked for dinner tomorrow. You and Bobby could do his flat then.'

Hendry was still reluctant to tell Wardour the truth about the fiasco of the burglary. He also hoped to survive Sweetman's paranoia. Hendry could see a time when the Wardour affair would blow over, and he would be on the street again. Members of Parliament, even if their names were Wardour and Sweetman, could supply useful references. So Hendry made noises of compliance, and avoided raising questions in Wardour's probing mind. But questions were all Wardour had left to drive him. He had forgotten that when Sweetman was briefly their guest-refugee at Regent's Park, Jessica had pencilled in a supper date to give Sweetman something to hang on to. Wardour intended to use the opportunity to rerun the events which had led up to the kidnap, and observe Sweetman's reaction.

When he mentioned it to Jessica, she said: 'I was just about to cancel it.'

'Why?' Wardour asked.

'I can't face it.'

'It would be very helpful to me.'

'You can see Jonah at the House. Or go round to his flat. I don't want to socialise at the moment.'

Rather than reveal anything, Wardour grudgingly accepted. But when he arrived home that evening, after finding the hours and aura of the Commons more oppressive than ever, Jessica had different news. She had tried Sweetman's number and, surprised at finding him in, had prepared to postpone the supper invitation. But Sweetman, sounding very strange, had misconstrued her call as a reminder, and had begun to evade it himself. He had sounded exhausted, and claimed to be unwell.

'Oh, I'm sorry. What's the matter?'

'Must be some damned flu,' Sweetman said.

Feeling sorry for him, Jessica said: 'Some time soon, then. Give yourself the benefit of the doubt and say yes. Rod could really do with cheering up.'

'Jessica darling, my entertaining days are over.' He sounded drunk, self-pitying and perverse. 'I haven't been worthy of you, your kindness, your goodness . . .' He became maudlin.

Although bad at insincerity, Jessica protested, 'Jonah, what is this? You're the life and soul of the party.' The not very good political joke was unintentional. But no humour came from the other end, only a deepening air of gloom and guilt.

'I don't deserve a friend like you, Jessie. You're different from all the others. All the hard-faced bitches.'

Jessica tried once more, in a complete reversal of her original intention. 'Jonah, why don't you come over and talk about it? Just you and me?'

'Temptation indeed,' Sweetman's slurred voice continued. 'But I have things to do. Politics. Dear Jessie, why did you marry a politician? All politicians are whores. But thank you for all your kindnesses.'

'Jonah – '

Helpless, Jessica had listened on while Sweetman hung up.

Sweetman's private strategy had failed. In spite of what he had written to Tony Gwyer, he was unable to set down a coherent account of his part in the Wardour affair. The combination of personal disgust and alcohol had ruined his mental focus. When he finally put words to paper, what took shape was a rambling letter to Roderick Wardour.

First, Sweetman gave an advance explanation of what he planned to do. He specified no single cause, only the culmination of several factors. Deepening cycles of depression, in spite of his public image, were making his life unliveable. Then, by getting caught *in flagrante* at that sex club, he had become a

361

standing joke at Westminster. Added to which, certain mal-functions of advancing age were, in his case, becoming serious. He had always intended to choose his own way of going, and now was the time. Professional pride kept Sweetman from mentioning that his constituency was about to deselect him. It would hurt too much to speak of that.

Instead of settling accounts, Sweetman produced an emotional and incoherent harangue, pleading with Wardour to accept what had happened, to take no further action which would jeopardise the party. The penalty Sweetman was about to pay at the hands of his constituency gave feeling to these words. Attempting to dignify his own humiliation, Sweetman insisted that a time came in the lives of all politicians when party interest had to take precedence over a man's private desires or hopes. For himself, he said, the future was a void, words which Wardour would understand soon after he read this, if not before. Wardour, on the other hand, still had the prospect of a happy life ahead of him. All the more reason for putting the party above impulses of retaliation, which would injure Wardour just as much as his colleagues. Half-remembered Shakespeare swam into Sweetman's drink-blurred mind, and he wrote how of all the conspirators Brutus was the only one who had killed Caesar not from envy, but for the good of the state.

These were the last words Sweetman was to write. The sound of a car door down in the street distracted him. From the edge of a curtain he watched people moving about. The thought of the Roman conspirators had brought his mind to Edmund Hendry. Sweetman turned back into the room.

Jessica summarised what Sweetman had said and how he had sounded. Wardour listened sympathetically, but secretly wondered if Sweetman suspected that he was on to him. The old bastard was the best actor in Westminster, and Jessica was not the most difficult person to fool. Wardour decided to call Hendry again.

To Hendry, Wardour suggested that Sweetman appeared to be unwell, that perhaps something had happened. A visit to his apartment might be to everybody's advantage. 'I'll see what I can do,' Hendry said.

Hendry was thinking around the best way to handle Wardour's request when the phone rang again. By a ghoulish coincidence it was Sweetman. Hendry cleared his throat: something sinister was coming. Hendry recalled Stanger's remark about the bottomless pit that kept opening up. Sweetman sounded like a pathetic windbag. 'Ed, my dear boy, I wanted to apologise. I was completely out of line accusing you like that. The thing is, there are people here – they're outside now, just waiting for the right moment. Then they'll come for me. I don't know what to do.'

'People?' Hendry asked.

'You're the only man I know who can handle them. They're closing in on me. Only you can help.' Sweetman was rambling, drunk. 'I'll be right there,' Hendry said.

'Don't leave it too long.' Sweetman's voice quavered. 'I'm scared.'

'It smells bad,' Stanger said, when Hendry relayed the call.

'What do I do, ignore it?'

'I'll come as back-up,' Stanger said. 'But there's no way I'm getting caught in that apartment again.'

Hendry said, 'It all depends on him letting me in anyway.'

'Not necessarily.'

'How's that?'

Stanger produced keys, replicas of the ones with which he had broken into Sweetman's flat, and which the police had impounded. 'Moral, whenever you take a copy of something, always take a copy of the copy. For luck.'

Meanwhile, Sweetman was not answering his doorbell. Lights were on, so while Stanger concealed himself outside, Hendry let himself in. Gingerly stepping into the flat, he called Sweetman's name. No one answered.

He began to search room after room, pausing, looking everywhere for signs. Before he got to the bathroom he knew what he would find.

From the bathroom doorway he muttered, 'Oh Christ!' Jonah

Sweetman's terrified dead eyes stared back at him. For a moment Hendry thought it was someone else. But he recognised the yellow-dotted tie. Sweetman had left his wig behind somewhere, that was it. Hendry had never seen the blotchy bald scalp before. This shocked him more than the fact that Sweetman was dead. Fully dressed, the old MP lay in an almost full bath. An electric heater rested half-submerged against his slumped body, its cord running under the door to a power socket outside.

Hendry retraced his steps and got out of the flat as fast as he could. Nobody had seen him enter, nobody saw him leave. The only trace of him they would find there was his fingerprints, and that was nothing new.

On the street Hendry walked straight past Stanger, shooting him the briefest of nods to get away from the vicinity of Sweetman's flat, with no delay for explanation. They stayed in town, drinking their way across London. For official purposes, Hendry had rung the bell, but not been able to raise Sweetman. Nor would anyone else. But that, Hendry thought, the world could discover in its own good time.

Roderick Wardour had already left, and Jessica was getting ready for a morning's committee work for one of her voluntary organisations when she caught the news of Jonah Sweetman's death on breakfast TV. By the time she collapsed in a chair, the item had passed. They had mentioned neither suicide nor suspicious circumstances, and Jessica managed to shake herself out of shock and continue her business.

Later in the day, Tony Gwyer rang. The two events were not unconnected.

'Hi, it's Tony.'

'Oh, hullo.' Jessica's tone was uncertain. Gwyer had always agreed not to ring the house. But he would have made sure that Rod was tied up at Westminster.

'Did you hear about Jonah?'

'Yes. I still can't accept it.'

'Some very strange things are being said.'

'Such as?'

364

'Can we meet?'

'Have you talked to Rod?'

'To get permission to speak to you?'

'No, I meant – '

'Time was, you couldn't see me fast enough. And I use the verb *see* to cover a lot of things.'

'Must you?'

'I think we should meet.'

'I can't.'

'It's in your interest. And that accident-prone husband of yours. You wouldn't want me to break my vow of silence, would you?'

An hour later they met in a municipal car park in west London. From there they drove out of the city in Gwyer's Mercedes.

There was one good thing about Tony Gwyer, he wasn't about to show off his bleeding heart. But Jessica recognised her own hypocrisy: she found repellent a man with whom only weeks before she had enjoyed a carnality that now frightened her, yet which she could not help constantly recalling. At one point Gwyer moved his hand from the gear lever to her thigh. Jessica eased it away. But his knowledge of her body made her uneasy.

No sentimentalist, Gwyer grinned. 'Finished using me, then?'

'What do you mean?'

'What a little puritan we are.' Gwyer accelerated through lanes of traffic. 'I was your revenge on Roddy, for his fling with that Yankee piece. Oh, it's all right, I don't mind. I'd have done the same.'

'Why did you call me?'

'Has it occurred to you that I might just want to see you again?'

'That's the last reason I would have thought of.'

'You know the police are treating Jonah's death as foul play?'

'I didn't know.'

'The informed whisper is that Jonah knew something about that Roddy business. And your scheming and ruthless husband took care of it. We of course know different, don't we?'

Jessica said, 'You hate Rod, don't you? That's why you enjoyed it in bed so much, isn't it?'

'You may find this difficult to believe,' Gwyer said, 'but that was the classiest sex I've ever had in my life. While we were in bed together I never thought of anybody else, my wife, your husband – they didn't exist. Afterwards, I admit, the trophy aspect gained some appeal.'

'Did you just get me out here to pump me?'

'Sweet Jessie, only one of life's innocents would phrase the question like that. But no, I wanted to warn you. Scandals stick, and Roddy's got a lot of question marks hanging over him.'

'Aren't you glad?'

'I don't want to see the party hurt. So if I had to cover up for Roddy to save the party, I'd do it. If you know anything about this Sweetman business, it might help if you let me know. Because everybody's pointing the finger at Roddy again.'

'If Rod's got anything to say to you, he'll say it himself. I don't have any power over him any more.'

'But do you trust his judgment now? What I'm asking you to do is act on his behalf, in the interests of all of us. I think Roddy lost touch with reality the day he started seeing himself as the future of the Conservative party.'

'Why should I trust you?' Jessica asked.

'Because you know I'm a bastard, but at least I'm willing to be *your* bastard. And you're still not sure about Roddy, are you?'

'Aren't I?'

'The Odell woman. Is that all over? He's not making any more unspecified trips abroad?' Gwyer asked pointedly.

'My marriage isn't your business.'

'A politician's married to the party, not a woman. And by the way, I won't tell Roddy about this meeting if you don't.'

Jessica said coldly, 'I've got nothing to tell you, so you may as well drive back.'

'OK,' Gwyer said. 'But if Jonah sends you any messages from beyond the grave, you'd be a fool not to let me know.'

★

366

'The word is suicide,' Wardour told Jessica that evening, over a meagre supper which neither of them had felt like preparing, or now felt much like eating.

'Because of the scandal?' Jessica was dismissive. 'It would take more than that to sink Jonah.'

'I wonder if somebody killed him,' Wardour said.

All day Jessica had prayed that it would turn out to be a natural death. 'Why?'

Wardour was reluctant to raise this again. But the pressure was too much. 'The weekend I went abroad – he was the only person who knew where and when.'

'The only one?' Jessica was not above this final stab. Holly's name hung in the air, unspoken. With lowered eyes Wardour tried to redirect the conversation to Sweetman.

'I don't say that Jonah was guilty of anything other than carelessness. But he might have told someone else.' Understating what he really believed, Wardour was shaken by Jessica's reaction.

'I think that's preposterous. He was just a sad old man. The idea of somebody killing him – '

'According to your version of common sense, Jessie, certain things can't ever happen. Except that they *do* happen, they happen all the time. And when it happens to you, you suddenly realise what it means to be a victim.'

'I don't mind you talking rubbish,' Jessica retorted, 'but do you have to sound so pompous?'

'I see,' Wardour said. 'Now I'm not an international statesman, I'm pompous. It's all about status, isn't it?'

'You don't think,' Jessica asked coolly, 'that you're suffering from just a hint of megalomania?'

'When I was on the up and up I was a man of destiny. Now they've thrown me out, it's megalomania. Amusing, isn't it?' One thing the Wardour affair had brought out was that Jessica did not appreciate irony. Determined to capitalise on his moment of grievance, Wardour added, 'When I talked of hope for Ireland, I was a man of vision. Then I got caught in bed with the wrong woman, and suddenly I was a filthy traitor.'

'You knew the score when you entered politics,' Jessica said.

'Yes. I'm not complaining.'

'Is running away any better?'

'What do you suggest?'

'I think the days when you took my advice are over,' Jessica said.

'You want me to swallow it, don't you?'

'Do I?'

'You expect me to take my medicine for being a bad boy, then spend the next ten years trying to crawl back into favour.'

'Do you have a better alternative?'

'Yes,' Wardour said, getting up, wanting no more of this. 'I don't know what it is, but there has to be something better than that.'

An hour later Commander Mike Wiley was at the Wardour house, after one of those brief warning calls that had become so familiar over the last few weeks.

'It always seems easier to come here than get you round to the Yard. Publicity, and all that.'

'Appreciate it,' Wardour murmured.

'Routine, really. The Sweetman business. You knew him well?'

'No more than many other people.'

'Any motives for suicide?'

'It was suicide, then?' Wiley's set expression refused to confirm or deny.

'The scandal?' Wardour suggested.

'People survive scandals, Mr Wardour. One way or another.' Wardour gave a chastened smile. At least Wiley could handle irony.

'If you don't mind me asking, how did he do it?'

'We're not quite ready to issue a statement yet. Would you know of any reason anybody had for killing Mr Sweetman?'

'Absolutely none.'

'You sound very definite.'

Wardour had attempted camouflage by over-statement. 'To

368

the best of my knowledge,' he said. 'But Jonah led a complicated life.'

'As people do,' Wiley replied.

'Surely,' Wardour said, 'suicide or murder, this case is hardly your territory? How does prevention of terrorism overlap with an old ham like Jonah?'

The unspoken, unsayable answer was that Wiley was still searching for a lever on the politician who sat in front of him. And they both knew it. 'Any threat to a politician brings me in sooner or later,' Wiley answered blandly. The Scotland Yard man got up. 'Any time you want to talk to me, sir, you've got my number.' It was the classic policeman's goodbye, a mixture of indifference, suggestion, and menace.

'Goodbye, Commander,' Wardour said at the door. 'Thanks for all you've done.'

A man who disliked wasting his time, Wiley left quickly, before his sense of irony failed altogether.

Days later, Tony Gwyer called Lucian Weidinger in Zurich. Although announcing the news was not his prime motive for calling, he began by saying, 'Sweetman's dead.'

'Yah?' The monosyllable was curtly indifferent. At Weidinger's end of the line there was a sound of tapping . . . a finger, a pencil.

'Sounds like suicide,' Gwyer said.

'Well, you know, he struck me as an unstable personality type.'

Gwyer had liked Sweetman more than he liked Weidinger and did not take kindly to this. 'This isn't a social call.' Gwyer's voice broke the words like bones. 'Sweetman left a confession.'

'Confession?'

'He sent me a note through the House of Commons internal mail, telling me that he'd written a document explaining everything. Before he killed himself.'

'Who's got it?' Weidinger asked.

'I don't know.' Since receiving Sweetman's note, Gwyer had talked to Jessica again, this time on the phone. Gwyer knew a liar a mile away, and anyway, Jessica couldn't lie to save her life. If she said she hadn't heard from the dead MP posthumously, that was proof enough for Gwyer.

'It's interesting,' Weidinger said, 'but I think it's not a big deal.'

Gwyer answered frostily, 'If Sweetman left a confession, and if the police found it when they discovered his body, then, frankly, first they'll get us, and then they'll get you.'

'You suppose the police have the letter?' Weidinger asked.

'No. We'd have heard about it by now. There's only one man Sweetman would want to get it. Wardour. And there's no way Wardour would have discovered the body. So Sweetman must have made sure he got it by some other route. That probably means Wardour has it already.'

At the Zurich end, concentration sculpted the planes of Weidinger's face. 'And this Sweetman knew everything?'

'He was probably the one link they needed.'

'May I ask you a question, Mr Gwyer?'

'Sure.'

'Can you keep your mouth shut?'

Bristling with offence, Gwyer said, 'Certainly.'

'That's all I ask. That's all you have to do. Then you leave the rest to me.'

Twenty-nine

McDade's flight was delayed, so to practise in the left-hand-drive hired Seat, Hendry suggested a drive into Malaga. It was soon evident that he knew his way around the Spanish town without consulting signs. Hendry had been here before.

Normally easy-going, Stanger took things as they came, but for the first time since he had agreed to come on this trip, he experienced a tremor, a feeling that whereas he, Stanger, was here as back-up muscle, Hendry had been drawn into a more sinister web, the origin of which lay in his past.

Hendry was certainly tightly strung, and it was not his usual military short temper when things refused to run smoothly. Nor was it an understandable lack of enchantment at meeting up with McDade again. Stanger read it as the stress of the soldier trained to fight, but forced to stand as a target for an invisible killer, against whom retaliation is next to impossible.

'Why are we here, Ed?' Stanger asked, as Hendry ploughed around the Malaga streets in search of a place to park.

'Because the man's paying us,' Hendry answered.

They drove around the one-way system a few times, channelled along palmy boulevards and the old port, till Hendry ran out of patience and took the Cadiz road out of town again. Sweating in the Mediterranean heat, they removed their jackets at a junction on the airport approach road. While they were stalled by other traffic, a thin ragged man of visibly Moorish descent leapt in front of the car. He sprayed foam over the windscreen, in spite of the fact that Hendry had seen him coming and was waving him away. Hendry would have turned on the wipers, but did not know which button to push. Meanwhile the cleaner, broken teeth above a wispy black beard, skimmed the window clean again and thrust his hand through the open window for payment. When Hendry brushed him away he grew threatening and protested that he had a wife and babies to feed.

'I said no. You understand? No, no, no.'

The Moor gestured and argued back. The traffic ahead refused to move. Hendry grabbed the Moor's hand and quickly spun the window up until the frame bit on his wrist. Then the Moor took the point, and Hendry released him.

'Hell,' Stanger said, 'what you need is a holiday. Go to the sun for a spell. A few palm trees might relax you.'

Hendry looked out the window. There was nothing but palm trees. 'When I tell somebody no, that's what it means.'

'Why are we here, Ed?'

'I told you.'

'If you got a bad feeling, would you tell me?'

'Like what, after a bad prawn? So you don't stand in a direct line with my mouth?'

'Don't smart-arse me. How are we coming out of this?'

'Meaning what?'

'Rich? Alive?'

'Hold out for both.'

'And settle for one.'

'Great thinking,' Hendry said. 'I'll buy it. And now for that little Irish bugger.'

McDade came past the car-hire touts, pushing a baggage trolley with his good arm. His other arm was strapped up to protect the gunshot wound, the bandaging largely concealed by an ample cotton jacket. For once McDade was clean-shaven, his hair unusually trim, his clothes new. The unobtrusive traveller. He met his welcoming party with an ingratiating grin. But his eyes contained a hunted suspicion, the look of someone arriving in a new place for all the wrong reasons.

Hendry resented Wardour's late request to meet McDade off the plane and taxi him along the coast. But McDade's injury foreclosed driving, and the Irishman had no other means of reaching Robleda. Wardour remained unaware of the subtleties of this arrangement. Stanger was all too aware, and saw that his

372

emerging role would be that of referee. With a long drive ahead of them, all Stanger could see coming was a war.

'Don't suppose you'd give me a hand with the bags?' McDade asked.

'No chance,' Hendry said and strode away to the car.

Stanger smiled and hoisted the heavier of McDade's bags. McDade was unsure what to make of him, and Stanger wanted to keep it that way. Too much certainty in the mind of people like McDade ended up doing a person no good.

Against a frieze of placid blue Mediterranean sea the coast road unwound above uneven beaches of mud or shingle, while on its inland side gleaming white villas with terracotta roofs ribboned for mile after mile. Finally Hendry took a road away from the sea, meandering north through a gorge of bleak rust-brown stone-faces that all but shut out the daylight. The road crossed and recrossed a dried-out river bed, then began to climb, its surface pitted from rockfalls. Stanger was navigating from the directions Wardour had given. In the back of the car McDade hummed to himself or stared with indifferent eyes at the landscape. Once the snow-capped peaks of the Sierra Nevada appeared, the road started to hairpin downwards, tortuously edging into the Azaroso valley, the valley of the guns.

Today everything was peaceful there, almond orchards fleck-ing the hills like lace, distant orange groves glowing, Robleda clustering across the valley where the real mountains began. Miles below, but distinct across a Romanesque bridge over the river, stood the yellow-fronted *venta*, an all-purpose roadside store and hostelry. Stanger folded the direction sheet. The *venta* was the final landmark. He broke the long silence of the gruel-ling journey.

'Well, guys, wherever here is, we're there.'

The Spanish word *cortijo*, smallholding, barely did justice to what the Coneforts had built up in the Azaroso valley. Cannily buying up adjoining plots and knocking down or modernising as they went, they had created a colony of low-lying single-storey dwellings, rough-plastered and whitewashed, some of them rendered hardly visible by their clumps of bougainvillea

373

and lemon trees. For a share of the produce, local labour farmed the almonds, oranges and olives.

As proudly as if it was his own, Roderick Wardour showed the three men round the property, noting their surprise as yet another ragstone outbuilding rose up from the fertile grass and luxuriant bushes. 'Yes, I know,' Wardour said, 'it's the end of the world, isn't it? The sort of place where you can't think of any reason for going anywhere else ever again.'

A punctual man who expected punctuality, Wardour had been waiting for them at the *venta* to guide them along the unmade lanes that led to the gates of the Conefort land. Wardour had food already prepared and waiting in the fridge. Don Federico, as he always did when English visitors were expected, had hung from the kitchen ceiling a prime *jamon*, the cured back leg of a pig, which Wardour demonstrated his skill in carving. On the enclosed patio, where geckos basked on the walls, the four men chewed the salty aromatic flesh, washed down with welcome glasses of beer.

Food relaxed them. If there was any unease, it arose from Wardour. Hendry and Stanger had discussed the MP at length and practically agreed on the conclusion that he was mad. But then the belief that half the bastards in the world were mad fitted the experience of both men, and insulated them from the unknown into which they had travelled. But in the presence of Wardour himself they became less certain, as they waited to learn his true reason for bringing them here.

The worst of the unknowns was McDade. Hendry had seen the Irishman in several settings, each one with its own persona, and the one he observed now disturbed him most. McDade ought to be feeling more threatened than any of them but he had a peculiar jauntiness as if he not only knew all the things that Wardour wanted to find out, but knew something more that Wardour had not yet even imagined.

Wardour himself, below his well-bred affability, had an autocratic manner which grated on Stanger and made Hendry feel inhibited. Having a drink with a commanding officer was an experience life had not prepared him for. Hendry was also

374

subdued by guilt at what they had done to Wardour, recalling in sharp focus the hopeless humiliated kidnap victim at the chateau. In Hendry's book revenge was like sex, a universal desire for which, sooner or later, Wardour must feel the urge. As he looked at the distant hills, hazy in a golden light above the roaring of the Azaroso river, Hendry reflected that Wardour had certainly chosen the right place.

Beds were available for the three men in separate outbuildings. For plumbing and cooking they would have to come to the main house. Wardour stressed that splitting them up was for strategic reasons, but observed that the arrangement came as a relief to all of them.

Bedtime was still a long way off as Wardour went from house to house to check how they were all settling in. Wardour asked Stanger to take McDade up to Robleda and see what a few drinks would do.

'I just want to talk to Ed about what happened in France,' he explained.

'Sure,' Stanger said.

'I trust you because you're the only one who came here freely. The other two are here because I have a hold over them.'

'I understand,' Stanger said. 'I'll see what I can do.'

Left to themselves, Wardour and Hendry drank coffee on the patio, whose walls created pleasant shade as the evening came on. Sunlight still played on the vines that ran overhead across wooden beams. The half-open gate of the patio afforded a view of the mountain road some miles away which, apart from the Robleda road, was the only approach to this part of the valley. Wardour's eyes returned to it constantly.

For different reasons neither man had much small talk. There was only so much to say about the landscape and the *cortijo*, and it had all been said in the first hour. Wardour broke the silence first, with a question whose answer he already knew.

'You were in the Falklands? And Ireland?'

'That's right.'

'Fighting politicians' wars? Is that how you felt?'

375

Hendry said, 'All wars are politicians' wars.'

'You felt the other side weren't your enemy?'

'Once they've killed one of your mates they become your enemy.'

'Quite.' Wardour sighed, grew reflective, then said: 'A tragic thing, about Jonah Sweetman. You'd become friendly, hadn't you?'

'Sort of,' Hendry replied.

'When I left, the police were talking about murder.'

'That's their business,' Hendry said.

'At one point I thought they were about to accuse me.'

'What motive would you have?'

'People invent motives for the occasion,' Wardour said. 'But what about you, did you believe it was suicide?'

Hendry took no pleasure in this style of conversation, all cut and thrust and talking around things. He said: 'Mr Sweetman was very decent to me. I didn't know anything about his life.'

'We're not in the Army now,' Wardour said. 'I want to talk frankly. It's all in confidence.'

'I don't mean to be offensive,' Hendry said, 'but to me there are people, and there are politicians, if you get my meaning.'

Wardour gave his slightly brittle laugh. 'You don't think much of me, then?'

'I read the papers,' Hendry said.

'Yes?' The laugh again. Now Wardour seemed defensive.

'And I don't like what I read.'

'About me?'

Hindered by his lack of articulateness, Hendry tried to explain. 'I don't like what happened to you, not because of who you are, but because I was involved in it.'

Here in Spain Wardour was more magnanimous than he would have been in London. 'Some people might say that I helped things along myself,' Wardour mused. 'I've noticed you never apologise.'

'What's done is done,' Hendry said. 'Apologies are lies.'

'A hard-headed view,' Wardour said.

Hendry shrugged. 'If I had the chance now, I wouldn't take

376

it. But when it was there, I did it. I helped fit you up. I can't deny it.'

Wardour was too well-bred and too shrewd to dwell on the fact that Hendry felt indebted to him. He knew this was Hendry's way of admitting exactly that. The time to draw on it still lay in the future. 'You know why I came back here?' he asked.

'With a place like this you don't need reasons.'

'I was here some months ago with my wife. We walked in the hills over there.' Wardour gestured at the moderately dramatic mountains through which Hendry had driven. 'Jessica reminded me of an old proverb: on each hill there can be only one tiger. I came back here to find out where my hill is now, and if I'm still a tiger.'

'And if you're not?' Hendry asked.

'Then I return home, resign from politics, get something useful to do with the rest of my life.'

'Fight,' Hendry said. 'It's all you've got.'

At the Bar Paradiso, across the square from the Café Nemesis, outside which Robleda's contingent of expatriate British were noisily having a good time, Stanger and McDade talked of Boston, of Barron Odell, of Vietnam and the Falklands and Ireland, of the random scars people carried.

'You, me, Ed,' Stanger was saying, as he pushed more local brandy McDade's way, 'we get caught up in these things we don't know nothing about. For some other guy's pay-off. We're just the dirty puppets, right?' He was aiming to coax out McDade's feelings about Wardour. But the Irishman took offence. His eyes stared, and the cigarette which he smoked right in the cleft of his fingers began to stab at Stanger's face.

'Are you telling me that the boys in Ireland are like the grunts in Vietnam? You got something the wrong way round there, my friend. It's people like you I've fought against all my fucking life. And don't call me no puppet. Whatever I do is down to me. Don't forget it.' McDade was getting drunk and his mood was more ragged than earlier. Stanger accepted the blunder and moved to calm him.

'Sure, sure. But the guy you're fighting, he's a victim too.'

'He sure to Christ is if I'm fighting him!' McDade bared his yellow denture and threw his head back in a loud rasping laugh that even stilled some of the noisy conversations at other tables around the square. Then McDade poured himself a lot more brandy, lit another cigarette, drank while smoke was coming from his mouth and nostrils, and said, 'Come on, Bobby, what's on your mind?'

'Well,' Stanger said, 'I guess I like to know what I'm working on, and here I don't.'

'Take it as a freebie. Wardour's footing the bill, who gives a shit?'

'You don't figure that he's planning to pay you out for the kidnap?'

'Ah, fuck it, let him.' The brandy was catching up with McDade now. 'Let the bastard. You know what I mean? What can he do to me? What have I got to lose? Wardour thinks he's lost everything, but boy, believe me, there's a whole heap more he can lose yet.'

'Like what?'

McDade leaned forward confidentially. 'The Odell girl.'

'Holly?'

'How many are there?'

'What about her?'

'She was in on it all the time.' McDade's small dark eyes watched Stanger for a moment, then his mouth exploded in sadistic laughter and a fume of rank breath. 'Your face, Bobby!' McDade looked round drunkenly and called out, 'Hey, any of you the village photographer? Come and shoot this man's face.'

'I don't believe it,' Stanger said.

'Everything they said was *true*. Ever since she was a kid, her Dad wanted her to do something for the old country. There are more ways of screwing the Brits than blowing them to shit. Believe me, pal.'

'Prove it,' Stanger challenged.

'Prove nothing, you fuck! I don't have to prove nothing to

378

you. If you got any brains, you worked it out yourself already. Why you think Wardour's here?'

'I already said, I don't know.'

'He wants to get to the truth. Except, baby, there's one truth he don't want to find. Holly was one of us. She set him up. You know how they met? The traffic jam story, you heard that?'

'I heard.'

'Real fucking romance, eh? Well, let me tell you, Holly had been following that guy for days. She had radio contact, she knew he was on his way back into London. She planned to stage a breakdown and flag him in but either she got the wrong road, or he did. So she headed back, and what do you know, she spots his Jag in a tail-back. Wardour did the rest. From all accounts he was a very hungry boy. After that it couldn't have been sweeter. The bastard walked straight into it.'

'What I don't get,' Stanger said, 'is that you had Holly kidnapped as well. All that Odell ransom stuff.'

'Holly's a good actress. The old man was right behind it. He played along.'

'So me and the StormWind men – '

'Credibility points.'

'You mean they were shot to pieces for nothing?'

'A detail that went wrong. Happens.'

Stanger said, 'Thanks. It's nice to know why I was there.'

Scornful, McDade said, 'Ah, what did you think you were? The Seventh Cavalry?'

'You mean Barron Odell went through all that – ?'

'Odell just wanted to help the cause. Why not? Why should any of you Americans like the Brits any more than we do?'

'Did you tell Wardour this?'

'Would you?'

'I might.'

'For what? This is the one thing the guy doesn't want to know. Ever since it happened, this is the one thing he's been dodging. Every time it comes crowding in, he looks somewhere else. While you're here, study him. He's a much nicer man than me, and a bigger man than you, but he's got one thing you and I don't. He believes his own bullshit.'

'You're telling me all this so I tell him, right?' Stanger said.

McDade shook his head. 'I'll say I was pissed and just feeding you a yarn. Just a heap of *fettuccine*. Face it, why should I upset him? This crap is not what he wants to hear.'

'I can't believe it,' Stanger said, in a tone that accepted the truth of what McDade said, although unwillingly.

McDade lit up again and punctuated the air with his cigarette. 'How long have you known Barron Odell?'

'Since – a few months.'

'Well, I used to run money from Boston back to Belfast. Sometimes more than money. Fifteen years ago. Holly was just getting bumps on her chest then. Bobby, there's nothing you can tell me about these people.'

Wardour and Hendry had been talking on. In corners of the patio geckos suctioned themselves to the walls, waiting for flies or moths attracted by the lamp above the stable-type door which opened from the kitchen. The men put on sweaters but stayed outside, where they felt less constrained. Gradually, Hendry began to feel like he was at the mercy of a ruthless and all-knowing lawyer.

'I asked you and Bobby,' it was all first names here in Spain, Wardour had even invited them to call him Rod, 'to search Jonah's flat.'

'Right,' Hendry said.

'A pity his death prevented that.'

Hendry wondered if in fact Wardour knew the truth and was simply trying to trap him into a lie which he could then exploit. Subtle verbal games were not Hendry's style. He had no objection to living in his own defence, or evading the truth for a quiet life. But through his reluctance to speak openly now, ran a streak of protectiveness towards Wardour, and perhaps himself, a fear that they might both be out of their depth. But he could see that Wardour was determined to push to the limit.

380

'We got into the flat,' Hendry said. 'Between us, we were there twice. Apart from when I was working for Mr Sweetman.'

'Twice?'

'Bobby got in, the way we planned. When I told you we hadn't been able to, I was lying.'

'Why?'

'The police were waiting for him. They must have been watching the flat.'

'They had Jonah under surveillance?'

'As soon as Bobby went in, they pulled him.'

'And then?'

'They came down the phone ordering me to Scotland Yard.'

Hendry gave a brief description of Mike Wiley. Wardour looked stunned and angry. This confirmed all his suspicion that the police had been keeping things from him.

'But they let you go.'

'There was a deal.'

'That you spied on me?'

'No. It was weird. You asked me to feed Mr Sweetman a message. So did the police. Different message.'

'You told Jonah what I instructed you?'

'Yes, and I guess it worked. I told him everything, including McDade's name. Then the police jumped on the flat. If that was a coincidence, it was very neat.'

'So Bobby got nothing?'

'No time. They were straight in there.'

'You kept my name out of it?'

'Absolutely.'

'You said something about a deal.'

'They did what you did. Like I said, give Mr Sweetman a message.'

'Which was?'

'They had Knight's killer on film.'

'But not under arrest?'

Hendry shrugged. 'I guess not.'

Wardour inwardly cursed the police. They knew everything, yet he had never been more certain that they had regarded him as just another suspect. 'You said there was another time you got into Jonah's flat?'

Hendry cleared his throat. 'You rang me, remember? The night he died.'

'I remember.'

'After you called, Mr Sweetman rang.'

'Oh?'

'Something about people were coming to get him. He wanted me to go round.'

Wardour looked grave, but clinical. Sweetman was dead. Wardour's hunger for facts contained no sentimentality. He gestured for Hendry to continue.

'There was no answer. But I had a key, from when we took copies for the break-in. He was dead when I got there.'

'My God,' Wardour said, thinking of a potential murder charge, 'you were lucky.'

'Yeah.'

'Tell me all you can remember.'

Hendry relived his arrival at Sweetman's flat. In the scale of horror he had witnessed in his life, the scene in Sweetman's bathroom did not rate highly. But his recall was total.

'From what you say,' Wardour commented, 'it could have been murder.'

'You said that's what the police thought.'

'If it was suicide . . . Why did he ask you to go there? Would he have known you could get in?'

'No. But he sounded confused.'

Wardour smiled. 'Or were you the one man he knew who would get in somehow?'

Hendry said, 'From what I read in the papers he knew all sorts of people.'

Wardour shuddered at the thought of the death Sweetman had met. It flickered briefly through his mind that Hendry was the killer. Only a man with that kind of strength and background could be so efficient. 'If it was suicide,' Wardour repeated, '*why?*'

Hendry had seen men driven to suicide, rifle barrel in the

382

mouth, the works, and understood why, but the idea of choosing it on impulse was beyond him.

'You see my thinking, Ed. Anybody who thought it worth killing Jonah would sooner or later have to kill me.'

'It wasn't mur – ' Hendry began.

But Wardour's head had already turned at the sound of voices. Two drunken men were stumbling back through the irrigation ditches and unpredictable pathways of the *cortijo*. They were making a bad job of it, laughing at each other's misjudgments, guided only by the outside lights of the house in the distance.

'To be continued,' Wardour said, attending to his duty as host and going out to meet Stanger and McDade.

Hendry felt both relieved and frustrated. He wondered if in fact Wardour had already heard more than he wanted, and was glad of the excuse to stop. Although he felt suddenly drained of all power to move or think, Hendry helped Stanger get McDade to his bedroom. Apart from pulling his shoes off, they dumped him on the bed with no further ceremony.

Stanger was still lucid, although unsteady on his feet. But he didn't want to talk, so after standing for a minute watching the headlamps of a car zig-zag slowly down the black mass of the mountain, they separated for the night.

Later, Stanger returned to the main house. Wardour was just shutting the upper half of the door when Stanger wandered onto the patio, brushing aside a creeper that grew over the entrance. Wardour was not feeling mentally receptive, but he saw that Stanger was not just socialising and let him in.

Yawning helplessly, his head spinning, Stanger had to sit down for a minute before he could speak. 'You'd better hear this,' he told Wardour.

Fighting off sleep, Wardour sat down and listened dumbly. Stanger outlined everything McDade had alleged about the Odells.

Coldly, Wardour said: 'Did you believe it?'

'He made it sound convincing,' Stanger said.

'And he said if I asked, he'd deny it?'

'Right.'

383

'With a man like McDade,' Wardour said, 'you have to make your own judgment.'

'Just tell me one thing,' Stanger requested. 'You and Holly met on some motorway. How could McDade have known about that?'

Wardour cast his mind back. 'Oh, I remember. We were talking about it at Odell's farm. McDade was there.' He shrugged. 'It's a mistake to let someone like him overhear anything.'

Stanger reflected, then held out his hand. 'OK, I'm with you.'

'Thank you,' Wardour said stiffly, but touched by the gesture. Stanger left.

Minutes later Wardour went outside. The black sky was brilliant with stars, an Arab sky. Ever since he was a boy Wardour had longed to be able to name the constellations. He guessed that now he would never learn. Here they burned with an intensity that, even on the clearest night, one never saw in England.

Wardour strayed into an olive grove at the edge of the *cortijo*. The Azaroso roared along its rocky bed, loud in the night's silence. As he thought of Holly and of what Stanger had just told him, Wardour buried his face in his hands and wept.

Thirty

Of the four men staying at the *cortijo* only Wardour and McDade were up early the next morning. Neither seemed the worse for wear from the night before . Wardour in particular had dragged himself back from the depths of loneliness in the small hours, determined to continue what he had come here to do. McDade appearing early and alone gave him his opportunity.

The Irishman required no breakfast other than coffee and cigarettes. Above the patio, vines rustled from timbers into which carpenter bees occasionally disappeared.

'Some place to eat, eh?' McDade said. 'Look at that now.' He was gazing at a square which had been knocked through one of the walls and stopped only with an iron grille, which framed the Sierra Nevada's westernmost white peak.

Wardour gave a relaxed smile and asked, 'How's the shoulder?'

'On the mend.'

'Can you walk?' McDade got up and took a few mocking steps in a straight line, thinking it a reference to his paralytic return last night. 'I mean some distance.'

'I can try.'

They went across the fields of the *cortijo* and followed unmarked paths that had been there hundreds if not thousands of years, along a tributary of the Azaroso. In the Koran, paradise is described as 'gardens watered by running streams'. No wonder the Moors had found their destiny here. Wardour picked oranges from a tree and peeled one for each of them.

With the derision that was never far from his speech, McDade said, 'The sunshine breakfast, eh? You're at home here, Mr Wardour, I can see that. Better for your health than the dumps we come from.'

'You and I have been in some strange places together,' Wardour said.

McDade spat a pip and agreed.

'Do you ever think back to that day on Odell's farm?'

'Which day would that be?'

Wardour felt that the one thing he had to do was dominate McDade, to cut through the barrage of mind games at which the Irishman was so adept. 'Why did you come here, Sean?'

'To clean the slate. So I thought.'

'That means doing it my way,' Wardour said. 'And if you change your mind, for example, or leave unexpectedly, I'll turn the anti-terrorist boys loose on you. Not to mention Ed and Bobby, who are just waiting for an excuse to take you apart.'

'OK, I hear you,' McDade said. 'What do you want?'

'That day in New Hampshire, you were about to kill me. Why?'

'I was confused and afraid. I thought the only way I'd ever get free of this mess was . . . I thought I could hide your body there.'

'You had a gun.'

'Odell's. I stole it.'

'He said nothing about that.'

'Guess he didn't want to be involved.'

Wardour shied away from the Odell theme. There would be time for that later. Wardour also preferred Holly's name not to come up. McDade probably didn't know yet what Stanger had passed on, and Wardour managed to give no clue of this. They scrambled up a bank and paused for breath, the air suddenly heady with the scent of herbs bruised by their legs.

Wardour asked, 'How long have you been in the IRA?'

McDade countered, 'How long have you been a freemason?'

'I'm not a freemason.'

'No, that's right. Well then, you get my point.'

'Was the kidnap an IRA job?'

'Got it in one.'

'What good could kidnapping me do the IRA?'

'Christ,' McDade said, 'you're asking too much. I'm just a

386

mechanic. You think the big fellers consult me about a job? No way. I just carry out my orders.'

'But what was the object of it?'

'The idea was, to trap you in with some heavy boys. Tapes, photos, that sort of stuff. That's why we zonked you when you came off the boat.'

'You mean it was a smear.'

'That's the word.'

'Who wanted to smear me?'

Irritably McDade said, 'There's no point keep asking me that, because I already told you I don't know it.'

'You organised it here in Spain.'

'You been talking to Hendry.'

'Naturally.'

McDade pretended affront. 'Get it all from him then.'

'But you were the brains,' Wardour said. 'Who approached you?'

'It was some guy – '

'The Swiss?'

'Is that right? I forget.'

'Here in Spain?'

'No.'

'Where?'

McDade shrugged with his good shoulder. Lying was a form of relaxation. 'Paris.'

'Who was he?'

'Look, in this business everybody's a middleman for somebody else.'

'British?'

'No,' McDade said, 'a continental guy. I can't tell you much about him. A long time ago.'

Wardour insisted, 'I want to know more about him.'

'It's all buried under lots of other things. You'll have to give me time.'

'A day, two days,' Wardour said. 'But I intend to leave here knowing everything I need to know.'

'You'll do that,' McDade said. 'I can guarantee you.'

387

'I can only keep Hendry off for so long.'

The threat hung in the air. McDade was surprisingly calm in the way he took it. Immediately, they had to traverse a steep, crumbling bank. Lacking an arm to balance him, McDade stumbled and would have fallen except for Wardour's support. Momentarily Wardour held McDade there, in a silent demonstration of his power.

By a rocky path along the river they approached Robleda. On the outskirts of the village, the shallow but wide and fast-running stream foamed through a debris of domestic garbage. Cans and bottles and bright plastic packaging littered the stony river-bed.

'Now that looks more like home,' McDade said.

'The villagers always threw their rubbish here for scavengers or the river to take care of,' Wardour explained. 'In the age of non-biodegradable containers the Robledans still leave it all to nature.'

'Proving,' McDade said, 'that nothing ever changes.'

'Except the river,' Wardour said.

Along a lane entering the village Wardour indicated something that had been pointed out to him the last time he was here. With one hand he traced scars in the side of a barn. 'Bullet holes from the civil war.' McDade peered at the wall. Before Wardour could deliver the really chilling detail McDade had spotted it for himself.

'All at chest height, see. Must be fifty of them. Firing squad, eh? All the village people on the wrong side, stood up against this wall and blown away.' McDade spread his good arm, crucifixion-like, along the wall. Wardour looked partly annoyed, partly impressed.

'Sorry,' said McDade, 'but I got a feel for these things.'

From a hillside several hundred feet above the Azaroso valley, Lucian Weidinger had been watching the *cortijo* since daybreak. Through powerful binoculars he had seen McDade wandering about, had seen the two men set off for a walk, the early stages of which were also visible from his vantage point. A simple reading of the distant terrain, and the fact that Wardour and McDade had no equipment for serious walking, suggested Robleda as their destination.

Weidinger stayed a while longer, long enough to log the appearance down there of two other men who were unknown to him. Undercover police, perhaps. Although Wardour's career had been crashed, there was no telling who he might have brought out here with him. Finally, Weidinger drove up to Robleda, where, partly disguised by dark glasses and a panama hat, he drank wine in the square, and waited.

Guessing correctly that in a small town like Robleda all paths led to the bars around the square, Weidinger did not have to wait long. When Wardour and McDade first appeared from a shaded back street into the strong but still benevolent sunlight, one tall and dark with a loose-limbed, self-contained dignity about him, the other short, dark and unkempt, with a bandaged shoulder and a shuffling walk. They looked like nothing more than Quixote and Sancho Panza. For a moment Weidinger's agile mind dwelt with amusement on this resemblance, then chilled over again to consider the business in hand.

For a few minutes the two men sat with their beers, not seeming to talk much. Then Wardour disappeared into a bar. Assuming this was a toilet visit, which gave him a maximum of two or three minutes, Weidinger left his drink and crossed the square in a hurry. 'Sean, hullo.'

McDade's face looked astonishment, apprehension and relief all at once. He had never addressed Weidinger by name, and did not do so now. 'How come you're here?'

'The same answer that I guess you'd give. We have to meet.'

McDade's eyes turned nervously towards the coloured plastic strips of the doorway. 'You know who's in there?'

Weidinger spoke rapidly. 'Sure, I know. I also know where you're staying. I have a view of the property. Can you signal to me?'

McDade forced himself to think, but before he could get out a word, Weidinger moved away and disclaimed all connection with him. Weidinger had seen Wardour parting the plastic strips in the doorway. With an icy, indifferent control, Weidinger approached the entrance of the bar. He held the strips apart for Wardour to come through. His head lowered, Weidinger momentarily raised his eyes to meet Wardour's. With a murmured '*Gracias*', Wardour passed from the dark and noisy recesses of the bar, which Weidinger then calmly entered.

McDade lit a cigarette. He had always been intimidated by Weidinger's self-possession. The way the Swiss had not only materialised here, but had rubbed shoulders with Wardour and not turned a hair, left McDade breathless, even beyond the ritual coughing brought on by his cigarette. After a minute he said, 'Me too,' and got up.

'The door doesn't lock,' Wardour said.

McDade answered, 'They never do.'

Weidinger had got a beer and was at the far end of the bar. In the atmosphere of chaos, trash and decibels he still managed to look fastidiously untroubled.

'I got a minute, that's all,' McDade muttered.

Weidinger had already anticipated this. 'Can we meet during the day?'

'I'm not in control of things. If I go off somewhere the boys will get suspicious.'

'At night, then. It will have to be at night.'

'OK.'

'Near your place, the other side of the bridge over the river, there is a sort of roadside cafe. I'll be there at midnight.'

With the merest nod of acknowledgement, McDade returned outside. By the time he and Wardour made their way back from the village, McDade had everything planned.

Hendry and Stanger looked up at the great hill across the valley. From the patio there was nothing else to compete with it in visual dominance. The early sun cast a heat-shimmer over the hill's deceptively rounded form. Then a light, compact and intense, flashed from somewhere a long way up the hillside. Both men saw it.

'We're being watched,' Hendry said.

'Why?' Stanger asked. 'So it was binoculars. Could have been anybody.'

'From the way glass flashes like that,' Hendry said, 'you can tell exactly where it's pointing. That's pointing at us.'

Stanger always discounted about ten per cent of Hendry's old soldier knowledge. 'How do you know?' he asked. 'Is there some law that says so?'

'My skin starts to crawl,' Hendry said. 'Somebody on that mountain is watching us.'

'So what do we do, go up there and take him out?' Stanger's constant mockery of Hendry's military idiom never made much impact. Hendry was already preoccupied with the bad strategic situation they had got themselves into.

'Of all the bloody stupid places. One man up there with a rifle has got us all at his mercy. Jesus!' After Bloody Sunday, 1972, they had kept the Paras out of the Northern Irish cities. The hated red berets did duty in bandit country, and if there was one thing Hendry had a feel for, it was terrain. All his training and instincts were revolted by this weak choice of position. Stanger, on the other hand, was a personal relations man, he found Wardour increasingly interesting and, although he had seen his share of violence and dead bodies in the line of work, they were usually domestics. Long-distance killing by faceless executioners was an idea his mind did not encompass.

'Why? I mean, why?' he asked. 'Somebody up there picking us off? What for?'

'Why do you think Wardour got us out here? Except he was afraid of something like that?'

'OK, but how about if there's some harmless citizen up there watching birds, and we tell Wardour that we're all about to be slaughtered by a long-range marksman. What then?'

A gecko padded swiftly across the wall, then froze again. 'Those little buggers give me the creeps,' Hendry said. 'So does this place.'

'Every place I've been in with you gave you the creeps,' Stanger said. 'It's your nature. Listen for a minute.' Hendry listened as Stanger told him about the previous night's revelation of Holly Odell's involvement in the kidnap.

'Oh Christ!' Hendry groaned.

'You believe it?'

'No. It doesn't add up.'

'Maybe they were fooling you guys as well. You're the only one still around to know.'

'Does Wardour believe it?'

'Yeah. But then he would. He'll believe the killer on the mountain story too.'

'If there is somebody out there,' Hendry said, 'that bastard McDade is tied up in it somewhere. The sooner I get him the better I'll like it.'

'Our problem isn't McDade,' Stanger said. 'Our problem is the not so honourable Roderick Wardour.'

'How's that?'

'I'm not sure why any of us came here,' Stanger said. 'But I know exactly why Wardour did. He came here to die.'

The wine which Don Federico had laid in as a hospitality supply was running out by the first lunchtime. Mixed half and half with sparkling mineral water, it had become the house drink at the *cortijo*, and between them the four men consumed it at a rate that, as soon as the last bottle hove in sight, became openly competitive.

About twenty kilometres along the valley there was a *bodega*, hidden away in the back streets of a village, locatable only with local knowledge. Wardour knew the place, and knew where the Coneforts kept their stock of plastic carboys, which from huge wooden casks the vintner would fill with the brown, nutty wine. But on his last visit Jessica had been there. Needing a Spanish speaker now, Wardour noticed that this was the first time, since he returned to Robleda, that Jessica had been in his mind.

'Don't suppose any of you speak Spanish?' he asked casually.

Stanger replied in Spanish that he did. Wardour looked pleasantly surprised. 'In the States it's the future,' Stanger said.

'So you can give orders to your servants?' McDade asked.

Stanger coolly ignored McDade's needling and with a facial gibe McDade left the gathering. Wardour fixed Stanger up as his interpreter for the afternoon and they left quickly. Hendry chose to stick around. When McDade returned to the main house, the hired Seat was already bumping down the track out of the *cortijo*.

'Just you and me,' Hendry said.

'I fancy a walk,' McDade replied. 'Alone, if you don't mind.'

'A pity about your arm,' Hendry said. McDade spat.

'A pity she missed,' he added.

'Grow up, Ed,' McDade said. 'You're a decent guy. Go home, get a day job, lead a decent life.'

'So Holly was part of the scam.'

'Oh, you heard. Well, live and learn, eh?'

'You fucking liar.'

'Don't be taken in by a pretty face, Ed. That's the mistake Wardour made.'

'You still owe me money from that job.'

'You'll get your money. Once we're out of here.'

This was not the answer Hendry had expected. 'How's that?'

'My friend, I've got access to money you never even dreamed of.'

'Filthy IRA money, covered in blood and shit?'

McDade remained cool. 'You work out what you figure I owe you, Ed, and I'll pay you back. No strings.'

'If Holly was one of us, why did we keep her tied up?'

'That's what Wardour would say. The man who can't face the truth. How long were you in France with the rest of us?' For most of the kidnap period, Hendry had been in America – exactly the point McDade was making. 'You think I had her trussed up all that time? That was just for appearances. Look, Ed, you were a Brit soldier. I don't hold that against you. But you got to accept people like me. OK, maybe you see us as scum that needs to be cleaned away, but a lot of other people believe in that cause, people you might look up to and respect. Barron Odell, for instance.'

'Odell?' Hendry said. 'That guy's crazy.'

'Sure,' McDade said, 'he's crazy, Wardour's crazy, I'm crazy, the whole fucking world's crazy except you, Ed. So what they'll do is lock you up in a special asylum for the sane, while the rest of us get on with our crazy business.'

'Are you going to tell Wardour about Holly?' Hendry asked.

McDade shrugged. 'Why destroy the man? It can't help him now.'

Hendry appeared to accept this answer. He asked McDade: 'Where are you going when you leave here?'

'I may not leave. Maybe I'll just go down to the coast again. Revisit the sort of place where I met you. A hungry man looking for work, remember? Maybe I'll meet you there again.'

'No chance,' Hendry said.

'You're straight now,' McDade said. 'Is that it? But what's your future, Ed? Roderick Wardour's chauffeur, that's you. I can see it now. Cap, gloves, salute. Yes, sir. Certainly, sir.' With a ghost of a sneer, McDade got up and walked away.

Every word McDade uttered contained its hidden message. The power the Irishman had always possessed over Hendry was his ability to suggest that he knew what the other man was thinking, to pick unfailingly on the nerve that would hurt most. Years of being a soldier in situations of guerrilla warfare had left Hendry susceptible to a fear that, however tough he was, people could get at his mind. In Belfast this had been common among the troops, as strong as the dread of bomb or bullet, this fear that the silent, invisible enemy would break them mentally.

This unease prompted Hendry to seek a private talk with Wardour when he and Stanger returned from the *bodega*. There was no pretence at a formal dinner. Bread, goat's cheese, slices of *jamon*, a now endless supply of the Alpujarra wine, sufficed for everyone. Wardour then retired into the main house and waited for Hendry to come to him.

Before Hendry could begin, Wardour demanded: 'What do you make of McDade?'

'The same as I always did.'

'A liar?'

'You could put it like that,' Hendry said.

'Mentally unbalanced?'

'I'm no expert.'

Wardour pressed further. 'Dangerous?'

'Even with one arm out of action I wouldn't turn my back on him.'

Wardour nodded with grim satisfaction and continued, 'You had something to say to me.'

'Last night we were talking about Mr Sweetman and we got interrupted. There's something I didn't tell you.'

'As I recall,' Wardour said, 'you were saying that you knew Jonah's death wasn't murder. I'm curious to know how.'

'He left a note.'

In the lamplight Wardour's jaw slackened and he grew pale. 'And you reckon a murderer would have taken it?'

'Yes.'

'Who has it now?'

Hendry waited a long time. 'I do.'

Wardour's eyes watched him with the intentness of the man who has all but given up on finding truth, only to have it walk in the door. 'May I see it?'

'It's not here.'

'Then where is it?'

'I left it in England.'

Wardour's hands clenched. Frustrated excitement made the veins on his face stand out. 'Why leave it there, for God's sake?'

'I thought it might be some kind of insurance.'

'Against what?'

'I want to come out of all this back on my feet again. If the police find out I was in that flat the night Sweetman died, they'll hang the lot on me. They'll fit me up with no trouble.'

'But by taking the note you made the case for them.'

'They don't have to know I've got it.'

'Who was this note addressed to?'

'You.'

'But it was still in his flat? After he died?'

'That's right.'

'How would you explain that?'

395

'I guess if he was about to kill himself, he was confused, thought he'd already sent it to you, something like that.'

'Or the murderer overlooked it.'

'He wasn't murdered,' Hendry said. 'You can't get a man to lie in a bath while you throw an electric fire at him. People don't cooperate like that.'

Wardour's tension was acquiring an unfriendly tinge. 'If the note was addressed to me, what business did you have keeping it?'

'I wasn't thinking straight. Maybe I thought I could sell it. I don't know. I thought it was best to get it out of there.'

'But two weeks later you still have it. My property, I think.'

Hendry was abashed, but mildly offended, having made the effort to bring this to Wardour's attention. 'If I hadn't found it, somebody else would.'

'Indeed. And you kept it for possible blackmail. I understand. Did you take a xerox?'

The world of high street technology lay outside Hendry's expertise. 'No.'

'And what did it say, this note?'

'Mr Sweetman was asking you to drop everything. He said all the things that happened were a mistake, although you'd asked for it. He said you should forget it in the interests of the party. If you kept digging, it would destroy you anyway. There were a few other things, but mainly that was it.'

'Why didn't you show me this in London?'

'I didn't think it would be doing you any favours.'

'So why now?'

'Because your unfinished business is mine.'

Wardour was clearly shattered, in spite of all his will-power and his gift for maintaining appearances. 'I understand. Thank you.' The audience was over. Hendry got up and left.

An hour later, kept awake by this conversation, Hendry abandoned attempts to sleep and went outside. The night was clear, and on a tree near his door, ripe lemons glowed in the starlight. Fifty years ago men had shot each other across this valley.

396

Difficult to imagine now. In the world's ugly places you could understand why people killed each other, but here . . .

Suddenly, a slight movement made Hendry melt catlike into the shadows. McDade had emerged from his house. Not for sleeplessness, plainly, because after a quick look around he took the track which led off the *cortijo*. Hendry's night-adapted vision marked McDade's path for some way. Then he began to follow.

Thirty-one

The bargain the police had made with Hendry had been that he would pass on to Jonah Sweetman the message that they had Knight's killer on film. They had assumed that this would be forwarded to Sweetman's contact, whose number the communication would enable them to trace. It would also, with luck, cause what Mike Wiley called a riot in the monkey-house. But their tap on Sweetman's phone produced no mention of the message, leading to the conclusion that either he had passed the information via some other channel, or had died with it still untransmitted.

Then, by a supreme irony, things started to happen anyway. A combination of technology and old-fashioned police work created a result.

Computerised image enhancement had to some extent made up for the poor quality of the video which showed someone entering Knight's shop – clearly being let in by the proprietor – but not coming out again. The tracksuited caller wore too much on and around his head for a convincing facial impression to emerge from the film. Nor did inquiries in the neighbourhood of Knight's shop produce any sightings of a man in a tracksuit leaving the scene of the murder. So far so bad. But the pathologist identified the instrument of Robin Knight's killing as one-millimetre steel cable of the type used on derailleur racing gears. A trawl of cycle dealers within a thirty-mile radius drew only a patchy response, except for one factor which sprang directly from Lucian Weidinger's desire for anonymity. The store where he had been able to buy the cable without speaking to anyone operated a computerised till which printed out date and time of purchase, description of item, price, means of payment and amount tendered, plus the name of the assistant who had processed the purchase. A retrieval of the store tape for the day in question threw up one sale of a replacement cycle gear cable. It had been paid for with a £50 note, and for that reason alone the salesgirl remembered it. She recalled that the customer had not looked much like a cyclist, although you could never tell. But also one of his fingers had a nail missing. He had kept that hand in his pocket for most of the time at the check-out, but for one brief moment, needing to use his wallet, the hand had been visible. The salesgirl was positive. Cycle gear, missing fingernail. More than that she couldn't say.

'Compared with what we've had so far,' Mike Wiley said, 'this is a bloody encyclopaedia.'

As if submitting to fate, he rang the Wardour household again. When Wiley called, Jessica Wardour had just returned from a few days away, an absence she had taken in order not to be there when Rod left for Spain. Wiley caught her just out of the shower, with unpacked things all over the place, and a stack of mail waiting to be sorted.

'I haven't any more to say,' she told him.

'No,' Wiley said, 'but I have. Is your husband likely to be home soon?'

Jessica did not believe that the police were ignorant of any move Rod made. 'He's away for a few days.'

Wiley insisted they meet. The discussion resumed as soon as he arrived at the Regent's Park house.

'Your husband's away on business?'

'Travelling.'

'Not one of the caring professions, politics, is it?'

'What do you mean?'

'Losing his post like that. And then the Sweetman business. You knew Jonah Sweetman well, didn't you?'

'I've already told the police all I know.'

'Yes. I didn't come here to reopen all that.'

'Why, then?' Jessica was crisp in her manner, pointedly not offering Wiley a drink. Even her invitation to sit down had been peremptory.

'I'm still trying to be on your husband's side,' Wiley assured her.

399

'I thought policemen didn't take sides.'

'There's crime, and there's injustice,' Wiley said. 'Ideally I'd like to avenge injustices, but not every injustice is a crime. The way they're treating your husband now is unjust, in my opinion. But it's not a crime, so I can't do anything about it.' Wiley had struck the right note at last. It got him the offer of a drink. He accepted a small vodka and continued. 'Some crimes are not injustices. Maybe the victim had it coming. But a crime it is, and we have to do something about it. Is your husband the victim of an injustice, or a crime?'

'Surely a kidnap is a crime.'

'Precisely. Don't quote me, but sometimes the only way you can remove an injustice is by a crime. By the same token, the investigation of a crime sometimes leads to injustices along the way.'

'I have a lot to do, Commander. Could you come to the point?'

Wiley continued, 'Every so often, things happen, bits of evidence come up, which point to your husband. I don't think he's ever been straight with me, maybe for very good reasons. But I'm still trying to tunnel out of this business. In the process I might do more harm than good, to certain people. For instance your husband.'

'A threat, Commander?'

Wiley replied, 'After what's happened to you in the last few months, what could I threaten you with?'

Jessica maintained the air of injured dignity with which she had outfaced all the affronts of the 'Wardour Affair' as the media now put it. She knew policemen made this sort of visit, pretending to have an errand but in fact casting around a cold trail for traces of activity. 'If that's all – '

'Just one more thing. Do you recognise the following description? Male, about forty with apparently no remarkable details except a missing fingernail on one hand. I'm not sure which. Not the sort of thing everybody would notice.'

'I don't know any such person,' Jessica said.

Wiley drained his vodka and got up. In the hall a shaft of

evening sunlight across her face showed how much Jessica had aged since Wiley had first met her.

'Check the missing fingernail with your husband,' he said. 'You never know. You've got my number?'

'Of course.'

Wiley liked Jessica. Behind her icy demeanour he saw an unhappy woman. A vulnerable man himself, he felt at ease with those in whom he sensed failure, confusion, loss. 'What does your husband want?' he asked. 'Except what we all want, to put the clock back?'

For the first time during this visit Jessica smiled, a smile of forbidding tightness, and said, 'Who knows what anybody else wants? Thank you, Commander. Goodbye.'

Jessica began to sort the mail into its usual stacks of junk, official, personal. She had noticed Wiley's eye resting on the pile of unopened letters. Relieved to be able to identify every envelope, Jessica gave way to yet another wave of indignation against Roderick. Each time Wiley cropped up, she feared that there were still things which the police suspected but which she would be the last to learn. Truth had become a tunnel which branched into an endless web of obscene subways. The phone cut short her growing disturbance at these thoughts. The caller was Tony Gwyer. He admitted that he had been trying to contact her for several days. Sensing a new receptiveness, he invited Jessica for a drink.

They met in the bar of a hotel off Hyde Park, a well appointed but not very classy place used by plane companies for senior aircrew. At least it was unlikely to have political or media people wandering through its doors. Her affair with Gwyer had left Jessica susceptible to his mixture of almost childlike amiability and cut-the-crap hard-headedness. From the outset she knew she was being manipulated. But somehow at this moment it was what she needed.

'I wanted to talk to you about Rod. I've been worried about him,' Gwyer said.

'Oh? Since when?'

'Particularly since Jonah died.' Gwyer took a long sip at his gin and tonic and went on, 'The party's in trouble, electorally for one thing, and all these minor scandals have started to add up to a terminal disease. Rod was a bloody fool.'

'To do what?'

'To risk his marriage to you, for starters.'

Jessica could not deny it, the compliment made her feel better. 'And beside that?' she asked.

Gwyer mused. 'Have you ever thought that Rod has a self-destructive streak? A lot of politicians have. Maybe it's because I'm not really the type – let's face it, the only way I'll ever see the inside of Number Ten is at a cocktail party – but I seem to notice things in my colleagues they don't see in themselves.'

Gwyer had planted the idea. Jessica asked, 'In what way self-destructive?'

'The way I see it is, he couldn't believe his luck. If ever anybody had a magic path through the political jungle, it was Rod. He was going to save us all: all the marginal seats, all the tired old hacks, all those of us who can't make it without a strong leader figure. You know my theory? He had to test his luck. It was as though he would never be able to accept the leadership till he knew how far he could go. And he made the two classic mistakes: flirting with the wrong woman, and the wrong cause. I believe it was deliberate. He figured that if he could get away with that, he could get away with anything. If not, at least he'd know how the cookie crumbled.'

'He's finished,' Jessica said. 'He could be an MP for another forty years, and that's all he'll be, just another MP. Don't tell me you're sorry.'

'In politics things change all the time. Rod hasn't always been my cup of tea. But in a year or two, five years, who knows?'

'You're not talking about a comeback?'

'I don't see why not,' Gwyer said. 'People have marched back from worse. Providing, of course – '

'Providing what?'

'He'll have to serve his penance, do the right things, cultivate the right people. Wipe the word *Ireland* out of his mind. When are you expecting him?'

402

'Perhaps by the end of the week, I'm not sure.'

Gwyer said: 'I don't know why he went there, but whatever the reason, he ought to forget it. Just tell him to come home and start again.'

'You may be right about the self-destruction,' Jessica said. 'But if I couldn't stop him going, I doubt that I could make him come back.'

'Well,' Gwyer said, 'whatever he's doing, I hope it doesn't make ripples at Westminster. Because next time the party won't forgive.' This was the one note which could trouble Jessica's inhibited personality and its tightly defined field of vision. She wanted to tell Gwyer that there was more to the party than him, but she had noted in the past how unerring his feel for his colleagues' prejudices seemed to be. And Roderick had always said 'Fear the clever back-bencher.' An uncertainty which she failed to hide prevented Jessica from speaking.

Gwyer went on: 'You and I are unlike. That's why we get on so well.' Gwyer could not resist a discreet leer, Jessica's open dislike of which only made him grin even more cheerfully. 'What I mean is, you're an old-style Tory. For you, some mystical thing exists called the Conservative party. It goes with fields and hills, dogs and horses, England's green and pleasant land, honour and all that rubbish. Me, I'm into money. Roddy is into *history*, and that's the most dangerous politician of all.'

Gwyer rarely just made conversation. Jessica asked: 'What are you suggesting?'

'Either reform him, or stop him.'

'How can I stop him?'

'Face it, Jessie, he'll take you down with him. He's already shown he's prepared to do that. There's one sure way you could stop him.'

Jessica guessed what was coming, but asked anyway. 'Yes?'

'Threaten him with divorce. You're well regarded in the party. If you divorced him, Roddy would never recover. Politically.'

'He might call my bluff.'

'So divorce him anyway.'

Jessica finished her drink and had to go. Through narrow eyes Gwyer watched her leave, his inward smile spreading across his face as he read Jessica's mind every step of the way to the hotel exit.

Wiley's visit and Gwyer's words brought Jessica as near to breaking down as she had ever been in her life. Even during Rod's kidnap her main function had been to hold out, not to give away any reaction. In the aftermath she had fallen back on the frosty dignity which people expected of her kind of woman. The affair with Gwyer had put the shine back on her self-esteem, but forced her to realise how much her ego dictated her so-called life of service. And now all her nerves seemed to be exposed at once, in a strain that, after many hours, she could only relieve by reaching for the phone.

There was no link to the *cortijo*. The Coneforts had always gone there to retreat from public life. But in their arrangement, Don Federico's place along the valley had a phone, which they used when they wanted to call the outside world. The issue of this number was severely restricted. Jessica only knew it because, impressed by her blonde handsomeness and her excellent Spanish, Don Federico had invited her to meet his wife one day, and Jessica had scored a small point over the Coneforts by committing Don Federico's number to memory. She searched through the filofax in which she had eventually scribbled it, and slowly, deliberately, tapped in the code.

Don Federico, higher up the valley, could see that the *senor*'s car was at the *cortijo*. Jessica said she would ring again in twenty minutes if Don Federico could oblige her by bringing her husband to the phone. The whole episode reeked of the leisureliness of the Alpujarras, which Jessica loved when she was there, but from London found trying.

'Rod?'

'What is it?'

Jessica had explained to Don Federico that it was not bad news, but the old man lacked the English to make this clear.

Having established this, but unsure how to refer to Wardour's absence, Jessica said, 'That policeman Wiley was here.'

'Oh?'

'He asked if we knew a man with a missing fingernail.'

After a momentary pause Wardour said, 'Why?'

'I didn't ask. They never tell you, anyway. But do you?'

'No.'

'That's what I told him.' Jessica visualised Wardour standing beside Don Federico's cool kitchen, with its ham hanging from the ceiling. What she could not see was Wardour's gaze become fixed, statuelike, as his thoughts ran elsewhere.

His mind had gone back to the previous day, to the square in Robleda. Once again Wardour benefited from, or was the victim of, his ability to recall details absorbed at random. In Robleda he had seen exactly such a hand as Jessica described. The hand had held aside the plastic strips in the doorway of the Café Nemesis as Wardour emerged into the daylight. And a few yards away McDade had sat calmly smoking. Aware of his silence, Wardour asked, 'Is everything else all right?'

His pallor as he recalled the moment came not from fear, but from an uprush of adrenalin at this imminent stripping away of the final veil. But to Jessica the tonelessness of his voice sounded like poorly concealed hostility. Unable to explore her real reason for phoning, distasteful of self-analysis, she had to stick with the excuse that she had rung to ask Roderick about the man Wiley had described. That done, the conversation had nowhere to go. An exchange of pleasantries would be insulting.

'Everything's well,' she answered.

'I'll see you next week,' Wardour said.

Jessica rang off with a precise, 'Yes. Goodbye.'

Within minutes of hanging up she was calling Gwyer's number. It was some time before she caught him at Ebury Street.

'Jessie! So soon!'

Jessica had listened to the phone ring unanswered too many times. She was not going to waste the moment now. 'I want to spend the night with you.'

'Well,' Gwyer said softly.

'At your flat.

'Yes, sure. But not tonight. Tomorrow.'

'Tonight. Please.'

Gwyer savoured the power Jessica had suddenly given him. The ultimate aphrodisiac, as a great politician had said. Ridiculous not to use it. Let the anguish build up, before he conferred relief. Make it clear who really called the shots.

'Tomorrow,' he said.

Lucian Weidinger drove with McDade for several kilometres, until they found a place to pull off the road. A long way down in the valley the minuteness of a few lights indicated the immensity of the massif on whose edge they had stopped.

McDade explained who the other men were at the *cortijo*, and Wardour's refusal to let things go.

Weidinger asked: 'What does he hope to gain from all this?'

'He wants to find out the truth. About everything.'

'An ambitious man.'

'He's one of those self-important guys who thinks the world owes him an apology for doing something he didn't like.'

'How did he get you here, Sean?'

'Let's just say there's pressure he can apply, and he applied it.'

'And what do you intend to tell him?'

'It doesn't really matter. He won't be taking it out of Spain with him.'

'How's that?'

'He's going to have an accident in the mountains.'

'As I understand from events in Britain,' Weidinger said, 'Mr Wardour could even be feeling suicidal.'

'That's it,' McDade said, 'just what I had in mind. Couldn't face going back, you see. Fell to his death, sort of thing.'

'What about his bodyguards? Isn't that why he's got those two men here?'

'They've got enough trouble already. Any more, they'll want well out of it. Another dead body they don't need.'

406

'So they sit down in the valley and suck oranges while you hit Wardour in the mountains?'

In the dark interior of the car McDade was enjoying this hugely. 'That's much too complicated. My idea is, Wardour goes into the mountains on his own. Hendry and Stanger are my alibi.'

'And Wardour doesn't come back?'

'That's about the score.'

'And on his body there is no bullet mark, no knife cut, only the normal result of falling off a cliff?'

'Got it in one.'

'Before *how*, tell me *why*. Why do you want him dead?'

'It's my return ticket,' McDade said.

'To Belfast?'

'Right. And with Wardour dead, we're all off the hook. Because I got to tell you, if he doesn't die, he'll get us all.'

'One thing I don't see,' Weidinger said. 'Why should he go up to the mountains?'

'To meet you.'

'Ah. Of course.'

McDade said, 'He knows I was only doing a job. He wants whoever gave me the job.'

Weidinger shrugged. 'We're all employees, all down the line.'

'He'll be happy to go one stage further than me.'

'He won't suspect a trap?'

'Maybe so. I'll tell him you're like God, to see your face he has to be alone. Shit, he knows he won't make progress without risk. Can you do it?'

'Oh, I think I can do it.'

'OK. And then I'll send the search parties in the wrong direction. Anyways, they'll only find what the buzzards have left. And the rest of us just go home.'

'And when you're back in Ireland, we can do some good business.'

'You're not joking,' McDade said. 'Believe me, when I walk along the Falls again, I am going to be big, very big.'

★

407

All the *cortijos* in the Azaroso valley were walled or fenced against wandering herds of goats. Even the narrowest footpaths were closed off. When McDade went out he unbolted the heavy steel-mesh gate and left it undone. Following the Irishman, Hendry was greatly helped by this piece of negligence. The last thing he wanted was to have to clank the gate open again. Any other sound of his pursuit was drowned by the river, which even in its low season ran fast enough in the wide boulder-strewn bed to make a continuous roar, amplified by the neighbouring hills. Besides which, McDade had the sloppy ways of the urban guerrilla, Hendry the neat control of the commando. For once he felt himself to be McDade's superior.

At McDade's approach, headlights flashed somewhere on the unlit road. Then everything went dark again. At the *venta*, a solitary outside light burned one small bulb to alert drivers, coming off the bridge, that here the road curved sharply. Hills hid the moon, but somehow whoever was in the car had spotted McDade. To avoid being equally conspicuous Hendry scrambled down a powdery embankment to river level. The thickness of the bamboo-like *cana* provided cover, but also screened the road ahead from Hendry's view. As he came to the wide Romanesque span of the silhouetted bridge, Hendry heard a car start up and speed away. By the time he got up to road level, even its lights had disappeared. The engine had a sporty sound, but otherwise Hendry knew nothing about car or driver. What he had learnt about McDade only confirmed what he had always known.

Hendry decided to walk some more before going back to tell Wardour what he had seen. But before he could cross the bridge another car came down from the direction of Robleda, travelling too fast for the bends in the road, with all the signs of a driver out of control, probably drunk. Hendry moved aside, ready to throw himself down the bank. The car shot onwards across the bridge, then stopped and turned round in the road. It was not the car in which McDade had left, but as it began to slow down, Hendry realised that it was his presence that had attracted the driver.

408

A window wound down. '*Por favor, señor* – ' Somebody lost. She was leaning across from the driver's seat. Hendry got ready to speak loudly in pidgin English. Then the woman said, 'Oh my God!'

At the same moment Hendry said, 'Jesus Christ!' It was Holly Odell.

'I don't believe this,' Hendry said.

Holly said, 'I found the village easily enough, but after that – '

Hendry was pleased and relieved to see her. In New Hampshire they had begun to get on well. But already his mind told him that Wardour had arranged this, and Hendry's old suspicion, his feeling that everybody else was one step ahead of him, came flooding back.

'Why are you here?'

'I have to see Rod. I guess he's here?'

'Is he expecting you?'

'No.'

'No?'

'Is McDade here?'

'He's here all right,' Hendry said. 'What's going on?'

'Can you take me to Rod? I ought to explain to him first.' She let Hendry in. Once they were bumping along the unmade tracks that led into the *cortijo*, Holly said, 'Now I know why I couldn't find the place.'

'It grows on you,' Hendry said. 'You soon start thinking you'll never leave.'

'Thanks,' Holly said. 'Very reassuring.'

'Sewer pipe,' Hendry said, indicating an abrupt mound ahead where treated waste from the village poured into the Azaroso. The car bumped over the barely covered concrete pipe. 'Anyway, how did you know the address?'

'Rod sent it to my father to pass on to McDade.'

'How is your Dad?'

Hendry explained the long silence that followed with the belief that Holly was concentrating on the driving. Finally she said, 'He's dead.'

Not a stranger to hearing that people he knew were suddenly

no longer there, Hendry still felt shock. For the second time in five minutes he said, 'I don't believe it.'

'Me neither.'

'How?'

'Coronary. His second. His blood pressure was high, he wasn't in good shape. The last few months took it out of him.'

'He seemed one of those strong, unbeatable people,' Hendry said.

Holly sniffed, and Hendry sensed that if her business there had not been so urgent, she would have cried. The news of Barron Odell's death plunged Hendry into silence for the remainder of the journey.

He let the car through the gate, which he left, as McDade had, unbolted, in case the Irishman noticed the detail. But from Holly's arrival Hendry guessed that events were about to overwhelm them all again.

The buildings of the *cortijo* rested in darkness, their flat white forms somnolent in the peace of the citrus groves. Winding down rapidly from the journey, Holly caught her breath.

'He's probably asleep,' Hendry said. 'What do you want to do?'

'Could you – ?' Holly asked.

Hendry went in, brushing aside the vines round the patio entrance, but found the split door into the house locked. About to knock, he saw a light through the crack across the middle of the door.

Wardour had pulled on a jogging suit. In the sudden glare of light he looked haggard. 'I heard a car.'

'I'd better tell you this first,' Hendry said. 'McDade's gone to meet somebody. I don't know who, or where they've gone, but he's up to something.'

Wardour was brusque, fatalistic. 'Doesn't surprise me.'

'I'll watch for when he comes back.'

'Good. Don't give anything away.'

Hendry concurred, then said: 'I think you had better come out here.'

Holly stood in the shadow of the vines at the edge of the

410

patio. Embarrassed but strangely moved, Hendry made his exit even quicker than usual.

Thirty-two

The sound Hendry heard behind him could have been laughter, or tears, or both. Within the walls of the patio Wardour and Holly, in a delirium of joy at being together again, held each other in an embrace whose breaking they feared would bring an inrush of bad news.

They went inside. In his over-socialised way Wardour began a nervous chatter about the place, how much the Coneforts had done . . .

Holly interrupted, 'Can we leave the small talk? I have to tell you why I'm here.'

'Of course, of course.' Wardour poured the house mixture of local wine and sparkling water. Finding it hard to say again so soon, Holly told him that Barron Odell was dead. Wardour put his drink down, untasted. For a moment he appeared to grow smaller. He muttered a few words of condolence.

To push back the silence, Holly explained, 'Once you'd left, all the kidnap and the StormWind business seemed forgotten. I think Dad liked you, but there was no way he and you could ever be alike. What McDade did was persuade him that they were the same kind of man. Maybe they were. For Dad that was always a fatal thing. Once he saw himself in McDade, he was finished.'

Wardour agreed. 'I could see that McDade was on a high as soon as he got here.' Then, changing the tack of his thinking, he added, 'You're sure your father's death was natural?'

'Yes. Although – '

'Although what?'

'He hadn't told me this. Maybe he felt he didn't have to, or maybe he couldn't. But after he died, his lawyers told me he'd made a new will.' Wardour nodded in anticipation, but what he heard still staggered him. 'McDade gets half. Of everything.'

412

'I've no idea what your father was worth.'

'The odd few million.'

'Well,' Wardour said, 'it could be worse. I assume you get the other half.'

'I'm fighting it,' Holly said.

'Of course.'

'Not for me. I just don't want that ghoul to profit from my father's instability.'

Wardour said: 'Perhaps the money will persuade him to give up terrorism. He'll become a respectable capitalist like the rest of us.' The joke was badly timed. Through her travel-weariness Holly was burning up to a high pitch of anger.

'He's a conman and a killer, and I don't want him to have anything of my father's. He exploited a sick man, and if I have my way –'

'You put a bullet in him,' Wardour finished. 'So, I understand your feelings towards him.'

Holly was jolted by this reminder. It seemed to come from another world. But from the back of Wardour's mind the accusations passed on by Stanger were becoming dominant.

'I'd better tell you that McDade is saying you were part of the team, that you were the bait to lead me into the kidnap and everything.'

'And do you believe that?'

'No.'

'When we first met, was the first time I'd seen you or thought about you. I fell in love, and if all these things hadn't happened I guess I'd have gone on falling.'

Trying not to give way to his own sadness, Wardour said, 'It would have been a long fall for us both.'

'Well, even if it didn't make eternity,' Holly said, 'it was good, and I haven't turned my back on it.'

Separated by half a room, they looked at each other for a long time. Wardour experienced again that sensation which only Holly had ever brought him, of looking undeviatingly into someone else's eyes. The moment faded, slowly but irrevocably. 'Why did you come here?' he asked.

413

'I'm on my way to the Sudan.'

'Work?'

'I've got a contract with the *Globe*. I figured I could take a day out on the way.'

Although disappointed, Wardour accepted the message in its subtle form: she was not staying. But equally she had not broken a journey to Africa just to say hullo.

'A day?' he asked.

Holly smiled. 'Or two.'

'And then?'

'Yes,' she said, 'and then.'

Wardour had always loved the way Holly teased him. But at this moment it was almost unbearable. 'See me through?' he asked.

'It sounds like a rough game,' Holly said.

'No rougher than what we've had already.'

'I'll stay on condition you don't turn your back on McDade.'

'I've got leverage over him. He needs my favour.'

Holly felt desperate to penetrate what she saw as Wardour's naivety. 'McDade was about to kill you. I have this terrible feeling he's about to do it again.'

Wardour objected. 'If he's about to inherit all that money, assuming he gets past the lawyers, what could he gain by killing me?'

To Holly it seemed, not for the first time, that Wardour had developed a morbid, compulsive focus on himself as the object of a political murder. If she had known of his demotion from the government, she would have been even more convinced that he now wished to die. That was how demented the world had become: only through being an assassination target could a politician know he was *somebody*. 'When I shot McDade, he was about to kill you. Did you forget that?'

'He and I have talked about that,' Wardour said.

Holly exploded. 'You've *talked* about it! My God, what are you into here, *therapy?* McDade is a twisted terrorist who will kill you if he can find the smallest reason for it. Can't you see that?'

414

Obtusely cool, Wardour replied: 'But there is no reason.'

Holly's lips parted to answer, but froze when someone tapped the door. Wardour went out. It was Hendry. 'It might be a good idea to move Holly's car, if you don't want McDade to know she's here.'

'Yes, yes, good.' Wardour came back in. 'Is that all right?' Holly had heard and had the keys ready.

Hendry said: 'Bobby's along the river. He'll flash a torch when McDade's on his way, so I'm ready for him. What do you want me to do?'

Wardour thought for a moment. 'Just let me know, then keep out of the way. Let me intercept him.'

'Right.'

Hendry moved the car to the back of the main house, returned the keys, then resumed his post.

'Sorry,' Wardour said. 'But I don't suppose you want to meet him.'

'I hadn't thought that far. But no,' she said.

'He's an animal, very cunning. He may sense that you're here.'

'If you don't care – ' Holly began. 'I keep telling myself I personally don't have anything to lose.'

'If you had nothing to lose you wouldn't be here.'

'OK. But now isn't the time to ask for a definition.'

'I'll take a raincheck on the definition.'

Holly drew a deep breath and, when her lungs reached their fullest expansion, shuddered. 'This is an unkind thing to say, but my father was an Ireland junkie. And I don't mean the green fields and haunting music. He couldn't hear anything bad enough. To his mind only a cataclysm could solve the Irish problem, so whatever squalor McDade described just stoked up the whole thing. Between them they made the IRA sound like a bunch of choirboys. And McDade had the right pedigree. He traced his family back to the Easter Rising, the Famine – for people like him, it all happened yesterday. And you know what, he could have been making it all up. My Dad was ready to buy anything. McDade was selling like crazy. And I'll say another thing for that guy, he can talk.'

Wardour said acidly, 'I've noticed.'

'They practically forgot I was there. And that was how I heard what I'm about to tell you next. My father kept trying to find out why McDade had left Belfast, and McDade wouldn't tell him. All he'd do was hint at things that made it dangerous for him to go back.'

Wardour seized on this immediately. 'But he went back. When they released you and me in Ireland, McDade returned to Belfast. I heard him refer to it in America. Something slipped out that made it clear he'd been back.'

'So maybe something happened then. He was telling Dad that he had to earn his right to go back. Dad asked, how much. McDade said, not money.'

'What, then?'

'That's all he said. Not money.'

'And your father said, there are only two things in the world, money and blood.'

Holly looked startled. 'How did you – ?'

Wardour smiled. 'Your Dad said that from time to time. It must have run very deep.'

'Well, that was the end of it. I never heard them speak about it again.'

Wardour shrugged, beaming almost genially. 'Don't worry. I'm not important enough to kill any more.'

'You don't understand people like McDade and my father,' Holly pleaded. 'They're like predators with robot brains. Once they've defined somebody as prey they'll trail them for ever, to the ends of the earth, to their own destruction if necessary. It's a sort of biological imperative, like they can't go on living until . . . Oh God, can't you see what I'm saying?'

As if he were fighting off a tough interviewer, Wardour replied: 'It would make more sense for McDade to buy his way back into Northern Ireland and cultivate me as a potential ally at Westminster.'

'People like McDade are not interested in building bridges.

416

If he kills you and they call it an IRA murder, it will cause more bad blood. Which is the general idea. Anything to feed the hate.'

'Then why hasn't he already done it?' Wardour asked. 'There's been plenty of opportunity.'

'He tried in New Hampshire, remember? Plus, he's incapacitated. Has he got a gun here?'

'I don't know.'

'You didn't have your boys check it out?'

'No.'

'They will have anyway. And McDade would expect that. Where do you think he's gone tonight?'

'As you observe, I've no idea.'

'He could be coming back with a gun, some plastic to put under your car – '

Suddenly Wardour's body language went from cold and aloof to vulnerable and confused, his fingers grating each other, his facial muscles contorting. 'What do I do?' he protested. 'The things that happened to you and me, I can't just leave. Even if the truth isn't about to do me any favours, I still have to know it.'

'Forget it,' Holly said. 'Put it behind you. I have.'

But Wardour insisted. 'McDade is the key. I brought him here for that reason. So what now? If I accept your suspicions, what do I do? Ask Hendry to kill him first? Get in the car and run? What?'

Holly saw the strange tortured loneliness of Wardour's position. For all she loved him, a man in search of his fate was doomed to isolation. She said gently, 'If I were you, I'd watch my back, that's all.'

With a smile Wardour said, 'I shall,' and the subject came to an end. He asked, 'You're staying here?'

'Is it OK?'

'Yes, there's a spare room, in fact there are five bedrooms – '

'One will do fine.'

Wardour was about to ask which way she meant this when

Hendry knocked the outer door. Quickly Wardour got Holly out of the way and went outside.

'Bobby just gave me the signal,' Hendry whispered.

Wardour set out into the darkness, heading for the boom of the invisible river. By the time McDade noticed the house light and became suspicious, Wardour would have met him. Acting as if he did not know who approached, Wardour waited till they were very close before exclaiming, 'Sean?'

Unabashed, McDade said, 'Oh, you're out too? I find I can't sleep here. Don't seem to need it.'

'Where did you go?'

'Towards the village. I'm a town boy, I miss the streets.'

Wardour suggested a drink. McDade accepted willingly. In the house they watched each other for a while as if the passage of time itself ticked off questions to which both men could by now supply the answers, so had no need to ask. Then, in the most casual way possible, McDade said, 'Tomorrow. If you still want it.'

His voice low with an emotion that surprised him, Wardour said, 'Go on.'

'Tomorrow,' McDade said, 'you will meet the man you have always wanted to meet.'

Wardour looked moved, his feelings stirred in a whirl of conflicting directions. McDade, in turn, had never been more pleased by his own psychological karate. He hated Wardour for more reasons than he needed, not least for Wardour's man-of-destiny self-regard, the vanity that refused to let him accept the triviality of what had left his career in ruins. Wardour genuinely believed that some crock of gold awaited him at the end of all this anguish. And there, McDade thought with disdainful relish, the fool had finally become his own worst enemy, the victim of his own thirst for vengeance.

Wardour requested further information, but McDade would only give the barest outline of the next day. He promised to describe a spot for Wardour to drive to, alone. What would happen after that, McDade could not say.

'How do I know I'm not being invited into a trap?'

418

McDade allowed impatience to show. 'Isn't it true that you were in the Army at one time?'

'Briefly.'

'Well, as an ex-soldier yourself, you'll realise the situation you're in here. You talk about traps. Don't you know that ever since you arrived, anybody with a rifle could have knocked you off from those hills over there, miles away? And nobody would ever know who fired the shot, or where it came from.'

'I had thought of that,' Wardour said.

'So if I was you, I wouldn't worry about traps.'

Wardour nodded his head slowly. 'All right. But why not tell me the details now?'

'My instructions are to give you the information only the moment before you leave. Just so you don't have time to set anything up. Oh, and you'll be watched on the way.'

'Of course,' Wardour said. 'Tomorrow, then.'

'Right. And after that you and me are quits.'

'Quits, yes.'

Outside, everything was dark, silent against the distant drumming of the river, as McDade returned to his quarters. Drained by the encounter, Wardour went into the room where Holly waited in darkness, stretched out on the bed, listening. 'Don't do it,' she said.

'I have to,' Wardour insisted.

'You've proved everything you needed to prove.'

Wardour reacted badly to what this implied. 'Such as?'

Holly expanded. 'OK, you're a good detective. You don't take things lying down. You're a difficult man to beat. Whatever. But tomorrow you'll just prove that you're a man who didn't know when to stop.'

Wardour switched on a lamp, then sat down on the bed beside Holly. It was less of a seductive moment than the action of a man who needed company and warmth. 'I think we can say that today's finally over.' He poured them both a drink.

Abandoning her attempt to change his mind Holly said: 'Here's to many more of them.'

'Live each one as if your last.'

As their bodies drew closer together Holly said, 'Only if it applies to nights too.'

Thirty-three

Sean McDade loved secrets. Even when it was to his advantage to let a secret go, he parted with it reluctantly. It had amused him not to tell Wardour of Odell's death and the estate which the Ireland-besotted old bull had left him. Here in Spain it suited McDade to appear more vulnerable than he really was. And he liked the thought of something ticking away, to blow up under Wardour later.

As he approached the *cortijo's* main house the next morning McDade heard Wardour's voice. This was nothing new. But what halted McDade in his tracks was the tone of that voice. He knew immediately that neither Hendry nor Stanger was the person being spoken to. There was only one person McDade had ever heard Wardour talk to like that. Then he heard her laugh. The light laugh came easily, attractive if McDade had thought about Holly like that. But he didn't. He had to assume that her presence here was another attempt by Roderick Wardour to outsmart everybody else. OK, McDade would take this as a challenge.

Acting as if he had heard nothing, McDade ambled onto the patio. He stopped suddenly, his face registering something midway between pleasant surprise and shock. 'Well, well. We're all here now. Good day to you, Ms Odell.'

As they had supervised the aftermath of Barron Odell's unexpected death, a hatred had flared up between Holly and McDade which no outsider could fully grasp. 'Hallo,' was all Holly could manage.

Wardour, who still had business to transact with McDade, stared impassively at the distant hills glimpsed through the patio's overhead vines.

McDade indicated the house. 'I just came to use the bathroom.' Wardour nodded. McDade went in.

Hendry and Stanger had already been over to eat. Now they returned. When McDade reappeared Stanger said: 'We figured on talking a walk, Sean.'

'I'm not in the mood,' McDade said.

Hendry's blue eyes were staring fixedly into McDade's own. McDade looked at Holly and Wardour, whose breakfast lay on the table untouched while he was there. He shrugged contemptuously. He had got the message. Some time soon these people would all get theirs, too. Something ticking away.

'Whatever you boys want,' McDade said. He jostled Hendry aside as he left the patio.

The hillside smelt of mountain shrub. Sun occasionally broke the haze. The silence was stunning. The three men had lost sight of the *cortijo*, of Robleda itself. The only building in view was the squat *pueblo* of a small Jewish sect which lived isolated in the hills, baking bread for the Robleda street market. As always McDade felt nervous in the middle of open spaces. 'How about we get back?' he suggested. 'The lovers have finished by now.'

'What's the hurry?' Stanger said. 'You want to make sure that Holly didn't fill your bed with those lizards?' Hendry and Stanger laughed. McDade's aversion to the geckos had become public after his first night there, when one dropped onto his sleeping face.

McDade lit a cigarette. Prevented by his inactive arm from rolling his own, he missed the habitual diversion. 'Better not be too long, for Wardour's sake.'

Hendry asked, 'How's that?'

'I don't have to tell you guys anything. But we're all working for the man and today I'd say he needs me more than he needs you.'

Stanger, restrained till now, drew McDade to one side, while Henry waited, next in line. On McDade's shoulder Stanger's hand conveyed all the strength it would require to send the Irishman down into the pine-cluttered ravine below. 'Listen,' the American said, 'you cost me a great deal of money and almost my life. You've caused I don't know how much trouble

422

to various people. And now we're standing out here in this goddamn wilderness, and you're talking to Ed and me like a pair of children who are spoiling your day off.'

McDade gave a self-deprecating laugh. 'Sorry, Bobby, that's not the way I wanted it to come out.' Hendry had moved closer. McDade realised that instead of passing, the menace was about to deepen. He attempted to level with them. 'Come on, lads. Roddy has an important meet today, and I have to be back there to tell him when and where. So let's stop psyching each other out, eh?' But sincerity was a mode in which McDade had no conviction left to offer.

Hendry's index finger gave him a not-so-playful prod in the chest. 'Get this, Sean. You're the psycho. We're the men who are coming to take you away.'

McDade's eyes flashed. 'OK, take your feelings out on me later. But if you keep me out here, Wardour won't be pleased.'

'You owe me as well,' Hendry said. 'Money, time, and the fact that I don't like being treated like an idiot.'

'Wardour's paying, boys, sorry. The stuff's his, first.'

'I'm taking it by force,' Hendry said. 'So that makes it mine. If I have to kick you all the way down that valley to get it.'

'Stay out of it,' McDade warned. 'Let these people go to hell what the fuck way they like. You and me, we're just their spear-carriers. As of today Roderick Wardour takes control of his own destiny, and the right place for a sensible man is as far away from him as you can get.'

Hendry was unimpressed. 'Whatever you've fixed up for him, I'm going to be there. So I'm entitled to know.'

'Can't be done, Eddie.'

'Says who?'

'The package is, he goes alone, and until he leaves nobody knows where, including Wardour himself.'

'I just changed that rule.'

'I got to make a phone call saying everything's all clear up to the moment he leaves. Otherwise no dice. And if you sabotage that it could get very nasty for your right honourable friend.'

423

Hendry was about to escalate the aggression when Stanger said, 'He's lying.'

'Not your fight, Bobby. Keep out of it,' McDade said.

'He's lying about the phone,' Stanger repeated.

Hendry's eyes moved from one to the other. 'How come?'

To McDade Stanger said, 'Where are you going to make this call from?' When McDade refused to answer, Stanger continued, 'You're telling us that you fixed up a plan that depends on a phone call. From a place that has no phone. That's real genius, Sean. You'll go a long way.'

Hendry was grinning and wagged a finger admiringly. 'Shit, you're right. There's no line into that place.'

'Mr McDade here of course wouldn't know that.'

'There's a public phone in the village,' McDade said. 'That's the one I planned to use.'

'Two miles away?' Stanger asked. 'But if you had to go to the village, you wouldn't be able to confirm that Wardour had left unaccompanied. Admit it, you bastard. You're lying.'

Taped inside his trouser leg McDade carried a knife. But with only one good arm, on an open unstable terrain, pulling the weapon would give the two men the excuse they were waiting for. So instead he tried charm. 'Come on, boys, don't let's live in the past. It's a whole different scenario, now.'

'Scenario,' Stanger echoed derisively.

McDade spat back, 'What do you reckon, Bobby? If you come out of this clean, Barron Odell might give you a job? Or forgive you getting his men blown to shit in France?'

Hendry had not been able to bring himself to tell Stanger about Odell. Before the fury in Stanger's eyes could translate into action, McDade said, 'Odell's dead.' He paused. 'That's right, dead. Why do you think his bitch of a daughter's here?'

'Does Wardour know?' Hendry asked.

'She'll have told him. Also, that he left half his money to me. You are looking at a millionaire, my sons.'

For Stanger and Hendry, middle-aged and never more than a few hundred pounds or dollars ahead of the next pay-by date, the magic of instant big money was the one thing that could

424

still suspend their breathing. And on this sort of scale they knew McDade was telling the truth. Going with the initiative, McDade said, 'Why fight each other? Who ever gave us anything?' He looked at Hendry. 'When your pals got burned in Ulster, who gave a shit? Let's work for people who are not ripping us off. Look at the background we can put together – me back in Belfast, you, Ed, with your military expertise, Bobby's American connection. We make one hell of a triangle. Let's buy into the big time.' He lit a cigarette and said more quietly, 'At least, don't close the option down until you've thought it through.'

Then, flashes of cunning glinting in his eyes, McDade started off back down the path.

When they reached the *cortijo* there was no sign of Holly, and Roderick Wardour had clearly been getting impatient for some time. 'Sean, can we get down to business now?' he said.

McDade made great play of looking at his watch and thinking. But Wardour's question had been an order. 'Now,' he repeated.

Inside the main house McDade asked if they were alone. Anticipating this, Wardour had asked Holly to keep out of the way. He took McDade from room to room, to demonstrate their emptiness, refusing to allow the Irishman the escape-route of paranoia. 'A map would help,' McDade said.

The Coneforts' shelves were good on two things, coffee-table books and maps. Wardour spread one out on a ceramic-topped table whose motif was Granadan pomegranate.

McDade complained about the map's small scale, then shrugged and said, 'Hell, you can't go wrong in these mountains. There's only one fucking road, and sometimes not even that.' He began to dictate at a speed at which Wardour could write. At moments like this McDade revealed the mental precision which operated inside the chaos of his exterior personality. Without questions Wardour noted down the instructions as given. 'This is the end of our long acquaintance, Mr Wardour,' McDade said finally. 'I'm only sorry it hasn't been more . . . productive.'

425

'You seem to have done well from it,' Wardour said.

'I'm a soldier in a great cause. For me the big questions have already been answered. To a guy like me it's just down to nuts and bolts. Anyways, I'll be here when you get back.'

'I thought you'd be leaving immediately.'

'I need Ed to drive me back to Malaga.'

'You could get a taxi in Robleda. A man of your newly acquired wealth.'

McDade grunted dismissively. 'The lawyers have got that locked up. Do I take it I'm not welcome any longer?'

'Of course not,' Wardour said. 'But as you say, our business is over.'

'I was in no hurry,' McDade said. 'I know I'll find you a man of your word.'

'Meaning?'

'I'm off the hook with the Brit authorities. That was the terms.'

'As far as it involves me,' Wardour said. 'But I can't answer for your other activities.'

'That's all I want. Just one word of advice, Mr Wardour.'

'Which is?'

'Go alone.'

'As you said, our business is finished. When I leave here, what does it matter to you how I go?' Hendry and Wardour had already spoken briefly when the three men returned to the *cortijo*, so McDade knew better than to threaten Wardour with mythical phone calls he had to make.

'I can't guarantee your safety unless you do it the way I told you.'

'Why should I believe you, Sean?'

'Why should I screw you now? All I want is to get this thing over. With the Odell money I can make a new start.'

'We all have to do that,' Wardour said.

They went out onto the patio. In view of what was to come, Wardour should have been nervous, but the agitation was McDade's. All the Irishman could do now was wait, a position

426

he had never enjoyed. His unease increased when he found Stanger and Hendry standing within the patio enclosure.

Before McDade could brush past, Hendry said, 'That's it, Sean.'

'What the fuck's this?' McDade shouted. His good arm was about to lunge down to the knife on his leg. But Hendry caught and pinned the arm while Stanger produced a length of nylon rope. McDade thought of everything, kicking, biting, but he knew there was no limit to what Hendry would do to him once the restraint was lifted. So with curses he submitted.

The only restraint was Wardour, who said, 'Don't take it as revenge, Sean. Although I know how uncomfortable this can be.'

'What's going on?' McDade demanded. 'What do you think you gain by this?'

Holly came along the path through the lemon trees and entered the patio. With a look of detached curiosity at McDade, this faceless man who had dominated so much of her own life, she followed Wardour into the house.

To McDade Stanger said, 'OK, sweetheart, walk.'

McDade gave a malevolent, near-hysterical chuckle, pitched loud enough for Wardour to hear from inside. Even with his arms bound, the intensity of the sound got to his captors. In Hendry it reawoke all the voodoo terror of Belfast duty, the fear that every kid or woman on the street, staring their hatred at the occupying army, could get into your soul and poison it. At least here he was not obliged to be tolerant. He clubbed a fist into McDade's back. The Irishman yelled and twisted in pain. 'You fucking Brit bastard. I was making you the best offer you ever got.'

'Hey, millionaire,' Stanger said, 'let's go.'

'You're a shrewd man, Bobby. Don't fall for this shit.'

'Your place?' Stanger asked.

They got McDade into his room and unceremoniously tipped him onto the bed, where they tied his legs.

'Come on, guys,' McDade protested. 'What's this all for? Is Wardour taking you with him, is that it?'

'It's worse than that,' Hendry said. 'He's leaving you here with me. And if he doesn't come back, I'm going to kill you.'

They had overlooked the knife. To McDade's quick interpretation this oversight revealed a gap in their assurance which he should be able to exploit. But with his legs trussed, the knife was no immediate help. 'You don't convince me, Ed,' McDade said. 'You're too smart to be used by Wardour. He's the same man that sent you into Belfast to get your face blown off while he drank champagne in his club. Why do you boys always fall for it?'

Hendy tried to appear busy, although once McDade was tied up there was little to do. For once McDade failed to get under his skin. Calmly checking the knots on the rope, Hendry said, 'It's personal. Let's just say I've got more against you than I've got against him. That's enough.'

Wardour, Holly and Stanger got into the blood-red Jaguar. A distinctive car even on the traffic-choked roads of Britain, here in the lower reaches of the Sierra Nevada it was outstandingly unusual. McDade had specified the Jag, and anybody watching the road along which he had directed Wardour would see this sleek car's approach from miles away. From this fact Wardour deduced two things, One, that whoever awaited him did not anticipate a car chase. The other was raised by Holly soon after they began the snaking climb towards the mountains. 'I never felt so much like a sitting duck,' she said nervously.

But by now Wardour had converted the vulnerable location of the *cortijo* into a plus point. Handling the car with easy skill he said, 'If anybody wanted to kill me at long distance, they've had plenty of opportunity. The danger will come when I leave the car.'

The road signs showing the recommended speed were becoming less frequent, their numbers lower. Small hilltop villages, clusters of white houses like distant patches of snow, came and went with startling suddenness, dropping away into mist-filled valleys that were soon left below as the ascent continued.

428

'We're near now,' Wardour said. His eyes were dilated, and all the blood vessels of his body seemed to tingle.

The map showed no more settlements this side of the high peaks. Wardour stopped where the road briefly straightened and let his two passengers out. He judged that this steeply angled section, cut diagonally across the face of the massif, was visible from nowhere except a similar spot a mile away across the gorge. What lay beyond the next bend, Wardour did not know. But the destination could not be much further. He dared not risk Holly and Stanger in the car till the last moment.

'Well,' he said, 'we'll meet later.'

'Sure,' Stanger said, 'we're right with you.'

Holly kissed him, and their eyes met. She got out of the car without speaking. The Jaguar disappeared round the next curve of road, through the steeply banking dwarf pines. Holly and Stanger started to walk.

Wardour had been right, the place he was headed for came into sight only half a mile further on. Here, before the road veered up into pine scrub again, it briefly ran into the open, with a view of Mulhacen's white ridge and what seemed like only a few miles of gently rolling country between him and the great mountain. On this open flank of hillside there was space to get a car off the road and as he parked Wardour knew that from here he was visible to half the points of the compass. Still, he made no show of looking around or searching out his observers.

From the verge a half-overgrown path led across a hillside of tough greyish-green grass. The thin mountain air filled the lungs like iced water. Shortly ahead lay the ruin of a stone hut, one complete wall with a staring window still upright, the remains of a primitive mine, or a shelter for the labourers who had once cut the road up the mountain. On the horizon immediately ahead, exactly as McDade's instructions had promised, stood a blue boulder, alone and menacing, unmistakable.

As soon as the Jaguar had left the *cortijo*, Hendry released McDade. As the ropes loosened from his legs, McDade

429

exclaimed triumphantly, 'I knew it! A performance for the benefit of the others, right? Dead cunning, too. You're a cute feller, Eddie.' He swung his legs off the bed. 'How about the arms now?'

But Hendry had felt something, and turned to McDade's leg again. 'What's this?' McDade twitched angrily away. Hendry slapped the Irishman's leg. 'Come on, what have you got there?'

'OK, it's a knife. I always carry it.'

McDade tensed himself to aim his boot at Hendry's face. Looking up, blue and emotionless, Hendry's eyes told their own story: one move in that direction and the reaction would be pitiless. McDade understood. Hendry stripped away the tape and exposed the knife, a narrow-handled blade in a leather sheath.

'Just my insurance, Ed, you know how it is.' Hendry took the knife from the sheath and kept it in his hand. McDade repeated, 'The arms.'

'You think I'm an idiot?'

'Are we making a deal, or what?' McDade demanded.

'You tell me.'

'Why are you letting me go, except you been thinking over my offer?'

'Tell me about it in the car.'

'Why go anywhere? We can talk here.' McDade was anxious not to depart from the *cortijo* coincidentally with Wardour's disappearance. His plan was to stay, to alert the police to the MP's non-return, to play out the part of bewildered friend. To the death, and no kidding.

'We're going,' Hendry said.

'We'll need to take a few things, then.'

'No.'

McDade realised Hendry's intention, and backed away. 'Forget it, friend,' he protested. 'No way.'

'In the car,' Hendry ordered.

'Wardour's taken over now. What do you think you can achieve? Or was this his fucking stupid idea?'

'It was my fucking stupid idea,' Hendry said. 'Now get in

the car.' He knotted his hand into the rope at McDade's back. McDade snarled and tried to shake him off, but Hendry's grip was firm as he pushed the Irishman onto the area of rough grass where the hired Seat was parked.

McDade turned outwards to ease himself into the car. Hendry waited to slam the door once he was in. Deceived by McDade's apparent helplessness, Hendry relaxed his attention for one instant. With snakelike timing McDade seized that moment. Both feet shot out into Hendry's groin. As Hendry staggered back, McDade leapt upright again and lashed out at any part of Hendry's body with which his feet could make contact, using to the maximum his advantage of surprise. Before Hendry could recover from the agony between his legs, one of his shins and the opposite ankle flared in pain. Just to remain standing, let alone retaliate, was next to impossible. And then McDade was at him again, saliva-flecked lips bared, his armless body like a killing machine run wild.

The voodoo fear got Hendry again: they could destroy you with their eyes, paralyse your nervous system, the weasel with the rabbit. As Hendry checked the ground beneath his feet, afraid of stumbling into an irrigation channel, McDade lunged again. This time his head butted Hendry's face. Hard skull bone struck the region around the bridge of Hendry's nose. It was enough to send him down, clutching his face, as his ankle refused to hold any longer. McDade took a short run and hooked a vicious boot into Hendry's stomach. Hendry had dropped both the knife and the car keys. McDade knelt for the knife, and clumsily but swiftly hacked himself free. For a moment he stared down at Hendry, all the instincts of the Ardoyne Stabber throbbing through every nerve of his body. Kill the Brits! But everything in McDade's mind was haywire. The thought that at this late stage Wardour, and that American bitch and her lawyers, might outsmart him, was too much for rational contemplation. Hendry was finished, the *cortijo* quiet, which surely meant that the Odell woman and Stanger had also gone to the rendezvous. Enraged at this sabotage of his plan, McDade slit the bandages to release his injured arm, scowling away the stiffness and pain, and got into the car.

As they climbed the winding road, Holly asked: 'Are you good at this kind of thing?'

'I don't know what this kind of thing is any more,' Stanger said. 'I take it a day at a time.'

'You're a little off your beat, aren't you?'

'I'm planning to write this down as my annual vacation.' Stanger nodded at the distance. 'There's the car.'

'So what do we do now?'

'What the man said, swing these walking sticks and make like Mr and Mrs Tourist.'

'You don't think it's a bit obvious?' Holly asked.

'Well,' Stanger said genially. 'I can stand being with you if you can stand being with me.'

'I didn't mean that. I meant that we'd hardly be seven thousand feet above sea level looking as if we were out for a Sunday stroll.'

'He just wanted to provide a diversion,' Stanger said.

'Or himself with witnesses.'

'Could be.'

'Tell me the truth, what do you think's going to happen?'

'If I knew that,' Stanger said, 'I probably wouldn't be here, because these things usually turn out badly.'

'These things?'

'The sort of affair where somebody puts his life on the line, to find out if the gods love him or not. Most of us have the good sense to steer clear of that.'

Holly asked, 'Do you think he's going to get killed?'

'Either he doesn't come off this mountain, or when he does come down he's in possession of the truth. Which I guess is the victory he's looking for. Or . . . nothing happens. Maybe there's nobody here.'

'Nobody! You're kidding.'

'The ultimate mind-game.' Stanger grimaced. 'That would be

432

something, wouldn't it? All this,' he gestured at the landscape of the Sierra, 'and nothing here, no truth, no enemy . . . nothing.'

'Except his own obsession,' Holly said.

'Absolutely. And he'd never recover. We'd be taking a madman home.'

Stanger's words mirrored a thought which had frequently passed through Holly's mind since they were airlifted from France. She did not take Stanger's point any further, but he had put his finger on her reason for being here. Her father's death and the McDade inheritance had only been an excuse. They reached the Jaguar, which for all its sleek glamour looked singularly abandoned against the crude strength of the mountains.

'Well,' Stanger said, 'he didn't see anybody when he got here.' Wardour's arrangement had been to park the car facing away from the road if he spotted anybody immediately on arrival. But he had reversed and left the Jaguar pointing back at the road from which they had come.

Stanger had also memorised McDade's directions and together with Holly he followed the exact path which twenty minutes earlier Wardour had taken, although by now he was already out of their range of vision.

Against a cerulean sky the white peak of Mulhacen floated in the distance like a Buddhist nirvana. Wardour's instructions, once he crested the ridge marked by the great blue-grey boulder, were to advance in a line with the white mountain-top for three hundred paces. Wardour counted out every step as he went.

There were tracks of a kind, but up here even goats were rare. It was serious walkers' country, and even then the route Wardour had been steered into was taking him into a walker's nightmare. Visibility could reduce to almost nothing in seconds; even Mulhacen itself repeatedly vanished and reappeared, as different ridges formed new horizons and the undulating ground took Wardour into the edge of a rocky wilderness. Still, he kept to his three hundred paces, traversing light scree or veins of marsh fed by narrow streams. Rapid rivulets, suddenly chanced

433

upon, howled in the stillness. Another ten yards and they became inaudible and lost to view again. The oxygen-thin air compounded the stricture in Wardour's chest.

Near the end of his measured distance, Wardour saw the rubble of the aeroplane. Some years ago a medium-sized passenger plane had crashed here and rusting shards of fuselage and other unidentifiable scrap still littered the mountain side, a gaunt landmark for the few who came here.

Ahead of the plane wreckage Wardour had been told to look for a crack between two red square-topped rocks. Another two hundred yards away, the fissure was striking, unmissable. Apart from the flinty rubble underfoot, there were no obstacles. The red rocks soon became towering, the split between them more than wide enough to pass through.

Then, perhaps half a mile away, Wardour saw another figure coming towards him. Initially his blood ran cold, but a moment later he felt dismay, even apprehension, because the man wore the simple economic gear of the proficient walker, and was swinging overland with a rhythmic gait unlike anything Wardour had anticipated. The walker came over a ridge above the red rocks, and angled his path across the scratchy terrain to coincide with Wardour's line of direction. Wardour tried to calm himself, but the stress of these last moments, added to the effect of altitude on his breathing, palpitated his heart. His pace slowed as his legs acquired a heavy, watery feeling, and he knew that soon he would have to stop. Meanwhile the walker came on, taking the ground in an even stride which declared someone who knew his way over here.

Now they were near enough to look into each other's faces, and closing all the time. Wardour noticed the features, a fit man in early middle-age, possibly Spanish, to all appearances a hiker, not anyone he had come here to meet. Feeling sick around his heart, partly from relief, Wardour steeled himself to pass by. 'Hola,' he muttered, the friendly greeting which was usual in these isolated regions.

The other man nodded briefly and repeated the 'Hola' as he strode by. Then he stopped. Fleetingly their eyes had met.

434

Wardour's nerves showed in the fact that he looked over his shoulder as the other man passed, and was still looking as the hiker turned back.

'Está usted extraviado?' the hiker asked.

'No Español . . . Inglés,' Wardour answered.

In English, with the faintest trace of a Swiss accent, the hiker said, 'I asked if you were lost.'

Wardour noticed that one of his hands had a fingernail missing. 'No. I know exactly where I am,' he replied.

'It's good to meet you, Mr Wardour,' said Lucian Weidinger.

As Wardour had outlined it to Holly and Stanger, it might be a good idea to have a couple of walkers appear on the horizon at the crucial moment. Better than nothing, anyway. But the suggestion had remained vague. And now Stanger was having second thoughts. 'I don't like it.'

Not having liked anything since they left the *cortijo*, but swept along by the unreality of it all, Holly said, 'You don't like what?'

'Do you run?' Stanger asked, ignoring her question. Holly looked fit, but she was finding walking on this terrain difficult. She shrugged. 'At the risk of not being a gentleman,' Stanger answered, 'I'm going on ahead.'

'Is that a good idea?'

'I don't know.'

'Rod told us to keep together.'

'Yeah, so I could comfort you when we found his body. All respects, Holly. I know how you feel, but I also know this man now. That's how he works.' Holly had gone pale. Her lips moved but could find no words. Stanger touched her arm and said, 'Since you arrived here, I think he wants to come out of this alive. He may need some help.'

Lips numb from the silent, stealthy wind that razed the mountain-side Holly said, 'Please bring him back, please.'

An untidy, ambling figure, Stanger loped away. Ungainly at first, he gradually adapted to the ground and picked up a stride. Surprised by his reserves of fitness, Holly walked as fast as she could after him. But the distance between them quickly widened, as Stanger's legs found the strength to scramble up the first ridge. There he threw himself flat, surveying what lay beyond. Then he was gone again.

Only once before had Hendry been beaten this badly, years ago in his Para days, by a drunken fellow-trooper outside a bar in Germany. That drunk had fallen victim to his own lack of coordination, and Hendry had been the one to walk away, but this time he was older and slower. Everything hurt more. He dragged himself off the ground. For a minute he needed all his remaining strength to keep him on his feet. The sound of the car as McDade drove away was only one of many noises drumming through Hendry's head. He had blood everywhere, mainly from the nose, which might be broken. One of his eyes was closing, and epicentres of pain throughout his body crowded out other consciousness. With each second an instinct to survive struggled through the physical agony. Hendry staggered onto the patio. A tap jutted from a corner of the rough wall. He splashed cold water over his face, head and clothes. The shock almost stopped his heart, but fragmented the pain. Then he might have sat down, allowed himself time to recover. But through the injuries Hendry snatched at one small hope: McDade might have made a fatal mistake.

Hendry limped into the house. McDade had grabbed the first keys he found, and had taken the Seat, of the two hired cars at the *cortijo* significantly the less powerful. Hendry had one chance. The bedroom Holly and Wardour had shared was perfectly tidy. In the wardrobe Hendry found a locked compartment. He staggered to the kitchen and brought back some heavy cutlery with which he soon levered the compartment open. Holly had left her bag in there, including the keys to her hire car. Brushing water and blood from his face Hendry stumbled out to the yellow Renault.

Hendry churned up dust as he screeched off in pursuit. McDade had left the gate open. Hendry caught sight of him at the bridge. Once he knew which way McDade had turned it was easy. After that junction the road ran for miles with no others joining it. On reaching the road, Hendry's superior speed soon brought McDade within his sights.

What now? The road wound upwards into the foothills. On the sudden tight bends McDade constantly disappeared from sight, but there was nowhere for him to go but up and on every straight Hendry pulled him back again.

It was personal now, all about the number of times McDade had used him. Hendry had no hatred for the Irish, he had left all that behind even before he handed in his uniform. Too many years in Ulster had taught him that the Catholics had received a bad deal, that the IRA was a fearsome enemy, and that somewhere within the psychotic violence lurked the ghost of a just cause. But the other way round it didn't work: to McDade, Hendry knew, *he* would always be just another Brit bastard. Had he not been in a hurry, back at the *cortijo*, McDade would have kicked him to death, for two hundred years of history. So if McDade was sweating now, at the pursuing car relentlessly hogging his rear-view mirror, so much the better.

More than sweating, McDade was shouting obscenities at himself for leaving Hendry the use of a car with a bigger engine. All his years as a Belfast joyrider had left McDade primitive about cars. He now punched and kicked the capable but modest-engined Seat as if, like an animal, it would respond to his savage goading. Or, McDade had to think now, he should have killed Hendry. He had had the knife, and hated Hendry for the way he had survived and kept coming back for more. It had been time to finish off the soldier boy for good. But the thought of Odell's million dollars, of how big that money could make him on the Falls Road, had stayed McDade's hand. In defence of that dream he had taken to the mountain road, and now a man he had left bleeding in a ditch had turned the tables on him, suddenly and overwhelmingly. However hard McDade jammed his foot to the floor, the chasing car remained steadfastly in his mirror. Once the gradient descended for a stretch and Hendry's intentions became clear. When it would have been easy to over-take him and force McDade to a stop, Hendry was content to keep his distance, knowing he had the power when he needed it. The threat which now hung over McDade was making him frantic.

Then he looked at the petrol gauge. The needle had dropped to the zero line. These things were never accurate, McDade told himself. But at the most optimistic he could only have a few kilometres left. The endless sequence of narrow road and hairpin bends provoked him into action that at least would solve the first part of his problem: to get Hendry off his back.

Choosing a moment when the curve of the road had blocked Hendry from his mirror, McDade braked and spun the wheel into full lock. His injured arm lacked strength, but the lightness of the car compensated. McDade leant forward to use his body weight against the wheel. The Seat lurched over the edge of the road, banging into the metal safety barrier. McDade had half turned when Hendry drove into view.

All Hendry saw was McDade's car pointing towards him, then starting to roll. Instantly he grasped what the Irishman was about to do. Hendry put the Renault into reverse. Beyond the road a sheer drop led down to tumbled rocks and a long way below that hectares of spectral almond blossom. And beyond that lay an apparently bottomless valley, down which you could drop for ever. McDade had seized two advantages: he was driving forward, and the slope was with him. And once again he had caught Hendry off guard. After negotiating one bend in reverse, Hendry realised that his success on the next, and the one after that, lay outside his control. Exactly what McDade wanted. Hendry cursed, clenched his jaw against the pain of his body, and stopped. For a second he held the car on the clutch, then stamped on the accelerator.

Hendry steered for McDade's car, not head on, but for a point between the Seat and the rocky hillside. Superior weight and engine power told. Panicking at the last moment, his face a silent scream behind the windshield, McDade braked. But this only slewed the car's rear end outwards. At the same moment, Hendry's impact tore open a space between McDade and the vertical cliff on the inside of the road. The lighter car spun

438

sideways, bounced as if poised to dive, then keeled over the edge.

Hendry braked, checked that his car would still move, then immediately drove on.

'This way.'

'You know my name,' Wardour said. 'I think you owe me yours.'

'It's not necessary.' They passed through the fissure between the red rocks and entered the outer reaches of a gorge, whose depths rested invisible below a complex interfacing of ledges.

'Do I take it then that you are not the person I came here to meet?' Wardour asked.

Weidinger answered, 'It's exactly because I am that person that knowing my name is not important. After all, this is not a social visit.'

Wardour stopped. 'I think we're alone enough here.'

'If you wish.'

'So, it was you.'

'No,' Weidinger said. 'We make the mistake of individualising things. As a politician you should know that what makes or breaks a man is forces operating in society. I was only an agent of something greater.'

'I'm here to find out what that is.'

'There is a thing called power. Those of us who want it all contend for it in our own way. Democratic politics is one of many methods of gaining and exercising power. There are others, one of which I represent. Sometimes they overlap and you find democratic politicians acting undemocratically.'

'Are you telling me that you were employed by someone in my own party?'

'You already suspect that, don't you?'

'Do I?'

'Who hates a rising politician as much as his colleagues?'

'Name them,' Wardour demanded.

Weidinger reached into his lightweight rucksack. Wardour expected him to produce documentary evidence. Instead in

Weidinger's hand he saw an automatic pistol. Weidinger looked apologetic, but behind the apology lay no emotion except mockery.

Wardour in turn looked unimpressed. 'Up here a gunshot will carry for miles. You'll never use it.' But Weidinger was already taking out a silencer, which he calmly screwed to the pistol barrel.

'We think alike, Mr Wardour. That's something. Now back, if you please.' Weidinger directed Wardour nearer the edge of the scree-littered path. 'A climbing accident or a suicide, how would you prefer them to think of it?'

'With a bullet hole in me?' Wardour said.

Weidinger shrugged. 'After the birds and animals are through, there won't be much left. Assuming anybody ever finds you down there.'

Wardour moved, but further away from the edge. Weidinger looked displeased. 'Names,' Wardour said. 'I'm entitled to that, surely.'

Weidinger quickly scanned the barren landscape around them. 'OK, why not?' He enunciated the names with contemptuous precision. 'Sweetman. Gwyer. Conefort. But men only take action because a greater tide is going their way.'

'And they paid you to kill me?'

'No. I have to do this to protect my associate McDade, myself, and those behind us. Your persistence has brought you here. Maybe death is what you sought all along. Now I must ask you to stand over there, and turn your back.'

The gun was a trick, Wardour realised. He would be thrown over bodily. Not even a tell-tale bullet graze would be left on his skeleton. A sudden exhilaration swept through Wardour, knowing that no end of life could be bitter that brought truth with it. This elation produced a huge release of physical energy. Desperate yet strangely carefree, Wardour hurled himself towards the gun and the arm that held it.

Weidinger was smaller, slighter. Before he could shoot, Wardour had deflected his arm and caught his wrist. Feet scrabbling on loose stone, the two men grappled to keep from sliding towards the edge. Wardour was angry, but Weidinger knew combat, and his mind remained steady. Regaining his balance, with his left arm he chopped Wardour's shoulder, then aimed a paralysing kick at his thigh. It worked; Wardour's nerves went numb. He looked confused as his strength suddenly drained away. Weidinger hustled him back, struggling to stay upright. Fragments of rock, dislodged by their feet, showered into nowhere. Wardour stumbled badly and skidded onto his knees. As he went down he made the mistake of looking sideways at the gulf, which yawned for him. Suddenly he was fighting off not Weidinger's gun, but mind-spinning vertigo. Screwing his eyes shut to drive out the terror of height, Wardour clung to any rock that promised security.

Meanwhile Weidinger had steadied himself and released the safety on the automatic. It irked him to change a plan, but if Wardour had to go by bullet, so be it. He took double-handed aim.

'Strike!' The yell came from the skyline, which a moment before Weidinger had scanned and found empty. Weidinger looked round. His head turned into the path of the rock which Stanger had let fly. The sharp chunk of stone had a diameter the width of a man's face. Flying downwards, it smashed obliquely into Weidinger's head, crunching bone, causing blood to spurt. Weidinger swayed dizzily, bemused, dabbing at blood. Once again he managed to raise his gun hand, tilting into the hillside to steady himself, the barrel point-blank at Wardour's eyes. His aim perfected by adrenalin, Stanger launched another rock. This one struck the side of Weidinger's head, which nodded with the graceful violence of a wind-buffeted flower. The gun spat in his hand as his finger achieved one wild shot. But already he was reeling sideways, and with flailing limbs slithered off balance.

After that the mountain took care of things. By the time Stanger had found a way down and joined Wardour all trace of Weidinger had gone. Wherever they looked, or for how long, his body had vanished, swallowed, it seemed, by the mountain.

★

Hendry had driven on as far as the road would take him. The car had structural rather than mechanical damage, and would get him to wherever he was going. Whenever there was a choice of road Hendry went for ascent, and eventually found Wardour's Jaguar. Parking beside it, he passed out in a mixture of concussion, pain and exhaustion. When he regained consciousness it was to see the three figures of Stanger, Holly Odell and Roderick Wardour making their way down from the distant horizon.

Somebody had survived, something had ended. Hendry remembered his daughter on her hospital bed, his tears falling on her hands at the thought that his life would never be anything he could present to her. Now, at least, his life was out of plaster. For him the Wardour affair was over. Fresh tears now, of fatigue and relief, washed the dried blood on his face, as Hendry sat back and waited for the tigers.